Praise for

Raven's Shadow

"A new novel by Patricia Briggs guarantees a good reading time. *Raven's Shadow* . . . lures readers down some of modern fantasy's less-expected paths . . . a great novel for grown-ups. I look forward to the next installment in the series." —*Crescent Blues*

"An excellent book . . . The characters have a real interior life, with thoughts and second thoughts and feelings, and the interaction between them is very good." —*SFRevu*

"Patricia Briggs is a talented storyteller who enchants her audience with a spellbinding tale. *Raven's Shadow* is going on this reviewer's keeper shelf." —*Midwest Book Review*

"Briggs's strength is in her characterization, but I appreciated the pace of action and the world building in *Raven's Shadow*, too . . . I'm a fan now, too, and look forward to revisiting the characters . . . recommended." —*Romantic SF & Fantasy Novels*

"An exciting and touching tale. It's self-contained enough to give the reader a satisfying sense of completion by the end while leaving room for a sequel that will be highly anticipated." —*Romantic Times*

Praise for the Mercy Thompson novels

Iron Kissed

"The third book in an increasingly excellent series, *Iron Kissed* has all the elements I've come to expect in a Patricia Briggs novel: sharp, perceptive characterization, nonstop action, and a levelheaded attention to detail and location. I love these books." —Charlaine Harris, #1 *New York Times* bestselling author

continued . . .

Blood Bound

"Once again, Briggs has written a full-bore action adventure with heart . . . Be prepared to read [it] in one sitting, because once you get going, there is no good place to stop until tomorrow."

—*SFRevu*

"Plenty of action and intriguing characters keep this fun. In the increasingly crowded field of kick-ass supernatural heroines, Mercy stands out as one of the best."   —*Locus*

"Briggs's world in which witches, vampires, werewolves, and shapeshifters live beside ordinary people is plausibly constructed; the characters are excellent; and the plot keeps the pages flapping."

—*Booklist*

Moon Called

"An excellent read with plenty of twists and turns. Her strong and complex characters kept me entertained from its deceptively innocent beginning to its can't-put-it-down end. Thoroughly satisfying, it left me wanting more."

—Kim Harrison, *New York Times* bestselling author

"Patricia Briggs always enchants her readers. With *Moon Called* she weaves her magic on every page to take us into a new and dazzling world of werewolves, shapeshifters, witches, and vampires. Expect to be spellbound."

—Lynn Viehl, *New York Times* bestselling author

"Inventive and fast paced . . . Mercy's first-person narrative voice is a treat throughout. And best of all, the fantasy elements retain their dark mystery and sense of wonder . . . entertaining from start to end."   —*Fantasy & Science Fiction*

Praise for other novels by Patricia Briggs
Dragon Blood

"It is easy to like Patricia Briggs's novels . . . Her books are clever, engaging, [and] fast moving."   —*Romantic SF & Fantasy Novels*

"It goes without saying, I suppose, that I'm looking forward to seeing what else Patricia Briggs does. If *Dragon Blood* is any indication, then she is an inventive, engaging writer whose talent

for combining magic of all kinds—from spells to love—with fantastic characters should certainly win her a huge following and a place on many bookshelves."
—SF Site

Dragon Bones

"A lot of fun."
—Locus

"A wonderful adventure tale written with charm, intelligence, and excellent plot twists that keep the reader off guard . . . an excellent read for everyone."
—KLIATT

"I enjoyed *Dragon Bones* . . . This is an enjoyable, well-written book with enough plot twists and turns to keep the reader's attention. This book is sure to appeal to lovers of fantasy."
—The Green Man Review

"[Briggs] possesses the all-too-rare ability to make you fall hopelessly in love with her characters . . . It's good stuff all the way . . . You find yourself carried away by the charm of the story and the way Briggs tells it."
—Crescent Blues

The Hob's Bargain

"This is a Beauty and the Beast story but unlike any I've ever read. Ms. Briggs blends adventure, romance, and innovative fantasy with a deft hand. Highly recommend this one to all my readers."
—S. L. Viehl, national bestselling author

"[A] fun fantasy romance . . . There's plenty of action, with battles against raiders and magical creatures, a bard who isn't what he appears, and an evil mage—but there's also plenty of humor and some sweet moments of mischief and romance."
—Locus

When Demons Walk

"An interesting cross between a murder mystery, romance, and fantasy . . . There are enough twists and turns in the plot to keep most readers' interest."
—VOYA

"Patricia Briggs proves herself a rare talent as she devises a clever mystery with appealing characters in a fantasy setting . . . top-notch reading fare."
—Romantic Times

Titles by Patricia Briggs

The Mercy Thompson Series

MOON CALLED

BLOOD BOUND

IRON KISSED

BONE CROSSED

SILVER BORNE

RIVER MARKED

FROST BURNED

The Alpha and Omega Series

ON THE PROWL
(with Eileen Wilks, Karen Chance, and Sunny)

CRY WOLF

HUNTING GROUND

FAIR GAME

MASQUES

WOLFSBANE

STEAL THE DRAGON

WHEN DEMONS WALK

THE HOB'S BARGAIN

DRAGON BONES

DRAGON BLOOD

RAVEN'S SHADOW

RAVEN'S STRIKE

Graphic Novels

ALPHA AND OMEGA: CRY WOLF: VOLUME ONE

ALPHA AND OMEGA: CRY WOLF: VOLUME TWO

Anthology

SHIFTER'S WOLF
(*Masques* and *Wolfsbane* in one volume)

RAVEN'S STRIKE

Patricia Briggs

ACE BOOKS, NEW YORK

THE BERKLEY PUBLISHING GROUP
Published by the Penguin Group
Penguin Group (USA) Inc.
375 Hudson Street, New York, New York 10014, USA

USA I Canada I UK I Ireland I Australia I New Zealand I India I South Africa I China

Penguin Books Ltd., Registered Offices: 80 Strand, London WC2R 0RL, England
For more information about the Penguin Group, visit penguin.com.

RAVEN'S STRIKE

An Ace Book / published by arrangement with Hurog, Inc.

Ace Books are published by The Berkley Publishing Group.
ACE and the "A" design are trademarks of Penguin Group (USA) Inc.

For information, address: The Berkley Publishing Group,
a division of Penguin Group (USA) Inc.,
375 Hudson Street, New York, New York 10014.

ISBN: 978-0-441-01312-8

PUBLISHING HISTORY
Ace mass-market edition / August 2005

PRINTED IN THE UNITED STATES OF AMERICA

22 21 20 19 18 17 16 15 14 13

Cover art by Gene Mollica.
Cover design by Annette Fiore DeFex.
Interior text design by Kristin del Rosario.
Interior illustration by Robin Walker.
Map by Michael Enzweiler.

For evenings of song and laughter,
Debbie and Tom Lentz, and Theo Hill
Jason, Sara, Jalen, and Chris Stejskal
John and Sue Wilson

And to my own Bard
Michael

This book is dedicated with love.

Acknowledgments

The following people read this book, or parts of this book, in its roughest stages and offered useful and necessary advice.

Michael Briggs, Collin Briggs, Dee Enzweiler, Michael Enzweiler, Jean Matteucci, Dan Matteucci, Ann Peters, Kaye Roberson, Kyle Roberson, Clyde Rowland, and John Wilson.

I'd also like to thank Robin Walker, for her wonderful artwork, and Michael Enzweiler, who provided the map of Colossae that Rinnie found.

Taela

Shadow's Fall

Korhaden

Colkern

Redeem

The Forum

Edren

Upsarlan

Erlandir

Eneweller '95

N

COLOSSAE

1. Merchant's District
2. Artisan's District
3. Old Town
4. University District
5. High Town
6. Merchant's Gate
7. Low Gate
8. University Gate

EAGLE: GUARDIAN

FALCON: HUNTER

RAVEN: MAGE

MEADOWLARK

HEALER

OWL: BARD

CORMORANT

WEATHER-WITCH

©WALKER&BRIGGS '03

PROLOGUE

In the eighth year of the Reign of Phoran, Twenty-Sixth of that name, the Sept of Leheigh died. His son, Avar, long having lived in Taela as a boon comrade of the young Emperor, traveled to the estate the Sept, his father, had bequeathed him. Hidden among those who traveled with the new Sept were a handful of mages who came for secret purposes.

They left one of their number, a mage-priest, to establish a new religion in the heart of Leheigh, a land old in power and well suited to secrets—this they thought the most important of their twofold assignment.

The second was to steal away a man gifted with the Bardic Order of the Owl, just returning to his family from a winter's hunt. The familiar task was no more difficult than many other such abductions they had accomplished—perhaps easier, for the Orders of Mage and Hunter were, either of them, more suited to resist the attack of wizards than the Order of the Bard.

They had no reason to suppose that this man was any different from the scores of such men and woman they had stolen in the past. No more did I—and I should have known, for Tieragan of Redern was no stranger to me.

The thought of his eventual death, needful though it was, saddened me. That his death meant anything to me at all told me that I had put it off almost too long. I would miss listening to him sing, I thought on the day I sent my wizards out to take him. I took some consolation from the knowledge that even if he had lived, I would not have been able to listen to him for much longer: he or his kin would have noticed what I was.

If I could not listen to his songs, it was fitting that soon no one would hear Tier's music. So I told myself, and put his death out of my head. I had forgotten, though, what he had been and had only remembered the farmer who sometimes earned a few extra coins by singing at the Hero's Welcome in the evenings.

So I left Tier to my wizards, who had always served me well, and concerned myself with the growth of my religion.

It had taken almost a full century before I realized that I could use power gained from things other than death. Death is what I crave, but I am chary of using it more than necessary. It draws too much attention, and the power that it brings is too addictive. It makes me reckless, when I want to be subtle. Instead I've learned to feed on strong emotions: envy, hate, and lust.

My temples are an endless supply of such emotions. What do people pray to their gods for, after all?

Let my father die so that I might inherit his wealth, says one, while another bows his head and asks, *Let Toren's wife look upon me with lust.* Some prayers are more desperate. *Please, let no one find out that I stole my lord's gold. I don't want to die.* I fed upon those desires, even as the gods must once have. They made me strong.

I am not the Unnamed King. They sometimes treat him as though he was the only Shadowed. But he was not the first Shadowed, nor, as, I can attest, was he the last. Unlike him, I do not need the adulation and the name of power when I have the reality of it. I don't want to be Emperor of the world. I have other plans. It suits me to allow others to accomplish my purposes. It amuses me.

I pride myself on knowing which men will serve my needs best. I grew dependent—no, not dependent— *complacent.* I grew too complacent because my people always obey me, always accomplish the tasks I set them to.

If I'd been paying closer attention to the wizard-priest Volis, I would have seen that his ambition was going to interfere with my own plans. I could have stopped the destruction of my temple in Redern.

But that temple was a convenience, not a necessity. It was formed as much to keep the ambitious and powerful wizard Volis where he could do little harm as for any other purpose. Thousands fed me from my temples in Taela. I did not need Redern, and so did not guard it as well as I might have. My neglect allowed Tier's wife to destroy it. My fault, true. But on the whole, I consider Volis's death to be as great a benefit to me as the temple was a loss. He was getting too ambitious, too curious. He knew too much.

The destruction of the Secret Path in Taela, though, was a much greater loss, but I am not at fault there. No one could have expected that Tier, who was not even a *Mage,* could destroy in a matter of months what had taken me centuries to build. No one.

It took the whole of humanity, wizards and warriors, to bring down the Unnamed King. I, who will become so much more than He was, will not have it said that I was brought to my knees by a *farmer*.

I burn with the humiliation of it yet.

I could have defeated them—a ragtag band of Travelers and a Sept's personal army would have been no match for the power I wield. But it would have been the first step in a war that I do not want. What good is it to rule the world when there is no world to rule? That is a question that the Unnamed King should have asked himself. But, I suppose by then he had already burned away most of who he once was and become nothing but an outlet for the Stalker's power. I have a better plan.

I can repair the damage. Rebuild the temple, rebuild my Secret Path. The destruction was not as great as it would seem: there are always ambitious men who will serve me. Tier has caused me no permanent setback; he is not so important.

But he must be punished for what he has done, what his family has done. He will wish he were dead before I am through with him. Perhaps I shall grant his wish.

CHAPTER 1

"Get that bucket filled for me, Lorra. Tole, bring more charcoal." Aliven knew his voice was harsh, but the world was a harsh place, with no room for people who did not work.

He watched out of the corner of his eye as his daughter snatched the wooden bucket from its place near the forge and left the smithy at a brisk walk for the well.

He would lose her soon, he thought, as he sorted through his store of metal. He'd two offers for her hand from neighboring farmers, but she hadn't made up her mind yet. He hoped she chose Daneel, who was soft-spoken and old enough to have proved his mettle, but she'd been showing a preference for Sovernt's youngest.

He would be happy to see her settled with either, though it would leave him only Tole and Nona, neither of whom was big enough to carry the bucket full of water or half a dozen other chores required to keep the smithy running.

"Step up, Tole," he said to his son, who had only half filled the forge coal bed. "The morning won't wait on your dawdling."

"Yes, Da," muttered the boy in a tone just this side of insolence.

"You watch your—"
Lorra's shrill scream cut through his voice.

"It doesn't look like much of a village, Papa," said Lehr.

Tier smiled at his youngest son, who had somehow crossed over from boy to man these past few months. His ash-blond hair, a legacy of his mother's people, was mostly tucked under a hat, but anyone with an eye to see could tell that there was Traveler blood in him.

Lehr's long strides had no trouble keeping up with Skew, though Tier's old warhorse was walking briskly. Tier shifted in his saddle, hoping to alleviate the steady ache in his right knee. He might believe the adage that any wound that hurt was a sign he wasn't dead yet, but that didn't mean he had to enjoy it. He took a deep breath of cool forest air to remind himself that he was free and on his way home: a little pain was a small price to pay.

He squinted at the small cluster of buildings in the little green valley. "It's small, but see that first building? There's a kiln behind it. It's either a pottery or a bakery."

"But, Papa," said Tier's older son Jes, who walked on Tier's other side, "Benroln said we need grain, not pots or bread."

"Very true," agreed Tier. "But so near to a great road, they will have trade goods, too."

"There are farms all around here," explained Lehr. "They'll bring grain here where they'll see higher profits from it than if they had to transport it to a bigger market."

Jes gave a puzzled frown. It might have been that he found Lehr's explanation too complex—or something else had distracted him.

It was ironic that Jes, who looked as Rederni as any village son, would be the one to pay the highest price for his mother's Traveler blood. The lesser part of that price was the slow thoughts and slower speech that set him apart as a simpleton—though he wasn't, quite.

"It doesn't look right," said Jes after a moment.

"What doesn't?" asked Tier. Jes's conversations sometimes were as difficult to follow as a hummingbird's flight.

"The buildings." Jes stopped abruptly and stared ahead.

Tier stopped Skew and tried to see what might have attracted Jes's attention.

"There's no smoke from the smithy," said Lehr.

"That's it," said Jes, nodding with his usual exaggerated motion. "Smithies have smoke."

"Maybe the smith isn't working today," Tier said. "We'll be there soon enough." Urging Skew forward, he squeezed a little too enthusiastically with his legs and couldn't bite back a yelp.

Shadow take these knees, the wizards who broke them, and the Traveler healer who can't fix them any faster.

That last wasn't fair, and he knew it. Brewydd had told him that riding Skew rather than one of the carts was making his knees take longer to heal than necessary. But it was bad enough to have to ride while most everyone else proceeded by their shoe leather—he was *not* going to sit in a cart.

"Are you all right?" asked Jes, his hand hovering just over Tier's leg. "Mother told me to watch out for you."

"Just my knees." Tier gave his son a smile despite the way his right knee was throbbing. "They're taking a long time to heal up—I must be getting old."

"Mother says you push too hard," said Jes frowning. Obviously Tier's smile hadn't been as convincing as he'd intended.

They had all taken to fussing over him, which Tier found both touching and annoying. He'd rather nurse his hurts in private if he could.

"Brewydd says that your mother is fretting too much," replied Tier.

"And Mother says to leave healing to the Lark," added Lehr, though he was looking concerned as well. "Brewydd knows what she's doing."

Jes frowned.

"I'm all right," Tier said again.

Lehr, he could have just told to leave it alone, but once Jes got something on his mind he could be amazingly stubborn. So Tier caught Jes's dark eyes with his own, and said firmly, "Even your mother agreed that I was fit for a visit to a village to negotiate for supplies—that's what we Bards are supposed to do. We owe this Traveler clan more than we can repay, but I can get them good prices on the things they need and ensure that they'll have a welcome here next time they pass through. My knees still bother me, and will for a month or two more, but they are a fair bit on their way to normal." It helped that he told the truth. Jes would hear it in his voice.

"I don't like those wizards," said Jes, and for a moment there was something dark, something alien in his voice.

"Nor I," agreed Tier, having no trouble making the connection between his knees and the wizards who'd caused them to be broken, because he'd just been thinking the same thing. "But they are gone for good and can do no more harm to anyone."

"We rescued you," said Jes in sudden satisfaction. "And you will be fine, and we are going home. Rinnie will be happy to see us. I wouldn't have wanted to stay with Aunt Alinath."

"Your aunt's a good person," admonished Tier. His sister was uncomfortable around Jes's oddities, and because of that, she mishandled his oldest. Nevertheless, she was his sister, and he loved her.

Jes set his chin stubbornly. "She is bossy and rude."

"Like Mother," said Lehr, with the quick sunny smile that he used all too seldom.

"Mother is Raven," said Jes, as if that explained and excused those faults, which, Tier thought, was largely correct. "And she is only rude to fools."

Lehr laughed. "And that's most of the people she meets."

Tier shook his head. "She's not usually rude, just intimidating."

"If you say so," said Lehr. "Weren't we going to negotiate with someone to buy some grain? Or are we going to stand here all day gossiping like old women?"

Jes grinned shyly and ducked his head. "Papa will negotiate, and you and I can watch. I like watching."

"Right. Just mind you don't say anything about Travelers unless Papa does."

Tier urged Skew forward again, this time with his weight and a click of his tongue. The patchwork-colored gelding paced forward with his usual glass-smooth walk.

There were three huts, the smithy, a small pottery, and a handful of small buildings in the village that Benroln had sent them to. But there was no answer from inside the potter's shed when Lehr knocked, nor did anyone come out at his shout. He opened the door and briefly peered inside.

"No one here."

So they went to the next building.

The smithy was a three-walled, open-face shed and appeared as empty as the pottery had been. Tier threw a leg over Skew's back and slid—slowly for the sake of his stiff knees—to the ground. He dropped the gelding's reins to ground-tie him and limped into the building, Lehr and Jes beside him.

Inside the smithy, tools were hung in an organized manner on one wall, rough steel lay scattered on the ground next to the forge, as if someone had just dropped it there. Tier put a hand over the bed of coals, then touched them cautiously, but not even the memory of fire lingered.

"What can you tell me about this, Lehr?" asked Tier. "How long have they been gone?"

It was an unreasonable question to ask of even the most seasoned tracker. The roof of the smithy kept the rain off and the walls protected the dirt floor. Tier wouldn't have been able to tell how long the steel had lain on the ground, abandoned to tend to whatever emergency had called the smith away.

But Lehr, like Jes and Tier himself, was an Order Bearer—and his Order was Falcon—the Hunter.

Lehr cast his Falcon's eyes over the scene and Tier felt the rise of magic as his son read the traces left by the people who'd lived here.

"No one's been in this building for at least two days, maybe as long as three," he said finally. "But there were chickens here until yesterday."

They'd seen no chickens when they rode up.

"There are people here still," said Jes after a moment, his voice crisp and alert. "I can smell them."

Something about the deserted place had alarmed his oldest son. Jes, his sweet-natured slow-speaking Jes, was gone as if he had never been, and in his place was the deadly predator who sometimes looked out of Jes's eyes. Jes's Order was a heavier burden than the others. Jes was Guardian, and the magic-induced dread that accompanied his secondary nature, unique to the Eagle's Order, sent chills up Tier's spine.

Lehr didn't even look up from the ground just outside the smithy. "Something ate the chickens."

"What kind of something?" asked Tier.

"I don't know," Lehr answered. "It's not very big—about the weight of a small wolf. See, here's a print."

Tier peered at the faint trace in the dust of the small trail. To his eyes it could have been any of a number of animals. "Could it be a raccoon?"

Lehr shook his head. "It's not a raccoon. No racoon has claws that size."

"Can you see where the people went?"

"There's someone here, Da," Tole said, his face pressed against a crack in the wall. "Out by the smithy. Strangers this time."

Aliven looked up from the damp cloth he was using on his wife's forehead. She hadn't opened her eyes since he'd brought her here days ago.

Because their home was closer to the well than the smithy was, his wife had been quicker to answer their daughter's scream. By the time he'd gotten to the well, Lorra was dead and his wife was struggling beneath some dark beast. When the strange creature noticed Aliven it ran off; at first he'd thought that the sound of his shout or the sight of his hammer had sent it fleeing—but he'd since learned the folly of that. Perhaps it only hadn't want to kill its food too fast lest it spoil. In any case, between the time he'd carried Irna into the house and returned for Lorra, it had come back and dragged her body away.

He'd sent his son for Tally, his wife's cousin, who'd been so immersed in his potting that he'd not heard Lorra's scream. As the other man had come hurrying over, it had attacked yet again, from behind the garden hut. If Aliven hadn't been carrying his hammer still, the beast would have gotten them both instead of just clawing up Tally's face.

He'd never seen anything move as fast as the beast did. Aliven had gotten Tally and the two children into their hut and barred the windows and doors. So far the beast hadn't torn through the wooden walls, but the smith was pretty certain the thin walls wouldn't keep it out when it finally decided it wanted in.

It had, after all, herded him back into the hut as neatly as a well-trained sheepdog putting lambs into their fold. Yesterday, a couple of farmers had come to pick up the plowshare he'd fixed for them. Aliven had left the hut to warn them, but he'd been too late. He'd found them both, dead, behind the potter's shed.

The beast had let him stay there a while. But when he'd gotten to his feet, it had pushed him back to the hut with unseen growls and noises. It wanted them there until it was hungry again.

Both Irna and Tally were dying. The initial wounds had been bad enough, but infection had set in with frightening speed. Irna hadn't moved for a day and a half, and Tally had been unconscious since daybreak.

Trapped inside the confines of the little hut, Aliven'd had to make do with what they had, and—he carefully wet the cloth again—he was running out of water.

Maybe these new people Tole was watching would be able to help. The Sept sent men out on patrols, soldiers who might know how to deal with the beast.

"Who is out there?" he asked his son.

"A dark man with a little grey in his hair, tall like Daneel. He's limping pretty badly. They've a horse—it's spotted like a cow, Da. There are two other men with him, younger. They look like they're all close kin. Can they help us?" Tole looked up with hope in his eyes; Aliven hadn't told either of his children about the two dead farmers.

He left his wife's side and put his own eye against the gap between boards for a minute. Tole, for all that he'd not seen a dozen summers, was sharp-eyed. The older man and one of the young men looked as alike as any father and son he'd ever seen. The second young man shared some of the same features, but his hair was—

Aliven pulled his head away and spat. "Travelers," he said.

"Travelers?" Nona, his youngest, looked up from tending Tally. "They'll kill it for us!"

"You've been listening to your mother's stories," Aliven said, disappointment making his voice even gruffer than usual. "Travelers only help themselves—and they help themselves to everything they can."

But he unbolted the door anyway and put his head out. He'd not see anyone, not even Travelers, killed if he could help it.

"Leave, Travelers!"

Tier looked up from where Lehr had discovered the marks of a struggle. Two men, he'd said, both of them dragged around behind the pottery.

"There's your people," Tier told Jes, spying a man peering out from a smallish hut on the far side of the cluster of buildings.

"We mean you no harm," Tier said, limping toward the man. "My son tells me you've had some people killed by an animal."

"Go away, Traveler," said the man again. "There's no gain to be had from this. I don't want your deaths on my conscience." His head retreated, and he pulled the door closed.

Lehr and Jes both followed Tier, flanking him. Lehr kept his eyes on the ground while Jes kept up a restless sweep of their surroundings.

"This place reeks of fear and blood," said Jes. "Fear and blood and something *wrong*."

Tier slanted a wary glance at his oldest son. "Stay back from the hut when we get there. This man sounds frightened enough. Your presence will only frighten him more."

Jes met his gaze but didn't say anything.

"It's no use, Papa," said Lehr, not looking up. "He's not going to leave you when he thinks you might be in danger. Trying to make him stay back is just going to frustrate you."

"I suppose I can't keep you back either," muttered Tier.

That brought Lehr's face up as he flashed a quick smile. "Mother told us to watch over you, remember?" His gaze caught on a shed set just outside the huddle of buildings, and he took a sharp intake of breath. "That's where it's laired," he said. "Over there in the well house. It's left dozens of tracks back and forth. And Jes is right, I can smell the taint, too. Whatever this thing is—it's shadow-tainted."

Tier looked, but all he could see was a narrow path through

knee-length, yellowed cheatgrass. "Can you tell what it is yet?"

Lehr shook his head. "Nothing I've tracked before."

Tier paused a moment, frowning. He loosened his sword for a quick pull if he needed it. "Lehr, keep an eye on that well while I'm trying to talk. Your mother would never let us live it down if I got you killed."

Lehr took his bow off his shoulder and strung it. "I'll watch."

Tier knocked on the door of the greying hut. "We're here to help if we can," he said, sliding as much Persuasion into his voice as he felt comfortable doing. He would force no man completely against his will. "Tell me what happened here."

The door jerked open, releasing an unpleasant miasma of wound-rot and sweat. A wiry man, as dark as Tier himself, peered out, squinting against the light, the same man who'd tried to warn them off. His beard was still dark although grey shot plentifully through the thinning hair on the top of his head. His hands were callused and bore the kinds of small scars working hot metal could give a man. This must be the smith.

"Traveler," spat the smith. "I know what your kind does. Fool with the weather, then beggar the farmers to fix it right again. Call up a curse and remove it for payment. If you've visited this thing upon us for gold, I'll see you dead myself. If you've not, then I'll tell you again. If you stay, it will kill you, too—though likely it is too late already."

"We're not that kind of Traveler," said Tier smoothly. "Though I know that there are more than one clan who do as you say. I am Tieragan of Redern and these"—he realized that he couldn't see Jes—a not-uncommon occurrence when Jes was on alert—and changed midsentence—"*this* is my son, Lehr."

The smith glanced around nervously. Tier didn't blame him, he felt it, too—but unlike the smith, he knew the source of his own unease. Jes was somewhere nearby. As if the menace that clung to the Guardian wasn't enough, his magic brought both cold and fear to anyone around him.

"My name is Aliven," said the smith, reluctantly responding

to the goodwill that Tier was projecting with all the skill he could muster.

Tier stepped forward and Aliven the Smith gave way, allowing Tier to maneuver past him and into the hut.

Two children, a boy not much older than Tier's youngest and a girl a few years younger huddled together near the pole in the center of the room, their smudged faces unevenly revealed by the light that filtered through between the boards. The boy had an arm around the girl and was keeping a sharp eye on Tier. The only other occupants of the hut were two adults, a man and a woman, lying on pallets crowded together on the floor.

Lehr came in behind Tier and knelt beside the blanketed man.

"What did this?" he asked, pointing to something that Tier, in the uncertain light, couldn't see.

There was a barred window just to the right of the door. Tier pulled the bar and pushed the shutter board to the side so that he could see what had so startled Lehr.

Under the improved lighting Tier could see the wounds on the woman, and the man's face had been sliced open by something sharp.

"It used three claws," said Lehr. "Just like the thing that killed the chickens and the two men by the pottery."

"The Fahlarn had a three-pronged fork with sharpened points that caused wounds somewhat like that," said Tier, kneeling to get a better look. "But see the way the bone is marked? Whatever cut him was sharper than the Fahlarn's weapon, sharper than any claw I've ever seen."

Jes entered the too-small hut in a wave of cold air that somehow pushed aside the smell of rot. The aura of dread that followed him brought the smith to his knees as surely as an axe fells a tree.

"What happened to them?" asked Tier.

"The beast," whispered Aliven. "It killed my daughter first, and clawed up my wife, who was drawn by Lorra's cries. Then it attacked Tally." He gestured to the man Lehr still knelt beside. He hesitated, looking at his children a moment, then said in a low voice, "When Kaor and Habreman came for the plowshare I'd repaired, it killed them, too."

"What did it look like?" asked Tier.

The smith shuddered from the memory or perhaps just the cold and fear that Jes wore like a cloak. "It was too fast. I can tell you it wasn't a wolf, boar, or badger. It was faster than a fox and maybe twice as big. It had four limbs right enough and a stub tail that looked fluffy and pale. The rest of it was dark brown or grey."

He stared at Jes, then let his glance fall upon Lehr's ash-blond hair. "I don't have much silver," he said slowly. "My cousin has a gold piece put back from when he fought for the Emperor when he was a boy, but I don't know where it is. You might apply to my Sept, since it's his well we're using, but I doubt he'll pay Travelers for anything. He has his armsmen drive Travelers away from his territory."

Tier opened his mouth to refuse to take payment of any kind but stopped. There were a lot of mouths in the clan of Travelers who were escorting them home, and helping people like the smith was how they earned their food.

"I don't know what the charge'll be if we rid you of this beast," he said finally. "That's not my decision. It won't be more than you can bear—my word on it." That much he could fight Benroln on if he had to.

Jes dropped to all fours and brought his face next to the wounded man's. The smith flinched at the sudden movement.

"It was a mistwight," whispered Jes. "I can smell it."

"What's a mistwight?" asked Lehr.

"A water imp," replied Tier. "It's not undead, despite its name. They're called wights because they are shy, and most people catch only a glimpse of them before they're gone. I've heard that they can be nasty if you corner them. I've never heard of them being shadow-tainted, but most people couldn't tell one way or the other on that, I suppose. Your mother will know for certain."

Mistwights didn't live around home, where the snow got too deep. He'd glimpsed one once when he'd gone a-soldiering, but he couldn't see how Jes would have ever met one. "How do you know what they smell like, Jes?"

Dark eyes looked up, and Tier saw Jes, *his* Jes, rise up to answer his question. "I d-don't know," he stammered. "We just smelled it and knew." A breath later, and the Guardian's sharp darkness was back in his eyes.

Tier had never seen him do that before, transform from Guardian to Jes and back again, though it happened the other way around from time to time. It made him wonder why it had been necessary for Jes to answer that question rather than the Guardian.

All of his children knew that, as a Bard, Tier could hear a lie as clearly as an off-pitch note. Would the Guardian have felt compelled to lie if he had answered the question and so had given way to Jes?

"It's all right, Jes," said Lehr. "It doesn't matter. Now we know what we're dealing with."

Lehr was right, time enough to worry about Jes when this mess was cleaned up. Assuming the Guardian was right about what they were facing—and he certainly hadn't lied about it—they had trouble enough facing them.

Tier looked around the hut and pulled together a plan of attack. "Jes, I want you and Lehr to go back to the clan and tell your mother and Benroln what we've found here. Tell them we need Brewydd for the wounded and whatever people it takes to get rid of a tainted mistwight."

"Both of us?" asked Lehr. "Jes can stay to keep you safe."

Tier shook his head. "Both of you." It wouldn't do to say that his part of this, soothing the smith, would be better done without his sons, so he chose another truth. "If Jes stays, I'll never be able to keep him away from the mistwight until your mother gets here. Take Skew with you, so he doesn't get eaten while we're waiting."

"What will keep you safe?" asked Jes.

"If these people have been snug in here for days, I expect I'll survive a couple of hours," Tier said.

Jes frowned unhappily, but in the end he went out and gathered up Skew's reins. After a brief argument about who would ride, they set off at a rapid jog, leading the horse.

Once his sons were gone, Tier closed the door and barred the window again because their being open seemed to make the smith nervous. Then he sat on the floor and braced his back against a wall, sighing with the relief of getting his weight off his knees.

He looked away from the oppressive fear on the face of the smith. The fear of the thing in the well was stronger right now than the man's dislike of Travelers, but he wasn't getting any happier trapped in the tight quarters of the hut with Tier.

Tier decided to give the smith time to calm.

"Hello," he said, directing his remark to the two children, who huddled against the opposite wall.

The boy responded with a wary nod, the girl just tucked herself closer to her brother's side.

"There's a healer coming now to take care of your folk. We'll get rid of the creature who hurt them, too," he told them. "I know that it's pretty scary, but so is my wife."

"Your wife is scary?" asked the boy.

Tier nodded solemnly. "She is."

"That man was scary," whispered the girl, then pressed her face against the boy's arm. "The cold one."

"Jes?" said Tier. "You don't have to worry about Jes, his job is to protect people. It's just that he has a special kind of magic, and one of the things it does is make people around him nervous. Travelers don't just have one kind of magic the way we do, you know."

"We?" asked the smith. "Aren't you a Traveler?"

Tier shook his head. "No. My wife is, but I'm from Redern in the Sept of Leheigh over in the Ragged Mountains."

There was a tug on his shirt, and Tier looked down to see that the girl had left her seat to get his attention. He smiled at her. "Yes?"

"What kind of magic did the cold man have?"

"Jes is a Guardian," Tier explained. "His magic makes him a good guard against all kinds of evil. He can turn into animals or make it hard for others to see him if he wants to. The other man, my son Lehr, is a Hunter; he has a different magic. He can track things, and his magic helps him aim his arrows."

"Traveler mages aren't as good as ours," said the boy. "Our mages can do anything."

"I wouldn't say that." Tier felt no guilt at revealing things the Travelers liked to keep secret. "They're just different. My wife, Seraph, is closest to our wizards. Travelers call her Order either Mage or Raven—each of the Orders has a bird associated with it."

"How many kinds do they have?" asked the boy.

The tension in the hut had dropped off. The girl was leaning against Tier's arm instead of her brother's, and the boy had quit hugging the post as if it were the only thing that could keep him safe. Partly, Tier knew, it was that he was a distraction from the thing they were afraid of. Partly it was Tier's own magic, Bardic magic, easing their fears.

"Six." Tier ticked them off on his finger. "You've met Guardian—that's Eagle, and Hunter the Falcon. Then there's Raven the Mage. Lark is for Healer—and you are lucky the Traveler clan we're with has a Lark for your mother. Cormorant is Weather Witch, and Owl is Bard."

"Why birds?" asked the girl. "Why not fish?"

The boy rolled his eyes. "Nona, don't be stupid. Why would they name their powers after fish? How would you like to tell people that you were a garbagefish or a trout? That's stupid."

"I asked my wife why they used birds," Tier said quickly, before they could start fighting. "She didn't know."

"You talk a lot for a Traveler," said the smith, with a shade less hostility than before.

"But then, as I told you"—Tier smiled as he spoke—"I'm not a Traveler." The smile had Aliven relaxing further. As Jes's job was protection, Tier's was winning over hostile strangers, and he would do it as he saw fit.

Not Traveler, but Owl and Bard, he thought as the smith eased enough to take a seat against the opposite wall. But there was no use confusing the issue.

It had taken Tier's wife years to adjust to the idea that though there was not a drop of Traveler blood in him, he was still Bard. Order Bearers, it seemed, did not have to be Travelers.

Tier was in the middle of a fine story of a Traveler hero who saved children from a rampaging demon-wolf when they all heard hoofbeats.

Tier started to rise to his feet, but fell back with a grunt because his knees had stiffened up. A hand appeared in front of his face, and, after a brief hesitation he grasped it and let the smith haul him to his feet.

"Thanks," he said.

"What's wrong with your knees?" asked the smith.

Tier grinned at him. "A bunch of wizards took a club to them when I was trying to save the Emperor."

It was the truth, but he wasn't surprised to see the smith

laugh. Tier had, after all, just spent the last few hours telling stories that sounded more probable.

"As if wizards would bother using a club," the smith said, shaking his head as he let Tier brace himself until he was certain his knees would hold him upright.

"They said the club would hurt more," said Tier lightly.

Days of hiding in the hut momentarily blinded Aliven as he stepped outside, with Tier leaning on his shoulder.

Looking down to save his eyes, all he saw at first was a confusing clutter of horses' hooves. It caught his attention because he'd never yet seen so many Travelers mounted. They generally came afoot and left that way, too—curling their lips at people who let horses do all their traveling for them.

As his eyes adjusted he looked up, and the confusion sorted itself into a group of about ten men and three women. All except Tier's son Jes were pale-haired, some yellow-blond, others the strange ash-grey blond that belonged only to the Travelers. One of the women was old, older than anyone the smith had ever seen. They all looked grim and cold as Travelers always did—a marked contrast to Tier's warm good cheer.

Aliven, who had been slowly moving forward under the gentle pressure of Tier's hand on his shoulder, stopped.

"Benroln," said Tier, stopping beside him. "I didn't expect you to come yourself. I didn't know that mistwights were so dangerous as to require half the clan's fighting men."

In someone else's voice, the words would have been sarcastic or biting, but Tier made them cheerfully teasing.

One of the younger of the men grinned and, evidently being the Benroln that Tier had addressed, said, "Our experts tell us mistwights who have a taste for human flesh are nasty dangerous: smart, with a few magic tricks up their a—" He gave a nervous glance to the old woman who sat beside him, mounted on the spotted horse Tier had sent back with his sons, and cleared his throat. "With a bit of magic, anyway. Your wife assured us that between Ravens and Falcon they could take care of it, but the rest of us decided not to let them have all the fun. There would have been more of the clan here if we had the horses."

Tier stepped forward a little. "Benroln, may I present

Aliven Smith? Aliven this is Benroln, Clan Chief and Cormorant of the Clan of Rongier the Librarian."

Cormorant was one of those magical birds Tier had spoken of, Aliven remembered belatedly, though he didn't remember which. He didn't know how to respond to the introduction without giving offense, so he ducked his head and hoped it was sufficient.

Apparently it was. The young man slid off his horse and shook the smith's limp hand briskly. "We've met," he said. "Though we've not been formally introduced."

It was possible, Aliven knew. But all those blond heads and subtly foreign features tended to look alike to him.

Tier gave the young Traveler a sharp look.

Benroln laughed and shrugged, flushing a little. "Just to trade for grain, Bard. Nothing more."

The horses shuffled, and a man came to the side of the old woman. Aliven was almost certain it was Tier's blond son, though it could have been some other Traveler—he hadn't paid so much attention to Tier's second son, not after the dark boy had come into the hut.

"I like this horse, Bard," the old woman said to Tier. "Like me, he's still kicking when his contemporaries have had the self-respect to die off." Now that he looked, Aliven could see hollows above the horse's eyes that told a different story than the sinewy hindquarters and alert stance.

Tier bowed to her, a low, sweeping bow that was court-polished. "The both of you are too stubborn to give in to time any more than you'd give in to anyone else. Brewydd, this is Aliven Smith. Aliven, this is our Lark, Brewydd." With his face carefully turned so that only Aliven could see, Tier mouthed the word *healer* and winked.

"Lehr, get me off this poor creature's back before we both fall down dead and are no use to anyone." The old woman hadn't acknowledged the introduction with so much as a glance.

Tier's son—for the old woman had called him by the same name as Tier had called his son—reached up and held her steady as she swung one leg over the horse's spotted rump with surprising grace. When she had both legs on one side, he caught her at waist and shoulder and set her gently on her feet.

She looked at Aliven for the first time and smiled gently.

"Don't let this mob worry you, my lad," she said, taking the smith's arm. "They just want to see the mistwight."

It took Aliven a moment to realize that he was the "lad" she referred to. No one had called him "lad" since his da died some fifteen years ago.

The old woman's words, for no reason that Aliven could discern, seemed to be the signal for the whole party of Travelers to hop off their horses and take them away to tie up somewhere.

"I'm going to quit sending you out on your own, Tier," said one of the younger women, handing off her horse to Tier's dark-haired son. She wasn't very tall, but carried with her an aura of power that made her seem larger than she was. If Travelers aged as regular folk did, she was younger than Tier. Only the fine lines around her eyes aged her at all.

Tier laughed and approached her with a quick stride that showed no sign of limp. He put his hands on her waist and swung her around once.

When he set her down, she continued, every bit as self-possessed as she'd been before Tier had assaulted her dignity. "I let you go hunting, and you got yourself kidnaped. I let you out to play with your boy-soldiers and, if not for Lark's help, you'd have been crippled. You left to get grain, and you find a mistwight who has taken up eating people instead of frogs and fish."

"It was either let me out to do some trading or suffer that some poor clansman be talked to death," Tier teased, then gave her a quick, smacking kiss in the middle of her forehead.

Beyond Tier's shoulder, Aliven saw a few of the Travelers lose their cool self-possession enough to smile.

"*Solsenti* bastard," said the woman without affection, staring at Tier as if he were something found in a midden.

"Not at all," he assured her. "My parents were married. Brave man, my father, just like his son."

She tried to hide it, but Aliven saw the corners of her mouth try to turn up.

"Where's Gura?" he asked, glancing around.

"We left him behind," she said. "The mistwight would make short work of any dog, no matter how big or ferocious. He was not happy with us when we left."

"I'd bet not," Tier said dryly. "Seraph, this is Aliven Smith, whose child was killed by the beast. Aliven, this is my wife, Seraph, Raven of the Clan of Isolde the Silent—though we're traveling with the Librarian's Clan at present."

To the smith's discomfort, Tier's wife stepped forward and touched his face, making him conscious of the grime of the past few days that covered his skin.

"We will deal with the mistwight," she said, "that it trouble you and yours no more."

There was such certainty in her voice that he found himself believing her.

"And you and I will tend your wounded," said the old woman on the smith's arm. She tugged him imperiously as she pointed her finger at one of the men. "You come, too. You'll be more help to me in healing than to the hunting of the mistwight. Bring my packs." If there was no sharpness in her voice, there was no politeness either. Aliven was surprised to see the man bow respectfully, then hurry to take a pair of largish saddlebags off the spotted horse.

"Brewydd."

The old woman paused to look at Tier.

"There are a pair of children in there who've been through a great deal. Be gentle with them."

The healer smiled, displaying a surprisingly complete set of teeth. "I'll bear that in mind, my boy."

Tier waited until the healer had Aliven in the hut before he said, "Something tells me that the mistwight's not going to be so easily gotten rid of."

Seraph nodded. "They're not easy. Smart and tough."

"I've never heard of one killing people," said Tier. "Though I know that people who live near them tend to leave them alone."

"When they are young they hunt fish, frogs, and other small animals," said Hennea, returning from tying her horse.

Hennea was a Raven like Tier's wife. She looked a decade younger than Seraph and was easily the more beautiful. There was a peacefulness in her face that Seraph had never managed, his wife's temperament not being well suited to peace.

"As they age," she continued, "they begin to go after larger prey. Usually they go to the sea and hunt the larger fish, but some turn inland and hunt raccoon or otters. I've never heard of one that fed on human flesh."

"The shadow taint explains that well enough," said Seraph. "Mistwights aren't as smart as humans, quite. But it's had several centuries to learn."

"Centuries?" asked Tier.

"Mistwights have been known to live four hundred years or more," said Hennea. "Since Jes says that this one is shadow-tainted, it might be even older. All of them have some magic of their own, which is probably why they live so long. Some wizards live halfway into their second century, and several of the Colossae wizards were four or five hundred years old."

"Or so it is said." Seraph caught his look and laughed, "Oh, not me. The Orders don't prolong life"—she cast a specula-tive glance at the hut where Brewydd had disappeared—"except, maybe, for Lark. When you're an old, old man, my love, I'll be an old woman."

Seraph and Hennea began pacing a double circle around the well in which Lehr told them the creature was living. Hennea took the outer ring and Seraph the inner.

"It killed easily," said Seraph.

"It's done this before. Doubtless Lehr would be able to track it back from one isolated farm or small settlement to another. If we hadn't stumbled upon it here, it might have continued for another few centuries before it attracted a Traveler's attention."

"Are you certain that it's in the well now?" asked Tier.

The Travelers from Benroln's clan had taken up a shady spot not too far away to watch. Not willing to risk Seraph get-ting eaten, Tier walked with the Ravens, careful to stay out of their pattern making.

He kept a weather eye on the well and noticed that Jes was doing the same. Lehr had taken a post not too far from the other Travelers, where he could see the wellhead. He had his bow strung and an arrow ready for flight.

"Hopefully," said Hennea. "Seraph and I will establish a net"—she waved her hand vaguely to indicate the paths they'd been establishing—"that will stifle its magic."

"What kind of magic does a mistwight have?"

Hennea shrugged. "Some illusion, a bit of water magic."

"They are nasty enough without their magic," Seraph said. "We'll hamper it any way we can. The most trouble we'll have with it is getting it out of the well since it almost certainly knows that we're here. It fed not long ago, so it won't be hungry."

"I, for one, have no intention of climbing down a well to face a tainted mistwight. What are we going to do about the well?" Hennea didn't sound overly concerned.

"Fire is nice," said Seraph. "It won't hurt the well itself."

"Can't it just submerge?" asked Tier.

Seraph pursed her lips. "Not without magic. They can't breathe underwater or hold their breath for long. If I scorch him fast enough, he'll not have a chance to call magic."

She stopped walking, and Tier's knees informed him it was none too soon.

"We've walked the round," she said. "Hennea, are you ready?"

He didn't see what they did, but he felt the magic right enough, sweeping through him like a cool wind.

"I thought you didn't need ritual for your magic," said Tier. "Isn't that the main difference between you and a *solsenti* mage?"

"We don't need it," Seraph told him. "But sometimes a few runes or a ritual walk to establish a warding is quicker and more efficient than doing it by brute force."

"Let's give a closer look to the well," Hennea said.

As they approached the well, Tier pulled his sword and dogged Seraph's heels again. Hennea had a wolf at her side— Jes sometimes became one of any of a number of predators when the mood struck him.

It looked like any other well to Tier. A three-sided building, much like a smaller version of the smithy, protected the well from weather and dust. A stout mud-brick wall ringed the wellhead about waist high on Tier. Before they came quite to the well, Jes put his front paws on the lip of the well and growled.

"Good," said Seraph. "It's there." She turned to Hennea. "I'll do the fire; you can deal with the mistwight."

Hennea usually held to her serene mildness under all circumstances, so the edge of fierceness that touched her smile surprised Tier.

"It's always nice to have plans," she said.

The wall of the well wasn't high, but neither was Seraph. Tier lifted her from the ground to the top of the well wall with a hand on each hip. He steadied her until she was stable with one hand on the post that held up the roof.

She gave him a quick, distracted smile for his help, then looked into the dark hole. Perched flat-footed on the old wall, she had to dip her head a little to avoid hitting the roof.

She was magnificent.

Her moonlit-colored hair was caught up in an elaborate crown of braids that he'd seen other Traveler women wear. Until this past month, she'd always adopted the simpler styles of the Rederni. The braids suited her, he thought. She was wearing Traveler clothing, too: loose trousers and a long loose tunic that hit the bottoms of her knees.

Hennea was beautiful, but Seraph stirred him more than a woman who was merely beautiful ever could. She had such inner strength that he was sometimes surprised by how small she was. He'd once seen her back down a roomful of angry men with nothing more than the sharpness of her tongue.

Watching her as she quivered with eagerness, like a fine hunting hound awaiting the horn, he was struck with a sudden, wrenching understanding.

This was his wife, his Seraph, who'd given up everything she was to escape from the endless battle her people fought against things like the mistwight. She'd married him hoping that it would keep her out of battles just like this one. Oh, she said now that it was because she loved him—but he knew Seraph. If she had not dreaded returning to the duties of a Raven, she would never have accepted his offer of marriage.

He'd always felt that he'd helped to save her from something terrible, but she didn't look like someone who needed rescuing.

She held her hands palm down over the well: tension flowed up her body from toes to fingertips, and the sharp, sparkling feeling that was magic brushed over his skin in an uneasy caress. With a hollow boom that shook the ground he stood upon, flame boiled suddenly out of the well in a searing wave of destruction. The roof caught fire first, then the walls of the sheltering building, the frail strands of weeds that surrounded the well house, followed an instant later by the post Seraph held on to.

Heedless of his damaged knees, Tier dove through the flames and caught Seraph around the waist, jerking her off the well and away from the fire. He had her on the ground and rolled her over twice before he realized that her clothes had not kindled and she was laughing.

He released her abruptly, but she sat up and kept her hands on him, brushing over his sleeves and quenching the smoldering fabric.

"I overdid it," she said, with a grin he recognized as the expression of action-drunk joy that sometimes caught warriors in the height of battle. He'd never seen her look more lovely.

He'd never been so angry with her, either—she could have killed herself.

There was a sharp crack of sound behind them, and Tier jerked around to see Seraph's flames whoosh out of existence as quickly as they had come, leaving the shed that protected the well blackened but unharmed.

As Hennea lowered her hands to her side after quenching the fire, something dark and smoking slipped over the rim of the well. It darted past Tier in an attempt to reach the nearby woodland; its pace so rapid he was left with scattered impressions of sparse wiry hair over wrinkled skin and sapphire eyes. The wolf who was Jes was only a little slower.

"The wight!" shouted Benroln.

An arrow intercepted the beast before Benroln finished the last syllable of its name. The thing rolled end over end several times, and Jes was upon it.

Dust and fur and darkness tangled until Tier couldn't tell one creature from the other. But evidently Lehr had no such problem. A second arrow found flesh, then a third and fourth.

Jes separated himself, then shook his fur to rid it of dust and dried grass. The mistwight struggled weakly for a few seconds more, three of Lehr's arrows stuck up from hip, neck, and rib. A fourth, broken off a handspan from the tip, protruded from its eye. Its ribs rose twice more and stilled.

Dead, it seemed to take up much less space than it had alive.

Seraph lay back down and laughed. She turned to Tier, and the smile slid from her eyes. "What's wrong, Tier?"

He forced a smile and shook his head. She didn't deserve his anger. It wasn't her fault that she enjoyed the spice of danger—he knew the feeling himself, but it unsettled him to see it in his wife. Not just because she had risked her life, either.

"Nothing, love. Let me give you a hand up."

This is what she had been born to do, he thought, as they strode back to the smith's hut like a small triumphant army after Hennea disposed of the mistwight's body with another bout of flame.

He could feel her outgrowing the home they'd forged together. He'd tried to ignore the changes in her since she and their sons had ridden to his rescue, but today had forced him to face them head-on. To save him, Seraph had taken up the mantle of her Order again.

He couldn't see how she'd ever pull herself small enough to live on the farm and be nothing but a farmer's wife again. Even if she tried to set her power aside a second time, he wasn't certain if he could allow it, not remembering the joy on her face as the well lit with flames.

CHAPTER 2

"No wonder he was out in the middle of nowhere. If
there were a good smith nearby, he'd starve to death," said
Benroln sourly as his sturdy bay kept pace with the little horse
Tier rode. Brewydd had appropriated Skew for the ride back
to the clan's camp with Tier's blessing. Lehr had had to carry
the exhausted healer back to the horses, but the smith's
wounded would recover.

"The smith's work is good enough by the local standards,"
Tier told Benroln. "You can't expect master-level bladecraft-
ing from a man who makes mostly nails and plowshares. If
you'd asked for a plow, doubtless you'd have been better
pleased."

"We have not the slightest need for a plow," grumbled Benroln. "Or nails either. But either would have done us more
good than three braces of ill-balanced, rough-handled knives."

"Then your own smith can use the metal to make something more suitable," soothed Tier. "You know as well as I that
the real benefit you gained this day is that next time you—or
any Traveler—comes by here, you will be welcomed and
treated fairly."

"Is Benroln still complaining?" Seraph came up to ride by
Tier's side. She gave Benroln a steady look. "If you'd really

wanted a good bargain, you'd have driven it before we killed the mistwight and Brewydd healed his family. Afterward, you get what he gives and be grateful for it."

Benroln muttered an excuse and dropped back to talk with someone who would listen to him with a more sympathetic ear.

"The knives aren't so bad," said Tier. "They're just not up to the standards of the clan's smith."

Seraph watched him closely. "What's wrong?"

"My knees," he lied. She saw too much with her clear-eyed gaze. "They'll be fine."

He would lose her, he thought. She would stay with him for a while because the children needed her and because she'd given her word to him. But the boys were young men already, and their daughter was no longer a helpless child. How long would his love cage her from the life she was born to?

She'd grown into a woman who could deal with the responsibilities she'd come to him to escape. She was Raven, and he thought perhaps for the first time he understood what that meant.

"We can stop for a while and give your knees a chance to rest," said Seraph. "Brewydd could probably use the rest as well."

"No"—he shook his head—"Brewydd is tired, but all she has to do is sit on Skew until we make it back to camp. As for my knees, I just walked too far today. My knees will be fine. No fun, but a long way from unbearable."

Unbearable was that he could see no way to hold Seraph without destroying her; by comparison his knees were nothing. "I'll be fine."

Midmorning the next day they came to a crossroads, and Benroln called a halt. As soon as everyone had stopped he strode directly to Tier and Seraph.

"We are called to the southern fork," he said in a tight voice.

Seraph smiled at him. "Is this the first time?"

Benroln nodded jerkily.

"Some leaders never hear the call," she told him, then glancing at Tier, she explained. "When the clan's help is needed, the leader of a clan knows. It spoke to my brother. He told me it's like a whisper or a tugging string."

"A string," said Benroln, his face a little flushed. "It pulls my heart. My father said his father had it—but I never really believed."

"You go on then," said Tier. "We'll continue west on our own. It's not far now."

Benroln's face lost the absent look it had held. "You have to come with us. Without you we have only me and the Healer. Brewydd says that there is another Shadowed."

Tier looked around. "I see a lot of people. Surely you don't dismiss everyone without an Order as useless?"

Benroln gave a huff of frustration. "You know what I mean."

Tier nodded. "I do. But I have a young daughter staying with my folk—who've no magic at all. Now, when my sons were chasing the Shadowed—"

"We don't know he was the Shadowed," said Seraph.

"All right," agreed Tier. "But if he wasn't another like the Unnamed King, then he was wearing the robes of one of the Masters of the Secret Path, so he must have been a wizard. I'm minded then, that he was killing off Travelers and stealing their Orders just as the others were. He's not going to be best pleased with the people who destroyed his work—and I've the nasty suspicion that he's going to hold me mostly to blame for it, despite the fact I spent most of the battle chained up and helpless. Benroln, my daughter Rinnie is staked out in Redern like the bait in a mountain-cat trap. I'll not leave her alone any longer than I can help."

"How do you know that he knows anything at all about your daughter? The wizard, Shadowed or not, was in Taela—that's a long way from Redern."

"The Path had someone watching our family," Tier told him, feeling a trace of the anger that he'd felt when he'd first found out. What if they had decided to steal away one of the children instead of him? What if he had died? Would the Path have been able to pick off the children one by one? The thought brought an urgent need to have his family together, where he could keep an eye on all of them. He needed to get to Redern.

"He knows about Rinnie," Tier said firmly. "I'm sorry, Benroln, but I won't risk her."

"You'll find a way to do what you are called to do without us," said Seraph.

Hennea, the other Raven, was not a member of Benroln's clan either, but had come to Seraph in Redern and traveled with his family when they rode to Taela, the capital of the Empire, to rescue him. She had no real ties to them.

"Perhaps Hennea will go with you," suggested Tier.

Jes had jogged over to see what the delay was, Gura at his heel. The big dog had been reluctant to let any of them out of his sight since they'd gotten back from killing the mistwight, and tended to race back and forth from one of his people to another—sort of like Jes.

Before Benroln could reply to Tier's suggestion, Jes shook his head, and said positively, "Hennea stays with us."

Tier raised his eyebrows, hiding the worry he felt about the budding relationship between Jes and Hennea. "Hennea's a Raven and will do as she wishes, Jes. I thought you'd know that, having grown up with your mother. Why don't you go find her and see what she says?"

Hennea usually liked to stay toward the back of the clan when they traveled. Jes found her there, talking with a half dozen or so people and Lehr, who smelled of mint and the herbs he must have been collecting for the Healer.

Lehr looked up, saw Jes, and asked, "Why are we stopped?"

Jes felt the weight of everyone's attention focus on him; their fear tangled with curiosity beat upon him. He didn't like it, and neither did the Guardian. He dropped his eyes to the ground and tried not to feel them or notice how they backed away.

"Benroln is called south," he told the ground. "We're going on to Redern because Papa is afraid that the Shadowed might try and hurt Rinnie."

The Guardian agreed with Papa. He also believed that the man they had chased was a Shadowed one, not just shadow-tainted.

Jes missed the first part of what Hennea said, though the

last of it—"I should go with Benroln"—was enough to bring
the Guardian boiling to the surface.

"No," Jes said, but that was all he could manage around the
Guardian's growl, unheard by anyone else.

<She comes with us! She is mine!>

Jes agreed with the sentiment, but was certain that the
Guardian's telling Hennea as much would be disastrous. So he
fought to keep control. It didn't help that as the Guardian had
arisen, the icy dread of his presence increased the fear of
everyone around him. Their emotions roiled around him like
the river in a storm, until Hennea put her hand on his arm,
bringing with her the cool relief that was a part of her. He
could still feel the others, but somehow, Hennea's presence
managed to shield him from the worst of it.

"Why don't you take him away from everyone," Lehr's
calm voice soothed him, too. "You're not going to get any
sense out of him with all these people around him."

Hennea must have agreed because Jes found himself following her through the trees. As soon as they were out of sight
of the others, their feelings died down to a murmur, but Hennea led him farther.

"I need you to come with us," he told her.

She patted him on the arm—a motherly gesture—then
crossed her arms in front of her chest and turned away. She
found something interesting in the bark of a tree and traced
patterns on the rough surface with a finger.

"You'll be fine," she told the tree, though Jes assumed she
was really talking to him. "There's no need for me to come with
you. I've repaid the debt I owed to your mother for tricking her
into killing Volis the priest. We've seen to it that the Secret Path
won't be killing any more Travelers and stealing their Orders."

Jes stared at her back. Did he mean nothing to her? Of
course not. She'd been kind to him, rescued him, and in the
process kissed him. Doubtless he wasn't the only man she'd
ever kissed.

How could she care for him? Had he forgotten what he
was? A madman who alternated between being a simpleton
and a ravening beast. He should count himself lucky that she
didn't run screaming.

<Let me talk to her.>

The Guardian had never asked him before, he'd just taken over if he could. Jes hesitated, remembering that first, possessive roar. But on the rare occasions when he was calm, the Guardian was better-spoken than Jes. Perhaps he could change her mind.

"We can't force her," he said. Perhaps he shouldn't have said it aloud because Hennea didn't look happy when she turned around to stare at him, but the Guardian wasn't as good at hearing Jes as he was at hearing the Guardian. Jes didn't want the Guardian to make matters worse.

<Please. She must come with us.>

With a sigh, Jes let the Guardian overwhelm him.

"You can't force me," said Hennea.

"No," he agreed, stepping away because he thought he might be frightening her—though her face was composed. He didn't want to frighten her. "What do you intend to do now that your debt to my mother is remitted and the Path is rendered harmless?"

"I will seek out the Shadowed," she said. "It may be that the man you chased through the tunnels of the Emperor's castle was just another *solsenti* wizard. But if not, it would be disastrous to allow him to run free."

The Guardian lowered his eyelids, trying to look unthreatening. It wasn't something he had a lot of practice at.

"My father told Benroln that the Shadowed is going to seek vengeance against us for the death of the Secret Path," he said. "If you want to find him, you are more likely to find him in our company."

"Or in Benroln's as he follows his call," she said.

But her voice wasn't as firm as it had been.

"There was no clue to the Shadowed's identity in the papers left by the Path," said the Guardian. "None of the servants knew anything, nor did any of the men the Emperor could have questioned. Only the wizards might have known who he was, and they were all killed the night the Path fell. There might still be records in the temples, but the Emperor could do nothing against either of the temples of the Five Gods in Taela because there was nothing that connected them to the Path. In Redern, though, there is a temple ready to be searched."

"We searched it already," Hennea said.

"Did you? I thought two tired Ravens went through and did their best to find all the Ordered gemstones and anything that might bring harm to villagers who might go exploring. Did you read all of Volis's correspondence? Did you search for journals? Were you looking for a new Shadowed One?" He knew the answers to those questions—she did, too, because she didn't say anything.

"Then there are the Path's gemstones, also," he murmured, trying hard to keep his triumph from showing. His relief. She was his to guard, as his family was his to guard. He could not have borne for them to be at risk and he not able to protect them all. He needed them to stay together. "Seraph will do her best to solve their secrets and free the Orders that are bound to the stones. She will not give them to you—I know her well enough to understand that she could never give that task to another, even if you do not. It matters too much to her." *And to you*, he thought.

She bowed her head shallowly. "You are right," she said serenely. "I will come. But I will not *stay* in Redern, Jes." She rubbed her hands over her face, and it seemed to Jes that the gesture rubbed away some of her composure. "I cannot be more to you than I am. You are so young. You will find someone else. I am—" She stopped. Took a deep breath. "I was Volis's leman, Jes." Her voice shook on the dead priest's name, though he could tell that she was doing her best to be impassive. It was fortunate for the priest that he was already dead.

She must have felt his reaction because she continued hurriedly. "I chose it because it seemed to be the best way to find out how to save my people. I would do it again. I am not your mother, who chooses her family over duty. *I* am a Raven first—and Ravens do not make good mates. Strong emotions are almost as dangerous to us as they are to Guardians. I chose not to love, Jes. Not ever. I can't afford it. You deserve someone who will love you."

The Guardian closed in on her, but she held her ground even when he put one hand on her neck and the other on her shoulder to hold her still. He bent his head and kissed her—gently at first, though that wasn't part of his nature. He let Jes return and take control of the kiss just as her shoulder softened under his hand and her lips parted.

Jes savored the touch, but withdrew before Hennea's snarl of emotions broke the spell of the kiss and made it something more complex.

He didn't look at her, didn't want to try and read her face. He didn't know what emotions she would decipher from his own since he wasn't certain what he felt.

His father would say that their conversation had resulted in a draw. He'd also say that sometimes, that was the best result you could hope for. Jes was pretty certain this was one of those times.

He didn't say anything, just stepped back so that she could lead the way back to where the clan waited. He followed her, making certain that she did not come to harm.

Tier fretted because they made slower time once they'd left Benroln and his people. Mostly that was due to Seraph's insistence on frequent rest stops to spare Tier's knees. Brewydd had not been so strict a caretaker. In the evenings, Seraph and Hennea continued to spend hours in the illusionary remains of one of the Colossae wizards' homes as they, and Brewydd, had done since they left Taela. They used Seraph's *mermora,* the house that had once belonged to Isolde the Silent.

Tier had known about the *mermori* for years, but Seraph had seldom done more than look through the graceful silver forms, which to him looked like small elaborate daggers. He'd seen Isolde's house once or twice, but that didn't make the sudden appearance of a house in the middle of the wilds any less fantastical.

They were looking for a way to free the Orders that the Path had bound to gemstones.

"It would have been easier," Seraph told him one night, "if the Path actually managed to do what they had intended. If they had managed to separate the Order completely from the Traveler they killed, the gemstones could probably just have been destroyed to free the Orders."

"But you can't do that now."

She shifted against his side to get more comfortable. He didn't tell her that her elbow was digging into his ribs where they were still a little tender because that would make her move away from him entirely. She'd wriggle around a bit more before she fell asleep anyway.

"No," she said, yawning. "Brewydd says there were only ever a few Orders in the world. When one Order Bearer dies, the Order is cleansed and passes to a new bearer. Because of the Path's interference, these Orders aren't cleansed."

"What do you mean?" he asked. He'd missed these late-night talks. When they'd first left Taela, he had been too tired by the time they stopped each night to do anything but sleep. He was tired tonight as well, but not with the kind of exhaustion that made him lose consciousness as soon as he quit moving.

"Most of the gems don't work quite right," Seraph said. "What was supposed to happen was when the gem was worn against a wizard's skin, that wizard could use the powers of the Order just as if he was the Order Bearer they had stolen it from. Brewydd thinks that they were stealing the Order too soon, before it was cleansed by the death of its previous bearer."

"So the gems are haunted?" Tier asked.

Seraph nodded. "Or so we surmise. Volis said that none of the Healer gems work right."

"If you break the stones, won't the Orders be freed?"

Seraph shrugged. "Probably. But they'll still have bits and pieces of their previous owners' experience—maybe even per-sonality. Brewydd thought it might keep them from bonding at all—or, worse, make the Order act more like a shadow taint." She took a deep breath. "Like the Guardian Order, maybe."

"I see why you can't just destroy the gemstones," Tier said, smoothing her hair.

"It might come to that eventually," Seraph said. "But I'm not anywhere near willing to take that risk."

The mountains were a mixed blessing, thought Tier a few days later. It meant they were getting closer to home—but it also slowed their pace.

Jes and Lehr had taken to ranging in front of them with

Gura, looking for chance game or wayside robbers—leaving the women to totter along with the cripple and his old war-horse, Tier thought sourly. Journeying with Benroln's clan, he had gotten used to riding while others walked, but it bothered him more when his only companions were a pair of women.

When they came to a fairly level stretch of road he threw one leg over Skew's rump and dropped to the ground with a groan.

"What are you doing?" Seraph put her hands on her hips and frowned at him.

"I'm going to walk a bit," he told her, and suited his actions to his words.

"Brewydd told you to keep off those knees." Seraph slipped an arm through his and walked beside him.

"That was a week ago," Tier said. "I'll only walk where the road is level. Skew needs a rest."

"He does not," she said stubbornly. "Tier—" She stopped herself. Her voice soft, she said, "I worry too much, I know. But I hate it. Hate that you were hurt. Hate it worse that I didn't get to immolate the men who did it until after they were dead."

He slipped the fingers of his left hand through her braids and ducked down to kiss her on the lips. "You're not responsible for everything that happens, my Raven. You can't prevent any of us from getting hurt or even dying. That is not your place. Best you accept that now, love."

She didn't say anything more, but tucked herself more closely against him as they walked.

"It is, though," she said, when they reached the end of the level path, and Tier stopped to mount.

"Is what?" he asked with a grunt of pain. Walking hadn't been too bad, but mounting was miserable. His left knee didn't want to bend enough for him to get a foot in the stirrup, and his right knee wasn't happy about holding all of his weight. He managed it, and managed to haul himself into the saddle, too, but only just.

Seraph waited until he was settled before she answered his question. "It is my place to keep others safe. It's what I was raised for and part of being Raven."

He kept Skew still for a moment as he looked down upon his wife. She was strong, and gods knew she was powerful. He knew that, but his heart saw how easily she bruised and how mortal her flesh. His eyes saw a woman who weighed half what he or either of her sons did.

He loved everything about her. If she were not a Raven, she wouldn't be his Seraph. If he could, he would not change that part of her, even if it meant she had to take up her duties and leave the farm, leave him. But he didn't have to like it.

"Is it?" he asked softly. "Maybe. But those stories are so old, Seraph. Older than the Empire. Older than the Fall of the Unnamed King. Are you certain that you are right? Maybe there's something else that the Ravens, the Owls, and all the other Ordered are supposed to do. Maybe there's a better reason that Jes suffers under the Guardian Eagle's talon. I hope there is. If it is only that some damn fool wizards decided they'd made a mess their children's children's children needed to pay for, then you are all paying too much."

Hennea stopped and picked up a rock that caught her fancy and put it in her pocket. The air was heavy with clouds, but there was no rain yet. Perhaps she ought to go back to the trail and join up with Seraph and Tier.

When the boys were both out scouting, Hennea tried to give Seraph and Tier what privacy she could. There was some tension between them to be worked out—and walking alone was no hardship for Hennea. She liked being alone because it gave her time to think.

She'd had time enough to decide the decision she'd made to stay with Jes's family had been the right one. The kind of man who could give up his humanity for power would not forgive the blow that Tier had dealt to his plans. Sooner or later the Shadowed would find them, and Hennea intended to be there when he did. That was the purpose of her existence after all—to keep the shadows at bay.

Her decision was the right one, but not for Jes. Not for Jes. She was going to end up hurting him.

She took the rock in her pocket and threw it as hard as she

could. It hit a tree and bounced off the bark and into the branches before falling to the ground with a dull thud.

"What's wrong?" asked Jes, startling her. Guardians were like that.

"Nothing," Hennea said, without turning to look at him. "I was just thinking it was probably time to get back to your parents. They're going to wonder where we are."

"I'm not my father," Jes said. He was close enough now that she could feel the heat of his body against her skin. "I don't know when you are lying."

"Always," she told him. It was the truth, but she kept her voice light.

Slowly, so she had plenty of time to move, Jes leaned against her back and wrapped an arm around the front of her shoulders above her breasts and pulled her against him. She could feel his breath stirring her hair and closed her eyes so she could feel it better. It had been a very long time since someone had touched her this way. There was nothing sexual in the embrace—if there had been, she'd have pulled away. But she couldn't make herself reject the comfort he offered her.

Her eyes burned with tears though she didn't know why.

"You are tired," Jes whispered in her ear, and tightened his arm.

"Seraph and I stayed up too late," she said.

He shook his head. "No. Not sleepy. Tired."

She was tired of fighting a futile battle that never seemed to end. They had managed to bring the Path down—a task that had seemed impossible to her when she'd started out for Taela with Seraph and her sons. They'd managed it somehow, but there was no triumph in a victory that left a Shadowed at large. And if they managed to destroy this Shadowed, another one would appear. Let ten years or a couple of centuries pass, and there would be another power-mad mage who wanted to live forever. Whatever she did, it would never be enough.

"Very tired," said Jes, rocking her slightly. "Shh. Don't cry."

She wanted to turn and bury herself in his arms. They were strong arms, which managed to make her feel safer than she could ever remember feeling. Only Jes. She loved the smell of woods and earth that clung to his skin. She loved . . .

She didn't want to hurt Jes.

She pulled away and turned to face him. "I'm not crying. It's started to rain."

He tilted his head then held out his hand to let a few sparse drops land on his palm. He gave her a gentle smile. "My father would know you are lying."

Impatiently, Hennea wiped her face. "It's a good thing that you are not your father then, isn't it?"

His smile widened further as he nodded. "Especially since my mother would be upset if you felt about my father the way you felt about me while I held you."

Empath. How could she have forgotten?

She didn't know what showed on her face, but it made him laugh. Even as her face burned, part of her observed that Jes's laughter warmed her cold center. It made her want to touch him.

"Look at that," said Tier pointing at a mountaintop. "See that peak? I'd know it anywhere. We're closer to home than I thought."

"Skew's been walking faster for an hour or so," Seraph told him, just as the first drops of rain began to fall. "I think that we're no more than an hour's walk from home. Maybe less. I've only been over this road once."

She glanced up at her husband and smiled to herself at the intent look on his face. It had been autumn when he'd seen Rinnie last, more than half a year ago.

From somewhere on the side of the trail came Jes's too-loud boisterous laugh. Branches rustled and shook, and Hennea burst onto the path, looking uncharacteristically disturbed.

She marched up to Seraph and shook her finger at her. "You tell that boy of yours that he is too young for me. I don't take babes fresh from their mother's milk."

"She likes me, Mother," said Jes, following Hennea with a wide grin.

"I can see that," said Tier. "But take it from me, son. It's time to let her settle her feathers."

Hennea shifted her hot gaze to Tier. "*You* will *not* encourage him."

Seraph had never heard of a Guardian stable enough to contemplate a romantic entanglement. There were any number of problems. Even simple touching was difficult—when the Guardian slept, its Order Bearer, who was always an empath, was too raw to allow anyone to touch him. When the Guardian was in control, the nameless dread that accompanied his presence was more than enough to cool the ardor of the most heated lover.

But Hennea's training as a Raven gave her enormous control that seemed to protect Jes from her emotions so that he could enjoy her touch. And as for the Guardian, Hennea didn't appear to be intimidated by him in the slightest.

It gave Seraph hope.

As Tier and Hennea exchanged a few words, sharp on her part and teasing on his, Seraph watched Jes, enjoying his laughter until it abruptly stopped. Amusement died in his eyes first, but quickly faded altogether, leaving a face that looked as if it had never smiled.

Before she could ask what was wrong, Lehr emerged from the forest on their left with Gura. "Papa, Mother, something—"

He was interrupted by the shrill scream of a stallion. Skew answered, half-rearing.

"Easy," soothed Tier, and Skew, his warning given, allowed himself to be gentled. "What's wrong?"

The storm chose that moment to turn from a gentle rain into a downpour; Seraph ducked her head involuntarily. When she looked up, there was a horse facing them in the middle of the path.

It was pale as death—a dirty off-white that darkened to yellow on the ends of his ragged tail. It looked cadaverous, with a full fingerspace between each rib and great hollows behind its sunken eyes.

"What's wrong?" said Jes, and at first Seraph thought he was just repeating Tier.

But then the horse spoke in a voice as rough and terrible as the storm.

"Come," it said, then dashed into the trees.

Both boys and the dog disappeared behind it. Skew took a bounce forward before Tier stopped him and looked at Seraph and Hennea.

"It's the forest king," said Seraph as soon as she realized it herself. "Go ahead. Hennea and I'll catch up."

He didn't wait for her to say it twice.

"That's Jes's forest king?" asked Hennea as she scrambled beside Seraph in Tier's wake. "Not exactly what I expected."

"He seldom is," agreed Seraph absently as she tried to pick a quick way through the undergrowth near the trail.

"Do we need to track them, or do you know where we're going?"

"Can't you feel it?" asked Seraph. "I wasn't paying attention until it worsened—but this storm is called."

"Rinnie?"

"Unless there's another Cormorant in the area. Something is very wrong."

They fell silent then, Seraph turning all her energies to climbing. The shortest path home was steep, forcing them to slow before they were halfway there.

"I'm going to the farm," she told Hennea, between gasps for breath. "That's where it feels like she is. I'll be able to tell for certain once we top this rise."

Hennea didn't bother to try and talk.

Seraph stopped at the ridgetop. The farm lay below, but she couldn't see it for the trees and the darkening skies. She had more than vision to call upon, though.

The first thing Seraph had done when she and Tier had moved to the farm was to walk a warding that surrounded it. The farm was too close to the old battlefield, Shadow's Fall, to be entirely safe without protection from the kinds of creatures attracted to shadow. Several times a year for twenty years she'd added to its potency.

Her warding traced along the crest just here.

Seraph knelt in the pine needles and touched the threads of her spelling. Power swept through her in a heady rush—something shadow-touched was trying to cross it at that very moment. Like a spider at her web, she waited, letting her breathing slow, while she waited for the warding to tell her more.

It settled back down after a moment, though she could tell that whatever shadowed thing had touched it was still near. There were some weak areas in the warding, she noticed, as if it had been much longer than the six months or so when she'd last reworked it: something or a number of somethings had been trying the warding while she'd been gone.

Thunder cracked almost instantaneously with the bright flash of lightning, and it was followed by a second strike and a third before the wind picked up into a howling force.

With evidence of Rinnie's distress, Seraph was unwilling to wait longer for more information, but she sent power surging through her warding, tightening it as a fisherman tightens his net. It wasn't enough to completely repair the damaged areas, but it would hold until she had time to do it right.

She came to her feet and started down the slope toward home.

"What did you learn?" asked Hennea.

"Not much, something shad—" Seraph's voice was broken by a torturous howl that rose above the wind.

"Troll," said Hennea.

Heart in her throat, Seraph started running again.

They came out of the trees still somewhat above the farm, but it didn't look as it had when Seraph left it. Instead of a half-plowed field and an empty house, there was a field of tents and her house was illuminated from within and without by dozens of lanterns. For courage, she thought, because it wasn't yet dark enough to require lanterns for sight, though with the rain it wouldn't be long before darkness had hold here.

Among the changes wrought since she'd been home last was a crowd of people that looked to be composed of the whole village, all confronting a troll that straddled the path leading to Redern.

Seraph pushed her way through the first group of people, mostly women and children, and into the clear space in front of them, where she paused to take in the enormity of her task.

It was a forest troll, moss-green and larger than its more numerous cousin, the mountain troll. By the earlobes which hung so long they brushed its stooped shoulders, it was older than any Seraph had ever seen.

That trolls had two arms and two legs had given rise to the rumor that the thing was related to humans. Anyone who thought so, in Seraph's opinion, had never seen a troll. Small red eyes were set deep and close on a head as wide as Skew was long above a nose that was merely two slits in the bumpy textured skin. Tusks curled out of its jaw and pulled the lower lip down to reveal fist-sized, serrated teeth that could snap a cow's skull open.

Seraph's long-ago teacher had speculated that they were hobgoblins or some other small creature morphed by the Shadowed King. He'd told her the first mentions of trolls in books and stories came after the Fall of the Shadowed.

However they came into being, Seraph could wish this one a long way away instead of pacing back and forth at the trail-head to Redern, with its head topping the nearest trees.

As far as Seraph could tell, almost every able-bodied man of Redern had gathered along the edge of the warding that had so far kept the troll from coming closer, almost as if they could tell where it was. Born and bred in the Ragged Mountain as these folks had been, it wouldn't surprise Seraph if they could sense her ward—though it could just be experience had taught them how far the troll could come. Some of them had bows or swords, but most of them held whatever implement had come to hand. She saw Bandor, Tier's sister's husband, with one of the big knives they used to cut bread.

She couldn't see the forest king—or Jes either, but it didn't surprise her. If either was here, he'd be in the forest, not in the midst of a crowd of people.

Tier was in the very front of the line of defenders. She could see him easily over the others because he was the only mounted man. Not many horses could be brought so close to a troll, but Skew was a warhorse born and bred.

The gelding roared the chill sound that belonged to fighting stallions—and geldings, too, apparently. Foam lathered his chest and neck, and the rest of him was wet with sweat and rain. Ears back, he rose to his hind legs in a slow, controlled rear. Warhorses, Tier had once told her, had been trained to turn their fear to anger—just as Seraph herself usually did.

Tier had his sword out, not brandishing it, but at the ready.

Some chance movement in the crowd gave Seraph a quick view of Rinnie, standing just behind Skew. She was a child still, with only the faintest of signs of the woman she would be. She should have looked pitiable next to the warrior and the troll, but her whole body glowed brighter than the lanterns Seraph had just passed.

For a moment Seraph let herself be awed by the beauty of the power a Cormorant could gather.

But it was just for a moment because Rinnie didn't have the control to hold that kind of power—nor was it doing any good against a troll. Seraph began threading her way between the men, who dropped away as soon as they saw who it was.

Lightning flashed and hit the troll. It rolled its eyes and shook its head, but other than that, the lightning did nothing. But while it was distracted an arrow found its target and the troll took several steps back with another of those agonized cries. It reached one of its arms up to bat at its face and pluck the arrow from its nose slit. It held the arrow up and shook it before throwing it aside and striding forward with a ground-shaking stride that boomed almost as loud as its scream.

Lehr, standing to Rinnie's left, nocked another arrow and waited.

The troll hit Seraph's warding and magic leapt up in a fine display of light and color and held it off. The creature stayed for a long count of two before falling back, covering its eyes; but it was obvious to Seraph, if to no one else, that the warding wouldn't hold it back much longer.

"Rinnie!" shouted Seraph, as soon as she was close enough that they might hear her over the storm. She stopped as close to her daughter as she dared. "Rinnie, let the storm go. Your lightning won't hurt it, and it prefers dark to light. Lehr, in the ear, eye, nostril, and ventral slit—if you can, get someone to make flaming arrows for you. A troll is partially immune to magic, so *I* can't set it afire, but real fire sometimes works." Sometimes.

Though her glow hadn't dimmed, Rinnie must have heard what Seraph had said: the rain and wind died, leaving an uncanny silence in its wake, but the storm and all its potential violence still hung overhead malevolently.

"There are a few spells that can hurt it," said Hennea.

In her anxiety for her family, Seraph had almost forgotten the other Raven.

She turned to see Hennea circle her hands as if she held a large globe, then make a tossing motion. As soon as it crossed the wards, her spell turned into a ball of fire so hot it burned blue. It hit the troll in the middle of its forehead with an impact Seraph could hear from where she stood.

Blinded by the light of the fire, the troll pulled the molten ball from its forehead, and at its touch the magic fell into nothing, leaving only a great blackened area in the troll's face. The troll howled its rage.

"You have to teach me that one," said Seraph. "But it's not going to help us much. They hunt by scent and hearing. Blinding's only going to make it angry."

Someone had heard her tell Lehr to use fire; she heard a voice cry, "We need flaming arrows!" Someone else yelled, "Eyes, mouth, and private parts, boys."

The troll charged the warding again. Seraph dodged past Skew to give the ward more power, ignoring Tier's shout of consternation. The troll saw her, too, and began wading through the barrier of magic to get to her.

Trolls were smarter than they looked.

A great mountain cat leapt onto the troll from the top of a tree, landing on the top of its head and sending it staggering back away from Seraph and the warding.

Jes, thought Seraph. A black mountain cat was one of the forms that Jes favored—and a normal great mountain cat would never have attacked a troll.

The enraged cry of the cat joined the howl of the troll. Before the troll could regain its balance, Gura joined in the attack, going for the tendon on the back of the troll's ankle.

The troll kicked out wildly and caught Gura with the edge of its foot. The dog yipped once and rolled a dozen feet to stop against a tree. He lay still.

Jes braced his hind legs on the back of the troll's neck and sank his front claws deep into the top of its forehead, then pulled back—forcing the troll's mouth open.

A troll's joints worked differently than most animals. It had no neck, and its lower jaw was fixed in relation to its body—so it chewed by moving the upper portion of its head rather than the lower. By taking control of the head, Jes's hold gave him effective control of the whole troll.

It was clever, Seraph acknowledged, but how did Jes know enough of trolls to use its weaknesses against it?

Someone had listened to her because a flaming arrow sank

into the troll's open mouth. Once she turned her attention to it, Seraph realized she'd been smelling burning oil for a few minutes. She turned to see the double handful of archers, including Lehr, were all shooting flaming arrows, which, inexpertly wrapped in oiled rags were awkward to shoot.

A number of the arrows smoldered in the damp ground in front of the troll, but the arrow she watched Lehr loose flew to lodge in between the troll's gaping jaws, just beside the first one that had hit it. He sent two more to follow the first in quick succession. Each hit was followed by a round of cheers from the rest of the villagers, who were beginning to find the target with their own arrows.

Maddened, the troll fought to close its mouth. Jes's claws slid through the tough skin, opening huge gashes, but also allowing the troll to close its mouth. It dropped to the ground and rolled, forcing Jes to leap clear. The smell of scorched flesh rose from the troll as it rolled again, trying to put out the fire of a dozen arrows.

The panther grunted and backed away until it stood near Gura, who was rising unsteadily to his feet. As soon as it was obvious that the troll was distracted by the fire that was eating it, the big cat disappeared into the woods, driving the dog before it.

Seraph heard Hennea murmur, "That's it, Jes. Away from us for the moment. The last thing we need is for anyone to be more panicked than they already are."

The wind began slowly, then gusted suddenly, fanning the small flames caused by stray arrows that had been slowly dying in the storm-dampened grass. Someone, it must have been Hennea, used magic to snuff out the fires.

"Rinnie," Seraph said in a biting voice. "That's enough."

But the sharp tones that sometimes worked did nothing as power shook Rinnie's small body.

"Is something wrong?" said Tier.

"Call her, Tier," she said. "Quickly."

"Rinnie?" he said.

"Not like that," Seraph said. "Like you called Skew the night the bear got into the barn. She's riding the storm, and it'll kill her unless you can summon her back."

He didn't make her explain further.

"Rinnie," he said, his voice somehow carrying the reverberating power of the thunder.

The children were not the only ones who had learned something about their Orders this past spring. Tier's voice sounded louder than it actually was—Seraph could feel it settle deeply into her bones, though it was not she whom he called. Even the troll stopped its flailing for an instant.

Seraph could sense the change in the weather even before rain began falling again, this time in a gentle drizzle that would eventually drain the power from the storm. She took a relieved breath. "Hennea, keep that troll dry so it burns to ash."

"Done."

"Papa," said Rinnie, dazedly staring at Tier. "Is it dead?"

Tier sheathed his sword and swung down from Skew's back, grunting as he hit the ground. But his knees didn't stop him from picking Rinnie up and pulling her tight.

"Shh," he said. "You're safe now."

But he spoke too soon.

The troll rolled across the wards and kept coming.

Tier, with his back to the burning troll, his eyes on Rinnie, had no warning. The dying monster struck him a glancing blow that knocked him off his feet. Tier rolled over until Rinnie was below him, protecting her with his body.

But the troll knew where they were now and brought forward a three-fingered hand and wrapped it around Tier's legs.

The troll still lay across Seraph's wards, and she spoke, using for the first time in her life one of the Words that had been passed down from the Colossae wizards to their Traveler children.

"Sila-evra-kilin-faurath!"

The wards shifted and became something else, called into being by her will and the ancient syllables.

For two decades Seraph had gone out each season to walk a path around the farm while her family slept. She'd set her blood and hair into the soil and called a spell to protect her family from harm. With the Word she called that power into a single act that was the culmination of the purpose of all those nights, all that magic.

Lehr's fire died completely, leaving the troll burnt and blackened, but alive. It roared triumphantly and tightened its grip on Tier.

Someone made a dismayed sound.

"Die," said Seraph, in a voice so hoarse and deep it sounded unfamiliar, as if something else used her throat. There was no room left in her for anger or fear, no room for anything except power as she touched the troll.

Blackened flesh turned grey and cracked around grass-green bones. Grey turned to white ash that slid to the ground under the gentle hand of the rain and the iron-shod hooves of Skew as the battle-trained horse protected his rider as he had been trained.

Seraph took in deep breaths and tried to contain herself, but there was too much power.

"Don't touch her, Lehr," Hennea said. "Look to Tier and the child. Seraph. Seraph."

Slowly, Seraph turned her head to look at the other Raven, who averted her gaze under Seraph's hot attention.

"What are you going to do with the magic, Seraph?" Despite dropping her gaze, Hennea sounded serene.

Seraph found herself clinging to that serenity for a moment. "Too much," she said. "Unwise to kill something that old with a Word."

"What are you going to do with it?"

The force of the power the Words had siphoned into her burned and felt wondrous at the same time. The troll had been old, too old. The power of his death rippled through her along with the magic she herself had drained from her wards. Too much power to be safe.

"The wardings," she said, her voice thick and still oddly deep. "I need to protect . . ."

"Papa?"

Lehr's voice broke Hennea's hold on her, reminding her why she'd killed the troll in the first place. She might have been too late. "Tier? Rinnie?"

Seraph turned to look at Tier, where Lehr and a couple of the bolder villagers were pulling the remains—bones—of the troll off them.

"They are alive." Hennea's voice was calm. "And they'll remain so if you can contain the magic you hold. Control yourself, Raven."

"Take care of them," Seraph said harshly, resenting the part of her that understood that Hennea was correct. She had to rid herself of this magic. "I'll walk the wards."

CHAPTER 3

Not letting herself look back, Seraph walked briskly through the storm-tattered camp that covered their fields, ignoring the people who scuttled out of her way. She stared at the ground to spare them her gaze until she made it into the woods that bordered the farm.

What had she been going to do?

She stood where she was for a long moment.

She had to protect . . . by Lark and Raven, she was power-sick. Couldn't think clearly.

The warding. She should reset the warding. Slowly she made her way to the place where the warding had been and knelt in the dirt.

There are two ways to set wardings. The voice of her old teacher was as clear as if he'd been standing over her shoulder. *For a night a warding can be a simple thing, a rope that surrounds the tents and wagons and keeps them safe. But for any longer, or where dangers are greater, a warding is best worked as a chain with interconnecting links, each subtly different from the one before so that if one link fell, the others will still be effective guards.*

She pressed her hands into the soil and began, ignoring the ugly whispering voice that tried to coax her to keep the power she held. If she could kill a troll with a whisper, how great was the good that she could accomplish with what she now held?

Her hands tingled as she carefully drew a curved line. She'd never held such power.

Only as the terrible rush of the troll's death died away did she really understand how old it had been. She felt his age in the burn of magic that was not lessened even when she set wards that should keep out the shadowed for generations.

She feared that just relaying the wards would not be enough to absorb so much so she began to feed it into the forest. Too much, and she'd harm as much as she helped, but a slow trickle of magic should not cause a problem.

Gradually the discipline of redrawing the wards absorbed her. Mathematical and artistic at the same time, they required enough of her attention that the part of her that desired the rush of power was reduced to murmurs she could ignore.

She became aware of him gradually, a pale form grazing quietly beside her. The pattering of the light rain was accompanied by the grinding of teeth and grass. The familiar, peaceful sound helped somehow, and she became aware of a deep inner contentment.

She was home.

She finished the link she was working and sat back, fisting her hands against her lower back as she stretched.

"You don't look well," she said.

"One of the tainted creatures attacked the priest," replied the pale horse who was Jes's forest king. His voice was velvety and very deep. "I saved him, but it was a near-run thing. Karadoc's not young by Rederni standards, and he's ill even yet. Without a priest, fighting the shadow-tainted has been draining, even with the help of your daughter."

She absorbed what he said and sorted through questions. The slowness of her thoughts told her that she was far from free of power-sickness yet.

"The troll wasn't the first of the shadow-tainted creatures to come here?" she asked. She didn't need Lehr or Jes to tell her that the troll had been tainted. Unlike the mistwight, trolls were shadow-born, creatures whose only purpose was to destroy and kill.

"No, there were other things, too, things I haven't seen since the Fall, though none as dangerous as the troll. They come to destroy and feed the Shadowed."

Seraph stilled. "I had hoped that we were wrong. You are sure there is another Shadowed? That Volis couldn't have set up a summoning spell?"

The horse snorted. "Creatures like that troll would only come to the call of a Shadowed." He rubbed his nose on his knee.

"You mean the Shadowed is here?" asked Seraph, then shook with the rebellion of her magic as her control of her emotions wavered. She took in deep, even breaths until everything settled down.

The forest king waited until she was through before he said, "Not now, I don't think. But he has been here. He left behind a rune in the old temple that was triggered a few weeks ago." He lifted his head to scent the air, then shook his mane and turned his attention back to her. "I don't pay enough attention to the town. If Karadoc hadn't called me when the first of the creatures appeared, it might have taken me too long to find the rune on my own. As it was, other than destroying the rune, I could do little for them in the stone of the town, so I called them here, where your wards could do some of the work while I took care of the tainted things. I wasn't expecting the troll, so I used myself up healing the priest and driving away the little things. A troll ⁀.." He sighed. "A normal troll would not have been too difficult, but that one . . . Your wards kept him mostly away from the villagers until today."

"There was a rune in the temple," Seraph said.

"To awaken and draw those things that bear the collar of the Shadowed," the forest king explained. "The priest took me to the temple, and we destroyed the rune. Not soon enough."

Runes were *solsenti* wizardry mostly. Seraph was only marginally familiar with the theory behind them—though there were a few useful ones that she used sometimes. She did know that they could be drawn and set to wait until something triggered them. The temple had only been built this past winter, though, so the Shadowed had been in Redern sometime since then.

A number of the Path's wizards had come with Volis, the wizard-priest she'd killed in the new temple in the village. The other wizards kidnaped Tier, then left for Taela. The Shadowed could have been among them.

Perhaps the mistwight that killed the smith's daughter had been drawn from whatever place it had been hidden and was traveling toward Redern. After the forest king stopped the call it settled in the smith's well. Unhappily, she wondered how many other creatures were even now preying upon defenseless villages—maybe that was what Benroln had been called to fight.

The burn of power slowed Seraph's thoughts, and she returned to her wardings. The forest king followed her when she moved, grazing while she worked.

Darkness fell under the trees, though she could see patches of light where the trees were thin. The birds quieted as they settled in for sleep, but there was music coming from the farm. She smiled; let more than two Rederni get together, and there would be music.

She examined the progress of her magicweaving critically and was satisfied. Her thoughts were a little clearer than they'd been, and the wards were strong and tightly woven.

"Tier told me once that he thought Jes's forest king shared a number of traits with Ellevanal," she told the horse casually.

Ellevanal was the god worshiped by the mountain peoples, including the Rederni. Though today was only the second time Seraph had seen him, Jes had spent his summers exploring the woods with a creature he'd called the forest king since he was old enough to run.

"Bards see things that others do not," agreed the forest king, taking another bite of grass.

"What would the Rederni say if they saw their god of forests eating grass?" asked Seraph.

"They are not Travelers," replied the god after he'd finished chewing. "They would not see what you do."

She laughed despite herself. "Now that's a properly mystical answer."

"I thought so," he said. "But it is true for all of that."

"Gods do not look haggard and sick to their worshipers?"

"You don't believe in the gods," Ellevanal said. "How would you know what they do or don't do?" The teasing note fell from his voice. "They say that the Travelers don't believe in the gods because they killed theirs and ate them."

"I've never heard that."

"Of course not," said Ellevanal. "You are a Traveler who doesn't believe in gods."

"How long have you been here, guarding the forest?"

The horse raised its head and tested the wind, his rib cage rising and falling as if he'd been racing rather than quietly grazing at her side an hour or more. There was mud on his legs and belly.

"A long time," he said. "Before the Shadowed King came and laid waste to the world. Before the Remnants of the Glorious Army of Man arrived here after the Fall and found safe harbor here, naming me god in their gratitude." Then he cast her a roguish glance. "Before the unthinkable happened, and Tieragan Baker was born Ordered and upset the Travelers' world."

"He hasn't upset the Travelers' world," she said.

"Hasn't he?" The horse snorted and tossed his head. "Wait and see what an Ordered Rederni may do. Already word of you is windborne, and some will come seeking you to destroy what you may become."

Seraph raised an eyebrow at him.

He dropped his head slyly. "A god may speak in riddles if He will."

She shook her head at him and went back to work because the power had begun singing to her again. The forest king went back to eating.

When she came to a place where she could see the farm she was reassured to note that the camp was orderly and relaxed.

A group of men were restringing tent lines and hanging the muddy fabrics over them. Another group was setting up fires for cooking—so many people could not be fed out of her kitchen. She didn't see any of her family, but there was a cheerful energy to the way the villagers moved that told her that no one had been seriously injured: and there was music.

"If you are a god," Seraph said, "shouldn't you have been able to take care of a troll far better than we did?"

"But I am only a small god," said the horse, sounding amused. "I could not destroy the troll—not *that* troll, which was a minion of the Shadowed and escaped the Fall to live centuries more than a troll ought, and still keep my priest alive. Death doesn't relinquish its rightful prey lightly, and healing is not my province."

"Why didn't you let him die?" she asked, though she had no desire for Karadoc's death. "No one has ever said that the priests of Ellevanal are immortal."

He laughed in soft huffs at her tart tone. "He is an excellent *skiri* player, which priests seldom are. Most of them are more given to things of the spirit rather than cleverness of the mind." The picture of a priest playing a board game with his god struck Seraph as extremely odd, but before she could ask him about it, the forest king's voice became serious. "There are no others to take his place. His apprentice will be fine in a few years, but I needed my priest now."

The rain had stopped, and rising warmth turned the moisture in the grasses to fog where the last light of the sun peeked through to light the small clearing where the god stood. Steam rose from the white horse's flanks and ribs, ribs that were a good deal less prominent than they had been when he'd first joined her.

"You've been feeding," she said.

The horse set his nose in a knee-high clump of grass and ripped some from the ground. He raised his head and chewed pointedly.

Seraph shook her head at him. "No grass pads ribs so quickly."

"Where do you think the power that you've been feeding into the forest goes?" He laughed, again. "Before the first of Rederni's Bards was born here, I was little more than a very old stag who wandered about. But a Bard is a very powerful thing, if subtle. There may be more than one reason that the Travelers never stay long in one place."

Seraph stared at him. Of course Tier wasn't the only Bard born to the Rederni, not with the way music flowed through them like blood.

"You feed off magic?" she said, setting aside the question of more Ordered *solsenti*.

"Did I say that?" asked the horse. "I would never lie to you, Raven. I feed off the land only." His eyes lit with wicked laughter at her huff of frustration. "Careful, Raven. Anger and magic are a volatile combination. I don't understand it completely myself."

"What *do* you understand?" she asked.

"Travelers have not come here in a long time," he said. "Not since the Fall and seldom before that. Only when you came to live here with Tier did I notice there is something about the Orders that makes the land . . . more alive. It is not magic, not that I can tell. There." He tossed his head. "I have told you as much as I know. The forest is my realm, and its secrets belong to me. Travelers belong to no gods and, I think, they have more secrets than most."

He stayed with her until she completed the circle, then wandered away, swishing his tail in mild irritation at an impious bug.

Seraph staggered almost drunkenly to her feet, sympathizing with Tier, as her knees throbbed, and her back ached. She'd worn a hole in her pants, but that didn't matter. Now that they were home she'd have to go back to wearing Rederni skirts.

As Seraph picked her way tiredly down the slope toward home, Jes ran up. She heard him before she saw him because he was chanting softly, "I found her," as he ran.

He was laughing when he stopped just in front of her. "I found you," he said. "I found you before Lehr."

She touched his shoulder lightly. "You did at that. Is everyone all right?"

He nodded and fell into step with her. "Hennea sent us out. She said it should be safe to find you now. She said if *someone* didn't, Papa was going to undo all the good *she* managed to do for his knees by coming out here himself."

Seraph remembered the troll's fist closing around Tier's legs. "Is he all right?"

Jes nodded. "He grumbled about his knees, so they must be fine."

Seraph smiled. "So they must." If he'd been really hurt, not a word would have crossed his lips. "And Rinnie?"

"She's asleep next to Papa, who's singing with Ciro. She has a bump on her head and a bruise on her shoulder about this big—" Jes held his hands apart to show how big, and Seraph hoped he was exaggerating, though that wasn't one of Jes's faults.

"Lehr was jealous of her," he said. "He said he'd never had a bruise that big. I have though. Remember the time I fell off the barn? That was a bigger bruise than Rinnie's."

"I hope none of us ever gets a bruise that big again."

Jes nodded. "Me, too. Here comes Lehr. I found her first, Lehr. I'll see you at home." Jes slipped off in the darkness, leaving Seraph alone with Lehr.

"Once I quit trying to track you and began to follow the sound of Jes's voice you weren't hard to find. Jes is happy to be home," said Lehr. "You look tired, Mother. Are you all right?"

Seraph nodded. "Fine. Just a little worn, I'm not used to handling so much magic. Jes said your father and Rinnie aren't hurt much?"

"They're fine—just a bit bruised and battered," agreed Lehr, and something inside of Seraph relaxed. "Ciro made Papa tell everyone the story of what happened while we were gone."

Ciro, the tanner's father, had been a close friend of Tier's grandfather, and had helped Tier learn to love music. Not that Tier had needed much encouragement.

"Ciro said he was going to make Papa's story into a song. Then they got in a contest to see who'd come up with the funniest verses." He turned his attention to the rough ground they were walking on for a moment, then said, "They've been having trouble here for the past few weeks. The troll was the worst of it, but there've been goblins and other things."

"The forest king found me while I was trying to get rid of the troll's death magic," said Seraph. "He told me the wizard-priest, Volis, had done something to call the servants of the shadow. Hennea and I must have missed that while we were going through the temple. Karadoc stopped the summoning, but he was hurt." She glanced at her son.

Lehr nodded. "He's staying in the house right now." He cleared his throat. "He's been staying in your room. Papa said to leave him there tonight. He looks pretty bad, pale and bruised, but they carried him out for the music, so he can't be as bad as he looks."

Seraph was tired, her clothes were wet, and she'd been looking forward to sleeping in her own bed. "Karadoc's not a young man anymore. If he's hurt, he'd better stay in our bed until they move back to town—which shouldn't be too long. The forest king told me Karadoc helped destroy the rune that summoned the tainted beasts here. The troll should be the end of it. I'd imagine tomorrow or the next day they'll all be back in Redern." She hoped.

"Jes will be glad to hear that," said Lehr. "He took one look at Aunt Alinath and hid behind Hennea."

"She took care of Rinnie for us," said Seraph, and stumbled over a branch she hadn't seen.

Lehr took her arm. "I know. But she's never known how to treat Jes."

"She wouldn't have been so bad if Jes hadn't gone out of his way to be at his worst with her."

Lehr snorted. "Papa says the same of Aunt Alinath and you."

There was a small gathering of people in front of the house, where someone had lit a small bonfire despite the damp. Tier, one knee tightly bound and stretched out in front of him, was playing the lute he'd brought back from Taela. Rinnie was wrapped up in a blanket and had fallen asleep with her head on Tier's unbound knee.

Ciro had a small drum out, and he and Tier were singing together. The old man's voice was as true as it had ever been, and Tier . . . Seraph had always thought that he had the most adaptable voice she'd ever heard. He could sing love songs in a tone of warm butter and sugar, then switch to harsh war songs in a voice that could cut stone. Right now he gave the old singer the melody and took a descant, softening his tone to flatter Ciro's—which hardly needed enhancing.

Just outside of the firelight, Seraph stopped. "Have you checked for a taint of shadow among the Rederni?" The Shadowed could be someone they knew.

Lehr nodded. "Hennea had both Jes and me do it. But not even Uncle Bandor shows any signs. Hennea said that like as not, if anyone had been tainted, they wouldn't have been able to cross your wardings—and all of the village is here."

"Good." She hadn't really been worried someone would have been tainted, though she probably should have been. And the Shadowed had been able to hide what he was from Lehr and Jes until the very last moments of their chase. It might be that he could hide himself from her sons.

It was, she thought, unlikely that the Shadowed was someone she knew from the village. She put thoughts of the Shadowed aside for another time, when she was less tired.

Tier's voice wavered when he saw her, and he fell silent, stopping the strings of the lute with his hand. After a few beats Ciro stopped, too.

"Is something wrong?" Ciro asked.

Tier shook his head, but kept his eyes on Seraph. "I'm just tired tonight. I'll leave the music to you for now."

"If Karadoc has our bed, we'll need to look for somewhere else to sleep," murmured Seraph, so she wouldn't interfere with Ciro's music. She bent down to touch Rinnie's face, then looked up into Tier's. Even in the dark, he looked pale and drawn—his knees must be hurting him.

"Somewhere private," agreed Tier. "But the house is full."

Seraph took a good look at the sky, but the storm had passed by. "I might be able to come up with something. Lehr, can you find our bedrolls and my pack? And make certain you, Hennea, Jes, and Rinnie have someplace to sleep."

He nodded. "I'll be right back."

He was as good as his word and handed Seraph both bedrolls before Ciro had finished his second solo piece.

"Rinnie still has her bed in the house, I'll carry her in," Lehr kept his voice soft, though Ciro was between songs. "The rest of us now have claim to space in the barn. Do you need more help, Papa?"

Tier levered himself to his feet and shook his head. "As long as we're not going too far, I'll be fine."

Seraph nodded to Lehr and bent to kiss the top of Rinnie's head. "I'll see you in the morning," she told her son.

She led Tier behind the house where the land rose to a narrow flat shelf of meadow that was surrounded by short trees and bushes. Tier was limping badly, Seraph winced inwardly with him at every step.

She set the bedrolls on top of a rock where they shouldn't get too wet, but stopped him when he bent to unroll his. "No. Wait a moment, and I'll have something better for us."

She set down her pack and took out the bag that held her *mermori*. Sorting quickly, she found Isolde's *mermora* and sank the sharp end into the ground. She stepped back and murmured the words that would call the ancient house of Isolde the Silent.

There was a pause, as the magic organized itself. She could feel the familiar weave of Hinnum's spells unfolding as they remembered the pattern of Isolde's dwelling, rebuilding rooms long since rotted by time. She felt as much as saw the house re-form in the shelter of the woods behind her house.

Isolde's had not been among the larger dwellings belonging to the Colossae wizards, though it was bigger than the house Tier had built Seraph. The front of Isolde's house was designed to please the eye, covered with decorative brick-work. The sides were flat and plain—so flat that Seraph was certain it had shared walls with neighboring houses rather than standing free. The contrast between gracious facade and flat sides made it look a little odd, especially standing alone in the woods instead of on a busy city street.

"We can sleep here tonight," she said.

"I thought you didn't do that," said Tier, though he followed her up the front stairs and through the ebony door.

"It can be dangerous," she said, though most of her attention was on her husband's slow progress. "This is an illusion—a very good illusion—but if the weather is unpleasant, you can freeze to death without ever knowing it. But the rain has stopped, and we'll use our own blankets for warmth."

"So why didn't we use it to sleep in while we were on the trail home?" Tier asked.

"Magic, any magic, tends to attract the attention of a variety of nasty creatures that I'd rather not wake up to," Seraph answered, moving a chair that Tier might have had to step around. "And the illusion is good enough you can't hear if anything comes prowling. Tonight—well, there was enough magic here to call anything looking for it, so Isolde's house isn't going to make any difference. With my wardings fresh, I don't think there's much that'll get through. We'll be safe and private here."

The house was lit with small lanterns. Tier limped behind her through the sitting room and into the smallest of the bed-rooms. There was less personality here than in the other bed-rooms. Seraph had always assumed it was a guest room, and felt more comfortable in it, less an interloper and more a guest.

"It seems wrong to put these dirty blankets on that bed," Tier said.

She could see his point, the bedding was pristine white. "It's all right. The dirt won't be there next time the *mermora* is called."

Tier shook his head, but he loosened the tie on his blankets and unrolled them on the bed. Seraph could see that more than his knees were bothering him tonight.

"You're hurting," she said. "Strip down and let me see."

It was a mark of how tired he really was that he followed her brisk commands without a word of teasing. She turned up the light on the bedside table so she could see better.

He moved slowly and she saw, in addition to the new damage to his healing knees, his left shoulder was hurt. When he was finished she walked around him once to assess the damage with an eye educated by three children who climbed trees and barns and other things more suited to birds than humans.

"Nothing a few days' rest and a good hot bath won't fix," she said at last with relief. No matter what Lehr had said, Tier's obvious soreness had worried her. "Lie down, and I'll see what I can do," she said.

He sat on the bed with a grunt of relief, and she helped him swing his legs up.

"Now," she told him, after she'd stripped off her wet outer clothing. "I'm going to see if I can't make you more comfort-able. If you tell Brewydd about this, I'll never hear the end of it. Pain is your body's way of telling you that you need to rest, or you'll do permanent harm. Nothing I can do will make you heal faster, but I can take away the pain for the night."

She touched the arches of his feet, then the ankles, working slowly up with just a breath of magic. When she touched his knees, his whole body relaxed.

"That feels wonderful," he breathed.

"It'll feel better before I'm done," she said, kissing him softly on the mouth. "But you'll curse me in the morning when I release the magic." She slid her hands up the outside of his thighs and over his hips.

"Have I told you I love you today?" he asked, eyes closed in bliss.

"You're just afraid of what I'll do to you if you don't," she said absently, her attention on the magic that she threaded carefully over his hurts.

He opened his eyes and put a hand under her chin. "I'm not afraid of you," he said, tugging her down for another kiss, this one carnal and knowing. "I love you," he said, when she lifted her head.

She found her lips curving upward on their own before she turned back to her work. "The forest king told me the shadow-tainted creatures were called by a rune in the temple. He said the only one who could have created the rune was a Shadowed."

"Ah," said Tier. "I know you were hoping against this."

She paused in her spell casting, blowing a stray hair that had escaped its braid out of her eye. "A Shadowed brings sorrow behind him in a blanket of death."

"Is the Shadowed a return of the Unnamed King?" asked Tier.

"No," she said. "He's a man who enslaves himself to the Stalker and takes power and immortality as his pay."

"There have been others?"

She nodded, tracing a faint scar on Tier's chest that he'd gotten fighting the Fahlarn before she'd met him. It came from a near-mortal wound that Tier seldom talked about. "A few."

"The Stalker is the thing that the wizards of Colossae imprisoned by destroying their city."

Seraph flattened her hand, warming it on his skin. "They didn't destroy the city, Tier. They sacrificed it."

He shifted restlessly under her hand. "You've told me that before. You mean they killed everyone who lived there except the wizards who cast the spell."

"Yes and no." It was an old story, but it wasn't one Travelers talked about much. "Every morning, Alinath gets up and the fires are lit in the bake ovens, just as your family has done since the bakery was built centuries ago. The whole village has tasks that have been performed every day—rituals of living. There is power in that, Tier, just as there is power in the spark of life that is the heart of the difference between your body and a clay pot. The wizards extracted the power of everyday rituals, of generations of living, as well as the deaths of their families and friends who had trusted them. The mages killed the people whom they loved, and there was power in that, too, more than death by itself would have brought. They used all that power and knew it wasn't enough to destroy their creation, only keep him in check."

"What does the Stalker want?" asked Tier, ever the storyteller. "What did it do to frighten the wizards into killing their families?"

"The Traveler word that translates into Common as Stalker also means the death of the prey that is stalked—not for food, but for the sheer love of destruction." She shrugged unhappily. "That's all anyone knows of it—just that the Colossae wizards named it the Stalker, then destroyed their lives in order to contain it."

"The Unnamed King nearly destroyed humankind."

Seraph nodded. "Mistwights live on small prey. They don't play with their food like a cat might. The tainted one we found was deliberately terrorizing the smith because it enjoyed it. So perhaps the Stalker drives those who serve it to terrible deeds. Certainly death follows the Shadowed and those who are tainted."

"You said Benroln was shadowed," said Tier.

She nodded. "It's unusual. Most of the shadow taint we Travelers see is still damage done by the Unnamed King."

"How did it happen?"

"I thought at first it was Volis who did it," she told him. "He was certainly tainted himself—as were all the Masters of the Path. But my old teacher, Arvage, told me once that he thought the Stalker was constrained from forcing his will upon others, a constraint not faced by the Shadowed for some reason. If that is true, then it was the Shadowed who was responsible for the taint that stained the Path wizards and Benroln."

"What is the difference between a man who is shadow-tainted and one who is the Shadowed?"

"A taint is imposed upon you," Seraph said. "It takes little sins—buried resentments and angers—and builds upon those until they are pulled to the forefront. Bandor hit your sister—peace, Tier, it wasn't his fault. I was just using that as an example of how much tainting can change a personality. If you fight the taint, it will eat away at you until you are little more than a beast and can no longer hide the madness. The Masters lived with it for years as far as I can tell."

"And the Shadowed?"

"We don't know how they are made. If we did, we might be able to stop it from happening again. All of the Shadowed have been wizards. I think they have to contact the Stalker in some fashion, perhaps there is a spell written in a *solsenti* book of magic somewhere. Or perhaps the Stalker is able to call a wizard who is suitable for his purposes. In any case the Shadowed willingly sacrifices the lives of people around him in order to gain power and immortality. I don't know what the Stalker gains, or what it wants beyond death and destruction. Maybe that is enough. People who are tainted gradually grow mad over a period of a year or even just months, but the Shadowed doesn't."

Tier was quiet, and after a moment, Seraph resumed her task of relieving his pain. It didn't take much magic, just finesse.

She touched a reddish splotch on his ribs that would be a bruise tomorrow and eased it with a caress of magic. Even battered as he was, she loved his body, sinewy and tough, bearing scars of war both old and new. When she'd finished with the spellworking she let her fingertips linger on his skin, trailing them over him slowly.

She had him home. Home and safe at last.

Her fingers trailed lower, and he caught her hand, murmuring, "If you want us to sleep tonight, I'd suggest you lie down beside me instead of petting."

She straddled his hips, the fabric of her underclothes a thin veil between her skin and his.

"Mmm," she said. "It doesn't feel like you are interested in sleep just yet."

He laughed, a belly laugh that didn't quite make it out of his mouth.

"Don't move," she said, bending down until her lips just brushed his. "You might hurt yourself if you move."

A long, satisfying while later, Tier said, "I've missed that."

"Me, too," she said. Reluctantly, she rolled out of the bed and dimmed the light. "It won't go out all the way. None of the *mermori* rooms can be completely darkened—I think it has something to do with the nature of the illusion."

"That's fine," he said. "I wanted to talk to you a bit, and if it were dark, I don't think I could stay awake."

"Oh?" She took her own bedroll out and spread the blankets over Tier before climbing back in beside him. With a sigh, she curled against the warmth of his body and yawned. "Talk fast."

"Tell me about Hennea," he said.

She lifted her head, but the light was behind him, and she couldn't see the expression on his face. "Hennea?"

He laughed. "If you could hear your voice. I've just noticed an odd thing or two, and since our son is so interested in her— I'd like to know more about her."

She settled back against him. "Odd things like what?"

He laughed. "You tell me about her first," he said. "Then I'll tell you what made me ask."

"She's a Raven of the Clan of Rivilain Moon-Haired," Seraph began tentatively. "That's a common heritage among Travelers. Last I heard, there are three or four of Rivilain's clans in the Empire and several outside. She came to us—" She stopped. "Do you want me to go through the whole history? I've told it to you already."

"Tell me again, please," he said.

She shrugged. "She came to us because she'd figured out that the Path had you and had taken you to Taela. She'd watched them kill her lover. She wanted revenge, and she wanted to stop the Path."

"But she didn't come directly to the farm on her own," he said.

"Right. She'd gone up to the place where you had supposedly died first. She was on her way here when the forest king put her to sleep, then sent Jes to bring her here."

"The forest king didn't want her in his realm?" asked Tier neutrally.

"I don't know what he wanted," said Seraph. "*You* ask him, and see if you can get a straight answer. If the forest king had thought she meant harm, I don't think he'd have bothered getting Jes to bring her here."

Tier didn't argue, so Seraph relaxed back against him again. "She helped me teach the boys what they could do while we were on our way to Taela. She saved Jes."

"You didn't tell me about that. How?"

"Do you know what a *foundrael* is?" she asked.

"No . . . wait. Isn't that the Guardian thing you told me about? The one that was supposed to keep the Guardian under control, but it drove them insane instead."

She nodded. "There were ten of them originally—nine now. Benroln—I told you how his clan was one of the ones who were preying upon *solsenti*. He felt he had reason enough for it; *solsenti* had killed his father and the rest of the clan's Order Bearers. He thought he could force me to help him by taking Jes and holding him with a *foundrael*. While I dealt with Benroln, Hennea managed to destroy the *foundrael*."

"Not an easy task?" Tier's voice was neutral.

Seraph shook her head. "I don't know. I've never tried it."

"Just how powerful is Hennea?" he asked.

"I don't know. There's no measuring stick for magic"—she frowned and continued irritably—"though *solsenti* wizards seem to think there ought to be. Training means as much as power, really—though less for Ravens than for wizards who don't bear the Order. She's been well trained; you can see it in her demeanor. People say 'self-contained as a Raven,' and that centered peacefulness of hers is what they're referring to." She couldn't keep the wistfulness out of her voice.

Tier heard it because he rubbed her nose playfully. "You do controlled well enough that most people don't think you have a temper at all. Now, me, I enjoy a good screaming fight once in a while."

She laughed. "You do not. I have a miserably hard time picking a good fight with you." She waited a heartbeat or two. "So what do you think of Hennea?"

"How old is she?" he asked.

It was not what she expected him to say, though it seemed to bother Hennea that she was older than Jes.

"I don't know," she told him. "She looks about ten years younger than I am. Twenty-four or -five maybe? Their age difference is less than ours."

He rolled until his shoulder was under her head. "I think she's a good deal older than she appears."

"Why do you say that?"

"It's in her eyes. When my eyes aren't reminding me of her apparent age, I feel that she is an old, old woman."

Seraph thought about what he'd said for a moment.

"The control that Ravens strive for usually only belongs to the very old," she told him. "I've seen it in other Ravens besides Hennea, though *I've* never managed to get it right." People thought Seraph cold, she knew, but it was so hard to keep her emotions at bay—and if she didn't, she would be very, very dangerous for everyone. Magic required a cool head, and her temper was too easily lit. "Hennea's control is the reason, I think, that Jes can tolerate her touch when most people bother him."

"Magic can make people live longer," said Tier. "I once met a seventy-year-old wizard who looked no older than forty."

"Wizardry, yes, but, as I told you, the Orders don't work like that. Healers like Brewydd can perhaps extend their lives, but not past reasonable limits."

"You said that wizardry runs in the Traveler clans," said Tier. "Could Hennea be a wizard, too?"

Seraph sat up, crossed her legs, and stared at his face in the dim light. "You seem awfully certain that she's old." Owls could tell when someone lied, but that was as far as their truth-seeing went—or so she'd always supposed.

"It's just a feeling," he said half-apologetically.

"All of the Raven Bearers are wizards," she told him. "Just as all Guardians are empathic. So, yes, Hennea is a wizard as well. But a Raven restricting herself to magic without using the Order . . . it would be like stuffing cotton in your ears to sing, Tier."

"I know difference between wizards and Ravens is that wizards use ritual magic and Ravens don't have to," said Tier. "But I've seen you use rituals."

Seraph nodded. "Right. Wizardry is knowledge, and Raven

is intuition. That's true as far as it goes, but it's really just the end result of the difference rather the real difference. It's like saying the difference between a dog and a cat is that a dog is obedient and a cat independent."

"Can you explain it to me?"

She thought a moment. "I have a very loose analogy. Imagine magic is a bakery that allows only some people in to make bread. These people can neither smell nor taste."

"Hard to bake bread that way," commented Tier.

"Very hard. But they manage because they study the recipe books very carefully and learn to measure each cup of flour, each grain of sugar."

"*Solsenti* wizards." Tier took one of her hands and played with her fingers.

"Right. Now a few of these wizards were given a ring that allowed them to smell and taste."

"And the ring is called the Order of Raven."

"That's right."

"But they could take off the ring."

Seraph rolled her eyes in exasperation and began speaking rapidly. "Only with caustic soap that burns. And the bakery is hot, so hot that some people die of it. Others learn to deal with the heat and manage to stay there a very long time—but only because all they do is bake bread, and they cannot leave or stop baking or they will die—those are the wizards who live centuries. But the ring protects you from all of the heat."

He threw an arm around her waist and rolled her under him as he laughed. "All right, all right. No Raven would think of working wizardry, and Ravens don't live for centuries."

"That's right," said Seraph, burying her face against his neck. "So Hennea is not a century-old wizard—nor is she the Shadowed. We would know—*Jes* would know."

Tier rolled to his side and was still for a while. She thought he'd fallen asleep and was halfway there herself when he spoke again.

"If Hennea joined you to help bring down the Path, why is she still here? Why isn't she looking for her clan to rejoin them? You said that the Path didn't kill them all, only her Raven lover."

Seraph started to answer him, but he continued. "It was Jes who made me question it. I think if she felt she was free to go, she would have left us as soon as she could simply because of Jes."

"What do you mean?" Seraph asked frowning. Tier was better with people than she was, but she was certain Hennea was attracted to Jes. "She likes Jes."

"She loves him," he said, with a certainty Seraph didn't feel. "Which is why she would leave if she could."

"That doesn't make sense." She hated it when Tier did that. She didn't doubt he was right—he usually was correct about people—she just hated it when he went out of his way to be obtuse, which was why he did it.

Tier grinned, his teeth flashing in the dimly lit room. "Not to you, my love. You take the world and shake it into a form that suits you. Most of us have too much self-doubt. She's worried about him. Not just that he's too young, but that he is Guardian. He's in the middle of a change—you must have noticed it."

"Yes." Seraph sternly repressed the fear that thought caused her. "He switches back and forth more often, and it's faster." She said the next part fast as if that could keep it from being true. "And I don't think the Guardian ever leaves entirely anymore."

"Jes, as Guardian, is the one who told us what lived in the smith's well," he told her. "He told me he smelled it. Has Jes ever encountered a mistwight?"

Seraph's fingers started to play nervously with the blankets. "Not that I know. There aren't any around here, and we didn't run into any on the way to Taela."

"That's what I thought. I asked him how he knew, and the Guardian deliberately switched to our Jes just long enough to tell me he didn't know, then switched back."

"Why would he do that?"

"I think that if the Guardian had told me he didn't know, he would have been lying."

"The Guardian knows things that Jes doesn't know?" Seraph groped for Tier's hand; when she found it she held it tightly. "That's not a good thing. If Jes is to survive, he and the Guardian have to be one." That's what her father had told her Guardian brother anyway.

"I'll talk to him," said Tier, as if talk could solve all problems.

Seraph let it make her feel better anyway. For Tier, talk solved a lot more problems than it ever had for her.

Tier tugged her until her head was on his shoulder, then pulled the bedding over her shoulders.

Hennea loved Jes. Seraph was fairly certain that Jes felt the same way, though it was sometimes difficult to tell.

"She's never said so much, but I don't think she has anywhere else to go," Seraph told him. "I don't know what Jes said to her to get her to come with us, though Lehr told me that at first she was going to go with Benroln. I know what would make her stay, though."

"What is that?"

"Duty. She's a Raven, Tier. She has responsibilities that supersede love and family. Somewhere out there is a Shadowed who wants to destroy you, my love. Doubtless he is hunting you down—and it is her duty to be here for the kill."

Tier laughed, bouncing her head gently. "His or mine?"

"Go to sleep, you," she scolded, to hide her worry.

When she and Tier approached the house the next morning, the priest was sitting on the porch bench with his eyes shut.

"You look tired, Karadoc," said Tier, waving at some people who'd shouted greeting to him from the fields, where they were taking down tents.

Karadoc's bright brown eyes opened. "You're a fine one to talk. From the way you're walking, I'd say you've bruises to rival mine."

Tier tilted his head toward the fields. "Is it safe for them to return to Redern?"

Karadoc smiled, a secret, pleased smile. "Ellevanal tells me that the village is safe, so I've told everyone to start packing. You'll have your home back to yourselves by nightfall."

Karadoc's prediction was a little optimistic, and Seraph and Tier spent another night in Isolde's *mermora* house. The villagers were more interested in celebrating their victory than in returning home. Then, too, Seraph thought, they were a little nervous about returning to the village. It would be a while before Redern felt safe to them again, despite Karadoc's assurances.

"Thank you again for watching Rinnie for us," said Seraph, as she helped Alinath gather her things from the corner of the house where Lehr and Jes usually slept.

It was the afternoon of the second day since they'd returned home, and Seraph was hopeful that they'd all sleep in their own beds tonight. To that end she'd sent her children and Tier out to encourage the stragglers to return to Redern.

"Rinnie is a joy," said Tier's sister, folding a shirt neatly and setting it into a pack. "Until we came here, she helped us in the bakery." She paused. "Thank you for finding my brother. If you and the Travelers hadn't found him, he'd be dead."

Seraph shrugged uncomfortably. She didn't know what to say to Alinath. The old animosity had faded, but she wasn't certain what to replace it with.

"Tier is resourceful," she said at last. "Did he tell you he had the Emperor asking him for advice?"

Alinath smiled, and the relief in the expression told Seraph that she was finding this no easier than Seraph herself. "Yes, he said something about it, but I thought he was exaggerating."

Seraph shook her head. "No. I've never heard him exaggerate about anything he's done—usually just the opposite."

"Really?" Alinath thought about it a moment. "Did he really take all the young thugs and turn them into an army for the Emperor?"

"They're still thugs. Most of them anyway. But they adored Tier and fought for the Emperor for his sake. Tier has a way with young men."

"Speaking of young men," said Alinath, "have you noticed the way that half of the village girls are swooning over Lehr? He's a hero for fighting and killing that troll."

"He and most of the men in the village," said Seraph dryly. "And *I* killed the troll."

Alinath grinned; the expression looked a lot like Tier's. It wasn't one that Seraph had seen on Alinath's face before—but then Alinath had seldom been happy in Seraph's presence since Seraph's marriage to Tier. "No one is going to chide you for using magic this time. But I doubt you'll have anyone swooning over you either."

Seraph stole Rinnie's favorite expression and rolled her

eyes. "Probably run the other direction. It took them twenty years to forget about the time I almost flattened the bakery— do you suppose it'll be twenty years before they forget the troll?"

Alinath put the last of Bandor's shirts in the pack. "I don't think they'll ever forget," she said seriously. "But I don't believe that is necessarily a bad thing that they are reminded you are not just a farmer's wife."

"That is what I am."

"No." Alinath tied the pack and lifted it. "You are a Traveler, a Raven of the Clan of the Silent."

"The Clan of Isolde the Silent," corrected Seraph. "I am also Seraph Tieraganswife. Isolde's clan is dead these twenty years and more. I have been Rederni for longer than I was a Traveler."

"Seraph," said Alinath. "You have always been Traveler— and Raven, too. We've known that since the day you almost flattened the bakery, all of us—even Tier."

She picked up her bags and left Seraph alone.

After a moment, Seraph shook off the effects of Alinath's words. Alinath wasn't Tier, with his fearful accuracy where people were concerned.

Seraph had given up her Traveler heritage and exchanged it for Tier and for her children. True, the time she'd spent in Benroln's clan this summer had been comfortable, like taking out a shirt stored for years and finding that it still fit. But here was where she belonged.

But she still wore Traveler's clothing rather than Rederni skirts.

With brisk movements, Seraph stripped the bedding from the bed for washing. She started for the ladder, then turned around. The room was small and spare, a third the size of the cell that Tier had occupied in the palace in Taela. It was the room in which her children had been born.

In a few weeks it would be harvest season. There would be no harvest this year, but that was all to the good because there was the Shadowed and the problem of the Ordered gemstones. Traveler business that had to be taken care of before she settled down and became just a Rederni wife again.

Then, no more magic except the seasonal strengthening of the warding.

"This is my home," she said aloud to counter the feeling of suffocation that made her chest tight. "I belong here."

Leaving Tier and her sons to expedite the villager's exodus—Tier restricted to a supervisory role—Seraph recruited Rinnie to help clean the house and take inventory.

"It's a good thing you've been taking care of the garden while we were gone," Seraph said, scrubbing at a new stain on the floor. "I was worried we'd have to send Tier to Leheigh for supplies, but with the garden we'll be all right."

"Aunt Alinath, Uncle Bandor, and I came out once a week." Rinnie climbed onto a table so she could get a better view of the cupboards. "The bakery is hard work. I see why Papa decided that he'd rather farm."

"Farming is hard work, too," said Seraph. "And the bakery brings in a lot more money."

"But at the bakery you have to be inside all the time." Rinnie pulled a jar out of a cupboard and peered inside it. "I missed Gura and Skew and the garden."

"But not us?"

Rinnie grinned. "I missed you, too. Next time you go on an adventure, I get to go."

"It looked to me like you had your own adventure," Seraph observed.

"Mother, Cormorants aren't any good for *anything*," Rinnie all but moaned, setting the jar aside. "Look at how Papa, Jes, Lehr, and you fought that troll. All I could do was *rain* on him."

"The Orders are all different," said Seraph. "We met another Cormorant—did your father tell you? He made a lot of money by manipulating the weather. He'd pick a wealthy village and let it dry out for a month or two, then have them pay him to make it rain."

Rinnie straightened up, aghast. "Travelers are supposed to *help* people, Mother."

"And so I told him," said Seraph serenely. "He doesn't do it anymore."

Rinnie grinned. "I wish people would listen to me when *I* tell them things, the way they listen to you."

The door banged open, and Jes came in. "They're gone, we're back," he said in one breath. "We took them to Redern. I'm glad they're gone."

Seraph raised her eyebrows. "Boots?" she suggested gently. "I've just swept the floor, and I have no plans to do it again soon."

He backed rapidly out of the house and sat on the porch. "Everyone kept touching, touching, touching. 'Hello, Jes.' They'd say. 'Good to have you back.' Touch. Touch. Touch."

"I'm sorry. You should have asked them not to touch you."

"Hennea said, 'Stop touching the man, you fools. It hurts him.' and they stopped touching me." He pulled off a boot and looked up with a pleased expression.

"Hennea yelled at them?" Seraph asked surprised.

He shook his head. "No, she just said it very firmly. But she can touch me. I told her so."

"In front of everyone?" asked Rinnie, horrified.

Seraph was hard put not to laugh.

Lehr and Gura stepped up on the porch on the tail end of Jes's story.

"Hennea blushed and walked off," Lehr said. "Papa laughed and told Jes it wasn't polite to tell a woman she could touch him while other folk were listening in. Everyone congratulated Jes on finding such a pretty girl."

"Poor Hennea." Seraph tried to suppress her smile.

"Papa told us to tell you he was staying in town tonight to help Aunt Alinath and Uncle Bandor. He'll be back after baking tomorrow morning. The bakery was in pretty rough shape. It looks as though something besides the troll took a run through town."

"Is everything all right?"

Lehr nodded. "The bakery looked like a pair of kids went through and tried to make the worst mess they could. One of the pots of breadmother was tipped over, but Papa says he thinks they can save it. If not, it's a local one, and Alinath can bargain with the beermaster for more."

"What about Hennea?"

Lehr grinned again. "I expect she'll be along. I don't know where she went, but she'll be over her embarrassment by now."

"Where is she going to sleep?" asked Jes.

"You and I can go get a couple of poles from the barn," Lehr said after a moment. "We can frame off Rinnie's alcove and put up sheeting. Rinnie and Hennea can sleep behind it. Papa was talking about doing that this year for Rinnie anyway."

"That's a good idea," said Seraph. "There's an old mattress out in the barn, I think. All it needs is stuffing. You might as well put your boots back on, Jes."

Jes heaved a sigh and shoved his foot back in his boot. "Off shoes, Jes, you'll dirty the floors. Then on shoes, Jes, I've work for you."

"It's for Hennea," Lehr reminded him.

Jes sighed again and retied his boot.

CHAPTER 4

Hennea came back a while later, a slender book in her hand. Warned by Gura's happy barks, Seraph met her on the porch.

"We didn't do a very good job looking through the temple," Hennea said, staggering a little as the big, black dog welcomed her home. "Down boy, good boy. Yes, I'm here. Now go lie down."

"You went to the temple looking for some way to find the Shadowed." The disapproval Seraph felt spilled into her voice, though she had no real authority to disapprove. Hennea was an adult, and a Raven. There was no reason she should feel obligated to talk to Seraph before she explored the temple. It should have been safe enough.

She cleared her throat, and said, "I know we didn't find the rune that summoned the tainted creatures. Did we miss something else that was dangerous? There weren't any Order-bound gems left, nor any shadow-touched items."

"The rune was my fault," said Hennea. "I should have thought to check for it." She wiggled the book she held. "And I certainly should have thought of the library. It just didn't occur to me that the books were dangerous."

A wizard would never have left the temple without taking every book in sight. Hennea was no wizard; she was Raven. All the Shadowed were wizards, so she wasn't the Shadowed either. Not that Seraph really believed the Shadowed could live so near Lehr and Jes without alerting one or the other of them.

Seraph hadn't realized that she had still been worried by Tier's observations—but she wouldn't have felt such relief otherwise. If Hennea was old, as Tier felt, there would have to be another explanation for it.

"What did you find?"

Instead of answering, Hennea handed her the book.

Sitting on the porch bench, Seraph opened the slender volume at random. On the left page was a drawing of a meadowlark. On the right was a page of closely written script in a language that looked vaguely familiar. The *solsenti* of the Empire spoke a little over thirty dialects in four languages—though Common was spoken by most of them. She spoke a smattering of them, some better than others, and read more than she spoke.

"I don't know this language," she said.

Hennea took the book from her and began reading. "Unto the Lark it is given to Heal all things and to make right the heart and head. First are fourteen things that all Lark are blessed to bear. Sweet breath for he who has breathed in water. Blood sealing—"

"The Song of Orders?" Seraph interrupted. "But it's forbidden . . . sorry, I'm being stupid. Obviously someone did write it down. But if he had the Song of Orders, why didn't Volis understand what the Orders were?"

"Maybe he couldn't read it either?" suggested Hennea. "Or maybe he thought it was wrong—as he thought we were wrong. It is incomplete—only the Lark, Cormorant, and Raven are here, and only in partial form. The rest of it is a hodgepodge of Traveler legends."

"Do we destroy it?" Seraph found herself curiously reluctant to do so; it was a beautifully bound book.

"Not until I read the legends to the Bard," Hennea conceded. "Let him hold the stories and pass them on to the next generation. What we need to do—you, I, and your Ordered family—is go through that temple from top to bottom. We can look for the Shadowed and search for less obvious dangers than shadow taint."

They headed out early the next morning, leaving Gura to guard the farm. Jes didn't want to go back, and grumbled to himself all the way to Redern. He did not like cities. But when Seraph told him he could stay home, he'd liked that even less. She kept a close eye on him, but the Guardian stayed safely asleep. Rinnie skipped next to her glowering oldest brother and tried to tease him into a better mood.

Hennea led—mostly, Seraph thought, to stay away from Jes. Lehr walked beside Seraph, giving her his arm. Among other things, Brewydd had taught him to mind his manners even with his own mother. It made Seraph want to smile, but she restrained herself and tucked her hand in the crook of his arm.

The Rederni greeted them as they climbed up the zigzag streets, mostly with shy smiles and averted eyes. When Hennea started directly for the new temple, Seraph caught her elbow.

"We need to talk to Karadoc. I should have talked to him while we had him at our home, but I didn't think of it. Ellevanal told me that he used Karadoc to destroy the Shadowed's summoning rune. He might know something interesting. I also want to stop and tell Tier what we're doing."

"Ellevanal?" Hennea stopped dead and stared at Seraph. "You believe a god directed the priest Karadoc?"

"That's what he told me."

"The priest?"

"Ellevanal," said Lehr with a small smile. "Didn't Mother tell you that she had a conversation with Him?"

"Ellevanal's the forest king," said Jes unexpectedly. Seraph hadn't known that he'd realized that much. "I don't know about being a god, though."

"He told me he was only a little god," Seraph told him.

"There are no gods, Seraph," said Hennea softly, almost to herself. "They are all dead."

Travelers did not believe in gods—demons and shadowed in all forms, but not gods.

Seraph shrugged, her years in Redern had softened her attitudes toward gods. "Hennea, this village has worshiped Ellevanal since Redern was settled. Ellevanal is most certainly the forest king—*ell vanail* means lord of the forest. From what he said to me, I think he was originally a Keeper or perhaps just an elemental who escaped the devastation the Shadowed King brought upon them. When men settled here after the Fall, Ellevanal used the forest to protect them from the shadow-touched things that escaped as well."

"He is no god, no matter what he told you," Hennea said.

Seraph shrugged. "I don't worship him, but I'm grateful that he fights at our side and not against us. If he wants to call himself a god, I can't see the harm in it. Come, we need to talk to Karadoc before we start messing around in the temple."

They found Karadoc wrapped in blankets and banished to sit in the sunshine outside of the temple while a number of people were cleaning inside.

"Greetings, Seraph Tieraganswife," he said with a mischievous grin that made him look more battered and pale in contrast. "Greetings also Jes and Lehr Tieraganson, and Rinnie Seraphsdaughter."

Seraph bowed her head. "Priest Karadoc, may I make you known to my compatriot Hennea, Raven of the Clan of Rivilain Moon-Haired."

"Priest," said Hennea in a low voice.

Karadoc tilted his head, and replied, "Welcome, daughter. I've seen you before, I think. In the new temple?"

She nodded. "I served the would-be-Priest Volis."

"Until she had Mother kill him," added Lehr in an undertone. But the old priest heard him.

"Yes," Karadoc said. "You look much healthier than you did that night." He turned back to Seraph. "How is it that I might serve you, daughter?"

That "daughter" grated. Even after all these years in Redern, the tendency of the menfolk to diminish any woman and patronize her bothered Seraph. Especially after the past months spent in Travelers' company.

Lehr's hand touched her shoulder—likely he knew just how she felt, having tasted something of the same treatment in the Traveler camp. Karadoc didn't mean to demean her, Seraph knew, but still it grated.

She squatted on her heels in front of him—something she wouldn't have done if she'd been wearing her Rederni skirts as she should have been, because they tended to tangle in her feet and make it difficult to rise again. The move put her head level with his, and gave her time to quash her temper. Anger had no place in the heart of a Raven—though it resided full often in hers.

"I need you to tell me about the new temple and how you stopped it from calling more tainted creatures to it," she said baldly.

He leaned back farther in his chair, and the merriment faded from his face. "Do you now? Why is that?"

"Because when Hennea and I went through the temple that night we saw no magic that should have called to the shadowtouched. Either we missed it, or it wasn't there then. That rune was drawn by the Shadowed."

"The Shadowed died five centuries ago," he said, not arguing exactly, more as if he were horrified than as if he didn't believe her.

Seraph nodded. "The Unnamed King died at Shadow's Fall. But he is not the first to contain the Stalker's curse, and, unfortunately, he won't be the last. We have a new one—ask Ellevanal if you do not believe me."

He stared at her and pursed his lips. But he didn't ask her what the Stalker was that its curse could create the Shadowed, he just said, "We'd already been having trouble—mostly with the kinds of things we'd usually only see in the outlying areas— goblins and the like. They killed a few goats, scared some boys who were too near the new temple. Then the bigger things started coming—an ogre that Ciro's grandson killed with that axe he's so proud of. We'd just finished burying one of the boys who died in the battle when Ellevanal called me to him."

He stopped and smiled with remembered pleasure. "I thought I was too old for him to call me that way anymore." He blinked and came back to himself. "He told me something in the new temple was summoning these beasts. He couldn't enter the building except through me, and he asked permission to share my body."

Hennea hissed in through her teeth. Seraph tapped the other woman's knee in a demand for silence. The Colossae wizards once had a word for such body sharing—*shadowing,* they'd called it.

"So you let him accompany you," Seraph said.

Karadoc nodded. "We went into the temple—I'd had the doors boarded up after Volis died, but Ellevanal pulled the boards off." He glanced at his hands, and Seraph saw his nails had been broken past the quick. He saw her look, and said, "It didn't hurt when he did it. He led me through the temple—" He closed his eyes as if he could see it again.

"We went from room to room. Sometimes we would stand in the middle of the room and do nothing—I had the feeling he was listening very hard to something I couldn't hear. We came at last to a room just barely large enough to stand upright in—almost a cupboard. We knelt in the hallway just outside the door. Ellevanal waved my hand over the floor of the little room, and I could see it, too—a scattering of strange shapes that looked almost like writing, except they weren't organized right to left in straight lines as we write. Instead the symbols were organized into odd shapes. Ellevanal put our hands on the shapes and . . ." Air left his lungs in a wheeze.

"Fire," he said in a low voice. "Ice and fire flowing through my veins like shards of glass."

"By Lark," whispered Hennea. "I wonder that he dared."

Karadoc looked at her.

"He worked magic through a man with no affinity for it," she said. "If you had failed him, it likely would have killed the both of you"—she looked at Seraph pointedly—"god or no god."

"I don't know how long it took," Karadoc said. "It felt like years. But I remember seeing the marks fade from the floor before I fainted. When I awoke, Ellevanal was there beside me."

"In the temple?" Seraph asked. "I thought he couldn't go there."

"He told me we'd cleansed it," said Karadoc. "He picked me up and brought me here to His own temple in the blink of an eye. Frightened my apprentice nearly to death." He smiled a little. "After that, few new creatures came. But the ones already here were bad enough. Something, I don't know what, attacked me here in the temple itself. I would have died if He hadn't saved me. That's when Ellevanal told us to go to your farm where your Traveler magic would help us. We hadn't been there two days when the troll came."

"I don't know much about wizardry"—Seraph turned to Hennea—"but I think I would have noticed such a spell if it were present while we were looking through the temple. That means that the Shadowed was here after we searched the temple the night the false priest died."

Hennea nodded.

"Thank you, Karadoc," Seraph said, getting to her feet.

He laughed. "I'm glad to be helpful." He tipped his head to the temple behind him. "They won't let me clean," he said. "I was feeling old and useless."

"Let them clean," said Seraph. "I have it on the best authority that if it weren't for you, a lot more people would have been killed."

"Whose authority would that be?" he asked.

She smiled at him. "He says you play *skiri* well."

He paused and looked at her thoughtfully before gifting her with a secretive smile. "Maybe your informant is right."

"So sit and rest," she told him. "Enjoy the fruits of your labors for a day or two more. They'll work you hard enough later. I expect that attendance at Ellevanal's temple is due for an increase."

He laughed. "That may be, daughter. That may be."

"Shadowed," said Hennea, when they'd left Ellevanal's temple behind them.

"Karadoc is not tainted," said Lehr.

"Ellevanal is not of the shadow," agreed Seraph. "He's been Jes's friend for years. But Hennea knows that already."

"What's wrong?" Seraph heard Rinnie ask Jes. "Why is Hennea so upset?"

"Ellevanal shadowed that priest," said Hennea, keeping her gaze firmly on the road before them.

"What?" asked Lehr. "The forest king isn't of the shadow. Jes and I would know."

Seraph sighed. "The Colossae wizards knew how to ride in the heads of others. They called what Ellevanal did with Karadoc *welaen*. Shadow, the kind of shadow that you see on a sunny day is *laen*. *Welaen* then, translates best into Common as 'shadowing.' Its meaning to the Elder Wizards was broader and encompassed a whole range of magical ability. For us, only the touch of the Stalker or the Shadowed brings shadow-tainting." She directed that at Hennea.

"What your Mother means," said Hennea, "is that the Colossae wizards could ride with unsuspecting people or simply take over their bodies without permission—just as the Stalker does. Because of the misuse of *welaen,* the Colossae wizards forbade it—and there wasn't much that they forbade."

Seraph had forgotten the endless debating about what kind of magic was allowable. It came, she supposed, because the lack of morality among the Colossae wizards had destroyed the city and began the endless guilt-bound wandering of the Travelers. The other Orders just used their abilities as they could, but Ravens must endlessly debate about what was right and proper.

"Here is the bakery," Seraph said, with something like relief. She'd always been a practical Raven, especially after her teacher died and she became her clan's only Raven. Whatever it took to survive was not a moral line she expected Hennea would approve of.

They found Tier elbow deep in dough. He listened as Seraph explained what they were going to do.

"I'll follow you in a couple of hours. We've a lot of hungry folk to feed."

Seraph leaned over and kissed him lightly, careful to keep out of the flour. "You'll do no such thing. I won't have you climbing the mountainside with your knees still healing. When you're through here, why don't you wait for us at the tavern?"

He thought about arguing, she saw it in his eyes. "Fine," he said instead. "Just you be cautious up there. I don't want to have to trek up there and find our Jes as a frog."

"Can't do frogs," said Jes seriously. "Can't do horses either. Only animals with fur and fangs."

* * *

They started back up the streets. Since Redern was dug into the side of a mountain, new buildings had to be built above the rest of the village, and Volis's temple was the newest building in Redern.

"Maybe Jes shouldn't be here," Hennea said. "There's a lot of people."

Seraph had been keeping an eye on him as well. She'd have left him home, but he wouldn't stay without them. He wasn't paying attention to them now, just staring at the ground with a distracted air.

"If you wrap a sprain for too long, you ruin the joint," said Lehr.

"What?"

"I mean," Lehr explained, "if Jes doesn't ever come to town—pretty soon he won't be able to."

"Jes," said Seraph, touching his sleeve.

He looked up with a jerk.

"Do you need to go home?" she asked. "Are the people too much for you?"

"No, Mother." Jes shook his head. "I'm all right. Everyone is so excited today it feels like I have bees in my head. But we think it wouldn't be a good thing to leave you alone in the new temple."

He used "we" just as the priest had. Lehr started to speak, and Seraph held up a finger for quiet so she could solidify her first, nebulous thought. There was a connection between shadowing and the way the Guardian Order worked, she could almost see how it was so.

Ellevanal had shadowed the priest. Was that the same kind of magic that caused the Orders to attach themselves to Travelers? She closed her eyes and thought, trying to work her way through an instinctive affirmative. The binding between the priest and Ellevanal had been temporary, but the Orders were permanent.

"I can *see* the Orders," she murmured out loud to clarify her thoughts. "But I can't *see* shadowing. I wonder if Lehr or Jes would have been able to tell that the forest king was riding inside Karadoc's skin? Or is it the evil of the Stalker's presence that they sense." That felt right.

"You think there is a connection between the Orders and shadowing?" said Hennea.

Seraph nodded and opened her eyes. "I think they are similar magics. Not twins or complements, but certainly in the same family of magics. Maybe, when you and I try to study the Order-bound gems again, we need to study the shadowing that the Elder Wizards did. There are books about shadowing in most of the *mermori* libraries. Isolde had four or five I've glanced through."

Hennea stared into the summer sky for a moment. "Yes, you're right."

Perhaps Hennea meant it to come out as if she'd just come to the same conclusion. But to Seraph, it sounded suspiciously as if she'd known all along.

"How long have you known?" Seraph snapped.

Seraph, Hennea, and Brewydd had spent days trying to discover what the Path had done to bind the Orders to their gems. There was nothing in any of the libraries on the Orders; they had been created after the Colossae wizards had left and were no longer writing down their studies. If Hennea had known there was a connection between shadowing the Colossae wizards had used and the Orders, she should have told them.

Hennea met Seraph's gaze. "A while. But I couldn't find anything specific. The wizards wrote a lot about how to get themselves into another person's mind and how to shield themselves from such abuse perpetrated by another wizard. Nothing useful in our situation."

"But you didn't mention it to Brewydd or me."

"No."

"Why not?"

"It was not useful."

"Or so you thought," Seraph said icily.

There was a connection, she could feel it; but that wasn't what bothered her. Tier liked to tease her about the secretive nature of Ravens, but Seraph had never had that facet of her Order turned on her before. She didn't like it. She'd become a Rederni—people who kept secrets couldn't be trusted.

Tier's suspicions of Hennea rattled around in Seraph's head, but she couldn't see any pattern to them. "Tier thinks you are older than you look."

"Why should he think that?" It was Hennea's turn to speak coldly.

It wasn't an answer, and Seraph had been a parent too long not to hear the evasion and the attempt to divert the conversation away from Hennea and direct it onto Tier.

"Mother?" said Jes.

He was swaying from one foot to another as he watched Seraph's face unblinkingly.

"I have questions for you," she told Hennea. "But they will wait for another time. Jes, it's all right."

"You are angry," he said.

"Mother's angry a lot," Rinnie told him. "Unless she's angry with you, it's all right."

Jes looked down at his sister. "Not at Hennea."

"Well," she said conscientiously, "you're right. I still wouldn't worry. She can do what I do, keep out of Mother's way until she calms down."

Lehr glanced at Seraph's face, and she thought she saw him hide a small smile before he turned to Rinnie, and said, "This might be a better conversation to have when Mother's not here."

Seraph brooded as she climbed. But the conclusions that she had come to earlier still held. Hennea was merely a Raven with secrets—and that was bad enough.

Willon's shop, the last building before the temple, was dark and empty when they went past it.

"He must still be in Taela," Lehr said, breaking the uneasy silence. "I'd forgotten that he went there, too. He was going to help us. I hope he's not still there waiting for us."

"He could hardly help but hear that a band of Travelers rescued the Emperor," said Seraph dryly. "I'm sure that he knows who that was. Though if I'd thought of it, I would have sent him a message before we left. He goes back to Taela every year to check on his family anyway. He didn't go there just to help us—though he would have if we'd asked. But we didn't need gold or information, just magic and swords; and those aren't something a merchant could help us with. He'll be back soon."

They climbed past the storefront and up the steep trail that led to the abandoned temple of the Path of the Five.

* * *

The temple burrowed deep into the heart of Redern Mountain, leaving only its head to mark where the bulk of it hid.

One door lay several feet from the temple, and the other was leaned neatly against a wall. It looked as though the troll had decided to investigate the temple, though when Seraph glanced around she saw no other sign of the creature. Then she remembered that Karadoc told her Ellevanal had used him to rip open the doors and was amazed he'd come out with no more than torn fingernails.

Seraph stopped just outside the entrance. "Would you check this to see if it is shadow-tainted, Lehr?"

"I already did. There's no shadowing I can sense."

"Jes?"

He didn't answer, and when Seraph looked for him, he was staring down at the roof of Willon's store which, because of the steepness of the mountain, jutted out of the ground only a few feet below where he stood.

"Jes?" Hennea reached out, but stopped just short of touching him. "Are you all right?"

He turned his face away from her and looked at Seraph. "There's nothing here," he said shortly. "Volis is dead. The forest king and Karadoc took care of the rest. Lehr says there is nothing here—why do you bother to ask me?"

Jes was usually cheerful unless the Guardian was present. He was very seldom sullen or moody.

"Hennea, take Rinnie and Lehr into the temple, Jes and I have some things to talk over," Seraph said, forgetting for a moment she wasn't just talking to one of her children. "Please," Seraph added hastily when Hennea stiffened. "We'll join you in a few minutes."

She waited while they filed in. Then she turned her attention to Jes, who had gone back to staring at Willon's roof.

She debated simply waiting until he was ready to talk—but this was Jes. It might be days before he was ready, and she didn't have Tier's patience.

"What's wrong, Jes?"

"Nothing is wrong." He didn't look at her, but she could see the stubborn set to his jaw.

Tier was better at this sort of thing than Seraph, but he

wasn't here. She thought back over the climb up Redern and tried to pinpoint when Jes's discomfort at being surrounded by so many people had turned to anger.

"Hennea is entitled to her secrets," Seraph said tentatively.

"Of course." The words were clearly enunciated, but Seraph knew that the Guardian was still at rest because she felt none of the dread that came with his presence.

"I don't like it when she hides things that might be important," she tried. She couldn't tell if he was angry at her or Hennea.

"Sorry."

Seraph picked up a small rock and tossed it down the mountainside.

"You'll hit someone," Jes said. "Papa says don't."

"Tier's usually right."

"Papa's always right," said Jes bitterly.

Ah, thought Seraph. "Your father doesn't disapprove of Hennea, Jes. He talked to me about several things he'd noticed about her—remember, he doesn't know her as well as we do. One of the things was that he thought she was older than she admitted."

"Does that matter?"

"That depends upon a number of things," said Seraph.

"Don't tell me," said Jes, kicking a clod of dirt onto Willon's roof. "I'm too stupid. If it's important, tell Lehr or Hennea or Rinnie. Or you could wait for the Guardian, he's smart."

Hmm, she thought.

"I thought your father was mistaken about Hennea's age until I asked her about it just now. She didn't answer me, Jes. She could have lied, but she didn't want to."

"Why does it matter?" he asked again.

"The problem is that I know of only three ways that Hennea could be older than she appears. At least, enough older that it attracted your father's attention." Seraph sat on the ground beside Jes, and after a hesitation, he sat down, too. "The first is impossible, because Hennea is no Healer. The second is equally unlikely. The Shadowed can be very old and still seem young. But Hennea touches you all the time. You'd know if she were the Shadowed. The third isn't much better.

Wizards—not Ravens—but *solsenti* wizards who are very powerful sometimes live longer than usual."

"Hinnum was centuries old when Colossae fell," Jes said.

"I've heard stories that say he was as much as three centuries old," Seraph agreed. "But he was the greatest wizard of Colossae, the wizards' city. Still, it is not uncommon for wizards to live to well over a hundred years."

"Hennea could be a wizard," he said. "You told me Ravens have to be mageborn, just like Guardians have to be empaths."

"I don't think she is," she said. "If she were a wizard, she'd never have left Volis's library the night we killed him. No matter how tired or anxious she was, a wizard wouldn't have forgotten about another wizard's library."

"You and she are using the *mermori* libraries to try and free the Order-bound gems," he said.

Seraph nodded. "But wizards are obsessed with books, Jes. Books are the only way they can do their magic. They have to know all about the nature of fire before they can light a candle. That makes books very important. Hennea knew about Volis's library—she'd lived here. But it was only yesterday she realized that his library might be dangerous."

"She came here when she ran away from me," he said. "I embarrassed her. I didn't mean to."

That was it, she thought, the real reason he was upset. Hennea had been avoiding him all day. Seraph looked at her son and wished she knew how to make the pain of living easier on him.

"That's right." She'd never found that lying about hurtful things made them hurt any less.

"But I embarrassed her, anyway."

Seraph considered it. "If, say"—she glanced down at the roof below—"*Willon* told me I could touch him anytime I wanted, do you think I would run off in embarrassment?"

Wide-eyed, Jes was obviously having trouble imagining Willon saying any such thing to her. He shook his head. "They'd be picking up Willon pieces for years."

She grinned. "Do you know what I think, Jes? I think if she hadn't wanted to touch you, they might be picking up pieces of Jes all over the place. I think she wanted to touch you, and that's what embarrassed her."

Jes gave a long sigh. "Maybe you're right," he said. "But you aren't always good at seeing why people do things. You're just like me."

"Probably," she conceded. She weighed the possible harm of telling him more. "But your father knows people. Do you want me to tell you the other thing he told me about Hennea?"

He looked at her, his dark eyes sad.

"He asked me why she was still with us. She came with us to Taela to fight the Path, but after the Path was gone, she still stayed with us."

"For me?" he whispered.

"Jes, I want you to listen until I finish, will you do that?" Seraph said. "Promise."

"I promise."

"Your father told me she would not have stayed for you."

Jes surged to his feet and took a step away, and Seraph continued quickly. "He said she would have left as soon as she could because of you, and I told him she was staying to help me with the Ordered gems and because of the Shadowed."

"She'd have left because of me."

"Because she's worried for you. Will you listen?" She kept her voice soft.

"All right," he said, not looking at her—looking away from people while he talked to them was a habit of his. But he was *not looking* rather more pointedly than usual.

"You know there are very few Guardians who live as long as you have," she said. "Of those who survive adolescence, most are women. As you said, the Eagle Order comes only to empaths, for whatever reason. Yet the Eagle, of all the Orders, is the most prone to violence—something that no empath can live with easily."

"Stupid," said Jes, with understandable emphasis.

Seraph shrugged. "The Elder Wizards created the Stalker, Jes. I don't know of anything more stupid, do you? Maybe there is a good reason for the Guardian Order to be so difficult to bear, but I can see none."

He didn't say anything.

"The Travelers have tried a lot of things to help the Eagle," she continued. "When an Eagle is born, the child is adopted out to another clan. They believe strangers won't have a strong emotional attachment to a child who is not of their blood."

"Sorry you didn't have a clan to give me to," said Jes hotly.

"*Jesaphi,* that's enough." Seraph snapped. She had no patience for self-pity. She took a deep breath. "Do you know that when your father and I were first married, I thought I had made the wrong decision when I accepted his proposal. I was Raven and had abandoned my duties out of cowardice."

Jes turned to look at her, obviously surprised.

"I *was* a coward, Jes. I had responsibilities, and instead of trying to fulfill them, I hid in your father's shadow, where I was safe from the consequences of further failure. I hadn't saved my clan. I hadn't even managed to save my brother. I was afraid to fail again."

"You tried. Trying is good enough," Jes told her.

Seraph shook her head. "Not when people die. When people die, trying doesn't feel like it is good enough."

He thought about it. "If Papa had died in Taela, I would not have felt like trying was good enough."

She nodded. "But when I held you in my arms and realized the gift I had been given, I knew there was a reason I was in Redern." She leaned toward him, willing him to feel the utter certainty that had come to her with his birth. "I *knew* your father would never make me give up my child in the mistaken belief that someone else, someone who didn't care as much, could do a better job of keeping you safe. From that day, I never felt I should go back to the clans. I had my home—in your father and in you."

"Is that why I'm not dead, like the other Guardians?" he asked. "Because you didn't give me away? Were they wrong to give away their babies?"

"I wish I knew," she said. "If there were a way to help other Guardians, I would tell the clans—but I think the answer is simpler. Too simple to help those others who bear the Eagle Order. The answer is you. You are strong, Jes, strong enough to bear a burden that would break other people. You can anchor the Guardian Order without losing your balance."

Jes sat down next to her again and stared at Willon's roof some more.

"Hennea knows I am dangerous?" he asked after a while.

"She knows Guardians are vulnerable," Seraph corrected firmly. "She knows there are things that are very dangerous for Guardians—very strong emotions, even good ones, are difficult. When you are falling in love, Jes, you have nothing but strong emotions. One minute you're happy, the next you're sad."

Jes nodded in emphatic agreement.

She wished Tier was here, to say the next part. But she needed to warn Jes, and this was as good a time as any other.

"Another thing that will be very difficult for you is sex," she told him.

Jes stiffened beside her, and Seraph kept her face a little averted so he couldn't see the rising color in her cheeks. She cleared her throat. "You have a hard enough time controlling the volatile nature of the Guardian without dealing with your own emotions running wild as well." And that was all she was going to say about that, she thought firmly. "Hennea knows this last adventure was dangerous for you, because the Guardian was called out so often. The Eagles who have lived the longest avoid situations that might call on the Guardian. We depended upon your abilities while we were trying to save Tier, and there were consequences. You must have noticed some changes in yourself."

"The Guardian is closer," he told her. "He used to sleep a lot, but now he's always near. We switch more often, too." He hesitated. "He listens to me better, though, and when he takes over, I can still be there with him. I used to wake up walking in the woods and not know why, but now he usually lets me stay if I want to."

"I didn't know that," said Seraph. "It sounds like a good thing to me."

He nodded. "To me, too."

"Hennea doesn't know about that part," said Seraph. "She only knows you are very vulnerable right now. She believes she is too old for you—however old that is. She thinks what you feel for her is"—her command of the Rederni tongue twenty years in the gaining failed her, and she waved her hands before she found the word—"mooncalf love; which is, maybe, even more emotional than real love, but not permanent. Something you would recover from if she were gone."

"She wants to leave to save me," he said, and, from his aggravated tone, he wasn't appreciative of the idea.

"She wants you to be safe because she loves you," said Seraph.

His head jerked around.

"Your father told me she loves you," she told him, knowing he'd trust Tier's judgment.

He took a deep breath, his shoulders softening with some emotion Seraph thought might just be simple relief.

"She loves you too much to trust in your strength when it is your life at risk. She doesn't see what a gift she is to you: a woman who is not afraid of the Guardian, a Raven who has enough control she can touch you without causing you distress, a woman who is strong enough to love an Eagle."

A slow smile crept across his face. "Pretty," he said, and Seraph felt an answering smile rise in her.

"Very," she agreed.

Jes stood up and started for the temple, but then stopped and turned back to her. Seraph got to her feet—slowly, because the hair on the back of her neck told her it was the Guardian who watched her out of her son's eyes.

"Why is she still here?" he asked. "If she wanted to leave to save us, why doesn't she just leave? The puzzle of the gems is more important than Jes is?"

"The gems are more than just a puzzle," answered Seraph. "Guardian, the Travelers are dying. We can't afford to lose so many Orders when the Orders may be the only thing that can save us. I don't know why she hasn't told me everything she knows, but I think she has earned the right to expect me to trust her judgment."

The Guardian nodded and retreated behind Jes's eyes. "It's all right if Hennea has secrets," Jes said in his usual cheerful voice. "Ravens are happier with secrets. Papa says."

Seraph raised her eyebrows and started walking toward the temple. "Oh, he does, does he?"

Jes laughed.

CHAPTER 5

The pristine antechamber of Seraph's memory was gone.
The temple flooring was covered with dirt blown in through
the open doors. The furnishings Seraph remembered were
gone.

Only when she and Jes entered the great domed chamber
with its frescoed birds flying in a circle around a false sky did
the temple match her memories, even down to the magelights
that illuminated the walls. She wondered how long the lights
would continue without the wizard who fed them.

Jes paused to look at the eagle that dominated the sky. "He
thought the Eagle was the Stalker, didn't he?"

"No," Seraph said, walking briskly toward a door on the
far side of the room. "He didn't know anything about the
Stalker at all, except that it was trapped. He knew even less
about the Eagle. You know Travelers don't talk about the Eagles because your Order has enough to bear, and the clans
try to protect the Guardians from the few things we can. Volis heard whispers of parts of the two stories and put them
together with a handful of straw and came out with nonsense."

Jes followed her out of the room.

They found the library and the others, thanks to Jes, who followed the sounds of voices through the labyrinthine series of narrow halls dug into the stone of the mountain.

Though it was a large room, it was sparsely furnished, as if Volis had just begun to fill it. One wall was lined with shelves that were half-filled with books. On the other side of the room were a bench, a chest, and several cabinets. Lehr and Rinnie were parked in front of one bookcase paging through books, Hennea was doing the same thing in front of another.

Hennea looked up when they entered. She saw Jes, humming happily to himself, and raised an eyebrow at Seraph.

Seraph couldn't help but smile at her a little smugly. "Ravens like secrets."

"Papa said," agreed Jes cheerfully.

He walked behind Rinnie and crouched just behind where she sat on the floor, a book opened to a colorful illustration of a Traveler camp.

"That's a *karis,*" he said, pointing at a picture of one of the little wagons. "The Lark, Brewydd, had one of those she rode in because she was very old." He looked up at Hennea. "Very old," he said again, and winked.

Hennea stiffened. Then she turned on her heel, grabbed Seraph by the arm, and tugged her out of the room into the hallway.

"What did you say to him?" she demanded, her usual aura of calmness gone as if it had never been.

In contrast, Seraph felt quite tranquil—an unusual state for her. She enjoyed it.

"His hearing is quite good," she reminded Hennea. "Though he'll pretend he didn't hear us because someone taught *him* manners." She looked pointedly at Hennea's hand.

Hennea let her go as if Seraph's arm had turned hot as a coal.

"Why are you doing this? Why encourage him?" Hennea asked in a harsh whisper. "You know it's not safe."

"My son doesn't hide from life," said Seraph, making no effort to shield her words from the three people in the next room, who were doubtlessly holding their breath so they could hear better. "You might trust him to know what he can bear and what he cannot. He is not stupid."

Hennea stared at her incredulously. "You *are* encouraging him."

"I told him nothing but the truth as I know it," said Seraph. "What he does with that knowledge is his business—and perhaps yours." She looked at the other Raven and sighed, putting away her secret amusement. "Life can be so hard sometimes, Hennea; it's easy to forget it can also be wonderful. Don't throw away gifts that come your way."

Deciding she had dispensed more advice than she was comfortable with, Seraph left Hennea and returned to the library, pulling a book out at random.

"Hennea's already been through that shelf," murmured Lehr. "It might be best if you moved over one bookcase. We're setting aside any books that are about the Travelers, and there's a big pile here for books written in languages we can't read."

"Thanks," she said, touching his shoulder. Instead of sorting through a bookcase, she sat on the floor and began going through the pile of books until she came to some she could translate.

To someone who was used to having the *mermori* libraries at her fingertips, this library was disappointing. Illusionary books were almost as useful as the real thing, and you didn't have to worry about tearing pages. The Colossae wizards had been wealthy and, being—by all accounts—*solsenti*-style wizards, they had spent their wealth in books. Even Isolde's library dwarfed this one—and Isolde had been one of the lesser wizards.

Seraph paged through a book about the Travelers by someone who claimed to have lived with them for a year. It was full of unlikely events and bits of nonsense that led Seraph to believe that if the author had ever met a Traveler, it was no more than a momentary encounter that allowed him to describe the clothing. There was nothing else factual that she could find.

Hennea came back into the library while Seraph was still paging through the first book.

"Have you decided what we're looking for?" Seraph asked Hennea, as if the conversation in the hall had not happened.

Hennea, having drawn her usual cloak of equanimity back in place, said, "The books about Travelers I think we should take with us so we can take more time to evaluate them. The books of wizardry that have nothing to do with us—I don't know. Most of what is in them is not very useful for us. It seems wrong simply to destroy them, but they are too dangerous to fall into just anyone's hands. There might be some correspondence—though he burned most of his letters after he read them. Keep your eyes open to anything that might point to the identity of the Shadowed."

"What if we don't find anything about the Shadowed here?" asked Lehr.

"We'll find him sooner or later if he doesn't find us," said Seraph. "A Shadowed lives by the deaths of others. Where he walks, the dead litter the ground. He can't hide forever, not once we are aware that there is a Shadowed once more."

"If the wizard books belonged to the Secret Path," said Rinnie, changing the subject for one she could comment on, "and the Secret Path people were all traitors, don't the books belong to the Emperor?"

Seraph had a brief moment of trying to imagine the logistics of getting a shipment of books of wizardry to the Emperor—who would have no more use for them than they did.

"Maybe your father will have a good idea," she said. "And, just in case Hennea hasn't already given you the lecture, if you find something that feels *wrong,* let Hennea or me look at it before you open it."

Lehr joined in the search through the books, but Jes, after picking up and setting down a few, paced back and forth restlessly. He could read, Tier had seen to that, but it held no interest for him.

"Go ahead and explore," Seraph told him.

"Can I go explore, too?" asked Rinnie, putting up the book she'd been looking through.

Seraph shook her head. "No. I want you here with me."

Jes, who'd paused to hear Seraph's answer, waved at everyone and left.

Rinnie's jaw set, much as her brother's had a short while ago. "I wish I were a Guardian, or a Raven or a Hunter. Being a Cormorant is *boring.*"

Seraph had no patience for any more drama. "Rinnie, you are too old to pout. Stop it."

"I don't want to look through boring old books."

Seraph sucked in her breath, but Lehr spoke first. "Why don't you look in the cabinets and the stuff on the other side of the room. There might be something interesting there."

Rinnie let out a martyred sigh, but crossed the room anyway and began to open cabinet doors. Seraph went back to searching through books, though she kept an eye on Rinnie's progress. She wasn't really worried, only cautious. She and Hennea had already gone through the temple to make certain there was nothing harmful.

Of course, the Shadowed had come back and set a summoning rune since then.

"Be careful, Rinnie," she said.

"There's nothing to be careful of, Mother." Rinnie sounded disgusted. "There's nothing here. Wait." She stuck her head farther into a cabinet and came out wearing dust and holding a leather satchel in her arms. "This is magicked!"

"Drop it, now!" Seraph let the book she'd been holding fall to the ground and hurried to Rinnie's side. "Being careful means don't touch, Rinnie."

"It's not very magicked," Rinnie muttered, but she dropped the satchel on the floor.

Seraph knelt beside Rinnie's find and waved a hand over it. The patterns of the spell were familiar with a few variations because whoever set the spell had been a wizard, not a Raven. "A preservation spell. You're right, Rinnie, there's no harm in this. Go ahead and open it and let us see what is inside." She handed the satchel back.

Rinnie tugged open the buckles and looked—keeping the cover flap up so that Lehr, who had come over when she'd first announced her discovery, couldn't see inside. "Scrolls," she said.

She took one out and unrolled it.

"It's a map." Lehr looked over Rinnie's shoulder. "I can't read any of the place names, though. Can you, Mother?" He moved out of the way so Seraph could take his place.

Seraph shook her head. "Although something about the language looks familiar. Do you recognize it, Hennea?"

Hennea set aside an oversized, red-covered book on the "*solsenti* wizard books" pile, and came over to have a look.

Her first, casual appraisal lasted only a second. Then she knelt on the ground and began tracing the markings with a fingertip.

"I can read it," she said in an odd voice.

Like Seraph, she took a moment to feel the shape of the spell on the satchel. Then she upended the whole thing so that eight rolls fell out, ignoring Rinnie's involuntary protest at her usurpation of Rinnie's possession of the satchel.

The map she unrolled first was a map of a city. "Merchant's District," she said, her voice shaking as her fingers ran over the spidery ink. "Artisan's District. Old Town. High Town. Merchant's Gate. Low Gate. University Gate."

Seraph stared at the upside-down map. She trying to place it in one of the cities she'd been in before. "University? There are only three universities in the Empire, but the layout doesn't fit any of those."

Hennea turned the map around and tapped the large writing on the bottom of the sheet. "Can you read that?"

Seraph frowned. The larger letters looked very familiar, she decided. It was the style of writing that was throwing her. She used her finger to trace the thicker lines of the letters. "This first letter's a *C* and the second . . ." She let her voice trail off as the pattern became clear to her.

"What is it?" asked Lehr.

Seraph touched the map with her fingers again. "Colossae." Awe filled her. "When this map was drawn, Colossae was a thriving city—before the birth of the Empire, before the Shadowed had ruled, before the first Travelers' feet touched a road—this map was drawn."

"It could be a copy." Lehr's voice was subdued, hushed.

"Maybe." Hennea's hand brushed it again. "Or it could be a fake—there's no way to tell."

"I might be able to tell," said Seraph slowly.

"How?" asked Hennea.

"I'm going to read its past." She reached out to touch it, but Hennea jerked it away.

"If it is that old, it is too dangerous."

"Dangerous how?" asked Lehr.

Seraph gave an exasperated huff. "It's a map, Hennea. I'll

be lucky if anyone has held it long enough to leave any kind of impression at all. Can you read objects?"

"No."

"Well then." Seraph pulled the map out of the other Raven's hands and set it on the ground in front of her. "Now if I fall to the ground shrieking, feel free to take it away again."

"Mother? Are you sure you should do this?"

She slanted a look at Lehr. "Allow me the courtesy of knowing my limits. Unless it was an object of worship, or someone used it to kill someone else, it will be fine."

Before someone else could object, Seraph sent tendrils of magic into the parchment.

"It's all right," she told them when the map's past came to her in whispered bits and pieces rather than an overwhelming wave.

Aside from a few barely formed images, the newest history came to her first, though that was not always the case. She felt Hennea's hands and the intense quiet that would have told her a Raven had held the map, even if she hadn't known Hennea.

"Volis had this." She could feel the cold sweat on his palms and the fear someone might see him. "He stole it." A new image, closer to her than the theft had been, and she knew that he hadn't been able to read any of the maps. "He had thought something so carefully hidden away would have been important, but he could see nothing useful in a pile of old maps."

The map had been undisturbed for a long time. "It was hidden away, for safekeeping. For secret. A wizard holds it, a *solsenti* wizard—but he understands what he has because language is one of his gifts. A gift that has served him very well in his search for power, for . . ." She quit talking because she didn't want to confuse her audience as her reading slipped from nearer past to older and back again. The years were so pale, sometimes it was hard to hold them.

"Mother?"

Seraph blinked up at Lehr's familiar face.

"Are you all right?"

She nodded. "This is a map made by an apprentice?" The word didn't fit quite, but it was close. "A student, perhaps. He was disappointed because his teacher judged it harshly and made him redo part of it." She touched a section in the upper right where he'd had to scrape the parchment and redraw.

"How old is it, Mother?" breathed Rinnie. "Is it really from Colossae?"

"It's that old." Seraph's hands felt cold and heavy from the deep reading. "Once it passed out of the hands of the young man who made it, there was a succession of owners. They held it for such a short time, so long ago, and with such little passion that I could get no more than an impression of a lot of people."

She looked up to meet Hennea's gaze and give her a small smile. "It's emotion that leaves traces behind on things, and a map hardly inspires great passions of any kind. I can tell the age, but not much more for a long time. It was hidden or lost."

Seraph reached out and touched the satchel that had held the map very lightly with her fingertips and a thread of magic. "It was in this satchel, which is nearly as old."

Rinnie gave her prize a look of respect. "It doesn't look old."

"The preservation spell," murmured Hennea. "Things can last a long time with a good preservation spell, and the Colossae wizards' magic was very good."

"They lay together in secret, the maps and the satchel, for hundreds of years. Then a woman, a *solsenti* wizard, held it and puzzled over it—she was hoping for treasure, I think. When she first held it as a young woman, but her last touch is dry and aged. She kept them in a secret place, and it lay there for a time, never managing to decipher what it was she held though she knew it was old. About two centuries ago it came into the hands of another wizard."

She swallowed and looked at the rest of the map scrolls lying about on the floor and touched them, looking for more answers. When she had read them all, she said, "He had a gift for languages. I saw the gates of Colossae, where he was searching for something he desired very badly—power? Not quite, but it was close enough." She returned her fingers to the first map, the city map. "The next time he touched this he was held by the Stalker's power; he was the Shadowed. He hid the maps somewhere secret, he didn't need them anymore. Volis found them and took them—but he couldn't read them."

"Can you see him?" whispered Hennea urgently. "Lark tell me you can see who it is."

Seraph shook her head in frustration. "No. I get scattered impressions and a glimpse of a young man's face, but not enough to identify him. He just didn't leave enough of himself behind. I can tell you he became the Stalker's child almost two centuries ago."

Hennea swallowed her urgency behind her usual cool facade, though she was paler than normal. "We've not had one get so old since the Unnamed King."

"There have been more?" asked Lehr.

Seraph nodded. "I know of three . . . four including this one. The Unnamed King was the second. The first one left Colossae with the Elder Wizards who became the Travelers."

"This is the sixth," said Hennea. "That I know of anyway. After the Unnamed King, we knew the signs to watch for. Death follows the Shadowed. I don't see how this one has been hidden from us for so long. Are you certain of the time, Seraph?"

"I may be off ten or fifteen years either way, but not more than that." She shared Hennea's apprehension. The Shadowed, like those who were tainted, gained power over the years. "There were the plagues a couple of decades ago—one killed Isolde's clan except for my brother and me. There were other clans lightened of their members, too." She hesitated. "The Path started killing Travelers for their Orders about the same time."

"That is not a coincidence," agreed Hennea. "Maybe we have grown so few over the last few generations that no one noticed the patterns of death."

"Mother," said Lehr suddenly. "If the Shadowed touched other things here, could you tell?"

Hennea answered. "The Path's Masters, the wizards who came and stole Tier away, left before the temple was finished. If the Shadowed was among them, he did not stay here. Only Volis used the rooms beyond the Great Chamber . . ." She cleared her throat. "Only Volis and I. I don't think we'll find anything else here on which the Shadowed left enough of an impression for Seraph to read anything."

"If we had not killed Volis, he could tell us where he got that map case," mused Seraph.

"I've apologized for that," Hennea said.

Seraph looked at her in surprise. "I didn't like being tricked, Hennea. I never said he didn't need killing."

She turned her attention back to the problem of finding the Shadowed. "However, I think if the Shadowed was able to hide what he was from Jes and Lehr for a time, if no Traveler has noticed his existence in two centuries, he has learned how to hide what he is. The impressions from the map are from when he was newly touched."

"He went to Colossae?" said Lehr. "I thought Colossae was destroyed."

"Sacrificed," agreed Hennea. "But the stones were sealed to seal the bindings."

Seraph hadn't heard that part before. "What does that mean?"

Hennea smiled suddenly. "I don't know. What did you see from the maps?"

"The Shadowed saw Colossae," Seraph said. "So the city must still stand."

"Do all the Shadowed go to Colossae to become what they are?" asked Rinnie.

"I don't know," Seraph said, turning to Hennea.

"I've never heard that," Hennea said. "I don't know how many people outside of the Travelers even know there was ever a city like Colossae."

"Have any of the Shadowed been Travelers?" asked Lehr.

"No," Seraph said firmly.

"The first one was," Hennea reminded her. "If he came out of Colossae."

"No," Seraph said. "He was a Colossae wizard."

Hennea smiled again. "That's slicing the roast pretty thinly, don't you think? We are all descendants of the Colossae wizards."

"I don't think so," said Seraph slowly. "I've always thought it was no accident that *solsenti* wizards are the only ones who have been driven to become Shadowed."

"You sound as if they are not making their own choices," said Hennea. "Are you making excuses for them?"

Seraph didn't bother arguing with the disapproval in Hennea's voice. "It must be a terrible thing to be a *solsenti* wizard.

Every little cantrip is a combination of ritual and components. Some wizards live their whole lives knowing they have enormous potential for power, but able to do only little magics for lack of knowledge. Most are not that unlucky, but for every major spell they have to spend hours in preparation and years in study. And here we are, we Ravens, flying free where they must crawl. It must be galling."

"You look for excuses where there are none," commented Hennea dryly. "Though I suppose you are right, and so should be grateful most *solsenti* wizards don't know enough about the Stalker to be dangerous."

She started rerolling a map as she finished speaking. Seraph took another and rolled it as well. When all of them were stored in the satchel, Hennea closed the buckles and handed the map case to Rinnie.

"You have maps to a world long lost, Cormorant," she said. "This bag is spelled by one of the Elder Wizards of Colossae. It is a treasure entrusted to you."

Jes stuck his head into the room. "I found something," he said.

Tier expected the tavern to be nearly empty, but it was full of strangers, mostly hired swords, he thought. They were probably from some merchant's caravan just passing through.

Maneuvering around the extra people, he found an unoccupied table in a corner and took a seat. Regil, the tavern owner, saw him and rushed over.

"Tier, welcome," he said. "I was just hoping you or Ciro would be stopping through to keep this lot occupied. Our midday meal is bread from your sister's ovens and fresh sausage—and you are welcome to it if you'll sing."

Tier smiled. "I'd be happy to, but I was helping my sister this morning. I didn't bring my lute."

"Would mine work?" asked Regil.

"That would be fine," Tier agreed.

Regil grinned. "I was worried I'd have to entertain them myself, and I have other things to do." He looked behind Tier for just an instant. "Master Willon, Tier will keep your men from too much trouble."

Tier turned in his chair, to see the old merchant standing

just behind him. "Willon, good to see you. I thought you'd be in Taela yet a while."

Regil backed a few courteous steps away, then turned and hustled off in the direction of the stairway to his apartment. Willon took the seat on the other side of Tier's narrow table.

"Once I heard some secret society had been brought low by Travelers, I figured Seraph had managed your rescue without my help." Willon grinned. "I had just heard the first whisper of rumor that made me think you might have been stored in the Emperor's palace itself, when the news of the Path's demise hit the streets. Seraph obviously had no need of my help—not that I was surprised. Your wife is a very capable person. My cousin had a trading trip scheduled through this way, so I caught an escort with his men. I'm getting too old to enjoy the big city; my old bones prefer Redern."

"I'm planning on growing old here, myself." Tier smiled when he said it, though his heart worried Seraph would not be here to grow old with him.

"Disappointing," Hennea commented, peering into Jes's secret room.

"You'd expect any place that Volis went to such trouble to hide would have *something* in it." Lehr brushed his hands on his tunic to rid them of the tingle of the power he'd used to open the lock on the hidden door Jes had found.

Seraph had thought it would have been magic he used, but it wasn't—at least it wasn't the same kind of magic that came to her call. Falcon's secrets, she thought, and smiled. It was a good thing that Brewydd had known more of the Falcon's Order than she did. She'd forgotten that locks and gates were something the Hunters did well—Brewydd had told them it had something to do with traps being a Hunter's art. Whatever the reason, Lehr seemed to enjoyed being able to open whatever locks came his way. If it hadn't been for him, for his tracking and lock picking skills both, they'd never have made it through the palace to the cell where Tier had been held.

Rinnie squeezed past Lehr and Hennea and darted into the room. "It's empty."

"Sorry," said Jes.

"Not at all." Seraph couldn't see the interior of the room,

but if it was big enough to hold Rinnie, it would be big enough for her purposes. "This is the perfect place to put the books on magic until we decide what to do with them. Lehr can spell the door shut, and Hennea or I'll put a 'don't look at me' on the removable panel. It'll be safe as a lamb in the fold."

"Then we don't have to carry them all." Jes gave her a bright grin. "Lehr and I," he said. "We would have had to carry them all. Two trips for all these books. Through the town to home, then back through the town to here. Back through the town and home again. There aren't so many Traveler books as there are wizard ones. Through the town just one more time."

"You'll still have the stairs," Hennea pointed out dryly as she started back down the narrow hallway.

"Only one set. Easy." Jes bounced passed her and ran up the stairway.

When Lehr decided to go exploring with Jes, Seraph relented and let Rinnie go with them. There weren't so many books in the library that she and Hennea couldn't take care of them.

"We'll get more done," she said, after the others had left.

"They're not so bad," Hennea said.

"Just not used to being cooped up." Seraph tapped her finger lightly on the page of the book she'd been paging through. "I've seen this book before, I think." She closed her eyes to aid her memory. "It was in a different language, but I recognize the illustrations."

"In Isolde's library?"

"I don't know," Seraph said. "For the first ten winters after Jes was born, I worked my way through the library of every *mermora* that came to me."

Seraph opened her eyes and set aside the book. "I had Isolde's after my brother died," she said. "Once I settled at the farm with Tier, I think I had three more. By the time Jes was nine, I had twenty-five. I went through all twenty-five libraries before I admitted my father was right when he told me that the Elder Wizards did not include anything about the Orders in their writings."

"You didn't say anything about that when Brewydd had us go through Rongier's library on the way to Taela."

"Rongier the Librarian might have had books in his library

that the wizards in my first twenty-five didn't," Seraph said. "Then, too, you and Brewydd know different languages than I do. We didn't find anything—but we might have."

Hennea stared off into space for a moment. "That was unusual, wasn't it? How many Travelers, whatever their Order, do you suppose can read in any language other than our own and Common Tongue? To the Elder Wizards those libraries were invaluable, but for a Raven they are mostly just a reminder of what Travelers once were, good only for invoking on ceremonial occasions."

"It sometimes seems to me that most of my life I've spent shaking my head, and saying, 'What are the chances?'" Seraph fought to imitate Hennea's calm and push away her anger. "My whole clan dies except for my brother and me—the very last of the descendants of Isolde the Silent. Then he is murdered, and I am rescued by the only Ordered *solsenti* I've ever heard of."

"There are probably more of them out there," Hennea murmured. "Who would look to *see* if a *solsenti* was Ordered?"

"Even the *solsenti* would have noticed a Raven when they tried to train him to be a wizard," Seraph said.

"Really?" Hennea tilted her head. "I'm not so sure of that. Ravens can use ritual, chants, and components for spells. We just don't need to unless we're learning something we've never seen done before and can't find the pattern of the magic any easier way. Affinities still apply. A mage whose affinity isn't metalwork won't be able to use magic to add virtue to a sword, whether he be Raven or just wizard. If a Raven thought he needed to use component and ritual, would he think to try spelling without it?"

"I see what you mean."

"What else has happened that is unusual?" Hennea turned back to the book she'd been looking at.

Seraph looked at her hands. *I should just stop the conversation here,* she thought, *because the rest of it is almost too painful to bear.*

"Tier and I had five children," she told her hands. "One was stillborn, and Mehalla, who died when she was three years old. Jes is Eagle. Lehr is Guardian. Rinnie is Cormorant. Tier is Owl. I am Raven. What Order do you think my

Mehalla who died of lung sickness bore?" She looked up as she asked the question.

Hennea was staring at her. "Lark?"

Seraph nodded. "I don't know of any *clans* who had all six Orders, let alone a small family. I've never heard of any family who birthed only Ordered children. The Orders don't follow parentage. That's one of the few things we do know about the Order. So why is my whole family Ordered? And why do we all bear different Orders? There are many more Ravens than there are Larks, or even Cormorants and Eagles."

"Maybe it is the *solsenti* blood?" Hennea hazarded.

"Or the magic that clings to the mountains here. Or that the Travelers generally avoid Shadow's Fall and our farm is only a couple days' journey from it. Or it is the will of the gods. Or it is fate."

"There are no gods," Hennea said flatly. "It is chance."

"Fine," said Seraph. "What clan did Kerine belong to? The Traveler Raven who fought beside Red Ernave at Shadow's Fall, do you know?"

"Isolde's."

"You might be interested to know that Tier's family claims to be descended from Red Ernave's only surviving child." Before Hennea could say anything, Seraph waved her hand impatiently. "I know, I know. Mythology. Every noble in the Empire, except the Emperor himself, traces their family lineage back to Red Ernave. But there's a stone in the bakery with a crude carving of an axe and Verneiar's name just below it. It's old, the carving on the stone, and the man who placed it there thought of himself as Red Ernave's son—I've touched it, just as I touched that map."

Hennea was quiet.

"I have over two hundred *mermori*, Hennea. Two hundred and twenty-four of five hundred and forty-two." Seraph felt tears touch her eyes, but blinked them away. "Why should I bear the burden of almost half the *mermori* Hinnum made? Why aren't they scattered among other clan leaders? Benroln had only three. Surely there are Travelers more closely related to Torbear the Hawkeyed or Keria the Four-Fingered than I am. Or how is it that my family—farmers from a small village half the Empire from Taela—became involved with the Emperor himself just when he was endangered by this new Shadowed?"

Seraph waited while the silence gave weight to her question, then she opened her neglected book to a random page. "I don't know either. But I can't help but wonder if there are forces shaping the events of our lives. I hope I'm wrong. I hope we all die of old age, but I don't think we will." She stared at a random page without seeing it. "Although maybe we'll be killed by lung fever or trolls first."

It felt good to talk about this to someone who could see the patterns only another Traveler would recognize. Not that Hennea would know anything more about what was happening than Seraph did, but it felt good to tell her anyway.

Seraph looked at the page she'd opened to—and suddenly remembered where she'd seen the book before. "Huh. This is a copy of a book I found in Kiah the Dancer's *mermora*— that's the fourth *mermora* that came into my hands. I used to keep track."

CHAPTER 6

Seraph wiped a hand across her forehead. No doubt, she thought, leaving an attractive smear of dust behind. She glanced at Hennea, who was picking through the contents of a chest, her face pale and set.

After sorting the books in the library and taking a careful look at the mostly empty rooms comprising the innards of the temple, they'd collected Rinnie and the boys and set them to hauling the books of *solsenti* wizardry and the books neither she nor Hennea could translate down to Jes's secret room. Then she and Hennea set out to look at the two rooms they'd left for last.

The closet where the Shadowed had set his summoning runes told them nothing. Given a few years, the dissipating powers might clear enough to allow Seraph to read the wooden slats and find out more about the Shadowed, but right now the only past that they wanted to tell her about was the past of Karadoc carrying the forest king into the temple and cleaning the runes.

She had learned something interesting though not important to their search for the Shadowed.

She'd thought the excavation was too extensive to have been dug in the short time between the arrival of the new Sept

of Leheigh, who had brought Volis and assorted mages belonging to the Path among his retinue, and the opening of the
Temple of the Five. She'd been right.

The lower tunnels told her they had been dug in secret,
many years earlier, as places to hide goods from the Sept's
tax collector. When Volis had brought hired men into Redern
to dig the temple, they must have happened into the tunnels
by chance. She wondered if Willon knew about the
tunnels here, since the lower layer should be on the same level
as his store.

By unspoken consent, they saved Volis's bedroom for last;
Seraph because it was the most likely place, after the library,
to hold something of interest, but she thought Hennea put it
off it for another reason.

Seraph found a yellowish sapphire set in a wristband,
fallen among the cushions of Volis's bed. It wasn't an Order-
bound gem, so she left it there. Dropping the bedding she'd
searched, Sraph looked at Hennea.

She was sifting through one of a pair of trunks that sat
against a wall and avoiding looking at the bed. If Seraph had
been in any doubt as to some of the uses Volis had put Hennea
to, one look at Hennea's face when they'd first come into the
room would have been all she needed. Hennea hadn't said
anything, and Seraph didn't pry. Sometimes silence was all
the help she could offer.

When they finished, Seraph let Hennea take care of
spelling Jes's secret room with its new treasure while Seraph
and Rinnie packed Traveler books.

Jes bounded into the library. "It's a good secret room, now,"
he said, as Hennea and Lehr followed him into the library.

"I'm glad it pleases you," Seraph told Jes. "Grab a pack,
and we'll start down."

"I get to carry my maps," said Rinnie smugly. Maybe it
was the knowledge she'd found the most interesting thing in
the temple, but Seraph suspected that at least some of the self-
satisfied expression was because the satchel with its maps was
a lot lighter than the books.

The tavern was a very old building, perhaps the oldest in Redern, and built near the bottom of the mountain. As Seraph put

her foot on the bottom step of the porch, Lehr touched her arm. When he had her attention, he nodded toward Jes, who was pale and swaying—always a bad sign.

"Why don't you head on home," Seraph told Lehr. "I can get Tier and follow the rest of you." She gave him her pack of books to carry along with his own. He gave her a half smile that told her he understood she didn't want to have to explain to everyone in the tavern just what it was she was doing carrying a pack full of books from the temple.

"Back to the farm sounds like a good idea," Hennea said. She took a step toward Jes, hesitated, then took his arm. He started as if he hadn't noticed her until she touched him. "Come, Jes," she said, her voice a little softer than usual. "We're going home."

Worried, Seraph watched them go. Jes had never liked the town, but she'd never seen him this bothered by it, either. Was he getting worse? Was there anything she could do to help? She felt like she'd spent half her life asking herself those questions, and she no more had the answers now than she'd had twenty years ago.

Searching for something more productive to think about, she found herself playing with the idea Hennea had broached earlier. What if there were more Ordered *solsenti*? Would she ever have recognized it in Tier if she hadn't met him under extraordinary circumstances?

Intent on her thoughts, the noise of the busy tavern startled her. It was full. Guards, she thought, judging by the number of weapons they carried. It wasn't all that uncommon to see so many strangers here; this was the closest tavern to the trail. It made her glad she'd sent her pack with Lehr—books were valuable, and some of these guardsmen looked as though they sometimes might have held other, less savory occupations.

She could hear a lute intermingling with the sounds of men talking, but whoever it was played stiffly and a little off pitch. She wondered when Tier would tactfully help him out a little.

The crowd shifted, and she saw the lute player. Shock caught her breath. It was Tier. Even as she watched him, he shook his head and put the lute down.

"Seraph," Regil, the tavern's owner, reached out to steady her, but didn't quite touch. "Are you all right?"

"Fine," she said, composing herself. "Excuse me."

Tier could play badly, she thought, but only if he wanted to. She'd spent the first two weeks after she'd gotten him back from the Path wizards surreptitiously checking to make certain that they had not damaged him, that they hadn't begun to steal his Order already. But after those first weeks, as he began to recover from the hurt they *had* done, she'd quit worrying, quit *looking*.

Unto the Ravens it is given to see the Orders. She called the magic and *looked*. The fine fabric of Tier's Order was wrapped around him as it always was, but there were holes in it.

She started toward Tier, but her exchange with the tavern owner had drawn several of the strange men's attention to her.

A man on her right surged to this feet. "A Traveler bitch? I thought the animals had to stay outside."

Seraph stopped and looked at him, waiting for him to do something else. Anything else. Rage surged through her veins and brought magic with it. Tier was home. He should have been safe. This guardsman had nothing to do with her anger.

Nothing and everything.

"Seraph Tieraganswife," said the tavern owner, trying to distract her from her prey, brave man. "As you see, your husband has been keeping us busy with his tales."

She didn't take her eyes off the guardsman. "I'm glad to hear it," she said.

"Seraph," said Tier. "Let the poor man alone."

If that "poor man" had tried his speech in a different place, with a different Traveler woman, one who was not Raven, he might have caused some harm. Benroln might have been right, maybe if the *solsenti* were more afraid of Travelers, they wouldn't have destroyed so many of the clans.

The Path wouldn't have begun taking Travelers, and Tier wouldn't have rents in his Order. She'd never seen anything like it, but then, until the Path kidnaped Tier, she'd never heard of anyone being able to separate Order from Order Bearer.

"Sit down." She told the guardsman.

Tier could put a compulsion in his words that made people obey him. Seraph's magic forced his body to comply with her demand. Same result from different causes. The guardsman dropped to his seat as if he'd been a puppet whose strings were cut.

"Shut up."

The spell would fade after an hour or so, she'd given it no extra push. The rest of the tavern had miraculously quieted, though she had been careful to direct the spell only onto the man who'd annoyed her.

She walked the rest of the way to Tier's table with Regil's anxious escort.

Willon stood as she approached the table. Her gaze locked on Tier, she hadn't even noticed there was someone else sitting with him until Willon moved. He took her hand and kissed it. He'd never done such a thing before, and it distracted her for a moment. "Seraph, so nice to see you. Please excuse the words of my cousin's guardsman. He won't be here long."

His words and his unusual gallantry were to let the guards know they were to leave her alone, she thought, and was dimly grateful.

"Willon." She couldn't manage to chat with the merchant, not when she was so worried about Tier.

She knew that Tier would have already thanked him for traveling all the way to Taela to help them, so she didn't need to. She inclined her head to him, but her attention was on her husband. "Tier, the children have gone on home, are you ready to leave?"

He smiled, but there was something off about his smile. He knew, she thought. Of course he knew there was something wrong.

"I think it might be best." He picked up a lute and gave it to the tavern owner. "Thanks for the lunch, Regil. I missed your sausage while I was gone."

He put Seraph's hand on his arm and led her back to where Hennea awaited him at the exit.

As soon as they were out of earshot of the tavern, Tier said, "Seraph, I was singing, and I couldn't stay on pitch." He shook his head. "I've never had that trouble before."

"There's something wrong with your Bardic Order," she told him.

His strides broke rhythm, then resumed his usual pace, though slowed a bit by his limp. "Something the Path did?"

Seraph gave a frustrated huff and slid her hand down until she was clutching his. "It seems likely. I don't know how to fix this. Until the Path's wizards proved differently, it was my understanding that nothing could affect the Orders."

"Coat it in sugar, why don't you?" Tier's voice was lightly amused, but his hand tightened almost brutally on hers. "If you can't fix this, I'm not going to sing on key anymore?"

"I don't know."

Tier didn't loosen his grip on her hand, but he quit talking.

They hadn't been so long at the tavern that the children had beaten them home by much. Gura was still bouncing with excitement when he spied them on their way. He tore up the path, going so fast that he had to run by them once before he could slow enough to get a proper ear rubbing from Tier.

In the house Hennea had a map spread out on the table, and the boys and Rinnie were gathered around, engrossed in their examination.

"Hennea," Seraph said. "We have a problem."

"Can you do anything, Mother?" asked Rinnie.

Seraph glanced at Hennea, who shrugged and answered, "I don't know. We'll try. The Elder Wizards managed to work with the Orders, obviously, since they created them. But as far as the *mermori* libraries that Hennea, Brewydd, and I have managed to get through, they wrote nothing about it."

"Brewydd might know something that could help," said Lehr. "I can go and find the Librarian's clan."

Seraph hesitated. Benroln's clan could be anywhere—and there was no guarantee that Brewydd could do anything for Tier.

"I'm Hunter, Mother. I can find them."

"He'll need a horse," said Tier. It was the first thing that he'd said since they came home. "Skew's not up to a fast trip."

"All right." Seraph got up to retrieve the purse the Emperor had given them from the loft. She scrambled back down the ladder and held the bag out to Lehr.

"Take this now, while there's still daylight. Go see what kind of a mount you can purchase from Akavith."

Lehr took the purse gingerly. "Akavith's expensive, Mother."

"He breeds horses for the nobility," she agreed. "He'll have something fast. Make certain he knows you want an animal for hunting, not farmwork." She glanced at Tier, he knew the crusty old horseman better than she. "Can he tell Akavith that he's riding for a Traveler healer?"

Tier nodded. "Tell him where the money comes from, too, though likely he knows already. After the verses Ciro sang the other night, likely the story of the farmer and the Emperor is all over the mountains by now. Akavith will be more likely to help if he knows the whole story. His mother's aunt was a hedgewitch and healer round about when I was a boy, and he has no grudge against Travelers."

"Tell him you'd like Cornsilk," said Jes.

Seraph felt her eyebrows creeping up.

Jes ducked his head. "I help him sometimes, Mother," he said.

"Akavith has a way with wild things," said Tier.

"Don't worry about the cost," Seraph told Lehr briskly. "If it is too dear, we can sell the horse when we no longer need it. But go now so you have the daylight—take Skew, he'll be faster than walking. In the morning we'll talk about the most likely places for Benroln's clan to be."

Akavith lived halfway to Leheigh. It would be dark before Lehr made it home, too late to start out on a hunt for the clan.

Lehr took the pouch and tied it to his belt. "I'll be back as soon as I can." He turned to Jes. "I'll tell him you told me to ask about Cornsilk."

After the door closed behind him, Seraph turned to Hennea. "Do you see any profit in waiting for word from Brewydd before we try anything?"

She shook her head. "I wish I could be more help. I don't know how the damage was done or how to fix it."

"Standing around wringing our hands won't do anything," said Seraph. "Tier, lie on the rug beside the fire. This could take a long time, and you can't move about. Get comfortable."

"Can we help?" asked Rinnie. "I could make some tea or soup."

Seraph started to shake her head, then stopped. "It would be best if we ate first. Bread and cheese then, Rinnie."

"And tea," said Jes. "I'll go get water."

* * *

Akavith was eating dinner when Lehr knocked on the door. He stuck his head out. "Eh, you're Tier's boy," he said.

"Yes, sir." Akavith was a formidable man with few kind words for anyone who had fewer than four feet. But Lehr had grown up with Seraph for a mother, and it took a lot to intimidate him.

Black eyes glowered at him from under bushy eyebrows. "What do 'ee want, lad. I've dinner to eat."

"I need a horse, sir. I can wait until you are finished."

"A horse!" He said it as if no one ever came to him for horses.

"Yes, sir."

He looked out at Skew. "Got a fine horse there."

"Yes, sir. But I need to fetch a Traveler healer for my father, who took more hurt than we thought from his stay in Taela. I need a fast horse who can travel a distance. Skew's too old for the trip."

The animosity faded from Akavith's face. "Do ye' now. Tier's taken hurt? Well, that's a different matter. Go on out to the barn and look for what suits ye. I'll be there as soon as I get my boots back on."

The horses in Akavith's barn were a choice bunch. Lehr stopped by a tall chestnut mare with a flaxen mane. She left her hay to come to the stall door for attention.

He leaned his forehead against her neck and drew in the sweet-salt scent of a healthy horse as he scratched gently along her cheekbone.

Gods, he thought, *I hope Brewydd can do something.* His faith in the healer was enormous, but the fear in his mother's eyes made his chest tight.

"That's a good, choice, lad," said Akavith, his voice the soft crooning one that he usually reserved for his horses.

Lehr straightened. He usually heard people approaching, but he'd had no idea that the horse trainer was nearby.

"I like the bay two stalls back, too," said Lehr. "And my brother told me to ask about a horse named Cornsilk."

"That's Cornsilk, right there, lad. And your brother has a fine eye for horses." Akavith grabbed a halter and opened the stall door. He haltered the mare and led her out so that Lehr could get a better look.

"She's coming five and fully trained—some of that training by your brother. I usually sell them younger than this— that bay is four and sold already. I've had offers for this mare, but . . . Ye see, lad," Akavith patted her red-gold shoulder. "Noblemen are too proud to ride a mare. They'd make her a lady's mount, trotting her from one party to another." He frowned fiercely. "She wouldn't be happy like that—she loves the trails and the challenge of a long run. Just don't be putting a harness on her and make her pull a plow like your father did to that Fahlarn gelding of his; Cornsilk doesn't have the bone for it. Tell your father to come see me, and I'll find him a replacement for the grey he lost, I've a few horses that should suit him."

"I doubt we can afford it, sir," Lehr told him, but he wasn't thinking about a new farm horse: he was falling in love.

Out of her stall, the mare was beautiful, fine-boned like a sight-hound, and nearly as tall as Skew. Liquid dark eyes examined him with curiosity and the sweetness of a horse who'd never been mistreated. Exotically long and silky, her mane and tail were the exact color of cornsilk. Her nostrils were wide to drink the wind.

"Tell your father, and we'll work something out," said Akavith. His craggy features relaxed a bit more, and Lehr felt as if those keen old eyes saw right through him. "Yes," he said, slapping his thigh. "You and this mare will do."

They bargained for a while, and Lehr knew the price they agreed on was far lower than the horse trainer would have gotten from one of those nobles who were looking for a lady's mount.

"Don't fret," said the horse trainer. "Your brother won't let me pay him, and these past few years he's as good as my best boy with the horses. Do you have a saddle and bridle that'll fit this mare?"

"No, sir."

Akavith put the mare back in the stall and led Lehr to his tack room. As he sorted through bridles, he said, "Had a man in here today from Redern. Told me Olbeck—the steward's son, do you mind him?"

Lehr knew Olbeck, but Akavith continued speaking without waiting for an answer.

"He killed a lad—a merchant's son, Lukeeth it was."

Lukeeth was one of Olbeck's sycophants, a Rederni merchant's son. Lehr hadn't known him well, nor liked what little he knew, but he hadn't wanted him dead either.

"Storne Millerson bore witness against him, I heard. If Olbeck's father weren't the Sept's steward, Lukeeth's father would have demanded his head and gotten it, too. But all he managed was to banish Olbeck from Redern. I imagine it won't take a month for the steward to have *that* judgment put aside." He spat on the floor of the stables. "Makes me glad I don't live in a town. One of my boys kills another, I take care of it."

"If you can't control your worries, I can do this," Hennea told Seraph as she sat beside Tier on the floor by the fireplace after they'd all eaten.

If someone was going to muck about with Tier's Order, Seraph preferred to do it herself. She knelt beside her husband and shifted until she was as comfortable as she was going to get on the slat floor.

When she was settled she took a couple of deep breaths and buried her fear and anger deep so that she could control her magic. Emotions made magic unreliable and dangerous.

"I am fine," she told Hennea.

Jes and Rinnie sat on the floor and leaned against a wall where they wouldn't interfere with anything Seraph had to do.

"Lie down," she told Tier, who was sitting up. "And relax."

She began by *looking*. Usually an Order appeared to her like a set of transparent clothes that covered the whole body, though she knew that all Ravens didn't see the same way. Her teacher Arvage had seen small crowns of woven vines, each Order bloomed with a different color flower. Only the colors were the same for each Raven. She wondered how her old teacher would have seen the damage to Tier's Order.

"What do you see when you *look* at his Order, Hennea?" she asked.

"Light," she answered. "With areas of darkness."

Seraph touched Tier's chest lightly, where her magic told her one of the holes was. "I see a break here," she told Hennea.

Hennea nodded. "That's one of the dark patches."

"Keep an eye on him," Seraph asked. "If you see any change at all, let me know."

Until this past season, Seraph would never have thought that there was anything that could alter an Order. When she'd been young, she'd tried, and she supposed that she wasn't the only one. She'd wanted to see if she could change the appearance of her Order so that any Raven who happened by would not automatically know what kind of Order Bearer she was.

Nothing had worked. Magic had just slid off the surface of the Order without affecting it.

Magic worked with patterns, she thought, patterns and symbolism.

Seraph stared at Tier's Order and pulled her magic to her as if she were spinning yarn at her wheel. She felt it soft and fine, like the best lambswool as it spun itself beneath her fingertips. She saw the Order as clothing, so she'd pattern her magic after that and see if it worked.

"Tier," she said. "Tell me if you feel anything—but most especially if something hurts."

"I'll do that." His wry tone made her smile, as he'd intended it to.

She set her yarn of magic against his Order, but her fingers sank through to touch his neck.

"Cold," said Tier.

"Very funny," she muttered, glaring at his uncooperative Order. Pulling her fingers away, she saw the glittering violet of her own Order, and it gave her inspiration. This time she took the end of her yarn with the lightest of touches, so light her fingers did not touch it at all, only the thin veil of Raven Order.

She laid the thread against Tier, and this time it rested lightly on Bardic Order and, at her will, the thread she'd spun began to take on the texture and green-grey color of the Bardic Order. When she tugged lightly on the yarn, it fell away from Tier. It wouldn't merge with the Tier's Order—she'd have to weave it through. Even as she put the yarn back to lie against Tier so that it could all absorb the aspects of his Order, she had an idea of how she might be able to repair the damage.

She hadn't darned socks or sweaters for a long time—not since she'd taught Rinnie how. Sewing had never been her favorite part of *solsenti* life. Travelers darned their clothing as well, but a Raven's time was too valuable to be taken up in such mundane tasks. For Tier, though, she'd have darned a patch that covered the farm with room to spare.

When all her yarn was blended with Tier's Order she pulled it away. From magic she formed a darning egg, visualizing a hard surface rounded just right to turn the edge of her needle away from Tier's skin.

Now all that she needed was a darning needle.

The only thing that had been able to affect Tier's Order was her own.

"Hennea," she said. "Would you sort through the Ordered gems and bring me one of the Lark gems? The tigereye ring, I think." That was the one that sometimes warmed in her hand when she and Hennea were working with them.

"You're going to try and use the gems?" Hennea's voice was neutral—a good indication of her disapproval.

Seraph shook her head. "I'm going to see if I can persuade it to help me."

She heard Hennea get up, but only peripherally. Most of Seraph's attention was on what she intended to do. There was no room for doubt when she worked magic. Only utter confidence would make her magic do as she desired.

Something small and warm was tucked into her cold hand, the ring.

She'd chosen the Lark, because Healing seemed very close to what she was trying to do.

Seraph thought through the problem she faced and what she needed several times, curbing her panic and her impatience as best she could. She'd begun on a third time when something sharp pierced the skin on the hand that held the gem. She looked down, and the rust-colored Order that had surrounded the gem had formed itself into the shape of a large needle.

She thought very hard about how grateful she was as she slipped her yarn into the needle. She set the darning egg beneath the largest of the holes in the fabric of Tier's Order. She had no idea what would happen if she pierced flesh with her needle, and had no particular desire to find out.

Carefully taking the needle in her Order-gloved hands, she used her will more than her fingers to set the needle into Tier's Order, two fingerwidths from the edge of the tear.

Like a tightly knitted sweater, the threads of Bardic Order slid away from her needle without harm and the egg protected Tier from the sharp point. The ring, which she held loosely between two fingers, passed through Tier's Order as if neither were affected by the presence of the other. The needle, though, worked as well as she had hoped it might. Carefully, she pulled it back through the weaving of Tier's Order, stitching all around the hole to strengthen the edge before she began reweaving the fabric of Tier's Order with her magic.

Hours passed, but she was absorbed in her work, painstakingly knitting Tier's Order together again. The familiar task was absorbing, and she didn't realize how tired she was until Tier's voice penetrated her concentration.

"Seraph, *listen to me.*"

"I'm not finished," she said stubbornly. There were still holes. Small holes that would turn into larger ones. She looked for her yarn, but she couldn't find any more.

"Hennea says you can do no more. Seraph, stop."

The needle faded away, until she held only a ring. Dazedly, she realized Tier was holding her wrists and shaking her.

"She's stopped," said Hennea, her voice little more than a hoarse mumble.

"I'll get them to their beds."

That was Lehr. What was he doing back already?

"Take Mother up," said Jes. "I'll get Hennea, then help you with Papa."

"I can get myself up," said Tier.

Tier. Seraph slid her hand in his loosened grip until she had a hold on his arm.

"Hennea," she said. "Can you *look?*" She was too tired to use any more magic.

"It's better," the other Raven replied. "It won't hold forever, but it should give us some time. I wouldn't have thought of using the Orders that way."

"You haven't darned many socks," replied Seraph. She wondered briefly what her weaving had *looked* like to Hennea, who saw light rather than fabric. But she couldn't hold on to the question long enough to ask it. Knowing Tier was better, even if just for now, let her collapse peacefully into the soft darkness of exhaustion.

Jes waited while Lehr picked up their mother and started up the ladder steps to his parents' loft. Then he extended his hand to his father, who got to his feet with a groan.

"Thanks, Jes," he said. "I was wondering how I was going to do that." He followed Lehr up the ladder steps, limping heavily.

Hennea was leaning against the stones of the fireplace—cool now, since there was no fire burning. Her eyes were closed, but he could tell she wasn't sleeping. Rinnie was, though. There hadn't been anything to keep her awake, just the heavy scent of magic that still hung thick in the air.

He left Hennea where she was and scooped up his little sister. As soon as he touched her, he could feel her dreams. She was flying in the night sky, with the land a dark presence far below her, dream-riding the storm winds in body as in reality she did with her mind.

<Some Cormorants can fly,> the Guardian told him, then abruptly withdrew.

Jes's hands curled protectively around Rinnie. It bothered him, this knowledge he should not have, that the Guardian should not have. How did he know Cormorants could fly when Rinnie was the only Cormorant they had ever known? But as much as it disturbed him, the Guardian was far more frightened by it. Jes couldn't think of anything else he'd ever encountered that had frightened the Guardian.

He carried Rinnie around the makeshift wall he and Lehr had built yesterday and laid her gently on her bed.

The unearned knowledge was part of the change that was happening, a change that frightened both the Guardian and him. Mother was worried about it, too. He'd always talked to the Guardian, soothing him, easing the constant rage the Guardian lived with. But it wasn't until they'd caged him with the *foundrael* that the Guardian had spoken back.

"She is too young to fly," Jes muttered softly. "We wouldn't be able to keep her safe."

The Guardian was silent, and Jes couldn't tell if he was listening, or if he'd closed himself off entirely. The latter was dangerous. When the Guardian emerged from such hibernations, he was gorged with anger, impossible to reason with.

But there was no answer, so Jes went back to put Hennea to bed. She was in a different position than the one in which he'd left her—she'd tried to get up, he thought.

Her hair was dark with sweat, and dark circles ringed her eyes. It looked to him as if she'd lost weight, too, as if the power she'd given Mother had come from her own flesh.

Tenderly, he picked her up into his arms.

<Ours,> claimed the Guardian.

"If she chooses," he told the other firmly, not hiding his relief that the Guardian had not retreated. "Don't push her away."

"Jes?" she murmured.

"Putting you to bed," he told her.

<Papa told Mother that she loves us.>

Jes felt a wide smile break across his face. "He did."

The Guardian shared the sweet scent of her skin with him, so he let the Guardian feel how strongly she desired to rest in their arms, safe.

He tucked her into her bed, next to Rinnie's. Like the wall, it was newly made yesterday. She was mostly asleep, and he brushed his hand lightly over her cheek because he could not resist both his desire and the Guardian's.

She opened her eyes, pale and unfocused. "Jes," she said.

"Yes?"

"Remind me. Tomorrow. Maps and Colossae. It's important. For your father."

He felt the Guardian swell with . . . some nameless emotion at the sound of the name of the ancient city.

"I'll remind you," Jes told her as he pushed aside a flashing vision of a city he'd never seen before.

The strange insights frightened the Guardian. Jes could feel that fear rising up and the anger that burned the fear to ash, rage that Jes swallowed and swallowed until it hurt to breathe.

"Jes?"

"We should tell someone," he muttered quickly. *Maybe someone could help us understand what is happening. Help us to prepare.* That was it, he thought. The Guardian was afraid of something that was going to happen when he remembered too much. Something bad.

"Tomorrow. We'll tell your mother," murmured Hennea, misunderstanding what he'd said.

The Guardian had heard him, too. Jes could tell because the other's towering rage dulled to a sullen burn that he could better tolerate.

Hennea subsided into sleep. Jes let himself pet her hair once before he left her to rest beside his sister and wandered out to stand in front of the fireplace.

<Tell whom?> asked the Guardian long after Jes had expected a response.

Mother? No, she hurts for us and feels guilty. I don't want that. Papa? Maybe Lehr. He's very smart. He deliberately didn't mention Hennea. If her worry for him was already keeping her away, he didn't want her to have anything else to worry about.

<No one for now,> the Guardian decided. But Jes could tell that the thought of sharing the change with someone made him feel better. *<But we could tell someone if we need to. We might need to.>*

CHAPTER 7

The Guardian appeased for the moment, Jes could pay attention to the quiet discussion in his parents' loft.

"I thought I'd just ride back to where Benroln left us," Lehr was saying. "I can track them from there."

"There might be an easier way," Tier said. "Your mother said Willon gave you a map before you set out for Taela."

"I'll get it," Lehr said.

"I can get the map," Jes told him. "I know where Mother put it."

Mother had stored it in the chest where Papa kept some souvenirs from the wars. He took it and scrambled up the ladder.

His mother lay in bed under the covers. Her hair was sweat-darkened, and below her eyes were rings of exhaustion so dark they looked like bruises. Her breathing was shallow, and she made small sounds, like a tired child.

The Guardian came out to see for himself that she was safe. Jes touched the covers just above her feet and felt her in a sleep so deep she didn't even dream.

The Guardian settled down once he was certain every care had been taken for her. Papa sat on his side of the bed and Lehr was cross-legged on the floor; both of them had watched the Guardian and allowed him the time he needed.

There was enough room for Jes on the narrow space between the foot of the bed and the ladder. He handed Papa the map and settled on the floorboards.

"Thanks," said Papa as he took the map and spread it on the bedding in front of him.

He studied it for a moment, then tapped his finger. "That's where we parted company. This is the road Benroln took." He let his finger slide down the map toward him.

Jes couldn't read the map upside down, the lettering was too fancy—but the Guardian could.

"Edren," said Papa. "Upsarian. Colbern." He hesitated, then tapped his finger on the last city he'd mentioned. "Willon took this lower road back here—" He drew his hand along the lowest of three roads that both ran east and west. "It's a better road for a wagon—there are bridges instead of fords. He passed by Colbern, he said. It's a town about the size of Leheigh. They'd closed their gates to visitors. Plague."

The Guardian, who had been amusing himself by pointing out the inaccuracies in the map to Jes, abruptly came to the alert.

Papa looked at Lehr. "I've been wondering what disaster called to Benroln when there was a shadow-tainted troll here they could have been fighting instead. A plague would do."

"Lehr can't go," the Guardian growled.

Lehr's eyebrows climbed almost to his hairline, but before he could give whatever retort was doubtless on the tip of his tongue, Papa said, "I agree. It's too dangerous."

Lehr clenched his fists. "I'm not a child. I know how to protect myself from plague. I won't touch anyone. I won't share food or clothing. Mother said to get Brewydd, and that's what I'm going to do." He got to his feet, and the Guardian rose up with him, blocking him in.

Lehr is right, Jes told him. *Father needs Brewydd, and Lehr is not stupid. He knows how to protect himself.*

He received a picture in his head of someone dying. Their face lay in the shadows so he couldn't tell if it was a man or woman, but he could feel the Guardian's consuming grief.

Brewydd will be there, he reminded him.

"Jes?" His father's quiet voice penetrated the internal argument.

<Brewydd will be there,> agreed the Guardian before with-drawing slowly. Brewydd would not let Lehr get sick.

"Brewydd will be there," Jes told Papa, and heard Lehr's relieved breath.

"Let me go," Lehr said to Papa. "I can do this."

Papa rubbed his face wearily. "All right. All right. Get a good night's rest and go in the morning. Take this map." He folded it and handed it to Lehr. "You can see the shortest route there."

Jes got up and began to go down the ladder stairs so Lehr could get past him.

"I want to talk to you, Jes," Papa said.

Jes nodded and jumped down to the floor, bending his knees so that he hit softly and didn't wake up Hennea or Rinnie.

Lehr, coming down behind him, said, "Thanks," softly.

Jes nodded and scrambled back up to his parents' loft. "Papa?"

"Close the door and sit down, son."

Jes shut the door, then took up Lehr's place because, with the door shut, there was no room for him where he'd been sitting.

"Remember the smith we helped on the way back?" he asked. Jes knew it wasn't really a question, but he nodded. "When the Guardian said he scented a mistwight, I asked him how he knew what it was."

The Guardian didn't like this conversation, and Jes did his best to think soothing thoughts at him.

"You told me you didn't know."

"I remember," said Jes. "I didn't know."

"Did the Guardian?"

It's all right, we were going to talk to Papa about this, re-member? All he got for an answer was a turbulent rush that wasn't quite an answer.

"Jes," said Papa, with just a hint of power in his voice.

It was enough to pull Jes's attention back to him. "He re-membered," Jes told him. "But we're not sure how. It makes him upset." He took a breath. "I don't think he wants to remember."

"Are you sure he doesn't know more?" asked Papa gently. "I asked the Guardian, Jes, and he had you answer me. I think that he might know more about it, and doesn't want you to—"

The Guardian pushed Jes away so far that he never did hear the rest of what Papa wanted to say.

"—know." Tier paused to adjust to the jumpy feeling that made him want to move away from the man who sat at his feet. Jes was gone, and only the Guardian was left.

"I don't want him frightened," said the Guardian.

"It's dangerous to keep secrets," said Tier. "Your mother was worried about you. She told me that it is important that you and Jes stay close to each other."

The Guardian stood up in a graceful show of strength that reminded Tier of watching an animal you thought was a dog and realizing it was a wolf instead. Jes and the Guardian didn't move anything alike.

"There are some things he doesn't need to know," said the Guardian.

"He's right," Tier said in some surprise. "You are afraid."

The Guardian hissed.

"You can't lie to me," Tier said, keeping his voice soft though his heart rate had picked up. "Everyone is afraid sometimes. It's all right if Jes is afraid, too. What is not all right is for you to hide things from him. You need to trust him more."

"You know nothing," the Guardian snapped. "You are a Bard—blessed, not cursed."

Tier raised an eyebrow. "You are not cursed. You were just given a rocky field to harrow. Seems to me that you are doing well at it. But you need to work as a team, or you'll not make it, son."

"I'm not your son," said the Guardian. "Jes is. I am the demon he is cursed with."

It was said without a flicker of emotion, but no parent could fail to hear the cry in those words.

"You are *my* son," said Tier, leaning close enough to the Guardian that his breath turned to frosty mist. "I love you. I worry for you."

"You worry for Jes," said the Guardian, turning his head away.

His absolute certainty suddenly reminded Tier of himself as he confronted his father two days before he went to war. His father had turned and left Tier standing with his despairing cry still echoing. *"You love the bakery more than you love me."*

He considered this volatile young man who was his son, then said the first thing that came into his head. "You remind me of my sister Alinath. No one ever convinced her of anything she didn't want to be convinced of."

"I am nothing like Alinath." The Guardian crossed his arms over his chest and rocked back on his heels.

"You are. The only times she ever changed her mind was when she stopped arguing and started thinking. So you go think about what I've said—tell Jes what it is you fear. The weight of most problems can be lightened a bit by sharing. Trust Jes."

The Guardian was swaying slightly from one foot to the next, the way Jes did when he was upset.

"Why don't you go out for a run tonight?" Tier suggested gently. "I sometimes find that exercise and solitude make a lot of things clearer."

Without a word the Guardian opened the door and slipped out of the room. Tier heard the outside door open and shut quietly, then turned to his sleeping wife.

"I hope that helped him." He kissed her, then blew out the lantern and settled in for sleep.

When Jes came back to himself he was stretched out on a tree limb with his claws dug firmly into the bark as if the Guardian had been sharpening them.

Jes managed to climb down from the tree before he lost the cat-shape. It was difficult, but so was falling out of trees.

Once again in human form, he bent and stretched, trying to decide how far he'd come. He didn't feel too tired—not with the deep weariness that sometimes hit him when he awoke from the times when the Guardian shut him away. Hopefully, it wouldn't take him too long to walk home.

He wondered what Papa had said to send the Guardian out running into the woods.

<We need to talk.> The Guardian seemed subdued.

"All right." Jes's too-human voice sounded wrong out so deep in the woods. He didn't have to speak aloud—but it helped him keep track of who was saying what.

<Papa says that I should not hide things from you. Even frightening things.>

"What frightens you?"

<I remember things.>

"I know that."

Impatience and frustration overwhelmed him for a moment. Jes tossed his head in the vain attempt to shake the feelings away.

"Explain it to me then," he managed. "Why is remembering so frightening."

<I was something else once, something more. Something dangerous that might hurt you.>

"You've always been dangerous," Jes said. "That's the point, isn't it? How can we protect them if you're not dangerous?"

The Guardian didn't answer, so Jes started for home. While they'd been talking he'd found landmarks in the moonlit night and had a pretty good idea where he was and how to find the shortest way home.

<I always assumed I was a part of you, a part held separate by the Order.>

"You are a part of me."

Negation swamped him, and Jes stumbled over a dead branch that lay in his path. He stopped.

<I am a part of the Order,> the Guardian said. *<But I was something more, once. Now I am a leech that will eventually destroy you.>*

The Guardian's shame brought tears to Jes's eyes.

"You are a part of me," said Jes. "You help me keep my family safe. Tomorrow we are going to follow Lehr and keep him safe, too. That is what we do."

<I make your life miserable. She won't see you because of me. Eventually, I will cause you to go mad.>

"No," said Jes.

<I remember. I remember the madness. I will drive you mad as I have driven others mad. I see their faces when I dream. That is the reason Hennea won't take us.>

"I'm not mad yet," said Jes. "I don't feel like I'm going to go mad. Maybe I'm different from those others. Mother says that she thinks I am." He smiled to himself. "She says it might be stubborn *solsenti* blood. She says that if Aunt Alinath is too obstinate to give in to reason, that I can be too obstinate to give in to madness."

<She won't have us because of me.>

Jes knew who "she" was. He let his smile widen. "Papa says Hennea loves us. Let's give her time to understand we are stronger than she believes."

He waited for a heartbeat or two, but the Guardian had said all he intended to say.

Tier rested, but he couldn't sleep. Had he said enough to Jes? Or had he said too much? He didn't know as much as he needed to about the Guardian Order—though from what Seraph had told him, neither did anyone else.

He heard Lehr tossing and turning in the room below. He was worried about Lehr, too. Lehr was not reckless; he wouldn't take chances unless there was no other choice. If Lehr were only going off to face a half dozen bandits, Tier would not be half as nervous. Skill and caution were of little use against plague. He'd have to trust to Lehr's Hunter skills to get him safely to Benroln's clan and to Brewydd's skills to keep his son safe from the plague.

It went against his grain to have his son risk his life for him. It seemed the wrong way 'round. A father should be willing to lay down his life to protect his family—he shouldn't have to rely on his son. But he'd had the whole of his stay with the Path, when he thought he'd not live to see home again, to decide that without him, his family was too vulnerable. In five years that would not be so true, but for now his family needed him. And for all Seraph's mending he could tell that he wasn't whole yet.

His stay with the Path had left him with more than just physical ills, and he was certain he stood to lose more than his ability to sing a few songs. Seraph had told him often enough the Order wasn't just a facade that could be easily separated from the man he was, but was as much a part of him as his right arm. He was afraid that if whatever magic the Masters had worked upon him succeeded in severing his Order, there would be no stanching of the flow of his life's blood.

Seraph rolled toward him and wrapped her arms around his arm, nuzzling her face against him until she was in her favorite sleeping position. She relaxed back into the stillness of exhausted slumber, but the warmth of her breath against his arm was comforting.

He drowsed, waiting for Jes to return so he could sleep, knowing his family was safe.

The door creaked open, and Jes said, "Papa, the Emperor has come to call."

Phoran noted that the main room of Tier's cabin would have fit five times over in his sitting room at the palace. He took a few steps inside the door behind Jes, and his guards followed.

"Jes?" A groggy voice came from the far side of the room. Then sharp and clear. "The Emperor?" Reason told him it was Tier's younger son, Lehr, though in the darkness of the room he couldn't see more than an outline of a sitting man.

A lantern was lit in a loft room, the light visible between the slats in the door. "Phoran?"

Tier's melodic voice rang through him like a bell. Phoran felt the fear that had been his close companion as they rode from Taela loosen its hold on his belly.

Holding the lantern, Tier slithered down the ladder from the loft, a lantern in one hand and broad smile on his face. "I didn't expect to see you here, my emperor." He held up the lantern and looked behind Phoran at his four guards, who had formerly been Passerines of the Secret Path and were now his personal guard. Tier, being Tier, knew them all. "Welcome. Kissel, Toarsen, Rufort, and"—he held the lantern higher—"oh, Ielian is it? Welcome to my home. What brings you here?"

"It's a long story," said Phoran. "If it is all right, I'd like to send my men out to find sleep in your barn for the night. We've been riding as swiftly as our horses could take us, and we're all tired."

"Of course," Tier said. "Jes, can you take them out to the barn? There is some canvas that can be laid over the hay in the loft. The horses—how many stallions, Phoran?"

"Two."

"Then put Skew and the new mare in the small pen. The stallions in the box stalls with a stall between them and the rest of their horses in the large pen for now."

"Beg pardon, Your Greatness," Ielian said. "But you need to keep a guard with you."

Phoran swallowed his irritation. It was easier to comply than it was to argue—and Toarsen and Kissel both knew everything he wanted to tell Tier anyway.

"Right," he said. "Toarsen, stay with me. Kissel, help Jes get the horses settled, then you all should get some sleep. This might take a while."

He waited until Jes had taken the three guardsmen out to the barn before he turned back to Tier.

"I'm sorry to bring my troubles to you," he said. "But you are the only one I could think of who might have a solution for my problems."

"The Path?" asked Tier.

"The Path is part of it," Phoran said. "Let's wait until Jes gets back—I don't want to have to tell the whole thing twice. Seraph probably ought to hear this, too."

"I'll make some tea, Papa," Lehr said, pulling on his clothes.

He rolled his bedding efficiently and set it off his bed—which transformed into a board on top of a pair of benches. Tier took an end of one bench and Toarsen the other and carried it to the large table by the fireplace. When Lehr started dragging the second bench over, Phoran lifted the other side and helped him put it on the other side of the table.

While Lehr made tea, Tier went up to the loft to rouse his wife.

"It might take a minute," Lehr said quietly. "Mother tired herself out this evening—we've had some troubles of our own."

"Nothing serious, I hope," said Toarsen. "If it's something the Sept could help with . . ." The Sept of Leheigh, the Sept who ruled Tier's corner of the world, was Toarsen's older brother.

Lehr shook his head. "Not that kind of a problem. I'm headed out tomorrow morning to find Benroln's clan."

Magic, then. Phoran felt worse for bringing his troubles when it sounded as though Tier had some of his own, but Phoran had no one else he could trust. Actually there weren't even untrustworthy people who could help him. Phoran paced and tried not to listen to the murmurs from the loft room.

Jes came in from the barn. If Phoran hadn't known better, he would have thought him a simpleton, but he'd seen what Jes had done in the battle with the Path.

Phoran knew the difference between a fight fought with brute strength and one fought with intelligence and skill. He'd also noticed none of the Travelers were surprised that this one lad could have been responsible for the terrible deaths of the Path's Masters. He hadn't been, but the Travelers had believed that he might be.

Tier had told him that Jes was gifted with one of those odd magics that belonged to the Travelers. Phoran had the feeling that it was a terrible gift.

"The horses are taken care of," Jes told him, looking at his shoes rather than meeting his eyes; it was a trick Phoran remembered from when he'd first met Tier's oldest son. "I put grain out for the stallions because your grey was restless in a strange place."

"Thank you," Phoran said. "He can be a problem. I should have gone out with you."

"Jes knows horses," said Lehr, lighting a few more lanterns. "He has a way with animals."

"Who's over there?" asked Phoran, noticing for the first time that there was a length of fabric hanging on the opposite end of the room from the fireplace.

"Hennea—she's another Traveler Raven like Mother," said Lehr. "You met her, but there were a lot of other people you met at the same time. You might not remember her. My sister Rinnie is there, too. She's ten."

He remembered Hennea, and any daughter of Tier's could be trusted. The murmuring had died down from the loft, and Tier climbed down. His limp was better than it had been when he'd left Taela.

Seraph followed him. When she turned, and the lantern caught her face, Phoran could see that Lehr hadn't been exaggerating. She looked as though she hadn't had any sleep in weeks.

"I'm sorry to disturb you," Phoran told her.

"Nonsense," she said—and somewhat to his discomfort she patted him on the cheek before shuffling over to the bench.

She sat down upon it and braced her elbows so her arms could hold her head up.

Everyone was there. It was time to begin his story, but he couldn't for the life of him decide where to start.

"I imagine cleaning up the Path was not an easy business," said Tier, after he'd seated himself next to Seraph. "Why don't you begin there."

Phoran found that he couldn't sit, and he couldn't watch them while he talked.

CHAPTER 8

Two Weeks Earlier in the Emperor's Palace in Taela

"My Septs, We thank you for your patience in hearing out this trial over the past weeks." The Emperor's voice rang in the huge chamber where most of the Septs of the Empire gathered.

Phoran had practiced this moment in the privacy of his own rooms. He had gone over the reasons for doing it this way with his closest advisors. Phoran had played out all the scenarios, and this one worked the best.

"We have acted upon Our Own powers to grant pardon to all the young men known formerly as the Passerines of the Path. First because of their defense of Our Own Person, and second, so We could use their eyewitness accounts to bring to an end the era of the Secret Path, a clandestine group that has been plotting the destruction of the Empire from within."

He paused, giving the Septs a chance to whisper with their advisors and colleagues. Some of the Passerines were sons of the Septs, mostly third or fourth sons who had caused their families no end of misery. Surely some of the Septs were glad Phoran had taken on the task of making useful men of their miscreants.

He'd offered each of the young men a place in the newly created Emperor's Own, his own personal guard. Most of them had accepted. He wasn't certain if that was a good thing or not—they had been chosen by the Path, after all, as the most amoral and corruptible young nobles of their generation.

"You have heard the testimony of these men, now Our Own, and also that of Avar, who is Sept of Leheigh and Our Own trusted counselor. We have also told you those things We observed Ourselves."

Phoran secretly loved speaking of himself in the first-person royal. It struck him as an absurd but utterly effective way to remind them all that he—however unsuited for the job they thought him—was emperor. He glanced casually at the Septs, who had been sitting in their seats off and on for the better part of a week and were doubtless looking forward to getting the whole business over with. Of course, they only thought they knew what was going to happen.

"These testimonies," Phoran continued, "were given to you to bring secret things out into the light where they might fade away and die, a threat no more. They were, moreover, given over for your judgment." They waited now, he knew, for him to call for a verdict, a vote of guilt or innocence.

He had practice in showmanship, Phoran thought, though most of the men sitting in their exalted seats would not have noticed the way he'd orchestrated his drunken revels, manipulating the attendees for his own jaded amusement.

"But these, Our enemy, will find their justice from Us." He gave the Septs no chance to murmur, but glanced down at the parchment that lay on his podium and began to read the long list of names aloud—merchants, guardsmen, generals, and minor nobles for the most part, but some few were royal servants. "These men all We find guilty of murder, conspiracy to commit murder—" and a dozen lesser charges that he recited with slow precision.

"These men We sentence to hanging. This shall be forthwith accomplished in the main market square, five each day until all be dead."

He could have left this judgment to the Septs. Then all those deaths would be on their shoulders, not his. He had no doubt that the Septs would have found each of those men guilty.

"But these are not the only men who stand accused." And this next group, no doubt, would have escaped justice if it had depended upon the Council of Septs. "Bring forth the Septs who stand accused."

During this trial, he had succeeded in proving at least one emperor—Phoran's own father—had been murdered. If he allowed the Council to set those murderers free, it would set a precedent he preferred to avoid.

He set the parchment down upon his podium and waited as his guardsmen brought in the thirteen Septs he'd been able to bring to trial. There were others who should have stood trial, guilty men who were too powerful for the evidence he could have brought against them. He was careful to keep his eyes off those men—among them Gorrish, the Council head.

The Septs came in, each man gagged and his hands bound behind his back. Each was escorted by two young men in green and grey, the colors of Phoran's personal Sept, hastily resurrected for a uniform for the Emperor's Own, a gold songbird in flight embroidered on the left shoulder.

Phoran thought it was the prisoners' gags that were responsible for the murmurs he heard echoing in the cavernous chamber. Gorrish, he saw, was not among those talking. A Sept's honor was considered above the need for bindings. Practicality, however, would have excused the tied wrists—the gag was an insult. Phoran didn't mean the insult, but he needed those men silenced to complete his task.

The Emperor's Own led their prisoners to the center of the floor, facing the ranks of seats where their peers watched them. Once they were in, Phoran stepped down from his podium and walked to the accused Septs.

The murmurs in the room quieted as the Septs waited to see what Phoran had planned.

"The Sept of Jenne," Phoran said, standing in front of the accused and meeting his eye before stepping to the next. "Sept of Seal Hold." There were thirteen of them in all. "Sept of Vertess." Some of them were old men, men who had known Phoran's father as he had not. Had known him and seen him assassinated as they'd assassinated also the uncle who had raised Phoran. Some of them were young men who had drunk his wine and eaten his food, thinking him a fat dupe—as he had been.

One by one he named them all.

This day, Phoran knew, he'd have to pay for the years he had allowed himself to be made into a fat capon. Phoran hoped the final cost of his sins would be something less than the price these men would pay for theirs.

"Your hands are bound," he said, "because this day you are powerless before Us. Your tongues are stilled because you have had the chance to defend yourselves and We no longer hear your words."

He turned to the rest of his Septs, letting his eyes roam the chamber. "We find these men, Septs all, guilty of murder and treason. We find this crime is more heinous than the crimes of lesser men, because the trust they betrayed was greater. We find their crimes dictate that the inheritance of their Septs will be Ours to do with as We choose."

That caused rustles among his audience. Oh, there had been emperors who had interfered with inheritances before—but not in the last two centuries, not even in cases of treason. He would allow most of the heirs to keep their Sept, but that wasn't the point. He wanted all the Septs to remember the power of the Emperor and set aside the memory of the fool they had believed him to be. He had to make them understand, viscerally, that their power came from him, and not the other way around.

"For their crimes We find that these former Septs shall be condemned to death."

There was, on the floor of the Council of Septs, a raised stone, where a statue of a rearing stallion, the symbol of the Empire resided. Phoran rather thought that most of the Septs had forgotten the raised stone had originally been something other than a base for the statue.

He held out his hand and Toarsen, First Captain of the Emperor's Own and former Passerine, stepped away from his honor guard position. Held at chest height and balanced upon his gloved hands was a rather large sword they'd tucked out of sight against the Emperor's podium.

It was not Phoran's own sword. They'd had to go into the storeroom and sort through dozens of weapons until they'd found something suitable.

Phoran took it from Toarsen and raised it, almost five feet of newly sharpened steel jutting out from a magnificently ornate two-handed grip. It was an awesome weapon—though not something he'd have cared to carry into a real battle against lighter, quicker blades.

Phoran let them all look their fill. A few Septs frowned or sat up, but most of them looked bored. They were waiting for a speech, he knew. Rhetoric was a common occurrence—even if the sword was a little more extreme than the usual props.

"We do not have a list of all the deaths these men are responsible for—though Our father and uncle are among them: emperor and regent to emperor. So We tell you instead the names of those who died fighting for Our life." These names he had memorized long before he decided to use them here. A man, it seemed to him, ought to know the names of people who died for him. He gave them the names of fifteen Passerines. Then ten men who'd belonged to Avar, the Sept of Leheigh, who had come to Phoran's rescue. "And of the Clan of Rongier the Librarian—" Eight names, and it took most of the Septs all eight before they realized the names belonged to Travelers.

Two of his counselors, Gerant and Avar, Septs both, had told him to leave those names off. Eliminating the "scourge" of Travelers had been a policy of the Council for generations. But those men had died for him also, and Phoran had decided their names should speak to the guilt of the accused.

"The first person to fall that night gains no justice from this. Lady Myrceria of Telleridge, daughter of the former Sept of Telleridge, died under torture, which was conducted by her own father. She died to keep Our secrets so We could bring about the fall of the Path. I would that Telleridge could be here to answer for his crimes, but he died that day, and he died much too easily."

While he was speaking, two guards, chosen especially for the duty, removed the statue of the rearing horse from its place of honor and pulled off the embroidered covering beneath it to reveal the cold granite stone that lay beneath.

Phoran nodded, and Jenne's guards led him to the stone. They jerked him off his feet and held his shoulders down against the granite, his head hanging over the end, with the smoothness of three days spent practicing that move on each other in preparation for this moment.

A Sept convicted of treachery had to shed his blood in the Council chambers. Traditionally the emperor would cut the Sept's hand and let the blood fall. A beheading would follow, usually the same day, in a courtyard of the palace reserved for such things. But, there were exceptions to that tradition.

With both hands, Phoran raised the old sword high over his head. The leather wrapping of the pommel kept his sweaty grip from slipping as he brought down that sword, a sword made for chopping rather than thrust and parry, and let it cleave all the way through Jenne's neck.

The whole thing had been accomplished so quickly, Phoran didn't think that Jenne had even realized what was happening to him.

Somebody shouted, not a protest, Phoran thought, but shock. When he turned to face them, the Council of Septs, he saw he *finally* had their complete attention.

In the silence that followed, Phoran let them get their fill of looking at him holding that dark sword with blood splattered about him; let them burn the image in their hearts and minds to supersede the picture of the weakling they'd thought him.

He kept his face impassive. It helped that this was not the first man he'd killed. *No matter how much it felt like it,* he told himself fiercely, *this was not murder.*

The guards pulled the remains of their former charge aside and covered the body with rough, dark-colored sacking—no fine linens for these men. When the bloodstained stone was emptied, Phoran nodded to the next pair.

After the first three, he found it was easier to keep down his gorge. He learned how to swing the blade so speed and the sword's own weight did most of the work. He only had to make a second chop once, when the Sept of Seal Hold struggled a little too vigorously for his guards and put his shoulder in the way of the sword edge.

While Phoran was waiting for a body to be moved, Toarsen brought up a clean, damp cloth and wiped the Emperor's face clean of blood and sweat: and that, too, Phoran had carefully staged beforehand.

He didn't want the Septs to see a madman, crazed by blood; but an emperor who was willing to kill to protect his Empire, a man whose power was to be feared.

At last the final body fell.

"In the name of Phoran, he who is emperor, the sentence has been carried out. Let their bodies be burned and scattered to the four winds. Let no one sing their way to the tables of the gods. Let their names be forgotten."

Phoran was never certain who it was who said those words. It was supposed to have been him—he'd written it out himself—but he was beyond talking. He cleaned the sword on the clothing of the last man he killed, then returned the polished blade to Toarsen's care.

Looking neither left nor right Phoran exited the room. Kissel, his Second Captain of the Emperor's Own, and Avar, the Sept of Leheigh, both kept a step behind him to serve as honor guard.

As soon as he was in the hall, Phoran quickened his walk as much as he could and still maintain the illusion of imperial dignity. He was grateful that neither of the men accompanying him said a word.

Once inside the privacy of his rooms, Phoran grabbed the basin he'd brought out for just that moment and vomited into it. When he was finished, he wiped his face with a cloth, then leaned against the nearest pillar and rested his forehead upon the cool stone. He wanted to be alone. Wanted to be anywhere but here.

Avar handed him a cup of water.

Phoran rinsed his mouth and spat in the basin.

"You were right," said Avar. "I was wrong. There isn't a man who was in that chamber today who will forget what happened."

Phoran wanted to forget, but he supposed that Avar was right.

There was a short, efficient knock on the door.

"Come," said Phoran, recognizing it.

The Sept of Gerant came in, followed by Avar's brother Toarsen. Toarsen still carried the sword, but it was sheathed and resting casually against his shoulder.

It was probably stupid, thought Phoran, that of the four people he trusted completely, he knew only one of them well. An unwitting tool in the Path's plan to ensure a weak emperor, Avar had been first Phoran's guide and then his companion in debauchery. Avar had never quite reached the heights of corruption that Phoran had managed, though. Like a gold coin in the mud, there was something pure and shining about his friend that nothing could quite smudge.

Until a month ago, Phoran had known Avar's brother Toarsen and Toarsen's best friend Kissel only to greet in the hall as they passed. Both of them were of poor repute—and from what he'd learned in the past month, their reputation for villainy was probably much less severe than they deserved.

He also knew they were, both of them, absolutely trustworthy. They were his, given to him as a gift by Tieragan of Redern—or else he'd been given as a gift to them: Phoran wasn't quite certain.

The Sept of Gerant, though, was very definitely Tier's gift. Gerant had come so seldom to Taela that Phoran wasn't certain he'd ever even met the man before he'd come in answer to Phoran's summons, a summons he'd written on Tier's advice.

Before Gerant arrived, Phoran had envisioned an aging Avar: big, charismatic, and physically gifted—especially after he'd done some reading about the victories Gerant had managed against the Fahlarn twenty years ago. But Gerant was no giant, no flashy hero.

He was shorter than average, and looked a dozen years younger than he was. He dressed modestly and watched more than he talked. At first Phoran had thought him a stolid sort of man, true as good steel but the kind of person who had to think things through before he acted. And Phoran had been right—except Gerant thought faster than most. Phoran's uncle would have liked Gerant, and Phoran knew of no greater compliment.

"You played that well," Gerant said.

Phoran took a sip of water. "Just give me a dozen virgins to rape, and I could have completed the show."

"He's never at his best after losing his breakfast," commented Avar.

"Good thing there weren't another two or three," continued Phoran. "Or I'd have had to start stabbing them rather than beheading them. Maybe I should have used an axe?"

Avar walked over to a pitcher and poured ale into the five goblets that waited. "Some ale, gentlemen? You can't make conversation with him when he's like this."

"It's hard," said Gerant. "Much easier to kill the bastards when they've a sword at your gullet than to do it cold when they're whimpering and shaking."

"I'd have done it for you," said Toarsen. Some trick of arrangement had taken the same features that turned Avar into the epitome of male beauty and made Toarsen look like a merry drinking companion—if you didn't look into his eyes.

Had Toarsen killed men who were bound and unable to fight back? Phoran didn't ask; he didn't want to know the answer.

"Nasty business." Kissel loosened the neck of his captain's uniform and accepted a goblet. "I like killing them when they're trying to kill you better," Kissel continued, giving apparent answer to Phoran's unasked question—though it was hard to tell: Kissel had a wicked sense of humor.

Kissel was the second son of the Sept of Seal Hold. When Phoran offered to let Kissel stay away from the executions, Kissel had offered to restrain the Seal Hold while Phoran struck the blow—or strike the blow himself. He was not, it seemed, fond of his father.

Taking a deep swallow, the big man relaxed into his usual seat. Somehow in the past few weeks, Phoran's sitting room had been arranged into a council of war.

"They'll fear you now, Phoran," said Gerant. "But they'll respect you more."

"I was watching Gorrish," said Toarsen. "Cold-blooded, that one. He wasn't afraid or impressed by the show. If he'd been a wizard, I'll wager our emperor would be lying in state now."

Avar nodded at his brother. "I know. I saw it, too. We're going to have to do something about him."

"We needed to kill that one, too," agreed Gerant, finding a small bench and taking a seat. There was a soft chair set out for his use, but, to Phoran's private amusement, Gerant was more comfortable with humbler furniture. "It's too bad there wasn't enough evidence against him."

Phoran gave a sour grunt and exchanged the water cup for a goblet of ale. "He was too busy running the Council for Telleridge to make many appearances below. The Path's servants knew, but I couldn't expose them to the kind of things that happen to servants who bear witness against their betters."

He wandered casually over to his chair and plopped down with a leg thrown over one arm. The company was steadying him, giving himself something to think about other than the blood that spattered his clothing.

"That reminds me," said Gerant, "I promised Tier I'd look after you, but you make it damn difficult. If Avar and Kissel hadn't thought to accompany you, you'd have been parading down the hall by yourself. You were supposed to wait and take half of your guard. Your performance today has made you a target—not just for the Path members who escaped us, but any Sept or merchant who liked things better while you were more concerned with whoring and drinking than matters of state."

"They had their whoring emperor for too long," agreed Phoran wryly. "It'll take us all time to adjust. I'll try to remember to take guards with me."

"Kissel and I picked out a few trustworthy men from the Emperor's Own," Toarsen said, and Phoran hoped he missed Avar's wince. It was likely that any number of the Emperor's Own were going to prove themselves untrustworthy. "They'll be stationed outside your rooms in pairs, day and night."

Gerant rubbed his face; he knew the Emperor's Own, too. He'd been conducting the morning training sessions (which Phoran attended), letting the captains conduct an evening session alone. "There aren't a dozen I'd trust, yet," he said.

"They'll stand twelve-hour shifts," said Toarsen. Phoran noticed he didn't argue with Gerant's assessment. "And Kissel and I will rotate with them."

Gerant shook his head. "The shifts are too long. And, by picking only a few, you're telling the rest they're not good enough. Pair them up—one trustworthy with another less so. Rotating three-hour shifts. Any longer than three hours, and a guard's not as effective."

One of the benefits, Phoran thought, of having these men was that they so often took care of the arguing so he could see around it to the real problem.

"Have them guard me in here," said Phoran.

Gerant raised an eyebrow.

"They're all noblemen," Phoran said with a faint smile. "Raised in noble households. They know which fork to eat with—and are probably more likely to do so than I am. Of course they make lousy door guards because that's not what they are. They aren't servants or castle guards. They'll come in and keep company with me, and we'll put castle guards at the door. Surely we can find a few castle guards who won't stab me in the back for having their captain hung. Find the ones he disciplined most often."

Avar snorted. "That'll be good. Pick out the worst of the castle guards to keep the Emperor safe."

"That's it," Gerant said suddenly. Phoran deduced that he was agreeing with Phoran rather than Avar. "That's what we've missed. We'll make the Emperor's Own something different from a guardsmen troop or an army. They're not suited to the kind of service a guardsman gives."

"I'm noble born," said Toarsen. "If someone gave me a uniform and expected me to disappear except when they barked out orders, I'd resent it." He grinned, and this time his eyes lit up, too. "Come to think of it, that's how the Raptors treated us, and look what it got them."

"That doesn't mean we'll let discipline go," Phoran told Avar, who was looking unhappy, "quite the opposite, I think. Tier said there isn't a man among them who isn't a decent swordsman. We'll find more experts, though, and teach them knives, staves, fighting dirty, and anything else we can think of. Tier said that they needed to be *valued*." He knew how that felt. He knew these young men who were looking for a purpose; he'd been one until very recently.

"So you make them think they are valued," said Kissel. "And then they become loyal."

Phoran shook his head. "I do *need* them, Kissel. All I have to do is show them that. They don't replace the castle guard— hopefully that won't be necessary, but if it is, I can find replacements elsewhere. I need them to be my eyes and ears, my hands and feet." He started to get enthusiastic. "Look how much trouble the city guards have with the wealthier merchants and lesser nobles. Let them appeal to the Emperor's Own—noblemen, gentlemen, men of rank who are listened to and respected."

"Noblemen," said Avar dryly, "who were thieves and vandals until just recently. I hope. Of whom your captains can find only what—fourteen trustworthy men?"

"Ten," said Kissel. "Including Toarsen and me."

"Noblemen who serve an emperor who was a drunkard and a screwup," said Phoran. "I certainly hope it is possible to change—and if you don't, you'd better pretend you do, or you might offend Us."

Avar grinnèd. "All right. But you need to keep at least one of them who is on the captains' shortlist of trustworthy souls near you."

Gerant chuckled. "They'll work out. Phoran's hit upon it, I think. That's what happens when people are around Tier for too long. They start expecting miracles—and usually get them."

"Before you came here, my lord," said Kissel, "you hadn't seen Tier since the Fahlarn War. Do you always answer summonses from commoners who served in your command two decades ago?"

Gerant smiled and ran a finger over his moustache to smooth it. "I answered a summons from my emperor, lad. Make no mistake."

Phoran tilted his goblet toward Gerant. "And they say you don't know how to play politics."

Gerant let out one of his soft chuckles. "No. What they say is that I don't like politics." To Kissel he said, "I do understand your question, though. Tier and I haven't seen each other since the war, but we've exchanged letters two or three times a year for twenty years and . . ." He shook his head. "You've met Tier. I'd trust his judgment before I'd trust my own—and I've done so. I expect that if I'd not heard from him since he left Gerant, I'd still come running if he asked."

"You've got it, too," observed Phoran. "That something that makes people want to do as you say. I don't know what it is, exactly. Avar has it upon occasion, but you and Tier carry it about your shoulders like a mantle of authority."

Gerant bowed his head. "Thank you. I've had to work at it. Tier was like that when he was a snot-nosed boy leading around men twice his age and experience and not a one of them thought to question it."

Toarsen laughed. "The Path didn't know what they were doing when they threw him down among us, did they, Kissel? I think they expected us to cow him or torment him like we did that poor Traveler bastard who was there before him. But instead Tier took us and made us into a weapon for the Emperor." He nodded at Phoran, who raised his goblet in acknowledgment.

"See that you serve him well," said Avar.

"Speaking of service," said Phoran, changing the subject. "I need an heir."

Avar grinned at him. "Do you have a lady in mind?"

Phoran rolled his eyes. "Please don't be stupid, Avar. Any wife I can contract right now is as likely to kill me in my sleep as anything. A blood heir will have to wait until I have a few more allies than those who are now present. Besides, a child would be of no use anyway. Too vulnerable."

He sipped at his drink and let them roll the idea around in silence a while, then said, "If I have a legal heir, an adult heir, the first thought in my enemy's mind won't be—if Phoran could just take a fall off his horse . . . or down the stairs, then I wouldn't have to worry about him."

Avar got it, but Phoran could see that Kissel and Toarsen were still working through it.

"It's not so much that I'm less vulnerable with an heir," he explained. "It's that there is less to be gained by my assassination—especially if my heir is likely to be more trouble than I am."

"It won't help with Gorrish or anyone else with a personal grudge," said Avar. "And, if you'll excuse me for saying so, you've gone out of your way to offend a lot of people, Phoran. But political enemies will be less likely to consider assassination as a solution. Do you have an heir in mind?"

"You," he said, and could have laughed at Avar's blank face. Avar wasn't stupid, but sometimes you had to grab him by the shoulders and make him look before he saw the wild boar charging him. "Come now, who else would it be? Your mother and mine were first cousins or some rot—which is how your father took over as regent when my uncle died. You're as close to family as I've got—you and Toarsen."

"I don't want to become Phoran the Twenty-Seventh," Avar said in dead seriousness.

"Don't then." Phoran leaned back and took the last swallow from his goblet. "Follow my tradition and include the first Phoran. You can be Phoran the Twenty-Eighth instead. Or, as far as I'm concerned, since I presume I'll be dead if you inherit, you can be Avar the First."

"That's not what I meant," Avar said impatiently. "*You* know it isn't. I don't want your place."

"No," said Phoran. "Which is the best reason for me to name you heir. Come, it's all right. Hopefully, you'll be deposed by the child of whatever poor lady someone eventually forces to marry me. But until then, I need an heir, and you are it."

Avar's handsome chin set firmly. "I won't, and you can't make me."

Toarsen grinned and raised his goblet at Phoran. "That's the first time I've ever heard him sound like a spoiled brat. Thank you for that—it's hard growing up with a big brother who is perfect."

"Come, Avar," coaxed Phoran. "The weight of the Empire is a heavy one, twenty-seven emperors deep. Since the first Phoran We have protected and served Our people. Who else's strong right arm am I to trust to keep the Empire safe and whole?"

"Gerant," said Avar.

Even as Gerant shook his head, Phoran said, "Gerant is no relative of mine, not even if you search back ten generations. The Council could overthrow the appointment even before it was announced."

"Come, my lord," said Gerant gently. "It is for every man to serve his emperor and the Empire as best he can."

"All right," he said, but he didn't sound happy about it.

Deciding it was best to get the business over with before he had to argue Avar around again, Phoran bounced to his feet. "Come then, all of you, let's go see if my scribe has the papers drawn up yet. We'll need witnesses."

"You've already had them drawn up?"

Phoran grinned at Avar. "I know you, my friend. Duty has never been a burden you've shunned."

Phoran had a new scribe. His previous scribe, whose duties had been far lighter than the scribe of a proper emperor ought to have been, was, nonetheless, one of the gentlemen due to lose his life by hanging in the market square sometime in the next week or so.

Phoran had found his new scribe himself via his archive keeper, who was not happy about losing his most promising journeyman. He'd given him several rooms in an underused wing with a secret passage to the libraries, where the young man worked during the day. It was after hours, and in any case, Phoran had requested this business be secret until he had the papers signed and witnessed.

As he led the way to the scribe's apartment, Phoran found himself wondering, not for the first time, what his ancestors had been thinking when they put the palace together. Small civilizations could flourish in unused rooms, and no one would be the wiser. Since the palace had been built over many generations, there was no pattern to how it was laid out.

He led his cohorts up three stories, over two halls, then down a floor, through several small doorways, the last of which led to a gallery where one could look down over waist-high rails to a pond three stories below. A raised section in the middle had obviously been a fountain, though the stone fishes' mouths were dry.

The whole pool—which was deeper than the pole Phoran had once pushed into it and large enough to swim a small whale—was covered with scum giving the whole gallery an unpleasantly fishy smell despite the fresh air that came from having no ceiling over the gallery.

"You put your scribe here?" asked Avar. "What did he do to you?"

"This is the shortest way," explained Phoran. "If you'd all quit gawking, we'll be there in no time."

"I think this might be why they keep getting pigeons in the art gallery." Kissel had his hand propped to shade his eyes from the bright sun that made quite a change from the dim halls they'd been wandering through.

"I haven't seen this before," said Toarsen, leaning over the rails. "I've been exploring this place for years. How could I not have seen this? Have you looked into fixing that fountain?"

"Fall over, and you won't have to worry about the fountain. Phoran has all the maps to the palace somewhere," said his brother. "He knows all sorts of odd places."

"Not all the maps, by any means," said Phoran. "Or if they are all the maps, then they leave out a great deal."

Irrepressible, Toarsen twisted until his back rested on the rail rather than his belly and looked up. "Three stories up? What does the outside of this look like Phoran? Are we in the North Central section or—"

The sound of a door thwacking against the wall pulled Phoran's eyes away from Toarsen in time to see armed men boiling out of the doorway.

He had a moment to wonder, stupidly, what they were doing here, wearing masks and waving swords, then Gerant shouted, "Assassins."

Avar bellowed out Phoran's battle cry twice to alert anyone who might be within hearing range that they were under attack. But rescue was a faint hope at best—in all the times Phoran had traveled this way in the last few weeks, he'd never seen anyone else here. Even if someone heard, the chances of their joining in on Phoran's side rather than his attackers was something less than fifty-fifty.

Kissel and Toarsen had their swords out, but none of the rest of them were armed with anything more lethal than eating knives. Which was stupid in retrospect, Phoran thought, as he ducked beneath a sword and set his hip behind his attacker's. A quick push and the man fell over backward just as Gerant had promised when he'd demonstrated the move the day before yesterday at morning practice.

It worked, but Phoran couldn't follow up his advantage because he was too busy avoiding another sword. Phoran wasn't able to wrest the sword from the man before he had to give up the attack or be hewn down.

A gleaming blade came from nowhere and slid toward his belly with snakelike swiftness. Phoran watched it with an odd detachment that had overcome him as soon as he realized that there was no way out, no rescue coming. He knew that he was dead and that this sword made him so.

The blade was touching Phoran's tunic when it jerked back and fell to the floor, along with the man who held it. Standing behind the fallen man was a familiar dark shape Phoran had hoped he'd never see again.

In a bewildering mixture of relief and horror, Phoran stared at the Memory, so much more solid than the last time he'd seen it. It returned his stare—or so he imagined, because it had no eyes he could see. Then it continued its hunt.

It should be gone. The Traveler healer had said once it killed the people responsible for its death, the ghost of the Raven he'd seen murdered would cease to exist. He had been so certain it was gone. He hadn't seen it since the night it had killed the Masters of the Path, the wizards who had killed a Raven to steal his power and loosed this Raven's Memory upon the only witness not protected against it: Phoran.

Looking almost like a man covered in an enveloping black cloth that flowed over the top of his head to the floor, the dark thing moved from one of Phoran's attackers to the next. It was more solid than he remembered, but no one but Phoran paid it any attention at first—but no one except for Phoran and the Travelers had ever been able to see it.

If it were still around, why hadn't it continued to feed off Phoran every night? And if it didn't need to feed from him, why had it protected him?

Phoran watched as his masked attackers fell, one after the other. A few were killed by human hands. Gerant and Avar had managed to arm themselves, and both were remarkable fighters. But many more fell to his Memory.

His arms folded on his chest, Phoran watched as the remaining fighters, on both sides, became gradually aware there was another killer present. Several attackers tried to run, but the Memory was swifter.

Phoran wondered what the others saw. For him the dying men were obscured, enveloped by the Memory, until they dropped bloodless to the floor. Toarsen and Kissel quit fighting the assassins altogether and flanked Phoran.

"It's all right," he told them. "It won't hurt me." Which was almost funny, as he carried the scars of the Memory's bites up and down his arms. But still and all, he knew it would not kill him. It couldn't. If he died, so would it.

The Memory turned its eyeless gaze back to Phoran.

Even as he moved to place himself between it and Phoran, Avar said in a hushed voice, "What is *that* Phoran?"

"It won't hurt me," Phoran said again. None of the others could see it, he thought, only Avar. He remembered the way the Memory had never come when Avar was around—was it because it knew Avar would see it?

But the others had seen the men fall dead, they'd know it was magic. Magic connected to the Emperor.

"I have fed this night," the Memory said, ignoring everyone except Phoran. "I will give you an answer to one question. Choose."

Why aren't you gone? thought Phoran. *If you didn't die when the Path fell, why have you stayed away? Why come back here now?*

But the question he asked was more important.

"Did anyone else see this?" he asked.

The Memory turned its attention upward, and Phoran followed its gaze. Two levels up he saw the gaze of a youngling so swaddled in rags it was difficult to tell if he were male or female. As soon as he realized they were looking at him, he took of in a scuttle of soft-shod footsteps.

There were any number of such homeless folk who found shelter in the endless unmapped rooms in the palace. His bad luck that one had found shelter here.

"Do I need to eliminate that one?" the Memory asked. "Does it pose danger to you?"

Temptation. But Phoran shook his head, and lied, "There is no more danger to me. You may go."

The Memory bowed shallowly and dissolved into nothingness.

When it was gone, Phoran looked at his men. *No use hiding it,* he thought wearily. Avar might have been the only one actually to see it—but there was no denying the bodies scattered on the floor.

"That was what the Travelers call a Memory," he told them. "One of their mages was killed by the Masters of the Path while I was secretly watching. The Masters had protected themselves, so it attached itself to me. It needed vengeance upon the wizards who killed the Raven, and I thought it had managed that when it killed the Masters when the Path fell; but it seems that is not the case."

There was an old law, immutable, written while the fell signs of the Unnamed King's reign, empty cities and barren fields, were still visible upon in the lands of the Empire: an emperor could not be touched by magic. The days when the Emperor had to wear the Stone of Phoran visible on the circlet that displayed it on the front of the imperial forehead were long gone. But Phoran had worn it on his forehead and ridden through Taela the day before his coronation as had his father before him. If one of the Septs chose, they could request he wear it before the Council.

He knew, because he'd tried it when the Memory first came to him, that the stone would not stay clear at his touch while he was bound to the Memory. If the Septs knew, he would be executed.

It was Avar who said it. "If that ragged child tells anyone about this, it will be all over the palace that the Emperor has a monster who slew assassins for him."

Phoran waited for their judgment.

Toarsen bent down and jerked the mask off one of the dead men. To Phoran's relief, the body was not shrunken and dried the way the Masters' bodies had been.

"First we'll have to dispose of these bodies," Toarsen said. "If anyone sees them, they'll know nothing human killed them."

"I thought Tier's son killed the wizards," said Kissel.

"No," said Phoran. "It was the Memory. Tier lied to save me."

Avar nodded. "If you'll help me, gentlemen. We'll throw them into the pond. They're wearing armor—that'll keep the bodies from floating. By the time someone finds them, any oddities will be explained by the water."

As Toarsen and Avar tossed one over, Gerant and Kissel picked up the next one. After the first several, Phoran helped, too—he tried not to watch as they hit the water below.

"It's a good thing that pond's so big," said Kissel, tipping another one over. "It'll be decades before anyone finds them—if ever."

"No renovation of the fountain," said Toarsen, with mock sadness.

"We'll have to rethink having the castle guard watch over your rooms," said Avar. "Did you notice most of them wear standard-issue boots? I don't see any faces I recognize, but I bet they are all from the castle guard."

"So," said Phoran, when they had finished. "I'm assuming that none of you has decided you need a new emperor."

Gerant patted him on the shoulder. "That law was not meant for this kind of situation. We'll help you."

"It'll be a few days before the gossip starts to spread," said Avar. "And even then, all they'll have is bits and pieces. Those pauper children don't associate with the Septs. It'll come from the servants upward."

"Unless I can get rid of it," said Phoran, "how long it takes won't matter. When the gossip hits, the Septs will demand I show them I'm untouched by sorcery—and I have no reason not to, except, of course, that I can't pass the test."

"The stone can be stolen," said Toarsen.

Phoran shook his head. "What we'll do is this. Gerant, Avar, and I'll go on to my scribe now. Avar might inherit a little earlier than I thought. Kissel and Toarsen, I want you to go to the Emperor's Own and have them make ready to go. Pick out a few of the most trustworthy to ride with me as my personal guard. I'll leave early in the morning. Gerant, if you would, I need you to take the rest of the Pass"—he caught himself—"the Emperor's Own to your home and train them. I won't abandon them here to rot, and I can't stay. I'll see to it that a suitable purse goes to you—"

"Not necessary," he said.

Phoran waved a hand. "I thank you for that, but they are mine, and I'll see to their housing and training." He took a deep breath. "I'm headed out for Redern. Hopefully Tier and his Traveler lady will be there and can help me. If not, I'll send word, and we'll fake my death—since I have no real interest in being beheaded, having lately gained a new aversion to the process."

"You can't leave," said Avar. "Without you to stem the gossip, they'll have you Shadowed and worse before you return, and you'll never live it down."

"I'm closing down the palace," said Phoran. "Kicking out the nobles and their families for six months, while a plethora of workmen redo the entry hall. Renovations." He tipped his head to Toarsen, who'd given him the idea. "They'll have to be gone by tomorrow noon."

"That's ridiculous," said Avar. "There's nothing urgently wrong with the entry hall—they'll all wonder why you didn't give them a month's notice."

Gerant chuckled unexpectedly. "Oh, that's all he'll have to say. They'll think he intends to search their rooms for signs of their guilt—and there's enough guilty or nearly so to cause considerable distress. Not one of them will think it an unlikely thing for the Emperor, who just beheaded thirteen ruling Septs, to do. They'll be far more worried about not leaving anything incriminating than they will be in discovering the Emperor's whereabouts."

Kissel smiled. "He's right."

Phoran gave a quick bow. "If I can't fix this in six months, it'll be too late."

"So you and I'll take some of your guard and my men—" began Avar, but Phoran shook his head.

"You're my heir," he said. "We can't afford to be in the same place. I won't travel with a large group of men, because I won't be the Emperor, I'll be some rich merchant's son. The people left at the palace will know I'm gone, but we won't tell anyone else. You'll stay here and supervise the work—or you can go with Gerant."

Avar opened his mouth to protest, but, in the end, he didn't say anything. Phoran was right.

"I have an objection," said Toarsen.

Phoran raised an eyebrow.

"I'm not certain I know how to find my way back to where you're housing the Emperor's Own from here. Can you give me directions?"

CHAPTER 9

*Tier watched quietly as Phoran fell silent at last, lean-*ing against one end of the table and watching the flames in the fireplace leap and crackle. He moved less like an overweight courtier and more like a fighter than he had when Tier had last seen him. He still carried extra weight that left his face soft-ened, but there was muscle now under the padded shoulders of his velvet tunic.

"I notice Toarsen and Kissel are with you and not at Ger-ant," commented Tier.

He saw Toarsen hide a grin.

Phoran smiled. "I told them to find a few of the Emperor's Own who could be trusted, and they decided they trusted themselves the best. Gerant and Avar are keeping the rest of the Passerines . . . of the Emperor's Own busy while we're off running about."

The smile died and he walked to the fireplace, bracing himself on the mantel. "I've come here," he said in a low voice, "hoping that you can save me again."

"I don't know much about Memories," said Tier. "Seraph might be more help, and Lehr is riding to find Brewydd to-morrow morning."

"Who is Brewydd?" asked Toarsen.

"The healer from the Traveling clan that helped us with the Path," explained Tier.

"The old woman?"

Tier nodded. "They left us before we got quite this far. It might take Lehr a couple of days to find them." He thought a moment. "Brewydd told us the Memory would leave when it had its vengeance. Maybe it doesn't feel its vengeance has been fulfilled yet."

"The wizard who escaped," said Phoran.

Tier nodded. "The Shadowed." Tier had told the Emperor about their suspicions before he'd left Taela, but Toarsen started at the name. "We're not happy about his escaping either. If that's what's keeping the Memory around, then maybe we can help. We've been looking for him ourselves."

"The Shadowed?" asked Toarsen harshly. "He was killed a long time ago."

"Not the same Shadowed," said Seraph, her voice husky with fatigue. "Not the Nameless King. This is another wizard who found a way to tap into the power of the Stalker. He doesn't seemed to have amassed the same kind of power yet—and we don't know why."

"You're certain there is another Shadowed?" asked Phoran.

Tier nodded, but he didn't tell the Emperor their certainty was based mostly upon the word of Ellevanal. Somehow he thought Phoran would find it more believable if Tier didn't explain too much.

"What is the Stalker?" asked Toarsen.

"The guilt of the Travelers," she said. "Though I'd ask you to keep it to yourself. A very long time ago, before there were Travelers, there was a city of wizardry, where mages collected to learn from each other and from the library there. They were an arrogant bunch, trusting to their great power to save them when they delved into things best not touched."

"They created something," said Lehr. "Something that all of their power and learning could not control. So the wizards sacrificed the city and everyone in it, except for themselves, and bound the Stalker. Then, knowing that the bindings were imperfect, the surviving wizards vowed to fight the damage it could still do. They became the Travelers—and the Shadowed is one of the things they fight."

Phoran rubbed his face, and Tier could see the fatigue that bore down upon him. "So we have to kill this Shadowed in order to rid me of the Memory?"

Tier shrugged. "I don't know for certain. Have you asked the Memory?"

"It hasn't shown up since it killed my attackers."

"It's not feeding from you?" asked Seraph, straightening. "That's dangerous, Phoran. If it's still bound to you and quits feeding, it will fade."

"That's good, though, isn't it?" asked Toarsen.

"It'll take the Emperor with it when it goes." Seraph's voice had a bite to it, but Toarsen didn't seem to mind.

"If it killed enough people, it wouldn't have to feed for a while. A mage might feed it for longer—and since the Masters were the ones who killed the Raven who spawned the Memory, that feeding might hold it longer than other people's death." Hennea's voice sounded calm and alert, with none of the fatigue that dragged at his wife's.

There was a rustle of her mattress, and Hennea emerged, her hair hanging in tangled skeins over her shoulders. It made her look nearer to Rinnie's age than Seraph's.

"Phoran, you remember Hennea," Tier said.

The Emperor nodded. "Of course. Raven."

"Your Highness," Hennea said, as composed as if she had been wearing court dress instead of a thin nightshirt. "Can you summon the Memory if you wish?" she asked.

"No." Phoran had tried to call it every way he could think of.

"Well enough," said Seraph. "It'll come eventually. Hennea, did you hear Phoran's story?"

Hennea nodded. "How much of this do your men know, Phoran?"

"Toarsen knows it all, of course, and Kissel," Phoran said. "I've told the others I've had a spell of some sort laid upon me by the Masters and you"—he swept his hand to include everyone in the room—"might be able to help me." His mouth tightened. "I don't dare trust them with the whole of it."

"It always surprised me that Rufort was recruited by the Path," said Tier. "I'd stake my life that he's as honorable as any man I've known."

"He's calmed down a lot this past year," said Toarsen. "He used to have a terrible temper. He'd go out and have a few at some tavern, then pick a fight with the biggest fool he could find. He quit doing that after Kissel beat the—"

Phoran cleared his throat and Toarsen ducked his head. "Beg pardon, my ladies. Kissel beat him pretty badly, and he stopped picking fights. Rufort told me once a man with a broken leg had a lot of time to lie on his back and think about what he was doing with his life."

Toarsen paused, then said, "They'd have had him killed soon—the Raptors and the Path's Masters. I think they might have already tried. One of the other Passerines was found dead not far from Rufort's room a few weeks before Tier was brought to us. He was a nasty piece of work, and no one missed him—but Kissel, who saw the body, told me the person who killed him was a big man like Rufort. We didn't think about it much, until you showed us the Path killed more of the Passerines than it graduated to Raptor status."

"Ielian I don't know as well," said Tier. "I remember him being quiet—and one of the better swordsmen."

"He's a good man," Toarsen said. "He gave an excellent account of himself in the battle in the Eyrie. There are few men I'd rather have at my back." He yawned.

Seraph stood up. "It's time for sleep. Phoran, you can take our room—"

But he was already shaking his head. "No, my lady. That I won't do. I'd never drive a lady from her bed. The barn is good enough for us—a bed of hay will be far softer than anything we've slept on these last weeks."

"Fast riding," commented Tier, "to make that trip in so short a time."

"Toarsen knows all the shortcuts, and our horses are grain-fed," said Phoran. He took a step toward the door, then stopped. "You didn't tell me why you were already sending Lehr out for the Healer."

"I brought back a gift from the Masters," said Tier. "Hopefully Brewydd will be able to take care of it. Nothing for you to worry about. Jes, can you take them out and get them settled with the others?"

"Wait," said Jes. "Hennea, before you slept you said to

remind you about Papa, maps, and Colossae. You said it was important."

She frowned. "I don't remember."

"You will." Jes said confidently.

Lehr closed his eyes and let his body absorb the rhythm of the mare's trot. He'd never ridden a horse like this one.

Akavith may have sold her for far less than she'd have fetched from a nobleman's house, but it was still more money than Lehr had ever held in his hand before.

The chestnut mare shied a little, and Lehr opened his eyes to see what startled her. He didn't see anything, but he watched her mobile ears. There was something in the woods to the left.

It might have been nothing. But they'd been moving for several hours, and she'd handled flapping pheasants and a startled rabbit with remarkable aplomb.

He asked her to walk, and she shook her head in protest before slowing to a prance. *See,* she told him with each dancing step, *I am not tired, and this is too slow.*

Lehr breathed in and out slowly, as Brewydd had taught him. *Quiet your mind, boy. Let your senses talk to you.*

He smelled it then, wild and frightening, the monster lurking in the shadows to eat you when you weren't cautious enough.

"Jes," he said, drawing the mare to a halt. "What are you doing here?"

The wolf emerged from the trees as if he had just been waiting for Lehr's call. Cornsilk raised her delicate head and watched him, but she didn't tense under Lehr's hands. The wolf looked at him with Jes's dark eyes.

"I don't need protection," Lehr said, answering his own question.

The wolf sat down and scratched his ear with a hind leg, then rose to his feet with a snort that might have been a mild sneeze. He trotted up to the mare, ignoring Lehr entirely, and exchanged a muzzle-to-muzzle greeting. Then he started on down the narrow hunting trail without a backward look.

"Curse it, Jes," muttered Lehr. "I don't need help."

The wolf had disappeared behind a curve in the trail.

"Company is not so bad, though," he told the mare.

She snorted and leapt forward into a canter when he shifted his weight. Lehr grinned and squeezed a little with his calves. With a joyful toss of her head, she took off like a startled jackrabbit. When they blazed past Jes, he gave a joyful yip and joined in the chase.

It took them three days to reach Colbern.

As promised, the city was walled. It looked to be smaller than Leheigh, but Lehr supposed that was an effect of the wall itself. The space within would be limited, so the people lived closer together.

The gates of the city were not as impressive as the wall, being both lower and less sturdy. A battering ram would have them down in short order. There hadn't been a war in the area for generations, though, so Lehr supposed the gates were adequate. They were shut tight with makeshift yellow flags hanging over the top as a clear warning to passersby that the inhabitants were fighting a plague.

Jes flattened his ears and growled low.

"I smell it, too," Lehr told his brother. The stench of death—disease and rotting bodies. He pulled his tunic up so it covered his nose and dismounted.

Cornsilk appeared undisturbed by the smell, but she had been trained as a hunter. Blood and death would not fret her as they would most horses.

"You'd better be a human, Jes, when someone opens the gate," Lehr glanced over his shoulder when he spoke—to meet his brother's bland, human face.

"I like this mare," Jes said as he rubbed underneath the cheek strap of Cornsilk's sweaty headstall. "She's pretty."

Lehr pounded on the gate again, but no one answered. He backed up a few steps and leapt up to catch the top edge of the gate. He swung his legs and hooked a heel, then rolled over the top and landed on his feet on the other side.

Two- and three-story buildings looming over narrow streets gave the town a claustrophobic air, which was not helped by the utter lack of movement. Lehr looked around warily, but saw no signs of watchers.

He pulled the heavy bars off the gate and opened it.

"I haven't seen anyone," he told his brother. "Keep alert."

The Guardian gave him a smile full of teeth and led Cornsilk onto the cobbles of the town road. "Can you tell if the Travelers were here?"

Lehr walked back to the dirt path around the gate. He took a deep breath and sat on his heels to contemplate the ground. It took him a while, because there had been a rainstorm sometime in the past week that had blurred and thinned the traces he was looking for.

"They're here," he said, coming back to take Cornsilk's reins. "They came in and never left."

The Guardian looked around the silent town. "I'm not sure that is a good thing."

Lehr had been feeling the same way, but he wasn't going to admit it. He tried to dismiss the eerie feeling of the town as a side effect of Jes's Order—but if that were so, why did he have such a strong urge to move closer to his brother?

He kept his eyes on the road, trusting that the Guardian would keep watch so that he could concentrate on following the traces the clan had left as they walked on the narrow, cobbled streets.

They came to an inn with a stable attached, and the Guardian caught his arm.

"Wait here a moment, I want to check something," he said then disappeared inside the stables. He was out almost as quickly as he was in. "The horses are all dead," he said briefly. "Killed, but not by disease. They've been dead at least a week judging by the maggots. No effort made to butcher them. There were a couple of people in there, too. One dead of stab wounds, the other of disease. I didn't get close enough to tell how long they've been dead."

"Let's find the Travelers and go home," said Lehr, increasing his pace down the road. He didn't think they'd find the Clan of Rongier the Librarian alive, but he had to find them anyway. He owed Brewydd that much.

As they got farther into Colbern, the stench grew worse. There were barricades across some of the streets, futile stacks of household goods to keep plague victims away. They saw scavenger birds, rats, and once, a feral dog, but no people.

They found Rongier's clan in one of the small squares of land left open for grazing and forage of such animals as the townspeople kept. The Guardian knelt beside the first body and sniffed, without touching.

"They've been dead for a week, more or less. Like the horses."

Lehr crouched by a woman who lay facedown, her pale hair reminding him too closely of his mother's. She, like the rest of Rongier's clan, hadn't died of plague. They'd been killed by the people they had been trying to help.

He touched her hair—as long as her face was downward, she was a stranger. "Someone thought they might carry the disease like the horses you found in the stable, and, I suppose, the cats, dogs, chickens, and goats we haven't seen."

He turned her body over gently, as if she might be hurt if he were too rough. He'd seen her cooking beside his mother, and straightening the shirt on a toddler, but he didn't know her name.

He rose to his feet and walked by the bodies, putting names together for the death roll running in his head. "Here's Ben-roln," he said.

Lehr could tell by the dead villagers who surrounded him— and by the way his body had been mutilated—that the clan leader had given good account of himself.

"Isfain," said the Guardian in such an odd voice that Lehr looked up. Isfain, he remembered, was the one who had been set to watch Jes when he'd been held by the *foundrael.*

"Are you all right?" Lehr asked.

The Guardian nodded. "I thought I wanted him dead," he said, then walked on to the next body. "Kors."

They were all dead, men, women, and—heartrendingly— children. The red-haired twins who had always been up to some mischief or other were laid out formally, their throats neatly cut. The toddler who had sucked her thumb whenever she caught his gaze was crumpled in a little broken ball.

There were townsmen among the dead here, too. A few armed with swords might be guardsmen, but most of them had been armed with cudgels or tools. *Desperate men do desperate things,* was one of Papa's sayings.

Lehr turned from the body of a dead man who held a sharp saddler's knife and almost stumbled over a woman's body.

Her ice-blue eyes had gone to the crows, but he recognized the sharply defined nose and wide mouth. Igraina, who had taken special delight in ordering him about and used the opportunity to flirt with him gently. Beside her was the clan smith, Lehr couldn't remember his name, but he remembered the man's shy smile.

By the time they were finished, the Guardian was leaving frost behind on the ground where he walked. Lehr couldn't tell if it was because he was angry or sad. There was no one left for the Guardian to defend or to seek vengeance upon. From the empty streets they'd seen coming through the city, the people who'd done this were most likely already dead.

The one person they didn't find was Brewydd. Lehr didn't find that a hopeful sign. Doubtless she'd been out trying to heal someone when the madness had taken the townspeople.

"There are too many for us to bury," said Lehr helplessly. "But we can't leave them like this."

The Guardian stared around them. "I remember . . . battlefields thick with bodies. Honorable soldiers who deserved better than to be carrion for the vultures. Come here, Lehr. Beside me where you'll be safe."

Lehr got as close as he dared, until the cold of his brother's talents bit his fingers, and dread made it hard to breathe. Cornsilk flattened her ears in distress, but she stood beside Lehr. Apparently they were close enough because the Guardian began singing, a strange atonal sound more akin to a wolf's howl than to any song Lehr had ever heard.

It hurt Lehr's heart, and the tears he'd been fighting fell from his cheeks as if he were a child no older than Rinnie. He'd known these people—hauled firewood with them, fought beside them. And they were all dead. Had died trying to save this town, who had killed them.

The ground shook beneath his feet in answer to the Guardian's song.

Magic surged up through Lehr's feet in a sudden, almost-painful wave that left his ears tingling. All around him the earth broke open around the bodies of Travelers and townsfolk alike and swallowed them down, leaving only turned earth to mark where they had been.

The Guardian's song ended.

"What—" Lehr abandoned his question and set his shoulder beneath Jes's as his brother, pale and sweating, started to fall. Jes sobbed hoarsely as Lehr helped him to a crude bench beneath a small maple tree.

"Shh," he said, kneeling in front of him, wishing he could do more. But Jes had pulled away from him as soon as he sat on the bench, and Lehr knew that no touch of his could comfort his brother. "They'll feel no more pain now, Jes. Nothing more can hurt them."

Jes raised his dark eyes. "So much sorrow," he gasped. "Brewydd, I think. Nearby."

Lehr remembered then that Jes was an empath.

He stood up and looked around slowly. If Jes felt Brewydd hurting, it meant she was still alive. His eyes fell on a small covered cart that could be pulled by hand or horse—Brewydd's *karis.*

He put Cornsilk's reins in Jes's hand. "Hold her for me," he said. "She's probably unhappy, too, Jes."

His brother leaned forward until his forehead rested against her front leg. The mare turned to lip the back of his shirt.

Deciding he'd left Jes cared for as best he could, Lehr made his way to the *karis*—mindful to avoid the places where the earth was soft.

When he opened the door, he was met by the smells of illness. Brewydd took up so little space he almost dismissed her as an odd lump in the bedding before she moved.

"You came, boy," she said. "I worried you would come too late, but then I felt the earth welcome her children home by a Guardian's call. I knew you were here then."

He gathered her into his arms and took her out into the sunshine, hoping its warmth would aid her. She looked as though she'd lost half her body weight since he'd seen her last.

"We should have come with you," he said. "Rinnie was safe with Aunt Alinath. If we'd come with you, this wouldn't have happened."

She reached up to touch his cheek, then patted it gently, and he realized she was blind.

"Who knows what would have happened? That is already written, boy, and not for you or me to change."

"Brewydd?" Jes had left his bench. Lehr looked up and saw that whatever had been tearing at his brother was better now. "We'll take you home, and Mother will fuss over you like she does Papa."

"No, boy," she said gently. "I stayed to talk with you. One of my gifts was farseeing—a weak gift, but it told me I had to wait. Don't mourn me, Lehr—" She brushed away a tear with her thumb. "I'm an old, old woman. Too old to see this illness for what it was. I should have: I knew there was a new Shadowed."

"What went wrong?" Lehr asked. He carried her over to the maple tree and its bench and sat, cradling her as if that might protect her somehow.

"I healed, and they were back the next day worse than before. It was shadow plague, boy. Deaths to feed the Shadowed's power. I knew what to look for, but I'd forgotten, old woman that I am. By the time I thought of it, I was sick myself and half the clan with me. Healed them, then healed myself, but it was too late. The healing took more than I had to give, so I'm dying anyway. Just as this town all died. Shadow-killed. I saw it."

"Mother said Lark can't see shadow," said Lehr, his voice gentle.

She shook her head. "Can. We all can a little, it's just hard for us who don't have Hunter eyes or Guardian instincts. Orders have more in common than not, for all that the Ravens like to pretend differently."

"The Shadowed killed this city," said Jes.

Brewydd nodded. "Those who weren't killed by knife or club. The Shadowed will be up to full strength now. Tell your mother to be careful of him."

"It is a man?" asked Lehr.

She shook her head. "Don't know. Shouldn't assume anything. Could be anyone. You had questions for me to answer. Important enough for me to stay for them, I think."

"Phoran's Memory isn't gone," said Jes.

Lehr explained about the aborted assassination attempt that led Phoran to flee Taela.

"Papa thinks that the Memory won't leave until the Shadowed is destroyed."

The old woman nodded again. "If the Memory didn't leave when the others died, that is probably so. But it'll get stronger, too, more like the man it once belonged to. It might be that even the Shadowed's death will not set it free—like the Ordered gems." She swallowed. "Tell your mother that. The Memory is like the Ordered gems—but the Order is attached to Phoran rather than a gemstone. It might help her."

She rested for a minute, her breathing slow and shallow. "What else?" she said, sounding impatient. "There were two things, I know there were."

"Papa," said Jes. "Lehr knows."

Lehr said, "Mother thinks something the Path did is weakening the connection between Papa and his Order. She said to tell you she sees holes in it as if it were fabric. She was able to patch most of them."

"She did? Tell me how?"

"She told me to tell you she persuaded one of the Lark gems, the tigereye, to help her. You'd know which ring it was." He cleared his throat. "She said she used magic to make yarn and the Lark's Order became a needle wielded by her own Order and she darned the holes to close them. Does that make sense to you?"

Brewydd made an odd sound that frightened Lehr before he realized she was laughing. "Audacious child," she said when she could. "She's lucky the Lark half-trapped in that gemstone didn't kill her while she held it."

"She says the mending is temporary and won't last. She was hoping you could do better."

"No, boy," she said. Her hand fell from his face, and he felt bereft of it. "Not even if I were twenty again. The Orders are beyond my touch as they should have been beyond hers. No. What she needs was lost when Colossae fell."

Lehr felt a chill go down his spine.

"Is it still there?"

Lehr jerked his head to stare up at the Guardian—but met his soft-eyed brother's gaze instead.

"In Colossae?" she asked. "I don't know." She gasped for breath while Lehr rocked her in his arms. She was too light; it was almost as if he held a child.

Her breathing settled. "I've been dreaming of Colossae

while I waited for you. I've never dreamed of Colossae before. You were there. You and your black dog and a tower."

"We found maps of Colossae," said Lehr. "In the Path's temple in Redern.

"Yes, yes," said the old woman smiling. "The dream was for you. That's why I had to stay for you. To tell you that you have to go to Colossae." She paused and relaxed. "Yes. That was it. You may not find your answers there, but if you do not go—you will find nothing." Power, raw and hot, slammed into Lehr's body where it touched the blankets wrapped around Brewydd, robbing him of breath as she said, her voice ringing through him as if he were a bell, "If you do not find Colossae, Tier will fade, and the Emperor's head will adorn his enemy's wall."

Her body went limp in his arms, and the strange power slid away until it was gone.

"Brewydd?" Lehr whispered.

He was afraid she was dead, but she stirred at the sound of his voice.

"I'm still here, boy. Tell your mother. I've been thinking about those Ordered gems. A few days ago something occurred to me. I didn't think it was important, but if you go to Colossae, maybe it will help."

She closed her eyes and breathed for a moment. When she opened them again her color was a little better. "Tradition has it that there is nothing about the Orders in the libraries of the *mermori,* and from the searching your mother, Hennea, and I have done over the years, I'd have to agree. Nothing. Yet when the Elder Wizards left Colossae after sacrificing its inhabitants, they were able to create the Orders. *Solsenti* magic—and the magic the Elder Wizards had was *solsenti* magic—requires great study and forms. Things to be written down. A great magic like the Orders, which have lasted for tens of centuries, would require, oh, so much work, my children. What else could the Elder Wizards have been working on?"

"The Stalker?" said Jes.

She nodded. "That might be, of course. But they knew how to create the Orders; they must have written something down. A Raven shouldn't need much. There was a library."

"Rongier the Librarian," said Jes.

She nodded. "Tell your mother this, too; if Tier loses his Order, it will destroy him. His body won't die, not if there's folk to care for it, but the Order will take Tier with it. Leaving nothing. Nothing. If that happens, you'd best take care of it, Hunter. Your father will be dead, his body should be as well."

She closed her blind eyes again and patted Lehr's hand. "There now," she said. "I've had my part in this. I can leave the problem of the Shadowed to those more fit." Her breath caught as if it hurt her. "There's a bag in my *karis*. Give it to your mother, she'll know what it is and what to do with it."

"Shh," Lehr said. "Rest."

Instead her left hand closed over his. "Jes," she said, holding out her free hand. "Come here, and take my hand. Now listen you both." But she didn't say anything, just sent her magic through him like a flame that warmed almost to the point of pain, but not quite. From Jes's startled expression she was doing the same to him.

"Safe now," she said at last, panting a little. "The plague cannot kill you or pass from you to anyone else. Best I could do. When you leave. Close the gates. Two weeks before this town will be safe to enter. Make certain. Keep people out."

"I remember how," Lehr promised. "I can keep people out for two weeks."

"Careful."

"Always, grandmother," he said.

She squeezed his hand, but didn't speak again. After a moment he felt her relax into sleep.

Jes cleaned out the *karis* while Lehr held the old woman. He found fresh bedding from somewhere—Lehr didn't ask where. Then Lehr put her in her *karis* and sat with her.

Jes put a hand on his shoulder, then left them.

When the light headed toward evening, Lehr bestirred himself to look after Cornsilk, but he found her unsaddled, brushed, and fed in a smallish corral that had, from the height of the fences, served to keep goats rather than horses. Jes was nowhere to be seen, so Lehr went back to Brewydd.

She had saved him when he'd been wounded to the soul.

He'd killed men. He snuck up on them under the cover of night and sliced their throats from behind before they had even known he was there. He'd killed them coldly, planning out each of his moves ahead of time. No honest, fair fight because he could not afford it at the price of his mother's life.

Brewydd had taken him under her wing afterward and taught him about being Hunter and human—and he was almost certain she'd practiced some of her healing art on his soul. Under her overbearing manner and sharp tongue lurked a soft heart.

"Here," Jes said.

Lehr looked up and took the dry flatbread Jes handed him. It was from their packs, not from this town. Lehr took a small bite and swallowed. "Where have you been?"

"Checking for the living," Jes said, his gaze sliding away from Lehr's. "We couldn't leave anyone. But everything is dead here. Human and animal."

"I won't leave her here," Lehr said. He didn't say that she was dying or that moving her would be senselessly cruel. Jes would know.

"I'll wait with you," said his brother, and sat down on the ground to do so.

She didn't awake again, but drifted off sometime in the night while Lehr was dozing.

Jes found a shovel and helped Lehr dig a proper grave near the maple tree. He buried her wrapped tightly in the bedclothes.

Jes stood beside him when he was finished. "Somewhere," he said, "a new lark flies." He squeezed the back of Lehr's neck with gentle affection, though he released him quickly. "We need to leave before others come."

Lehr saddled Cornsilk and walked beside her and Jes until they came to the gates. Then he sent Jes out with the mare while he shut the gates and barred them. Climbing over the top from the town side was easier than from the outside, and he dropped to the ground near Jes.

He put both hands against the wall and did the easy part first. Walls are built to keep people out, and he reinforced that with power. No one would be able to get over them or through them until the energy he left here wore away. That would probably take a month or more, he thought. Those walls had been stoutly built: they wanted to keep people out.

The gate was more difficult. By the time he finished, both the mare and Jes were getting impatient.

"At least there's only the one gate," Lehr said, when he was finally satisfied. The wall had shown him that much.

"Walls and gates," said Jes. "Why, Falcon?"

"Because Hunters set traps." Interpreting Jes's aborted speech without much trouble, Lehr climbed tiredly into the saddle. He patted an apology on Cornsilk's neck for his awkward mount. "Brewydd told me that fences, walls, doors, locks, and gates listen to me because they keep things in, so they fall under my Order."

"Hunters trap or cage their prey," said Jes thoughtfully.

Lehr set Cornsilk on the trail toward home and concentrated on staying on. He'd not slept much last night, and the magic he'd worked had drained him.

"The bag," he said suddenly worried. "Did you get the bag Brewydd wanted us to give mother?"

"Yes," Jes said. "It holds *mermori*. Rongier the Librarian's and the others that Benroln had. There were five of them. Mother won't be happy. She already has too many of them."

The sun was warm, and Lehr found himself fighting to keep his eyes open. His eyelids burned, and his throat hurt.

"Go ahead and doze," said the Guardian at Cornsilk's shoulder. "Jes and I'll keep you safe. There's nothing more you have to do."

"I'm sick," said Lehr in surprise.

"Yes," said the Guardian. "Rest."

CHAPTER 10

"You should have gone out fishing with the children,"
Tier observed mildly, without looking up from his carving.

That of the "children"—Hennea, Phoran, his guardsmen,
and Rinnie—only Rinnie really still qualified—didn't make
them any less his children, Seraph knew. Everyone Tier cared
about, he took under his wing, up to and including Ciro, who
was a contemporary of Tier's grandfather.

"You're as anxious as I am," she told him, turning to pace
the other direction. "That's the only time you ever carve."

Tier held up the unrecognizable object he'd spent the better part of the morning shaping with his knife. "Obviously a
good decision on my part," he said.

Seraph sat down next to him on the porch bench and rested
her head against his arm. She sighed. "It has two eyes, but the
right one is too big and a little lower than the other."

"That's the mouth," he said. He set the carving on his lap
and ruffled her hair. "They should have been back by now—
even if they were bringing the whole clan here."

"According to the map," she reminded him. "None of us
have ever been that way. Maps are unreliable."

They'd had several variations of this conversation over the
past week. This was the second one that morning, and it was

her turn to point out the harmless things that might have delayed the boys—at least, she assumed Jes had gone off with Lehr.

At their feet, Gura lifted his head and turned his head to look at the trail that Lehr had taken away from the house. Seraph felt Tier's pulse speed up to match hers, but then Gura flopped over on his back to expose his belly to the late-morning sun.

Tier sighed. "At least Hennea took everyone else, so Phoran's not pacing the floor, too. For a man with a reputation as a lazy womanizer, he sure doesn't sit still for long. I thought the two of you were going to start colliding."

"When he's still, he manages to look as though he'll never move again," Seraph said.

Tier laughed. "I'll grant you—"

Gura rolled to his feet and gave a soft woof, staring at the trail. Seraph looked with him, but couldn't see very far down the trail because it curved back and forth up the forested hillside.

Tier set his carving aside and walked to the end of the porch. He put his hand up to shadow his eyes as if that would improve his chances of seeing around corners. Gura's tail began to wag.

"It's the boys," said Seraph.

"Or the others returning from fishing by a roundabout way." Despite the laconic words, Seraph heard the eagerness in her husband's voice.

Gura's tail wagging doubled in speed, and he let out a series of thunderous barks.

"Go get them," said Tier.

Gura didn't wait for a second invitation before he took off up the trail as fast as he could run. Tier gave Seraph a wide, relieved grin and waited for the boys to appear around the corner.

But they didn't.

"Too long," said Tier, echoing Seraph's thoughts.

"Go ahead," she said.

He leapt off the porch with much the same speed as Gura had exhibited, and ran up the trail with the wolfish gait that she'd seen him use to eat up miles in the woods. There was no sign of his limp, and she hoped he'd been truthful about how much better his knees were doing. Knees or no, he'd not stop running until he found them.

Seraph went into the house and got out the bread she'd baked last night and began to slice and butter it. The boys would be hungry; her boys were always hungry.

They would be fine. She repeated it to herself like a mantra.

The front door opened at last, and instead of the cool greeting she'd composed to cover her pleasure, Seraph said, "Lay him on the bed. Did you carry him all the way down the hill?"

She stripped Lehr's bedding down so her grim-faced, sweat-drenched husband could lay their son in his bed.

"No, the horse did that," Tier said as he helped her strip boots and dirty clothing off Lehr, who didn't even twitch. "Jes is out tending the mare."

When they were through, Tier helped Seraph tug the bedding around Lehr.

"I'll go out and finish taking care of the horse," Tier said. "Jes doesn't look much better than Lehr—though he's still on his feet—but he wouldn't leave that damned mare to wait on me."

"Someone taught him to be stubborn," Seraph said coolly.

Tier grinned at her tiredly and touched her cheek. "They're all right, Empress," he told her. "Worn-out, not hurt. Relax."

Seraph waited until Jes finished the stew and bread she'd warmed for him before she folded her arms, and said, "Tell me."

Jes smiled faintly in her direction, the expression making him look even more exhausted. It made her feel guilty for pushing him. Guilt always made her angry. Even when she had no cause. She raised her eyebrows.

"Don't know where to start," he said, the smile dying more quickly than it had come. "Rongier's clan is dead. So is the town of Colbern. Lehr sealed the walls so that no one will go in there until it's safe again."

Seraph sat down, careful to keep her back straight and her face controlled. Control was important.

"You found the entire city dead?" asked Tier. "Of plague? There aren't many diseases that will kill that many."

Lehr groaned from the bed, then sat up. "Gods take it," he swore—a common Rederni oath, though Seraph had never heard him use it. "If I let Jes tell it, you'll never figure out what happened—but when I'm finished I get to go back to sleep."

He sat up cross-legged, put his elbows on his knees, and rested his head on his hands as if it ached. "Jes showed up before I was a full day out. We followed the map, and it was a shortcut to Colbern."

In concise, tired sentences Lehr described what they had found. Seraph listened without interrupting as he told them about Brewydd and shadow plague.

"I think she thought she'd made us immune to it," Lehr mumbled. "But we caught it right enough, both Jes and I. I don't know why we didn't die like everyone else."

"The Guardian thinks that Brewydd saved us," added Jes. "I'm not a healer, but I could drive the shadow away—he says that if—if it were buried in illness, I wouldn't have been able to do it. So we got shadow-sick, but not the actual illness that the Shadowed used to carry the taint." He took a bag off his belt and handed it to Seraph. "Brewydd told me to give you this."

She could feel them though the leather of the bag. *Mermori*. Each one standing for death and more death. Benroln had had five, he'd said.

"Both of you go to sleep, now," said Tier, his eyes on her face. "Your mother and I are going for a walk. Lehr, do you want food? Jes has put enough food away for any four men. You have to be hungry."

Lehr shook his head, once, very firmly, rolled back flat, and pulled his bedding over his head.

Seraph left the bag on the table when she got up to go to the door. It wouldn't matter. If she threw them in the sea, they would still come back to her. She couldn't escape them. The symbols of her dying people and of her guilt.

Seraph let her grief-fed anger power her strides as she walked up the steep path that the boys had ridden down. As she walked, she remembered the faces of the people of Rongier's clan. They were all dead, as her own clan was dead. As Tier would be dead. All her fault.

Control, she thought.

It was dangerous to be angry when you were a Raven. Ravens don't cry. Tears don't solve anything. Angrily, she wiped her eyes.

She was aware that Tier followed behind her, letting her set the pace, letting her keep a little distance between them.

If we hadn't been in such a hurry to get home, she thought. *If we'd gone with Benroln, then there would have been Jes and Lehr to see the shadow and Hennea and me to help fight it.* A Traveler shouldn't have a home—it was just one more distraction from their job of fighting the Stalker and his minions.

"What's done is gone, lass," said Tier. She didn't know if she'd spoken her thoughts out loud, or if he just knew what she was thinking. "Your clan had Raven and Eagle and assorted other Orders, and no one was able to stop the plague that killed them. If we'd gone with Benroln, like as not, we'd only have died, too. Of all the people in the city, Brewydd managed only to save our sons. If I die from this problem with my Order, that won't be your fault either. You didn't put the spells on me—the Path's wizards did."

Seraph stopped. The thought of Tier's possible danger had put an odd icy calm between her and her anger. It was soothing to feel nothing.

"You're right," she said. "The plagues that killed my clan and so many others—and allowed the Path to sew its minions amongst the Septs like poison weeds—it was all shadow-driven. The Shadowed is . . . *has* destroyed my people apurpose. Is trying to destroy you."

Pain flared through her as she spoke the last sentence.

A pain that was buried behind ice, she reminded herself swiftly. She didn't feel anything now. She was Raven. She was in control.

"That's how I see it," Tier said, his voice wary.

The tone surprised her: she was calm now, why was he worried? She turned but before her eyes fell upon him there was a loud crackling pop beside her.

A rock on the trail beside her exploded into powder. Bits sliced by her, leaving small cuts in her Rederni skirts and the skin within them. Had she done that? The shock of it broke through the ice.

"Emotion and magic don't mix," said Tier softly, taking her hand. "Burying the anger and grief just makes it worse— haven't you learned that much from Jes?"

She closed her eyes. "I can't be angry. I can't grieve. I can't—" She bit her lip. "Whining doesn't seem to help either."

Hard arms closed around her and surrounded her with his scent and his warmth. "Let me help," he said. "And I'll let you help me, too."

He led her off the trail and through the trees to a small clearing with a small creek, soft grass, and shade. In that small private place he took her anger and his own, turning it to something else with touch and soft murmured words—something warm and alive and triumphant.

Afterward, naked, breathless, sweaty, and temporarily at peace, Seraph said, "We are going to Colossae to find the wizards' great library. Brewydd thought that was the advice she'd stayed alive to give us—such things have their own power. We'll find what we need to fix what the Path has done to you. We'll find the means to combat this new Shadowed. Then we'll destroy him so that he will cause no more harm."

She didn't tell him they didn't know where Colossae was. She didn't tell him that even if they managed to find the library, it was unlikely either she or Hennea would be able to find what they needed or even read it if they did. She didn't tell him that even if they found everything Brewydd had told Lehr they might find, the chances that she could help Tier with it were poor. She didn't tell him a Shadowed who had lived almost two centuries was unlikely to be easily dealt with. She didn't have to—he already knew.

"All right," said Tier, his voice a comforting rumble under her ear. "Where do we start?"

Jes was sitting on the bench on the porch when she and Tier returned. Although his face was still grey and drawn, he all but vibrated with repressed energy.

"They're all here," he said. "Hennea, Phoran, and his guardsmen. Lehr woke up long enough to tell them about Colbern and Benroln's clan, but he went back to sleep."

"Are you all right?" Tier asked. "Are you getting sick?"

Jes shook his head. "Lehr got it first, and the Guardian cleaned the shadow from me when he cared for Lehr. Just tired. Too many people inside."

"You can stay outside," Seraph told him. "Brewydd told us we needed to find Colossae, so we're going to get out those maps and see if we can figure out where it is."

"I'll come in," he said. "The Guardian sometimes knows things that I don't."

Seraph opened the case and, with the help of a dozen rocks to weigh down the corners, laid the maps out on the table where everyone could see them.

Brewydd had told the boys that they needed to find Colossae if they wanted to save Tier and Phoran, though she hadn't been certain just what it was in the city that would help them.

Looking at the maps, Seraph was less optimistic than she had been. Other than the city map, there were four maps that had Colossae on them in the satchel Rinnie had found. Three of them were normal-looking, but the fourth was covered with so many lines it was hard to tell what was road and what was city. Even on the maps that were easily read, the roads and landmarks were a thousand years out-of-date.

Tier surveyed his troops.

"Between all of us," he told them, "we've ridden over most of the Empire. We're going to study these maps and see if anyone finds something familiar."

Jes sat down next to Hennea, but rose almost immediately to pace behind Hennea's side of the table until Rinnie recruited him to help her make dinner. She gave him a few things to do, but when he leaned against the wall and closed his eyes, she let him be. *Good girl,* thought Seraph.

Lehr had retreated to the loft, and not even the noise of all the people in the room below him seemed to disturb his slumber.

Phoran and his men argued quietly over the resemblance of a hill near Taela though nothing else on the map seemed to fit.

Hennea, who had spent much of the last week searching through these maps, was composed and silent, much like Seraph herself, but Jes hadn't been able to stay near her. Seraph wondered if the death of Benroln's clan made her angry, too.

Rinnie, who knew the Travelers only from stories, kept her eye on the boys while she cooked. She'd just gotten her brothers back and wasn't going to chance losing them again.

Seraph turned her attention to the map Tier had. After a while, with a few glances at the other maps, she picked out the slightly thicker lines that were the roads.

"Maybe if we used Willon's map," said Tier. "It doesn't have the whole of the Empire, but it covers a good two-thirds. And it's mostly accurate as far as we've used it."

"What if this city isn't in the Empire?" asked Rufort, the older of Phoran's two guards.

He was, perhaps, a year younger than Jes, and nearly as big as Toarsen's comrade Kissel. Like Kissel, he gave the impression of a life hard-lived, but Seraph could see why Tier liked him so much.

There was something solid about Rufort, as if he were a person who, once having given his word, would keep it at considerable cost to himself. This past week, he'd turned a willing hand to any of the farm chores Tier had give him.

"Tradition places Colossae in the Empire," said Hennea, without looking up from her map. "Unfortunately, there's at least a six-century gap between the time when the Elder Wizards left the city and the founding of the Empire, so we can't count on that."

The younger guard, Ielian, looked at the maps and shook his head. "What is this supposed to accomplish? Phoran came to you for *help*. Not to be dragged around the Empire on a seek-and-find game looking for a city that might never have existed. You don't even know that there is still a city—or ever was one for that matter. It is just a story on the tongues of a couple of women." He didn't add the adjective *silly* to *women*, but it was in his voice.

His eye caught Seraph's, and he saw what she thought of his disparagement. Instead of backing down, he just got angrier. Since Seraph always did the same thing when she said something stupid, she had a certain amount of sympathy for him.

"I thought we were waiting for the healer—" He aimed his accusation at Seraph. "But now your son says she is dead. If we do find Colossae, I suppose you will want us all to go there. But how does that help us kill this Shadowed, who needs to die to free the Emperor from your *Traveler's* curse?"

He knew a little more about Phoran's problem than Phoran had thought—or maybe Phoran had explained it to Ielian and Rufort sometime this week.

"It's not a Traveler's curse," Seraph told him in an almost-gentle voice. "I could demonstrate the difference for you if you'd like."

"Behave, Seraph," Tier said, and she was certain she was the only one who heard the amusement in his voice. He didn't think she was serious. Perhaps he was right.

"Ielian has reason for his worries." Tier pushed his stool a little back from the table so he could see Seraph and Ielian at the same time—like a referee at one of the Harvest festival wrestling matches. "He doesn't know Brewydd or Traveler magic, and we haven't taken the time to *explain* them."

Seraph tapped her foot, but Tier had a point. She just wasn't used to justifying herself—or being referred to as "silly" even if only by implication.

"Fine," she said. "First, the city exists beyond the legends. I am Raven, Ielian, and one of the things I can do is touch an item and get a feel for its history."

Behind Ielian, Phoran was watching her with vague eyes. She'd been learning that the expression really meant he was thinking very hard.

"When we found these maps—"

"*I* found the maps—" said Rinnie, who was efficiently chopping up greens.

"When Rinnie found the maps," Seraph corrected herself, "I read them with my magic and found these maps are from the time of Colossae. Moreover, that around two centuries ago a wizard held the city map in his hands as he stood outside the gates of Colossae. That is not legend, or women's stories. My own magic told me this."

"The city exists," agreed Phoran, leaning his elbows on the table and bracing his chin on his folded hands.

"Maybe it's near here," said Rinnie. "That could be the reason that the Path built its temple here."

"Volis told me that it was because of Shadow's Fall," Hennea said.

"He told me that, too," Seraph agreed.

"Fine," said Ielian, throwing up his hands. "The city exists. How is finding the city going to help the Emperor?"

Seraph wondered if he realized that Jes had unobtrusively moved until he was leaning against the wall just behind Ielian.

"I don't know. But if Brewydd, Lark of the Clan of Rongier the Librarian, tells me if we don't go to Colossae, Phoran will lose not only his throne, but his head as well—then I will go to Colossae. If something in Colossae can help us rid this world of the Shadowed, then I will go to Colossae."

"On the word of this bird woman?"

"Lark," said Seraph, biting off the ends of her words. "A healer who dedicated her life trying to save people in need. She died to save the people who killed her."

Hennea's sharp "Control, Raven" and Tier's "Easy, love" came one atop the other, followed by a thump as the heavy slab table lifted a handspan off the floor, then slammed down hard enough to vibrate the floorboards.

Seraph took a deep breath and fought to calm herself.

Ielian's next question was considerably more respectful. "Finding the city is the easiest way to discover who this shadow-man is?"

"He's not a man, not anymore," Hennea told him. "No wizard who drinks at the Stalker's well stays human for long."

"Mother, did the wizard have to go to Colossae to become Shadowed?" said Jes suddenly, and Ielian jerked—answering Seraph's questions about whether or not he'd noticed her son creeping up behind him.

"I don't know." Seraph was grateful to him for asking the question, though. This wasn't a subject likely to stretch her ability to control her temper. "I've learned a lot this summer from working with Hennea and Brewydd. They knew different things than I did—but some of the information we shared was contradictory. There are things we just don't know and others we disagreed on. A lot of Travelers believe that the Unnamed King was the Stalker of our oldest stories."

"Only stupid Travelers," murmured Hennea.

Seraph continued blandly, "I can tell you my grandfather was certain that the Unnamed King had never walked the stones of Colossae—something supposedly passed down Isolde's line, on my grandfather's mother's side, all the way from Kerine, who fought at Red Ernave's side at Shadow's Fall."

Ielian made a disbelieving sound.

"Ielian." Phoran's command was quiet, but Ielian nodded and subsided.

Seraph shrugged. "It doesn't matter what you believe, Ielian. Phoran came to us for help, and we'll do whatever we can for him. I believe finding Colossae is the best thing that we can do, both for Phoran and for my husband. I believe it because that's what an old, dying woman told my son." She looked at Phoran and softened. Ielian was doing his duty and trying to protect Phoran. She was glad that his men were that loyal.

"What I can tell you, Ielian," she said, "is that we will do our best to find the Shadowed and kill him or die trying."

Something, maybe the truth in her last statement, at last satisfied Ielian.

"All right," he said. "All right."

"Is Willon's map still in the packs you boys took?" Tier asked Jes, breaking the small silence.

Jes bestirred himself and went to his still-full pack and unearthed the map, set it on the table, and retreated to a wall nearer Rinnie than the people crowded around the table.

"Can't you go sleep, Jes?" Rinnie asked, not for the first time. "I can make dinner by myself." She tactfully refrained from pointing out that he was getting in her way more than he was helping.

"Go use our bed, son," said Tier, an invitation that held the force of an order. "There's room next to Lehr. If you can't sleep, you can at least lie down for a while."

Jes stiffened. "There are too many people here. I can't sleep with everyone awake."

That was probably true as well; Seraph looked thoughtfully at her son. "Would it be easier outside?" she asked. "Or does the sun bother you?"

Jes shook his head. She could tell he was feeling bad because his gaze carefully avoided touching anyone in the room.

"He's too tired," Hennea said suddenly. "If he goes to sleep, he'll sleep too deeply. He can't protect himself in the forest, and the Guardian won't allow him to try." She pushed aside the map she'd been looking at and continued briskly. "But he'll allow me to stand guard."

"Yes," said Jes, very softly.

"Get a blanket or two then, Jes." Hennea stood up and cast a sharp look at Tier, then Seraph—perhaps waiting for them to object.

Seraph thought a walk in the woods might do Hennea as much good as it had earlier done for Seraph. She'd noticed that the collected expression on Hennea's face was beginning to fail her. She needed someplace private to grieve for Benroln's clan—and Jes needed rest.

"I'm not doing any good here," Hennea told Seraph, almost angrily. "Whoever drew these maps knew less about mapmaking than I do. They don't even agree with each other."

"We'll keep working on it while you're gone," said Seraph steadily. In the Traveler tongue, she added. "I entrust my son to your keeping, Raven."

A wild spectrum of emotion flashed over Hennea's face. "You trust too much," she said in the same tongue.

"I don't think so."

Tier opened the door for them. "Jes?"

Their son turned, so obviously operating on the last of his reserves of strength that Seraph had to fight the need to go to him. Her touch would only hurt him, though, so she stayed where she was.

"Thank you for going with Lehr to Colbern, son," Tier said. "If you had not been there, he would have died."

Jes clutched his blankets a little tighter and nodded.

Hennea let Jes choose his own path, and walked far enough behind him there was no chance of accidentally touching him. He was too tired to deal with her lack of control.

Time was such an odd thing. One moment you could talk to someone, then, suddenly, they were gone. Somehow it always seemed to her that there ought to be a way to turn back time and change the events. An hour, a minute, they were so simple in passing . . . reversing them should not be impossible. But she'd never found a way to do it.

Another clan was dead. More people that she had known and would never see again. She felt . . . empty.

Jes was silent as he walked. With his shambling gait, he should have been stumbling all over, but somehow his foot always seemed to land on the other side of fallen debris, rocks, or holes.

Hennea kept quiet as well. She didn't know if she could have spoken to him if she'd tried.

She understood what Seraph had just done, though she rather suspected neither Jes nor Tier knew Seraph had chosen the last words of a Traveler marriage ceremony. The ceremony where parents turned the care of their son to his spouse.

Hennea didn't want to think about it, or about death, or the Shadowed.

She tilted her face into the sun and let her mind go blank, as if there were nothing more than this moment: the sun in her face, the smell of trees and grasses, the sound of birds and insects, and the sense that told her where Jes was that had nothing more to do with magic than the power of the ties between a woman and her man.

He stopped on a gentle slope covered in yellowing grasses that looked no different to her eyes than several other places he'd passed without a pause. He shook one blanket out, handed her the other, then lay down on his face, leaving his back to absorb the late-afternoon, summer sun.

Rather than shaking her blanket out, she folded it and set it on an unoccupied corner of his. Sitting on its soft folds, she pulled her legs up to her chest and settled her chin on her knees, prepared to watch over him while he slept.

"I remember when Papa used to have nightmares almost every night."

Jes's voice was so soft it could almost have been the breeze that rustled the leaves on the trees.

Hennea didn't say anything.

"He still has them, from his time as a soldier, I think. Though maybe some of them now are from being a prisoner of the Path."

"I'll watch over your dreams." Hennea almost touched his shoulder, which was so close she could feel the warmth of his body. "I'll wake you before they get too bad."

"Thank you," he said, and slept.

Sitting in the sun, trying to think of nothing, Hennea instead thought about what Seraph had said about all the strange coincidences that had shaped her family's life.

It had angered Seraph, the thought of someone meddling in her life, someone she had no control over. But Hennea found it to be a curiously uplifting thought. If there was such evil in the world, was it possible that there was good, too?

The gods are dead, she reminded herself fiercely. But she couldn't, quite, kill the hope that Seraph had given her.

After an hour or so, Jes began to stir restlessly. She'd been avoiding watching him sleep, because some people could feel when they were watched—and, given Jes's abilities, she assumed that he belonged to that group. But a soft sound drew her eyes, and she watched the subtle motions of muscle in his face, searching for a clue to his dreams. Slowly his face hardened into that otherness that told her the Guardian had come. She'd never seen that happen to an Eagle while he slept before.

"Jes," she said softly. "Guardian, wake up. You're dreaming."

He rolled so fast she almost hit him by reflex. Two arms, strong and hard wrapped around her hips so tightly she knew she'd have bruises tomorrow. His head burrowed against her midriff, and the rest of him curled around her.

"Shh." She touched his hair lightly, but then decided if her touch were bothering him, he wouldn't have wrapped himself as close as he could get, and she let fingers sink through the dark strands in a caress. "Can you talk about it?"

He shook his head firmly.

She leaned over him and put her arms around him as best she could, given the awkwardness of moving while he was still wrapped around her middle.

"Shh," she said. "It's all right."

"He remembers," said Jes hesitantly after a while. He'd relaxed somewhat, and she'd thought he was sleeping again.

"What does he remember?" she whispered.

Jes shook his head. "I don't know, but it frightens him."

Phoran watched Jes and Hennea leave the house. He knew that something had happened, but, not speaking the Traveler tongue himself, he wasn't certain what. Later he could ask

Toarsen, who like quite a few of the former Passerines could speak a little Traveler.

For some reason, he thought, as he turned back to the map in front of him, he'd expected Tier to solve his problem overnight. Instead, he'd spent the better part of a week working on the farm. He suspected many of the tasks Tier had given him were merely to keep him busy—but not all of them. Survival, he'd discovered this week, took time and effort even when you weren't the Emperor. A farmer didn't have to worry about assassinations and political maneuvers, but Phoran found cutting wood, gardening, and washing required as much time and effort.

Toarsen hadn't been best pleased when Seraph sent them all to weed the kitchen garden—Phoran savored the memory of the expression on his captain's face—but since Phoran had gone out without a murmur, Toarsen had to do the same.

Now, he thought wryly, when Rinnie had had to show them all what to do—her eyes wide at the thought of someone who couldn't tell the difference between dill and reaverslace—*that* had stung Phoran's pride. But she hadn't laughed at them—at least not openly—and the memory of Toarsen's face had kept Phoran's sense of humor stronger than his sense of pride. Kissel hadn't needed supervision: he said his family's cook had taught him how to garden when he was a boy.

He'd learned a lot; but when Lehr and Jes returned, somewhere in his heart of hearts, Phoran had expected his trials to be over.

Lehr should have come back with the old healer in tow. She'd take one look at Phoran and give him a mysterious potion or tell him to turn around three times while wailing some unpronounceable word—like half the doctors in Taela. The Memory would leave him, and he could race home to rule in peace. He smiled to himself. At least until someone decided on a more effective method of assassination sometime when he wasn't guarded by his men. His men.

He cast a quick glance at Ielian. The man had surprised him with his passionate attack on Seraph as Phoran's advocate.

It seemed that the Emperor's total number of loyal followers was growing. At this rate, in ten years they might number over—say—twenty. Phoran was amused at himself for the pleasure he found in knowing that Ielian, at least, served him out of something more than desire for gainful employment.

He turned his attention back to the map, but it looked the same as it had earlier. Sighing, he gave up. "If you have a sheet of paper, I'll start making lists of places this might be. There's nothing unusual about the placement of the roads. Maybe Master Willon will have more maps we can use for comparison."

"I'll do it, Mother," said Rinnie as she wiped her hands clean on a rough cloth.

She rummaged around, then set a sheet of paper, an ink pot and a well-trimmed pen beside him with a smile—she'd been shy of him at first. That day in the garden, though, had robbed her of any awe she might once have felt.

"Good idea," agreed Tier. "We might see if Willon will take a look at these maps, himself, if we don't come up with anything. He's had more than half a century running all over the Empire. Maybe he'll see something that we've missed."

"Dinner will be done soon," Rinnie announced.

"As long as you used dill instead of reaverslace, we'll not flog the cook." Phoran started scratching out place names. He wished that at least one of the maps had some kind of scale so he knew whether he was looking at ten-leagues mapped in great detail or a hundred leagues.

"If it's reaverslace, it's because someone weeded out the dill," returned Rinnie complacently. "*You* can try it first. If you don't go into convulsions, the rest of us will eat."

"Threatening your emperor is treason." Phoran scratched out a place he'd written because it was too near the coast. If Colossae had been that near the sea, certainly one of the maps would have shown it. "Kissel, should we string this girl up?"

"Not until she finishes our dinner," rumbled Kissel. "I'll even eat reaperslace if it tastes as good as that fish smells."

Tier stood up and stretched. "I'll bring some water for washing to the porch," he said. He took a step away from the table, glanced back at his map—the one covered in fine lines that seemed to be meaningless—and he froze.

"Seraph, can you hold that map up?" he said.

Phoran looked at Tier's map as Seraph pulled it from the table, but it hadn't changed. It still looked as though someone had, very carefully, drawn hundreds of meaningless lines all over the parchment.

It was big and had been in a roll for a long time and kept trying to curl up. Phoran got up and helped Seraph hold it flat while Tier took slow steps away from it without taking his eyes off whatever had caught his attention.

"Lehr?" he said. "Son, I need you to get up and help me a minute."

Lehr groaned and muttered something that sounded rude to Phoran, but he rolled out of the bed in the loft and dropped to the main floor without bothering with the ladder. Staggering across the room, he stood next to his father and rubbed his eyes.

"Look at that map," Tier said. "Tell me what you see."

"Lines," said Lehr grumpily. "What am I suppose to . . ." He frowned, coming to alertness just as Tier had.

"It's the distance that helped me see what it was," Tier explained.

He walked over to the map and put his finger on the lower left-hand corner. "The lines are elevations," he said. "I bet they used to be different colors, but age turned them all dark."

"What do you see?" asked Phoran. "Can you tell where it is?"

"It's here," said Tier simply. "Not Colossae," he brushed his hand over the star that marked the wizards' city. He dropped his hand until he pointed to the lower left-hand corner again. "Right here, this is Redern Mountain and the Silver River. Here's our valley." He ran his hand up to a section about the size of his palm that had a single thick line running through the middle of it, but none of the thinner lines. "This must be . . ."

"Shadow's Fall," said Lehr. "If the distances are right for Redern and this valley, then that's right where Shadow's Fall would be."

Tier let his finger follow the line that bisected the flat plain of the battlefield. It connected to a second road, then took an abrupt turn north. About a finger length from Shadow's Fall, Tier's finger stopped and rested on the strange symbols that Hennea told them represented the ancient wizards' city of Colossae.

"I can take us there," he said.

CHAPTER 11

"You want journey bread?" Alinath came out of the
baking room, her face tight with dismay after overhearing
Tier's request to her husband, Bandor.

Seraph took a step back and let Tier deal with his sister.

Tier picked up a piece of bread left out as a sample and
tried it. "I'll need it as soon as you can. You know, Bandor, if
you put a bit less salt in this bread"—he motioned to the plate
of sample offered—"it would allow some of the other flavors
to come out."

"I'll try that," Bandor said. "Does the journey bread have
anything to do with your guests?"

Tier nodded easily, but Seraph could feel his arm tense under her hand. "Who told you about them?"

Five strangers were a hard secret to keep, but they hadn't
told anyone about them, and no one had been to the farm since
Phoran and his men had shown up.

"Apparently some youngsters—who should have work to
keep themselves busy—were out that way a week or so ago
and came back into town spouting nonsense," said Alinath.

"Spying on us, are they?" Tier grinned, and Seraph could
tell that he was honestly amused. "I hope they saw something
more interesting than our guests."

"They said they were nobles," Bandor said. "And one of them the Sept's own brother. We had the tale from the steward, who was convinced you are after his job."

"Gods save me," exclaimed Tier with honest horror. "What idiot would want that job?"

"Exactly," said Alinath with satisfaction. "And so I told the steward when he came whining to me."

"Toarsen, the Sept's brother, *is* there with a group of bored young noblemen whom Tier met in Taela," said Seraph, having found a story that might satisfy some of the curious. "They had nothing to do, and knew Tier would come here too late for planting. They've asked him to take them hunting in the mountains."

"You can't take the Sept's brother up there," said Alinath, horrified. "If something happens to him, the Sept will—"

"It's all right," said Seraph. "We're all going. I doubt there will be trouble with all of us there."

Alinath stopped fussing and frowned thoughtfully at Seraph. "Very well," she said slowly. "Two dozen dozen loaves of journey bread. It'll be ready the day after tomorrow—I've put all the breadmother up for today." She gave Seraph a sudden conspiratorial smile. "And any who ask, I'll tell them about the nobles who are paying my brother's family for an adventure up in the mountains. Only you'd better make it somewhere more interesting—like Shadow's Fall. Bored young boys might very well be stupid enough to ride from Taela to have Tier take them to Shadow's Fall. They'd have the money to tempt anyone, too. I can take Rinnie, if you'd like."

"No," said Tier instinctively, and Seraph smiled to herself—then at Tier when he looked at her with second thoughts in his face. *Is it fair to take her?*

"She'll be as safe with us as she would be here with Alinath," Seraph said. "I think if we try to leave Rinnie again, she'll just follow us."

"Besides," said Tier, relaxing a little, "the summer's getting old. Up high it's possible we could run into early snow. A Cormorant might be a very useful thing to have."

Bandor patted his wife on the back. "She'll have a story to tell her children, if that's where you're going. I'd like to see Shadow's Fall once before I die."

"I'll take you there," agreed Tier. "But I've only been once myself. It's not easy to get to—and it is not a comfortable place to be. If you're serious, though, I'll take you next summer after the crops are in."

They left the bakery with a sweet roll each.

Seraph hummed her pleasure at the sticky, warm bread.

"See," Tier said. "If you'd been nicer to my sister all these years, you'd have had a sweet roll every time you came to the bakery."

"Liar," she told him cheerfully. "Until I saved her husband, it didn't matter how nice I was to her—she was convinced I used magic to steal away her big brother."

As they wandered up the road to Willon's, Tier grew more serious. "I don't like it that those boys were out by our farm, Seraph. It was Storne and his lot, I suppose. He used to be such a nice boy before he took up with Olbeck."

"They're not boys anymore," Seraph said. "They're Lehr's age—Olbeck's older than that. If the Path had taken over here, doubtless they'd have recruited those boys as Passerines."

Rinnie went out to find some tingleroot for the trip. Whatever she found this late in the year was likely to be woody and weak, but it was better than none at all—which is what they had.

Lehr was still looking thin and pale, and he was sleeping too much. Jes hadn't returned with Hennea yesterday. He was out walking, she'd said.

So Rinnie slipped out of the house while Lehr was napping and Hennea was brooding over the maps again. She hushed Gura with a stern command. She thought about taking him with her, but he didn't always listen to her when he was excited the way he listened to the boys and her mother. She didn't want to spend the day out chasing after him if he found a rabbit, so she commanded him to stay on the porch and started across the fields.

Phoran and his men were seated on the ground in front of the barn, playing some sort of game that seemed to involve a lot of laughter and wild grabbing for bone-dice. But when she walked past them, Phoran stood up and motioned his men to stay where they were.

"Rinnie Seraphsdaughter, where are you going in such a hurry?" he asked courteously.

She liked it that he never treated her like a ten-year-old brat (which was what Lehr called her in moments of extreme provocation).

"I'm hunting some tingleroot," she told him without slowing her pace. "We've run out."

"And this tingleroot is important?" he asked, rolling his tongue around the herb's name.

Really, she thought, *an emperor shouldn't be so appallingly ignorant.* Then she was horrified and embarrassed when he laughed because she hadn't hidden her thoughts better.

"It's for packing in wounds," she said quickly. "It helps keep infection out. Mother makes an eyewash with it for smoke irritation, too."

"My eyes are delicate," he said, batting his eyelashes at her. "By all means let us go fetch this *tingleroot.*"

"It gets its name because it makes your tongue tingle, then go numb if you chew it," she told him. "You really don't have to come. I know the way."

"If Jes or your parents were here, would you be off alone?" Phoran asked.

"It's perfectly safe," she said, miffed that he'd think she wasn't capable of gathering herbs on her own.

"I should hope so. I wouldn't go with you else." He glanced back at the barn. "I'd send Kissel, surely. He's ugly enough to frighten anything away. Or Toarsen, he's just mean."

"Toarsen's not mean," she said, then realized he was teasing.

"No." Phoran agreed. "Toarsen's not mean—but don't tell him I told you so."

She laughed. "All right, come on then."

Rinnie was one of Phoran's favorite things about Redern. Children weren't something he had much experience with, and never having had a childhood himself, he was fascinated by her.

For one thing, she was competent, with skills that many a grown woman in Taela would envy. She could cook, sew—and weed gardens. She knew how to work and how to play, too.

He liked it best when he teased her into her grandame manner that he recognized she copied from her mother. But what was intimidating in Seraph was touchingly amusing in her daughter.

He wasn't about to let anything happen to her. No matter what she said, anyplace where a troll had been killed only a few weeks before wasn't safe. He had no idea what he'd do if they ran into a troll, mind, except run. He wasn't sure that his Memory was up to killing a troll with the same dispatch as it had disposed of his would-be assassins. Against a chance-met wolf or boggin, though, Phoran felt himself to be more than enough of a guard.

Rinnie hiked fast enough that Phoran was hard put to keep up with her—making him glad that he hadn't allowed any of his guards to come with him. More humiliating was that she noticed and slowed up. And apologized.

"Sorry," she said. "I'm used to walking with Lehr or Jes. And you're from the lowlands—Papa says that lowlanders have trouble breathing up here near the mountains."

"Hmm," Phoran said. "You don't need to make excuses. Emperors aren't expected to be able to hike out in the woods."

She turned around and walked backward so that she could see his face. "Papa says you like it here."

He smiled. "Your papa's a pretty wise man."

To his delight she gave him a solemn look that made her look like an owl just waking up. "My papa knows people."

Just then a sharp sensation slid up his leg, and he jerked it reflexively away from . . . bare ground.

"That's Mother's warding." Rinnie grinned. "It didn't used to do that until she reset them after killing the troll. You should have seen Lehr jump the first time he set foot on it afterward."

Phoran stepped cautiously past, but other than a brief, pain-less jolt, nothing happened to him. "I'm still alive," he said. "I guess that means I'm not what she was warding against."

When Rinnie finally stopped it was none too soon for Phoran. He dropped to the ground, lay on his back, and panted. Most of it was for her benefit because it made her laugh, but lying down felt good.

"Quit fooling around," she told him. "You can help gather."

When he obediently rolled to his feet she drew him over to

a plant that looked somewhat like all the other plants around.

"Look, this is tingleroot, you can tell it because it has lacy edges on its leaves. It blooms with small yellow flowers in the spring—that's the best time to harvest. But even a late-harvest root is better than none." She looked at him sternly. "We never pick more than one plant in three—so that there will be more here next year."

"I promise not to pick them all," he told her.

Her eyes narrowed, and she leaned forward. "Your eyes are laughing. This is serious."

"Yes, princess, I know," he apologized. "I'm just not used to taking orders."

"All right," she conceded. "I can see that. The boys don't like it when I tell them what to do—but they don't usually laugh either."

"Possibly because they don't need your directions as much as I usually do."

She tilted her head at him, then grinned. "You like it. All right. Go harvest. Remember to get a stick and loosen the dirt around the plant 'cause it's the root we need."

With the first plant as a template, Phoran found two or three others that were probably tingleroot. He took the whole plant though, so Rinnie could make certain that's what he had. His search took him around a pile of boulders higher than his head, and he found a whole grove of tingleroot. Or something that looked like it to his untrained eye.

He was in the process of loosening the dirt around a stubborn plant when Rinnie's squeak of surprise brought him into a crouch. He waited to hear something more, not wanting to charge out and make an idiot of himself.

"Hey, little girl, where's your crazy brother this time?" It was a deep voice, a man's voice, and the tone had Phoran setting his harvest on the ground and loosening his sword.

The stranger's tones quieted, like a cat stalking a bird. "Or is it Lehr's footsteps I've been tracking instead? Tracking the great hunter himself, the hero who slew an ogre. Did he leave you here while he went off hunting? Did he leave behind such tender meat for me?"

The avarice in the man's voice tightened Phoran's hand on the hilt of his sword. Phoran knew that he was going to hurt this lout now. Kill him if he was given enough excuse. Rinnie was a child; only a sick man sounded like that around a child.

"It was a troll, and my mother killed it." Rinnie sounded calm, only a slight quiver betrayed her fear. But then she knew that Phoran was listening to them, knew that Phoran wasn't as incompetent with steel as he was with plants.

"What are you doing here, Olbeck?" she said stoutly. "Shouldn't you be in the middens with the rest of the swine?"

Something happened. Phoran heard it in the stretch of time between Rinnie's comment and Olbeck's next words. Maybe he'd struck at her, and she'd dodged his hand.

Phoran worked his way quietly around the boulders and the evergreen tree that grew next to them. He didn't want to give Olbeck warning that she wasn't alone and give him a chance to take her hostage before Phoran could get between them.

"My father will have your family out of that farm now," he said. "I told him that Toarsen is here. Don't you think I'd rec-ognize the Sept's brother? I'm the steward's son, bitch. I know that Toarsen and his brother don't see eye to eye. My father will tell Avar that his brother has been sniffing around here and planning treachery. Avar will believe him. Maybe he'll have your father beheaded."

"You are so *stupid,* Olbeck," said Rinnie in disgust. "I wonder that you can put your clothes on right-side out every morning—or is that something one of the boys who follow you about does for you?"

"That may be," Olbeck agreed silkily, and there was a sound of ripping cloth. "But you're—" And then he used some words that Phoran hoped Rinnie didn't know the meaning of.

The sound and Rinnie's surprised cry were too much. Rather than working his way into a better position, Phoran rushed out from behind the boulders and used his shoulder to knock the stranger two or three paces down the hill—away from Rinnie, who was huddled on the ground. He didn't take time to assess her condition before he stepped between her and the stranger.

Olbeck was nearly as big as Kissel, and Phoran found the cool resolve he'd discovered in the heart of the battle with the Path. He smiled.

Regaining his balance, Olbeck drew the sword that hung at his hip.

"Don't hurt him," Rinnie whispered frantically. "If he dies, it'll go hard for my family. He's the Sept's steward's son."

"That's right," said Olbeck with a sneer. "Who are you? One of the twelfth sons of a fourteenth that Toarsen likes to hang about? The Sept will crush you and your friends when he comes, summoned by my father's letter."

Phoran hadn't drawn his sword. He'd prefer to keep swords out of it if he could. It was better for his cause if Tier's noble guests remained a curiosity rather than a news item. Killing this scum might just send news of Tier's unexpected guests all the way to Taela. If Phoran ever managed to rid himself of the Memory, he didn't want the whole of the Empire knowing where he'd been, not if he could help it.

"Rinnie's right; you are stupid aren't you?" he marveled out loud. "You do realize that if you were correct in what we're up to here, you've just given me the ultimate provocation to kill you? That's obviously the only thing that would keep your mouth shut."

"He doesn't think you can kill him," Rinnie said in a small voice. "He's had some training in sword work, and it impresses the other boys."

"Since he's outnumbered now," said Lehr, coming around the same boulders that Phoran had crouched behind, "he'll likely run."

Lehr had Tier's sword in one hand and was breathing hard. "Go back to Leheigh, Olbeck. You aren't welcome in Redern anymore, I hear. No more are you welcome here. If your father has problems with us, I expect that he will come himself. Run back to your father, coward."

Olbeck snarled wordlessly at Lehr, and Phoran saw the intent in his body before he charged—not at Lehr, but straight at Phoran. He probably thought that he could bull through Phoran to get at Rinnie.

Phoran dropped him cold with a fist to the chin.

"Stupid sot ran right into it," he said, rubbing his knuckles to dull the sting. "Are you all right, Rinnie?"

The memory of the sound of ripping cloth kept him facing away from her.

"Yes," she said. "I wish I were a Guardian like Jes. Lightning only works if I have *hours*."

"Too bad," agreed Phoran. "If someone deserved a bit of lightning to strike him down, it was that man."

"Here, Rinnie, take my tunic." Lehr pulled the article in question over his head and tossed it to her. "Nice right cross, Phoran. Did you kill him?"

There had been enough force to have broken his neck. Phoran bent down and rolled the big man over with a grunt of effort.

"Not so lucky," he said. "Likely he'll be awake in a minute or two. I could kill him for you—we could hide the body."

"Much as I hate to admit it, Rinnie was right. Olbeck dead by human hands or missing around here is even more of a problem than Olbeck alive. Too bad about the lightning, Rinnie. That would have been an answer. I suppose we'll just leave him."

"Why isn't he welcome in Redern anymore?" Rinnie, safely covered by Lehr's tunic leaned lightly against Phoran's arm and stared down at her attacker. She sounded collected, but she was trembling like a bird. Phoran thought again about killing Olbeck.

"Remember Lukeeth, the mercer's son?"

"He's one of the boys who follows Olbeck."

"Not anymore. Olbeck killed him. Storne says it was murder, but Olbeck claimed it was self-defense. He got away with it, but his father agreed to keep him out of Redern. Get your herbs—I assume that's what sent you hurrying out of the house this morning. We'll leave him here."

Rinnie nodded and turned and began picking up the scattered bits of plants. Phoran saw her wipe her cheeks when she thought no one was watching. He saw that Lehr had noticed, too.

"Likely, I broke his jaw," he told him as consolation. "He'll remember this every time he tries to eat for a long time."

Lehr sucked in his breath, two red lines forming on his cheeks from gritting his teeth. "You should have pulled your punch so we could have broken a few more bones for him."

Phoran went back behind the boulders and gathered the three plants he'd unearthed and presented them to Rinnie on one knee, holding the limp greenery stretched across both hands.

She laughed as he'd intended. "This one isn't tingleroot." She sorted through what he had and broke off a very few small bits. "You can leave the rest."

She put the bits in her pouch and started back down the hill. Phoran and Lehr followed her.

"I tracked you until I figured out where Rinnie was heading," Lehr said. "Mother left her to sort out our herbs, and I knew we were out of tingleroot. This is the best place to look for it. I'd just decided to head home when I ran across Olbeck's trace. Thanks for escorting her."

Phoran gave him a mock-surprised glance. "I wasn't escorting her, she was educating me. I can harvest tingleroot now—and dill."

"Only if there's no reaverslace nearby," Rinnie said repressively. "Thank you, Phoran. Someday, I'm going to tell Olbeck that it was the Emperor who broke his jaw."

"He'll never believe the Emperor went out herb gathering with you," said Lehr.

A creak of a branch overhead had Lehr spinning around to get a good look. Then, with a procession of quiet thumps, Jes dropped down in their midst, hitting the ground in a roll that ended with him on his feet.

"Olbeck found his horse. I think he's going home. He won't get past the wards anyway." Tier's eldest son looked better than he had the last time Phoran had seen him. His dark skin wasn't so grey, and he moved well as he strode beside his brother.

Phoran sighed. They were both going to have to slacken the pace for him, but he'd wait to ask in case they'd notice and slow down on their own.

"What do you mean he won't get past the wards?" Lehr asked.

"He's tainted," said Jes. "Didn't you smell it? Not so badly as Bandor was, but he still stinks of shadow."

"You two need to slow up," said Rinnie. "Emperors don't run through forests like some peasant farmer's boys."

Phoran grinned.

* * *

Willon was alone in his shop and looked up with a smile to welcome Tier and Seraph.

"My friends, what can I do for you?"

Seraph let Tier do the talking, and turned her attention to the display shelf that Willon had set up near the front counter. Small animals of blown glass in bright colors danced across the scarred wood shelf.

"I brought those back from Taela," Willon said. "Broke half of them getting here, but I thought they'd sell well. You didn't come in here for glass animals, though."

"No," Tier agreed. "We need forty pounds of salted dried beef or venison. I'd also like to look at any other food you've got that will keep."

"Are you going out trapping already?" asked Willon as he led Tier to the section where he kept foodstuffs.

"No. Seems I made some friends among the young lads that helped overthrow the Path. A group of them came down and persuaded me to give them a guided tour of the Ragged Mountains. They want to see Shadow's Fall, but I suspect I'll be able to talk them out of it once they see the country they're going to have to walk through."

Seraph left the glass animals and began sorting through the herbs on the shelves.

Pepper, she thought, and took one of the small packets. She and Tier would stop by Loni the Herbalist's shop before they left town, but Willon carried exotic spices and Loni only the things she could grow in her garden. That meant Loni's herbs were fresher, but Willon's were more diverse.

"I'd like to see Shadow's Fall myself," Willon was saying.

"No," Tier shook his head. "It's a rough trip, Master Willon. I'll take these young rascals and wear them out—it'll be good for them. But the mountains are no place for someone not ready for them. I'll take you next year, if you'll spend the summer hiking with me to get into shape. I've already promised Bandor."

"I travel a lot," said Willon. "You might be surprised at how tough an old man like me can be."

"I'm sure that's true," Tier said.

For a moment Seraph thought Willon wasn't going to let the matter drop. But then he laughed and patted Tier on the shoulder.

"All right, all right. Next year then, mind. I won't forget."

Tier paid for the food and Seraph's herbs after a little bargaining. When they were through, Tier gave Willon back the map he'd given Seraph.

"It was a gift," said Willon.

"A valuable gift," said Tier. "And as we don't have any plans for another trip across the Empire, it won't do us much good. Give it to someone else who needs it."

Willon bowed and accepted it. "It's always a pleasure to do business with you," he said.

"Olbeck is shadowed?" Seraph sat down at the table and tried to figure out what that might mean.

Lehr, Jes, Phoran, and Rinnie had greeted them at the door with the tale of their afternoon adventures.

"He wasn't shadowed when he attacked Lehr and Rinnie just a few days before we left," said Jes.

Hennea sat on the table near Jes and looked at him. "You can tell that easily? The other Guardians I've met have to look for it."

Jes shrugged. "They smell wrong, then I look."

"The question is, what do we do about it?" asked Tier.

"Nothing." Seraph said decisively. "Olbeck will wait until we get back. Though it is interesting that he was tainted after we left for Taela. Every unappealing person doesn't pick up a shadowing just because he's nasty. Bandor was a more usual case. A nice upstanding citizen who causes as much damage as possible for as long as the Stalker can hold him."

"There are several ways a person can become tainted," Hennea said. "The Shadowed is only one of them."

"Well, we certainly have had a Shadowed around here."

"Rinnie," Tier said. "I think that for a while you're going to have to make certain that someone is with you when you leave the house. Take Gura if you have to."

"All right," she agreed. Her lack of protest was a testament to how frightened she'd been.

Seraph caught Phoran's eye and nodded her thanks.

They spent the next day packing and repacking sacks and bags, balancing them in pairs to be attached to the saddles in the morning. Seraph carried the Ordered gems in a bag that would ride on her hip. The *mermori* went into one of the horse's packs.

Lehr and Tier went out and brought back three more riding horses for the trip, two mud-brown and a grey. That left them one horse short, but Jes could outwalk most horses anyway. None of the new horses were the quality of Lehr's Cornsilk, but they were tough little mountain horses and would do just fine for the trip.

As if in omen, Alinath and Bandor appeared in the afternoon with the journey bread half a day earlier than she'd promised.

"Tomorrow," Tier said.

CHAPTER 12

They left the farm while the sun was still a faint hope in the silvery sky. Phoran's horse danced and pranced and pretended to be afraid of the packs that hung here and there from his saddle. Seraph's horse, one of the new ones, started and skittered in response.

She whispered reassurances and talked to it. It was a little inexperienced, but basically even-tempered and settled down quickly. Unlike Phoran's stallion.

"Warhorse," explained Phoran, when his horse finally began walking instead of bouncing.

"So was this one," Tier said, motioning to Skew, who had only twitched an ear toward the misbehaving animals. "If you ever actually go to war, you might consider a different horse."

Phoran smiled. "He settles down fast enough when there's work for him. He's just showing off for the mares."

Tier shook his head. "The Fahlarn used to ride mares to war just to give us fits because so many of our nobles rode stallions."

"I'd heard that," Phoran said. "But if I rode around on a gelding or, worse yet, a mare, my protocol minister would have fits." He hummed a happy little tune to himself as the big grey reared up then quick-stepped sideways. "Might be a good reason for doing it, at that. But Blade does his job—which is to make me look like a good horseman and make himself look athletic and expensive."

He sounded disparaging, but Seraph noticed he had enjoyed the performance at least as much as his horse had. Once they had been riding for a few hours, the hot-bred stallion settled down to a few jitters.

Hennea watched the sun bring out gold and red highlights in Jes's dark hair and wondered at the unexpected gift of him, an *almost* unwelcome but greatly desired gift.

Jes walked beside Hennea's horse, Gura at his heel. The pace seemed to give Jes no trouble, though the horses had set out at a rapid walk. She hadn't exchanged a private word with him since the afternoon when she'd guarded his sleep, but somehow she felt as if they had both accepted that as a new step in their courtship.

He was hers now.

The natural rhythms of travel had broken them into small groups—Seraph and Tier at the head: Phoran, Rinnie, Lehr, and Ielian: Toarsen, Kissel, and Rufort: Hennea, Jes, and the dog bringing up the rear.

She could hear the sound of the conversations in front of her, but could make out only a word here or there. Since she and Jes traveled behind them with a light wind in their faces, no one else would hear anything they said to each other.

She didn't know what to say to him. She was seldom awkward, though it was getting to be a familiar state around Jes. Not that she talked all the time—like Tier—but she was comfortable with her silences. Or had been. Now she wanted to speak to Jes, but she didn't know what to say or how to say it—so she stayed quiet.

Jes patted her knee. "Don't worry so much," he said.

It was so unexpected—although why she couldn't have said, since she knew he was an uncommonly powerful empath—that she laughed.

"I'll try not to," she said. She couldn't see his face to read what was there, but his shoulders were relaxed and easy. "It's just that I feel as though there is a lot to say—but whatever I need to talk about won't reach my lips."

"I do that a lot," he said gravely. "Usually I wait it out. If it's important, it'll come sooner or later. Running helps."

"I think I'll just enjoy the sun on my shoulders," she told him.

He turned his head then so she could see his smile. "I told you about the sun," he said.

"Sometimes you're a wise man."

He laughed. "Sometimes. Usually I'm stupid."

All desire to laugh left her. "Who says so?" she asked.

He turned around to walk backward and grinned. "No need to draw your dagger, sweet lady. I say so. Most times I can hardly hold a conversation."

"You're not stupid," she told him.

His grin faded into a gentler expression that she couldn't read—though for some reason it caused her pulse to quicken.

"All right," he said. "I'm not stupid."

Then he turned around, and she could think of nothing more to say: but she wanted to, if only to see that unreadable expression on his face again.

They set up camp while the sun was still a few hours from setting because Tier knew from experience it would take them longer to set up camp the first few days than it would later on. Also, Lehr was still recovering from the illness he'd suffered at Colbern, and the lowland horses that Toarsen and his boys were riding were tiring faster because they weren't used to the heights. An early day or three in the first part of the trip would give them time to acclimatize and Lehr time to heal completely.

"Besides," he explained to Seraph, as he stretched out beside her on a fallen tree with a twig in his mouth. He put his head on Seraph's lap. "I like this camp. There aren't a lot of rocks in the ground, and that lake is full of trout for supper."

"The boys are enjoying it," said Seraph, as a wave of excitement rose among the intrepid fishermen as Toarsen jerked on his fishing line—but Tier was watching his daughter.

"For a man who's likely never been around a child, he's good with Rinnie," he said.

". . . not like *that,* Phoran," Rinnie was saying, trying to teach the Emperor how to bait his hook. "If you don't get the grub stuck on good, it'll just fall off."

"He lets her get away with ordering him around," said Seraph dryly. "I think it amuses him, but it's not a habit that'll serve her well with her brothers."

Tier took the twig out of his mouth and pointed it at Rinnie, who had both hands on her hips and was shaking her head in exasperation at something Phoran had asked. "He'd better be careful. I know my Rinnie. If he loses that meek posture and starts laughing, he'll be in for a drenching."

Gura barked at a flopping fish that Toarsen pulled onto the shore.

"Toarsen's been fishing before," Seraph said. "And Kissel, too."

"Leheigh's right on the river, same as Redern." Tier adjusted his head so he could watch the boys more comfortably. "It would be more surprising if Toarsen couldn't fish—and Kissel does whatever Toarsen does. Rufort can't fish, but he's been in the woods—did you see how quickly he had that fire built? You don't learn that in the city. Our Ielian, though, is a city boy through and through. Sensitive, too. We'll have to keep Rinnie away from him—*he* won't think it's funny when a ten-year-old girl tells him what he's doing wrong. I'll have a talk with Lehr."

"You can talk to Rinnie, too," advised Seraph. "She's pretty considerate of people if she knows what will bother them."

"Where did Hennea and Jes go?"

Seraph bent her head toward him and brushed his cheek with hers. "Since we had more fishermen than hooks, Hennea said they'd go out and gather firewood or greens."

He wiggled his eyebrows at her. "We could go gather firewood."

She laughed. "My mother told me about men like you."

When the fish were all caught and eaten and the sun setting, they gathered around the fire. Tier tuned the lute he'd brought back with him from Taela.

"Play 'The Marcher's Retreat,' please, Papa?" asked Rinnie.

And so began the singing. They were into the second verse before Seraph's soft alto joined in. She didn't like to sing in public, he knew, though she sang with him when it was just family. It was a sign of how much she'd taken to Phoran and the boys that she sang at all.

The soft lamenting tones of "The Marcher's Retreat" gave way to the rollicking "Big Tag's Dog's First Hunt." He liked that one especially because he'd spent a whole month learning the quick-fingering for the tricky runs from his grandfather the summer before he'd left to soldier. It was the last song his grandfather had taught him.

Lehr pulled out his pennywhistle and played the descant, while Rinnie used a pair of sticks for rhythm accents. It was too fast for the boys who didn't know it, but Toarsen kept up with them until the last chorus, which was sung twice as fast as the rest.

Tier picked a soft ballad next, a common one that everyone would know. There was a duet on the second chorus that Jes and Lehr took. Their voices were almost identical in timbre, and Tier always enjoyed listening to the unusual texture that similarity added to the music.

On the third chorus, Tier's fingers failed him, and he missed a note.

He continued as if there were nothing wrong, and no one seemed to notice. It wasn't as if he played the wrong note, after all. His fingers had just hesitated a moment too long.

He'd played it hundreds of times and never missed a note—still, a missed note should have been nothing to worry about. That is what he told himself as he finished the last verse and swept into the chorus again, but he couldn't put aside that for that bare instant, while his fingers stilled, he'd had no idea who he was or what he was doing.

He finished the song with a flourish and a grin, then sent everyone to bed.

"Morning comes early, and we'll not wait for the sun," he told them.

He smiled at Seraph and teased her about something that he forgot a moment later. He hid his fear behind a smile and words as he'd learned to do during his years as a soldier. But this was an enemy that he had no idea how to engage in battle.

When Seraph curled beside him, he held her too tightly. She kissed him, wriggled to loosen his grip, patted his hand, and went to sleep. He held his wife against him and hoped the warmth of her body could relax the knots in his belly.

He'd been so worried about losing her, he hadn't thought he might lose himself first.

Jes got up from his bedroll and walked to him. He crouched down by Tier's head. "What's wrong, Papa?" His tone was soft as the night air.

"I'm fine," Tier whispered. "Go back and go to sleep."

Jes shook his head. "You don't think you're fine. I can feel it."

Tier found himself wishing it were the Guardian he was dealing with because Jes was the more stubborn of the two. He wouldn't leave without an explanation for whatever he'd sensed of Tier's fears.

"Tonight, while we were singing, I felt the effects of what the Path did to my Order," he said finally, hoping his voice wouldn't awaken Seraph. He didn't want her to worry any more than she already did. "It didn't last long, and it didn't hurt. It just frightened me."

Jes nodded his head, "All right. Don't worry so much. We won't let anything happen to you, not if we can help it."

Tier smiled, feeling absurdly better for talking to Jes. "I know that. Go on back to sleep."

Two days later, Tier was in the middle of telling the story of a boy who found a phoenix egg when it happened again. One moment they were riding up the trail, Kissel laughing, and the next the horses were stopped and Kissel had his hand on top of Tier's.

"What's wrong?" Kissel asked urgently.

Tier shook his head, smiled, and hoped he hadn't done anything too stupid. "I just forgot the next part of the story. Likely, I'll remember in a bit and finish it for you tonight after supper, if you'd like."

Kissel nodded slowly. "That would be fine."

Toarsen caught up to them. "Why did you stop?"

"Waiting for you," Kissel said, and started a conversation with Toarsen about the relative merits of two different types of saddles as he urged his horse forward.

Seraph had been just behind Toarsen. She coaxed her gelding until she and Tier were riding shoulder by shoulder. "My mending isn't holding," she told him. "I'll try to fix it later."

After dinner, she tried to patch it again, but, to her frustration, the tigereye Lark's ring would not or could not cooperate again, and she could do nothing.

Even so, when he took out the lute and played a few tunes, he had not the slightest bit of difficulty. Seraph didn't sing, just sat near him and stared out into the darkness.

When it was time to try and sleep, Tier held her and wiped the tears from her eyes. "If I can't sing, will you still love me?" he quipped.

"I'd love you if you couldn't talk." She thumped his chest lightly. "Perhaps more."

He stifled his laugh so he didn't wake the whole camp. "I love you, too."

The next afternoon they came to the beginning of the worst part of the trip, a high pass that lay between them and Shadow's Fall. The steep climb spread the distance between riders until Tier could look down the face of the mountain and see nearly a half a league between him and Jes, who was walking behind the last rider. Tier stopped Skew at a wide spot in the trail and sent Lehr, who had been with him, riding on ahead while Tier waited to bring up the rear with Jes.

Lehr's chestnut mare's coat was dark with sweat, but her breath came easy. It bothered her not at all when Skew stopped and she had to go on alone.

There was a small flat area a couple of leagues ahead, just before the highest and steepest part of the pass, where Lehr could start setting up camp while the stragglers trailed in. Tier was worried about how Phoran's men's horses were going to handle the climb. In his experience, the horses felt the height of the mountains worse than the people.

Rinnie's horse, with its lighter burden, was the first to appear down the trail. She stopped it next to Tier while Gura dropped to rest, panting happily.

"Papa," she said. "There's a storm front coming behind us with snow. I'm trying to send it around us, but I need to know which direction we'll be heading."

"East," he told her. "East and a little north for a couple of days yet. If you can hold it off us for the next two days, we'll be back down, so it'll come down as rain rather than snow."

"There's some snow on the ground that direction already," she said. "We might have trouble coming back this way.'

"We'll find that trouble when we come to it," he told her. "We might have to come back a different way. This is the most direct route, but riding home, a few extra weeks won't make much difference."

She nodded. When her horse started on up again, Tier said, "I'm glad we thought to take our Cormorant rather than leave her in Redern, where she'd be useless."

She gave him a grin and turned her attention to riding the uneven surge of her horse's uphill scramble. Gura hesitated, gave Tier a long look, then took off after Rinnie.

Seraph appeared before Rinnie was quite out of sight. He kissed her as she passed and told her Rinnie was trying to hold off a storm.

"It's never quite warmed up today," she said. "I'll make certain there's something hot for you when you come into camp."

"I'll look forward to it. See you tonight," he said.

When she was gone, he dismounted and slipped the bit so Skew could graze on the sparse edible vegetation. The trees so high up were all fir and pine, and grass didn't grow well under evergreens. All the horses would be a little hungry for a day or two.

He sat on his heels and waited.

Phoran came next, with Toarsen at his side. Phoran's hard-headed stallion looked none the worse for wear, but Toarsen's horse was breathing hard.

"This is hard on the horses," Tier said. "You might have to walk some of the steeper bits."

It was a longer wait for the next rider, Ielian.

"Is someone riding with the Emperor?" he asked.

Tier nodded. "Toarsen was. It looked as though Phoran was holding Blade back so Toarsen could stay with them."

"Good," said Ielian.

Hennea came next. "Jes told me to go ahead and let you know that the others are fine. Kissel and Rufort are taking the climb slower to save their horses. Jes told them to."

"He's right," said Tier. "Seraph and Lehr should have camp mostly up by the time you get there."

It was getting dark by the time Tier and the others caught first sight of the campfire above them.

"Not far now, lads," Tier told them, standing in the stirrups to loosen his knees which were stiffening from the strain of the ride.

"What's that?" asked Rufort. "Down there below us, see that flicker of light? Is there someone following?"

"Ah," Tier said, stopping. "I'd wondered if we'd see them."

"See whom?" asked Jes.

"What, not whom, I think," Tier said. "When I was up here last time there were lights and voices and . . . other things all night. I thought it might have been altitude sickness. I was coming from the other direction—we haven't hit the high stuff yet—and I was pretty well exhausted."

"So we shouldn't worry about it?" Rufort's horse took advantage of the pause to rub its nose against its knee.

"I wouldn't say that," replied Tier. "These are the Ragged Mountains, and there are some unpleasant things round about. But these didn't hurt me last time, so we'll hope for the best. Come. Camp awaits us."

The camp was just as Tier remembered it, full of small rocks that were ready to punish people for trying to sleep and little grass for the horses.

The odd lights continued to flicker here and there, as if there were men carrying lanterns a hundred yards away.

"There's something here," Seraph said, after Tier told them all about the lights that had followed him down the mountain the only time he'd come this way. "It doesn't feel quite like magic to me. It has no pattern."

There were rustles in the bushes, too, that set both Jes and Gura off a couple of times, only to come back frustrated.

Seraph was banking the fire after everyone had set out their bedrolls and was trying to sleep when she jerked abruptly upright. "Did you hear that?"

"No," Tier said, sitting up to look around.

"I heard nothing," said the Guardian.

Seraph crawled into the bedding with Tier, and muttered, "It's bad enough to hear voices no one else does, but it's worse when you don't know what they're saying."

"Names," said Hennea, and Tier realized that she hadn't said anything since he'd come into camp. Travelers were like that. "I started hearing them at dusk. Don't you recognize what this place is, Seraph? When the wizards who lived fled Colossae, some of the ghosts of the dead followed them. The wizards bound them to the side of a mountain to guard the way. They called the place the Mountain of Memories or the Mountain of Names, and the ghosts stayed and kept any other spirits from following their killers. The lights, rustles, and a few voices that try to bind you to this place with their names. The magic that holds them here has faded, and in a hundred years there'll be nothing here at all."

Seraph shook her head. "I never heard that story."

"I've heard of the Mountain of Names," said Tier, "though nothing that told me just what or where it was. I wish I'd known that it was some magic or other when I came here before. I thought I was losing my mind."

"Why did you come up here in the first place, Papa?" asked Jes. *No,* Tier corrected himself, hearing the darkness in his voice, the Guardian was the one who asked. "This isn't the kind of place you find a lot of animals to trap."

"I was on my way home," Tier said. "It was a particularly mild winter, so I'd traveled farther than usual hunting winter furs—that's when I ran into Shadow's Fall." He paused. "It spooked me when I realized where I was, and I headed home by straight directions rather than backtrack the way I'd come. This isn't the easiest route, but the only other way I know would take us weeks longer."

"How did you know it was Shadow's Fall?" asked Phoran.

"It could be nothing else. You'll understand what I mean when we get there," said Tier. "I left as fast as Skew could go, and I don't think I slept a wink until I was home again."

"You scared Mother," said Lehr. "I remember that a little. I think I was younger than Rinnie is. You came home and collapsed without a word. Mother thought you'd caught some illness and sent Jes and me for Karadoc."

"That was the only time you were here?" asked Ielian. "How do you know where you're going?"

"There speaks a city man," said Rufort, but the smile in his voice robbed it of any offense. "Men who roam the mountains learn fast to tell east from west and gauge how far they've traveled—or they don't survive."

"You've been in the mountains?" asked Phoran.

"Grew up not far from the Deerhavens. I had an uncle . . . well he was my mother's cousin, really. He knew the mountains."

"Tier's a Bard," said Seraph, snuggling down against Tier. "He remembers things."

They tried to sleep again, most of them. Tier listened to the camp quiet down. Jes didn't bother lying down, and Tier tried to convince himself the rustlings he heard were Jes, so he could sleep. But Jes seldom made that much noise, so Tier lay awake most of the night.

The next morning Tier made everyone bundle up and had Jes double-check the horses to make certain they were in shape for the day's travel.

Peaks rose, icy-covered and barren around them as they started on the worst part of the trail. Lehr took the lead again since there was little chance for Lehr to miss where they were going: until they were on their way down, there was only one way the horses could take.

This part was hard on the horses, and Tier could make better speed on foot. His knees weren't any worse than they'd ever been after a day of riding up a mountainside; they'd handle walking better than riding.

They hit snow at midday, but it was all a few weeks old. So high up, Tier could look off and see the storm clouds that Rinnie was holding off as best she could.

"Papa, my head aches," she told him.

"Mine, too, love. It's the heights and the glare of the sun off the snow. Close your eyes, your horse will follow the others. We'll find the top in a few hours. Once we get down the other side, you'll feel better."

She swayed a little. "The storm doesn't like me pushing it away. It wants to come this way."

He didn't know how much she could do without risk, and Seraph and Hennea were farther ahead.

"Be careful, love. You don't have to hold off the storm forever, just a little bit. Whatever you can do helps."

She nodded and closed her eyes.

Ielian rode up. "My horse is sound," he said. "She can ride with me for a while if that helps."

"Thanks." Tier smiled. "There's another steep climb just over that ridge, though. Best she stay where she is."

Ielian cupped a hand across his forehead to block the sun and looked up. "Ridge? I thought that was the top."

Tier shook his head and smiled. "Not for a little while yet. My best reckoning is that we've a league or so before we see the top."

He wasn't off by much. A little over an hour later, he leaned against Rinnie's horse and watched as Toarsen and Kissel staged a snowball fight at the crest of the mountain. It didn't last long because it was too cold, but everyone was cheerful as they started down.

They were an hour from the spot Tier thought they should camp when Rinnie tapped him on the shoulder.

"The storm's coming," she said.

"That's all right." He patted her leg, then swung up behind her. "Go ahead and sleep."

Rinnie slept until they stopped for the night. She grumbled when Jes pulled her off the horse's back, and fell back asleep as soon as he set her down on her blankets.

Lehr made sweet tea and saw to it that everyone drank two cups while Seraph busied herself making a stew of a little water, salted venison, and turnips. It took forever to soften the meat, and the tea, though it had boiled furiously, was not very hot.

With Rinnie's warning in mind, Tier sent Phoran and the boys out collecting tree boughs while he tied up the oilcloth tarp to provide some protection while they slept. The storm hit in the night and followed them down the mountain, turning from snow to rain before letting up at last.

A day off to rest and dry their clothing followed by five long days of travel found them riding on a game trail through heavily forested but mostly level ground. They saw no sign of other people. Everyone knew if they settled too near to Shadow's Fall, crops didn't grow right—as if the Unnamed King had robbed the land of some virtue. Evergreens did all right. There might have been some way to make a living cutting trees and hauling them to the grasslands in the southeast, but the Ragged Mountains made people uneasy if they stayed in them too long.

There were several other Rederni besides Tier who collected animal fur in the fall and winter, but most of them stayed out for a shorter time than Tier. They had stories to tell about things that followed them for weeks without leaving a track or sign. Tier'd had a few odd encounters himself.

Though the trail they were on was flat, towering peaks rose around them. When Tier looked back he could see the highest mountain, a long ridge with a barren red top edged in snowy white with a narrow notch that almost bisected it—the pass they'd taken over the mountain.

Hopefully, Tier thought, as Skew forded a shallow stream, they would be riding back that way in a few weeks and return to Redern—just as the people who'd survived the fall of the Shadowed King had forged their way over that same pass to a place where they felt safe, protected by the steep slope of Redern Mountain.

Then he'd be able to sing again. Skew tossed his head, and Tier loosened his reins, letting them lie slack.

Last night Tier had been singing and lost himself—at least that's what it had felt like. One moment he was singing, and the next he was lying on the ground with Seraph patting his face.

They said he'd just stopped singing, stopped moving, then gone into convulsions. Phoran and Jes had held him down until they stopped. Hennea and Seraph had conferred for a long time last night, then decided that the fit had been brought about by his use of Order while it was under attack by the Path's mages' spell.

Tier didn't want to do anything ever to put that look in Seraph's eyes again, so he'd decided to stop telling stories and singing songs until—well, just until.

Seraph tried not to watch Tier all the time, tried not to *look*. She and Hennea had spent most of the evening trying to locate the magic that was destroying Tier's Order, but they couldn't. There was nothing to be found, just as there had been nothing to find when they had cleaned Tier of spells when they'd freed him from the Path.

Hennea knew something of the spells they'd used because she'd been there for the first part. Tier remembered a little about it as well, though the Masters had tried to blank his memory of it.

Rufort, who was older than the other three former Passerines, had been there at a ceremony when the binding of Order to gem had been done in front of an audience. He did the best he could, but he wasn't a wizard and, as Tier said dryly, about half the things the Masters did on stage were performance rather than magic.

If Phoran's Memory were to show up again, it might be able to tell them more. However, it hadn't come back to feed since it killed Phoran's would-be assassins in Taela, though Seraph didn't know why. Since Memories were rare, formed only sometimes when a Raven died by murder or betrayal, no one knew much about them. They formed quickly after the Raven's death, usually while the killer was still in the room. Then they avenged the dead Raven and dissipated. With the Masters protected from the Memory by magic, if Phoran hadn't been nearby to feed upon when the Raven died, it would have been attached to the gem as they had planned—and become one of the gems that none of the wizards could use.

She'd never heard of a Memory feeding from anyone other than its intended prey, so she didn't know the rules that governed what it did to Phoran. Until the Memory returned, she and Hennea could only use what information they had to understand how the spell on Tier worked.

From information the former Passerines gave them, they believed the spell had been done in three parts. The first, which Hennea had seen, was a binding ceremony. It hadn't worked on Hennea, and neither the Masters nor Hennea knew why. She hadn't seen the gem bind to her Order, so she didn't know how they managed it. Tier, being a Bard, knew only that it hurt and left him feeling sullied.

The Path kept its Ordered prisoners for a year and a day before successfully stealing the Orders to bind to the gems. Some of that was because magic worked better on a person who is known to the magic wielder. Seraph could work magic on one of her family far easier than she could ensorcel someone she didn't know. But, some magics just took a long time to work. The binding of Order to gem had to be as strong or stronger than the binding of Order to Order Bearer; it probably just took time.

The second part must have been when the gem gradually started pulling the Order to it. That's the phase Tier seemed to be in. Toarsen said both of the Ravens who had preceded Tier in captivity had begun having episodes toward the end of their stay. Hennea believed that meant someone had worked a second spell, after they'd left Taela. There was only one Path mage left after the Memory had gotten through with them: the Shadowed himself. He must have the gem that was bound to Tier's Order.

The third part of the Path's spell was where the wizard severed the tie between Order and Order Bearer. It might not need magic at all, just the death of the Order Bearer.

Both Phoran's and Tier's fates were tied together: destroy the Shadowed and both would be safe. Brewydd's last message indicated either the Shadowed was in Colossae, or they would find some way to deal with him there. Seraph glanced at Tier and away before he noticed. She would find the Shadowed, she vowed silently. She would find him and she would see that he never bothered her or hers again. Tier was riding alone in front today. He wasn't talking much, and, though she knew that he could be as comfortable in silence as he was in a storm of words, she worried about him. However, she knew her fussing bothered him more than it helped, so she let him avoid her for now.

The game trail they'd been following emptied into a broad, flat meadow half a league across and, as Seraph could judge it, three or more leagues long. Seraph's horse took four steps onto the meadow and stopped. Seraph realized she'd pulled the horse to a halt, but couldn't say why.

"I know this place," said Jes, who'd been walking beside Hennea just behind Seraph.

Phoran came up next and stopped just beyond Seraph. He turned Blade in a rapid circle and looked through the trees as if he expected to see a waiting army. But there was nothing except a gentle breeze that moved the tops of the evergreens.

Tier looked back and saw them stopped. He turned Skew around and began cantering back to them.

"Shadow's Fall," said Ielian in an awed voice, as Tier rode up.

"There are the remains of buildings on somewhere ahead," Tier told them. "I don't know if we'll pass by close enough to see them. According to the map, our path lies directly through this valley. The first time I came here, I came into it from the north about two leagues from here and cut back toward home before I'd gone very far."

"It's just a meadow," Kissel said, sounding a little disappointed. "Though it's bigger than I thought."

"Five hundred years doesn't leave much behind," Toarsen said. "Leather rots and steel rusts."

He was right, but something was calling to Seraph. She dismounted and walked forward a few steps. It wasn't magic, not really. Just something that cried out to her affinity with the past. Kneeling, she put her hand on the ground and came up with a gold ring. There was a deep mark on it such as a knife or sword might make upon the softer, more durable metal. As soon as she touched it, more of them tried to attract her attention. She'd always thought the reading of objects was a passive thing, but these remnants of a long-ago battle waited for her to read them.

"They're calling to me." She felt as if the air she was breathing was too heavy. "All of the things left here with stories to tell, stories ending here." She closed her hand on the ring. "He was too old to fight, but there was no one left. No one but old men, women, and children. He had arthritis in his shoulder, so he used his old sword with his left hand. His first wife, his childhood sweetheart, gave him this ring when the world was different, and he was the privileged son of a . . . some sort of mercer, but the cloth he dealt in came from across the seas."

She dropped the ring and remounted. "It will take more than five centuries to clean Shadow's Fall. I don't want to linger here."

Jes, who'd been shifting from one foot to the other, abruptly swung up into the saddle behind Hennea as they started off again. "I can't walk on this ground," he said.

Gura, his tail down and tucked between his hind legs, kept close to Rinnie's horse rather than bounding around exploring as he usually did.

"I wonder if their bones still lie here," Tier said to Seraph, his voice a little dreamy as they rode through the old battlefield. "Red Ernave and the Shadowed King, I mean. Did the remnants bury their hero, or were they too afraid of the Shadowed's dead body? Were there scavengers? Wolves and mountain cats or other things, things that had served the Shadowed like the troll Seraph killed."

"I'd have let the dead lie," said Rufort, who was riding beside them. "There would have been too much to do, trying to ensure remnants of the Army of Man survived. It would be a poor repayment of the price Ernave and all their beloved dead had paid to be so busy burying the past they lost their future. I've heard said that a battlefield's as dangerous a month after the battle as it was during the fighting."

"Disease," said Tier. "I agree with you. Best to save the living and let the dead lie. Remember them in song and story—that's a better memorial than any grave marker."

They saw the remains of buildings, though they didn't ride close enough to see more than a few broken stone blocks that looked to be as large as their horses.

"I can almost see it," said Phoran in a hushed voice. "The smoke and the sound of screaming. The terrible task of fighting foes who died so hard."

But even as great a battlefield as Shadow's Fall had to end sometime. There were trees in front of them, marking the boundary between old floodplain and foothill, when Seraph stopped her horse again.

"Wait," she said. "There's something."

"Yes," agreed Hennea. She rode off to the right a little, where three ragged blocks had been stacked one atop another. They were sunk into the soil a little. Hennea handed Jes her reins and, throwing a leg over the mare's neck, slid off, leaving Jes still mounted. She crouched down so she could get a good look at the stones.

"*Doverg* Ernave *atrecht venabichaek,*" she said, then translated, "Red Ernave defended us here and died."

"They left a marker after all," said Tier. He looked around, then he turned his horse in a slow circle, and an expression of growing astonishment appeared on his face. He gave a disbelieving laugh. "It's just as I pictured it," he said.

"I wonder how much of the story of Shadow's Fall is true?"

"I don't like it here," said Rinnie. "And there's a rainstorm coming soon. I don't want to be here if the sun's not shining. I don't think it would be a good thing."

Hennea dusted off her hands. Jes gave her a hand, and she swung up behind him this time.

"I don't think so either," Seraph told her daughter. She wanted away from the things that beckoned her with their stories of the long-ago dead.

They had to stop, though, at the end of the battlefield because, where their maps had shown a road, there was no trail at all.

Rufort got off his horse and stretched, while Tier and the women tried to compare the old maps to the current reality. He took the opportunity to look behind them at the wide flatland with its short yellow grass.

Shadow's Fall.

How had he, Rufort Do-Nothing, come to such adventures? The third son of the fifth son of the Sept of Bendit Keep, Rufort had fought for everything he had, fought siblings and cousins until he was banished to Taela.

He'd joined the Passerines when the place was offered, hoping for somewhere to belong, to be valued. The Path had valued him, all right. He wasn't stupid. It hadn't taken him long to see that the Passerines were throwaway troops in a game the Masters of the Path were directing, but by then he'd also known there was no way out except death. But he had nothing to live for anyway, and the Path gave him a way to use the anger he kept bottled inside.

It had taken two things to make him rethink his attitude. The first was a beating that had taught him that, no matter how big and tough you are, there is always someone bigger and tougher. The second had occurred one night in the hall just outside of his room in an almost-forgotten corner of the palace, when he'd looked at the dead body of one of his fellow Passerines and decided he didn't want to die.

Rufort was a survivor.

He looked over at Phoran, who'd given up on a quick resolution and stripped his big grey stallion of its saddle and was inspecting a place where the horse's hide had rubbed thin on the ride over the mountains. Who'd have thought that Rufort of Bendit Keep would find himself embarked on an adventure with the Emperor—and such an emperor.

Rufort had honestly thought that in the Emperor's Own he would be a simple guard, a glorified servant—which was better than dead. But Phoran had never treated him that way, not in the practice fields before this trip, and not during it. Phoran asked his advice and followed it—or explained why he didn't.

Oh, Rufort knew the things that people said about Phoran. He'd seen the Emperor passed out in a drunken stupor more than once. Had watched the careless cruelties spawned by dissatisfaction and boredom—and hadn't Rufort done the same and worse for the same reasons?

But all that had changed. Rufort wasn't certain exactly how or why it had changed—except that Tier, a farmer of Redern and a Bard, had been loosed among the Passerines and changed Rufort's life forever. He had a place now, a position he was honored to serve in, and honorable men to serve with and under.

Toarsen and Kissel were men he could follow. He looked at them a minute as they chatted softly together. Men now, both of them, not the boys that they, and he also, had been at the beginning of the summer, men directed their own destinies rather than dancing to the tune of another's piping.

Rufort *chose* to serve his emperor. He'd follow Toarsen and Kissel as his captains gladly. But Phoran, Phoran was a man that Rufort of Bendit Keep, Rufort Survivor, would lay down his life for.

He laughed softly to himself at his overwrought (however true) thoughts. He looked around and saw there was a place not far away where a line of dwarfed willows outcompeted the fir trees. Probably a creek, he thought. They'd filled their water bags and jugs that morning; but he was from drier country than this and had learned never to pass water by.

He left his horse with the others and went exploring.

Ielian found him staring down at a mostly dry creek bed.

"They're still trying to decide which way to ride," Ielian said. "The maps disagree."

Rufort grunted. "What do you see when you look here?" he asked.

"Rocks and mud," Ielian said cautiously, in a manner of a man who'd been the butt of too many jokes. Being a Passerine made you wary after a while.

"I don't want to move, or I might lose this perspective," Rufort said. "Would you go get . . ." Whom? Tier? Toarsen or Kissel? "Lehr. Would you get Lehr for me?"

Ielian nodded and ran back the way he'd come. The others weren't far, so it didn't take him long to come back with Lehr.

"What is it?" Lehr asked.

"What do you see?" Rufort asked again, nodding at the creek bed.

Lehr looked, and when he crouched, Rufort knew he was right.

"You see it, too?" he asked.

Lehr nodded, stood up, and picked his way down the bank and stood in a dry part of the creek bed, looking first one way, then the other. He reached into the sluggishly flowing water and came up with a large, squarish rock, which he carried back to Rufort.

"Good eyes," Lehr said.

"What is it?" Ielian peered at the rock.

"A cobble," said Rufort, patting Ielian on the back. "A cobble put in a road to keep it from getting muddy. Streams meander, Ielian, my city-bred friend, but this one runs straight as an arrow. Straight as a road."

Lehr grinned, "Rufort's found the road to Colossae."

Rinnie was right, it did rain. For the next four days water drizzled from the skies as if it were spring rather than late summer.

"There's too much water to keep it from raining, Mother," she told Seraph. "And the storm is going the same direction we are. It's better for it to fall now when it can do it gently, than if I hold it off, and we get flooded."

Everything they owned was wet or damp by the second day. Since they had been heading more north than east since they left Shadow's Fall, Seraph figured that they would be fortunate if they didn't run into more snow before they found Colossae.

In some places, Rufort's road had become so overgrown it was impossible to tell roadbed from undisturbed forest floor, as it disappeared under years of soil and reappeared a half mile later. Following the old road was made harder when the forest thickened until it was difficult to see more than a hundred yards in any direction.

In the early afternoon of the fourth day of rain, Jes, who had taken Gura ahead to check out the trail, came loping back from his explorations.

"River ahead," he said. "Road goes across."

"We can't get any wetter," said Phoran, with a grin. "I just hope it's shallower than the last river we crossed. I'd hate to float away when we've come so far."

Seraph looked closely at Jes, who was even wetter than most of them from the waist downward. The dog panting happily at his feet was soaked through. "Did you try to cross it, Jes?"

He nodded. "It's fast," he said. "Not too deep for the horses, though."

"We could have sent one of the horses across," complained Hennea. "You don't have any more dry clothes."

Seraph, who had been about to make the same complaint, closed her mouth.

Jes looked down at himself and shook his head. "It's only water, Hennea. We are all wet."

"Wait until you're chafed in all the wrong places from wearing wet clothes," Hennea said. Then, "I'll try and dry out some things tonight when it isn't raining."

Seraph smiled to herself.

As Jes promised, the road took them to the edge of a river, where the bank led gently down into the water. Upstream and downstream, where mountains arose on either side, the river was narrow and swift, but here it spread out to twice its normal width.

"They must have had a bridge here," said Tier, riding beside Seraph. "In the spring you wouldn't have been able to ford it at all. I'd not want to try and take a wagon across here even now."

"It feels as though no one has ever been here before," said Ielian, just behind them.

"I feel it, too," Seraph agreed. "Even the things that are man-made—the road and such—feel as if they've been around so long that they've been cleaned of human touch."

"We'll find a good flat area to camp," Tier told Seraph, when Jes, who had waited until everyone else had safely crossed, arrived dripping and smiling. Tier started up the rise of land that edged the river, still talking. "If Rinnie can put a hold on the rain for a few hours, we'll rig something to hang up clothes around a fire . . ." His voice trailed off, and he stopped his horse.

Seraph stopped her horse beside him and looked down into the valley stretched below them. It was a sight worthy of a Bard's silence.

Colossae.

CHAPTER 13

If the trip had taught Hennea anything, it was the power of time. Five centuries was enough to bury Shadow's Fall, where tens of thousands, perhaps hundreds of thousands, had died—she'd forgotten which. She'd seen that a thousand years was enough to hide a road built to last through the ages by mages more powerful than the world had seen since before the dawn of the Empire. It was time enough to reduce a great city to rubble.

She'd constructed possibilities for what they would find in the wizards' city a hundred times on this trip. She'd been prepared for anything except what they found.

Three-quarters of the way across the lightly wooded valley, perhaps a full league away, a hillock arose, cliff-edged and flat-topped. The city covered the entire ridge of the higher land, and spilled out to the valley below, as perfect as it had been on the day the Elder Wizards had destroyed it to save the world from their folly. Rose-colored stone walls surrounded the entire city, protecting it from invaders who had never come.

Even from this far away, the city felt empty and waiting.

"Anyone could have found this," said Ielian.

Hennea turned her head to look at the smallest of Phoran's guards. "No," she told him. "Only Travelers."

"Only if the city wanted to be found," said Jes, in an odd voice. It wasn't the Guardian, not quite.

The gates of the wizards' city were built of polished brass and were nearly as tall as the wall. They looked just as they must have when the wizard Hinnum had spelled them closed so many centuries ago. Etched into the top of the left gate, in the language of the Colossae wizards, were the prosaic words *Low Gate*.

Hennea looked up at the gate towers that loomed on either side of the gate and could almost imagine a face looking down at her.

There were few cities in the Empire older than the Fall of the Shadowed, and few cities that old outside of it; the Shadowed King's claws had sunk farther than the boundaries of the Empire. The older sections of Taela were supposed to have been built by the first Phoran, and they proved that even well-built stone buildings shifted and moved over centuries. The stones in the walls of Colossae sat squarely one atop the other, as if they'd been placed there yesterday.

She shivered, and Jes wrapped a warm hand around her calf in a manner that had grown familiar. "Are you cold?"

"No, it's not that," she told him. "This is wrong. Where are the cracks in the wall? Why is the brass still bright without people to polish or wizards to preserve?" She could feel the power here, but it was oddly distant—a memory of magic rather than the real thing.

"Illusion?" said Seraph, dismounting. "It doesn't have that feel, though there is some magic here, right enough."

She touched the gates, then jumped back as they began to open. Not swinging inward or outward as the city gates of most places did; nor did they rise up like the smaller gates of a keep or hold. These slid back on oiled tracks set below the road surface and into the walls themselves until the only remnant of the gate was a handspan-wide bar of brass up the middle of the wall edge.

A wagon length in front of them was another wall wider than the gate, that blocked them from the city so people entering would have to go to the left or the right of it. On either side of it, set between the city walls and the inner wall were two wooden gates of the sort a farmer might use to keep livestock in or out. One was open, the other shut.

Tier dismounted and crouched beside the brass door's track, bending down to sniff. "If this is an illusion, it's on par with the *mermora*," Tier said. "This oil smells fresh."

"There are people here," said Kissel. He loosened his sword and tipped his head from side to side, loosening his neck muscles in preparation for battle. "This can't be a deserted place. Not looking like this." He pointed at the dirt just the far side of the gate and Hennea saw what he had—there were lines on the ground as if someone had just finished raking the ground clear of debris.

"It's too quiet," protested Toarsen. "A city is never this silent, Kissel. Not even a city the size of Leheigh. You can hear the sounds of Taela miles away."

"It's magic," said Jes quietly. "The city was left this way. That's what the Guardian says."

"He's been here?" Tier gave his son a surprised look.

Hennea was startled as well. She knew the Guardian had been remembering things he should not have known, not if the Order had been cleansed after the death of the previous Guardian who bore it. She'd started to believe that might be most of the trouble with the Guardian Order.

If so, then when she and Seraph solved the mystery of what to do with the Ordered gems, they might also stumble upon a way to help make the Guardian Order less dangerous to its bearer. Not that she wanted to change Jes or the Guardian, just keep him safe. But if the Guardian knew about Colossae, then it wasn't just bits of the previous bearer that the Order contained— it was the first one, one of the survivors of the death of Colossae.

Jes stared determinedly down at the ground for long enough that she thought he'd not answer Tier's question. Finally, he said, "He doesn't know. He just remembers that the wizards left the city as it was."

"Let's go in," said Phoran, with all the impatience of a young man, reminding Hennea that, for all his cleverness, he was only a few years older than Jes. "Let's see what this wizards' city looks like."

Tier got to his feet and stared at the rake marks before he nodded. "All right. Loosen your swords, boys, those of you who have them. Be alert. Remember that according to Traveler stories there is something evil here. It may be bound, but the Travelers didn't trust those bindings."

Jes didn't wait for the others but went to the closed gate and jumped over it; his dog followed him. Seraph led her horse through the open gate.

Hennea hung back. Let Jes and Seraph see to the front guard, she would take the rear. There were other people thinking about safety, too. She noticed Toarsen rode in front of Phoran and Kissel behind. Since Rinnie was riding next to Phoran as usual, that left the most vulnerable of their group well guarded from physical harm. Rufort and Ielian looked at her, and she waved them through ahead of her.

Lehr waited.

"Go ahead," she told him.

He smiled. "I'm not telling Jes I let his lady take rear guard."

She stiffened. "I can protect myself."

"Doubtless," he agreed, and held his chestnut mare where she was.

She smiled and shook her head, but urged her gelding through the gate ahead of him anyway.

The narrow passage dumped them in a large plaza cobbled in the same reddish stone as the walls. Water puddled in the spaces between the cobbles and splashed under the horses' hooves.

In the small houses that crowded together around the plaza and continued to line narrow streets were some of the signs of age Hennea had expected when they'd approached the city. The wood of the doors and windows was cracked, and weeds poked up here and there around the houses. Roofs looked as though they were decades beyond where they had first needed rethatching. Decades, though, not ten centuries.

By the time Hennea and Lehr arrived, everyone else had dismounted and was looking around.

"It still doesn't look deserted enough," said Phoran, rubbing his stallion's neck absently. "There are places in Taela that look worse than this."

"And it doesn't smell," agreed Toarsen.

Lehr hopped off his horse as well and wandered over to one of the houses. "I can't get the door open," he said in surprise.

"Is it locked?" asked Tier, going to see.

Hennea dismounted slowly, still waiting for some danger or attack. The vast emptiness of the city gave her chills.

"I tried that. I can feel locks, and there are none here, Papa," Lehr said. "It just won't open."

Hennea bent down to look at weeds growing along the edge of the wall between them and the gate. A raindrop fell on a leaf, joining a puddle that had formed there. The weed was knee high and fragile-looking, but it didn't bend at all under the weight of the rain. It didn't move.

She reached out to touch it, and it didn't give under the weight of her finger either, even when she pressed down on it.

"Try the window up there," she heard Phoran say to Lehr. "It's got an open-air window."

She glanced behind her and saw Lehr jump to catch the lintel of a window and chin himself up. He dropped back down after a moment. "There's a curtain across, but it feels more like a wall."

"I know what's wrong with your door and the window," she said, standing up and looking around the streets again. When she knew what she was looking for it was obvious. The thatch on the houses was dark and grey with age, but not with rain. The wood of the walls of the houses was not wet either—and none of the horses were nibbling at the weeds.

Seraph frowned at her.

"The Elder Wizards somehow froze the city in time," said Hennea certain that she was right, though she could barely feel a trace of magic. "Everything is exactly as it was the day the Elder Wizards sacrificed it. You'll have to find an open entrance if you want inside these buildings because there isn't a door that will open or a curtain that you can move."

They spent a while exploring the little square. None of them seemed to feel the way Hennea did about the city—except for Gura, who whined and settled in the middle of the square with his muzzle on his paws. It made him sad, too. She left Jes and Lehr trying to figure out how to get across a small yard full of grass time-stiffened to sharp spikes so they could take a closer look at a shed with an open door.

Seraph had taken the map satchel under the overhang of a building for protection from the rain. When she saw Hennea wander back toward the square, she called her over.

"You're the only one who can read this," she said, handing Hennea the city map. "Can you figure out where we are and how to get somewhere that might do us some good?"

Hennea took the map and looked at it. "The gate said 'Low Gate,' so we must be here." She pointed. "It calls this area Old Town."

"I'd have thought they'd build first on top of the ridge," said Seraph, distracted from her original question.

Hennea looked around again and saw, not the dilapidated buildings, but how they once had been built against the solid wall of cliff face that curved around them protectively.

"They might have wanted to be near their fields," Hennea said. "Or maybe the oldest sections had been on top, but were razed and built over."

Seraph grinned at her, an expression Hennea still wasn't used to seeing on the face of a Raven—but Seraph herself admitted that she didn't have the control she ought. It didn't seem to hamper her—much, thought Hennea, remembering the table that had slammed the floor when Ielian had made Seraph too angry.

Seraph's expressions tended to be sudden, breaking out of the cold reserve that should have been a Raven's calm like the sun from a storm cloud or lava from a volcano, then gone just as quickly as they had come.

"Tier will make up stories for us," she said, then lost her grin, and, at first Hennea thought it was because she'd remembered that Tier had quit telling stories or singing.

But then she said, "Tier?" and thrust the maps at Hennea.

Hennea looked over at Tier, who stood near his horse looking at nothing, his face as empty as any she'd ever seen. Hennea shoved the map back in the case and set it on the dry ground beneath the overhang before following Seraph. Not that there was anything she could do to help.

He'd been having this kind of episode a couple of times a day. Nothing as dramatic as the thrashing fit he'd had a few days before they'd come to Shadow's Fall, but frightening even so.

"Tier?" Seraph's quiet voice was pitched so as not to disturb the happy explorations the boys were pursuing. Jes, Hennea saw, looked up anyway.

Seraph touched Tier's arm. "Tier?"

Gradually, personality leaked back into his face, and he blinked, looking slightly surprised. "Seraph, where did you come from? I thought you were looking at maps with Hennea?"

Seraph smiled as if there were nothing wrong. "This is Old Town, Hennea says. These buildings were already old when the city died."

Tier must have seen something in her face Hennea had missed because he touched her cheek, and said gently, "I did it again, didn't I? That's the second time today."

Third, thought Hennea, but she didn't correct him.

"Let's look at the map and see if we can find the library," he said, when Seraph didn't speak. "If we're here looking for information in a wizards' city, the library is the place to start." He looked up at Hennea. "Can you read the city map well enough to tell us how to get there?"

There was nothing in his face except for cheerful interest. *Brave,* Hennea thought. She cleared her throat and answered from memory. "It's in the north center of the city. Several miles away, if the map is to scale. Let me go look at it and find the shortest path there."

If she hadn't summoned them to continue through the city, Seraph thought that the others would have been content to spend the rest of the day exploring Old Town. But, once she'd caught their attention they were happy enough to mount up and set off to look for the library instead.

The horses' hooves rang unnaturally loud on the cobbles, the sound echoing off the buildings that rose around them. As they got farther from the gate, the houses grew larger and more elaborate, some as large as the richest of the merchants in Taela, and, for the first time, Seraph saw the green pottery-tiled roofs that she recognized from the *mermori*.

On one street where all the houses were built wall to wall, there was an empty place where a building should have been. As they got closer to it, Seraph could see that not only was a building missing, but there was a hole half a story deep filled with the crumbled bones of a building. Seraph could see the marks on the walls where a roof had once touched on either side of the hole.

"It's as if, in this one place, the magic didn't protect this building, though the ones on either side are fine," Hennea said. "These ruins are what the whole city should have looked like."

They found other holes in the perfect preservation, places where buildings should have been but were no more. Sometimes there was nothing except bare earth, other places they could see stone foundations or piles of rubble.

"Papa, look. It's an owl." Rinnie said, pointing down a narrow side street that ended at the base of an open building made of granite. A pillar stood before the center of the building, in front of the door. On top of the pillar was an oversized carving of an owl, its wings half-furled, as if any moment it would take off in flight.

Unable or unwilling to miss the call of curiosity, Tier turned Skew down the street.

A few moments more or less would make little difference, Seraph told herself. Even if they found the library and managed to get into it—something not as promising after their troubles with the buildings they'd tried to explore so far—it might take months before she found what she was looking for. Years.

Tier wouldn't have years. Maybe not even months.

She kept her face blank and rode after the others, reminding herself, a little desperately, that Brewydd had believed something here could help them.

"The door's not closed," announced Lehr, who'd taken the lead. He disappeared into the building before Seraph could caution him.

Seraph dismounted.

"Leave the horses," suggested Tier, though Lehr had already done so. "Skew, Cornsilk, and Blade will all stand, and the other horses won't leave them."

He offered his hand to Seraph and escorted her up the half flight of stairs and through the double doors. Despite her worries, she found herself hurrying, eager to see the inside of one of the buildings here at last.

Mosaic tiles of vibrant colors covered the floor of a cavernous room. Great, sweeping arches lifted a ceiling far above them. There was light coming in from somewhere, and Seraph searched for a while before she saw how it had been done.

Shaded by yellow glass, glowing stones cast their light as brightly as the sun had ever shone through an open window.

"It's a temple," said Tier, when no one else found words to speak.

"I don't know anything about Colossae's gods," Seraph said. "None of the books in the *mermori* talk about them." But all of the *mermori* books she'd read were about magic. They gave little insight into the lives of the wizards who had written them.

"Look over there." Tier nodded toward the far side of the room, and she followed his gaze. She'd been too dazzled by the lights and color to notice the raised dais on the far side of the room. On the dais was a statue.

"She looks as though she might breathe," said Phoran, striding across the room and bounding up the steps until he could touch the robes of the goddess caught in stone, then painted with such attention to detail that Seraph almost expected the fabric to move.

Phoran's head just reached the goddess's knee. Above him she rose, bare from the waist up. Her skirts, painted bright blue with green-and-yellow geometric patterns, were caught in a belt at her hip—the belt clasp was in the shape of an owl. In one hand she held a small harp, the other hand was stretched out toward the room.

Her hair, very nearly the color of Seraph's own, was cut short, and either some quirk of accident or the subtlety of the artist made the fine strands look like the hairs of a feather. But it was her face that really drew Seraph's attention. The artist had depicted her with a gamine grin so full of life Seraph had to fight the urge to smile in return.

"The goddess of music," said Hennea. "Kassiah the Owl."

Seraph turned to look at the other Raven because she'd sounded a little tense. "How do you know that?"

"It's written on her belt." Hennea sounded like her usual self again, and Seraph could read nothing in her peaceful mien.

"I always wondered why the Bardic Order was the owl rather than a songbird—like a lark or canary," said Tier.

"It still doesn't really explain it," said Lehr after a moment. "I mean, why does she have an owl rather than a songbird?"

He ran his fingers over the stone of her skirts. "I like her."

"She's dead," said Hennea. "It doesn't matter whether you like her or not."

Tier frowned at her. "I thought Travelers didn't have any gods."

"Travelers don't," said Seraph. "But it looks like the Elder Wizards did. I wonder why they left them behind?"

"Dead gods don't need believers," Hennea said tightly.

Seraph frowned at Hennea's odd agitation—she wasn't the only one who noticed. Jes, who'd been wandering around the room, turned abruptly and strode across the room to Hennea.

"It happened a long time ago," he said. "Don't be angry."

Hennea closed her eyes and took a deep breath. When she opened them again she'd regained her usual air of peacefulness. "I'm sorry. I don't know why this should . . ." Her voice trailed off as her gaze crossed Tier's. "You're right, Jes. It's stupid to get upset about something that happened so long ago. Let's let the past lie behind us, where it belongs. It's just this city. It's so empty." She took a deep breath. "We need to find the library and see if we can get in."

There were no sounds but the ones they made, none of the smells that Seraph associated with human habitation: beer brewing, bread baking, smoky incense mingling with the less pleasant smells of sweat, sewage, and rotting food. That was not to say that there were no smells, but they were the *wrong* smells.

The former inhabitants of Colossae hadn't bothered with a small zigzag path up the cliffs like the Rederni. Instead they'd built a giant ramp. Seraph, looking up the gradual slope of the ramp marveled silently at the wealth that would allow such construction.

Though at first everyone had been pointing out the wonders of the city, they'd all eventually fallen silent. Not even the massive ramp, cobbled with rough-surfaced stones that gave hooves good purchase on the climb and must have required replacing on a regular bases, drew comment. Overwhelmed, she thought.

But she wasn't here as a tourist. She let her eyes return to Tier, who was talking with Phoran. She'd have to put her faith in Brewydd's foresight and believe that there were answers here.

The houses were more spread out on the upper reaches of Colossae than they had been below, and, to Seraph's eye, the curious holes in Colossae's magic where buildings had fallen into rubble were more common, too. Sometimes there were two or three in a single block.

The road they followed turned abruptly, and the houses fell behind them as they rode through elaborate gardens full of varieties of flowering plants Seraph had never seen before.

"I wonder what season it was when Colossae was ensorcelled." Tier looked around them dreamily, and Seraph could almost hear the story he was composing in his head. "I don't see many flowers that I know. I wonder if it was spring or summer."

"I don't like this," said Jes. "It's like Colbern."

"Shadow-touched?" Seraph straightened in the saddle.

"No," Lehr said. "Dead. I feel it, too."

"There's the library." Hennea pushed her horse into a trot and headed for a large building in the center of the gardens.

"It looks like the palace in Taela," Phoran told Rinnie, as they took a slower pace than her parents and brothers, who had rushed off after Hennea. "Though the palace is considerably bigger."

Toarsen, who'd overheard his comment, took another look at the building. "It is smaller," he said. "And it looks like some effort was made to make it pleasing to the eye. But I can see what you mean. This started as a small building and just kept growing."

"Your palace is bigger than this?" asked Rinnie, and looked as though she might be awestruck by him again. Phoran couldn't have that.

"Stupidly big," he admitted. "And ugly. And impossible to keep repaired. There's a leak in the eating hall that has been there for three generations. No one can figure out where the water is coming from."

"I expect we'll find out someday when the entire ceiling falls in," said Kissel comfortably. "Hopefully the Sept of Gorrish will be seated under a suitably heavy bit and be crushed to goo."

Toarsen cleared his throat and tipped his head meaningfully toward Rinnie.

"Eh, sorry, lass." Kissel ducked his head in embarrassment that might or might not have been real.

"That's all right." Rinnie hopped off her horse and gave Kissel a mischievous smile. "I'm sure anyone you want smooshed to goo would deserve it."

They tied their horses to a railing that might have been set before the university for just that purpose—or it might have been decoration. Phoran couldn't tell. He tied Blade as far from Toarsen's stallion as he could, though the two horses had learned to tolerate each other for the most part.

Tier, Seraph, and Hennea were talking quietly together. Phoran didn't see either of their sons, but he knew them well enough to know they'd gone off exploring.

"—where the library is in this building," said Seraph.

Hennea raised her eyebrows. "I'm pretty sure this *is* the library, Seraph."

"The whole thing?" Seraph didn't sound overjoyed about it.

In Phoran's experience if there was anything a wizard appreciated more than a building full of books, it was a bigger building full of books.

"Most libraries are organized," he offered. "Especially libraries run by wizards."

Seraph drew in a breath and gave him a shallow bow of thanks. "I'll hope it is very well organized."

Phoran continued to look at the library while Seraph went over to talk to Tier. As he thought of all the wondrous things he'd seen since they left Redern he realized two things.

The first was that he was almost certain he was not going to be rid of the Memory soon enough to do him any good. He'd been listening to Seraph and Hennea and realized that, for all of Seraph's earlier arguing with Ielian, neither of the Ravens really expected to find the Shadowed here. They were almost certain that *he* would find *them* eventually, because he wanted to punish Tier and his family for the fall of the Path and Seraph's killing of the Shadowed's minion in Redern. They didn't expect the Shadowed to find them soon, though: Why would the Shadowed hurry to avenge himself, when he had all the time in the world? The Shadowed would be patient and strike when he felt it was time.

The second thing he realized was that he was glad the Memory had forced him to flee to Tier. Even if it meant his death at the hands of the likes of the Sept of Gorrish when he returned, as he must, to Taela. He would not have given up the opportunity to see Shadow's Fall and the wizards' city for his throne or even his life. He turned from the library and glanced at Tier and Seraph. And the opportunity to be someone other than the Emperor was something he could not begin to put a price on at all.

Lehr came jogging back, having evidently run around the perimeter of the entire building. "I can't find any open doors," he said. "There are some windows up higher that—"

He broke off when the door they were standing in front of opened wide, revealing Jes. "This building is different," he said, unnecessarily. "It's not frozen like the others."

Hennea walked to the nearest wall and put her hand on it. "He's right," she said. "This building is thick with magic, but it's a preservation spell of some sort."

"Like the maps," Seraph said. "Of course the wizards would preserve their library."

"Of course," murmured Tier. "If we couldn't open doors and windows, I bet that we wouldn't have been able to take books off the shelves. I can't see wizards willingly making a library unusable."

Phoran waited until most of the others walked into the building, motioning Toarsen, Kissel, Rufort, and Ielian through ahead of him. Instead of obeying him, Ielian waited beside him.

"Why do you do that?" Ielian whispered.

Phoran slipped through the door, but hung back to give Ielian the illusion of privacy as they talked. He'd learned Lehr and Jes would probably hear every word anyway—but they'd pretend they hadn't.

"Do what?" The entryway to the library was not impressive, Phoran noticed—though maybe this was the back door. There was only a small entrance hall edged in businesslike doors and stairways.

"Let Tier take charge, follow where you sh—could lead? You are the Emperor."

"Sometimes being Emperor is tiring," Phoran answered, then he grinned. "And it's always safer to let the Ravens go first into a wizards' library." He smiled at Ielian. "It's all right. They know who I am. I don't have to enforce protocol among my friends."

The others had taken the central stairway, so Phoran followed them leaving Ielian to trail behind him. The stairs went up only a single flight to a room that was as impressive as the entryway had not been. The ceiling, far above, was covered with decoratively shaped skylights, which illuminated the huge room.

The library in the palace at Taela held five thousand volumes and was accounted the largest library in the Empire. Phoran estimated that this room alone held ten times that number. The entirety of the walls was covered in bookcases, mostly filled with books, and ladders and narrow walkways spider-webbed around the walls to provide access to the shelves. On the floor of the room were more bookcases, set so closely together there was scarcely room to pass between them.

Only a small section of the room near the stairway they'd entered by was free of bookcases. Instead, a number of small tables were set up so that library patrons could take the books and read them on padded benches and a couple of carved chairs.

Seraph was holding on to Tier with obvious dismay.

"It appears that we'll be staying here for a while," Tier said, sounding mildly amused.

Phoran, bending over to rub Gura's belly, noticed that they were all leaving muddy tracks on the polished floor.

"Let's leave this for today," said Tier, glancing around. "The map shows another of the city gates on the other side of this building. I'd like to set up camp while it's still light."

"Why not stay in here where it's dry?" asked Ielian.

"No," said Hennea.

"No," said Lehr. "No one has brought back stories of an empty city, not in all the centuries this has waited here. Perhaps it's not because no one ever found it—but because no one ever left it."

"We'll camp outside of the city," said Tier. "We might as well go now and pick a good site since it looks like we'll be here for a while."

The University Gate was located just where the map had promised. After Lehr's little speech in the library, Phoran was relieved when the brass gate, like the one they'd used to enter the city, opened at the first touch.

In the end, a campsite wasn't difficult to find. There was a small pond fed by a creek not a quarter mile from the gate. The ground was free of rock, and there was grazing for the horses. Best of all, sometime while they had been in the library, it had stopped raining.

"We'll set up a permanent camp, here," said Tier, in satisfied tones. "Tomorrow we'll see about building a few corrals so we don't have to worry about the horses. And a shelter or two to keep the rain off our heads."

"Except for Hennea and me." Seraph had already started to pull the packs off her little mountain horse. "We'll go to the library while you set up camp."

"Not alone," said Jes.

Seraph turned to her oldest son and raised a cool eyebrow, and Phoran was caught between being thankful her look wasn't turned on *him* and wishing he could use that expression on encroaching Septs—but he'd never managed to learn to raise a single eyebrow, and he didn't think the expression would look quite the same with both eyebrows raised. Doubtless he would just look surprised.

"Do not forget who and what I am, Jes," Seraph said icily. "There are weapons other than swords."

Tier cleared his throat. "We'll need you at camp, Jes. I'm going to send you and Lehr out hunting. If your mother can kill a troll, I'm certain she can handle a library."

That night, after the rest of them were sleeping, Phoran found himself restless for no reason he could determine. He set aside his blankets and pulled his boots on. Jes opened his eyes, then closed them again as Phoran walked past him. Toarsen and Kissel were both fast asleep, and he stepped lightly around them because they, unlike Jes, would not have just let him walk off alone.

There was a little rise to the land fifty yards from camp, and he walked in that direction. When he topped the rise, the Memory was there waiting for him.

It was darker than the night and taller than he was. Its oddly gracile form bent down, and thin wisps of something strong wrapped around his wrist.

His sleeves were loose, so it had no trouble pushing one of them up and exposing the inside of his elbow. Phoran hissed as the Memory's fangs sank deep. He'd forgotten how cold it was, forgotten how much it hurt.

When it had finished with him, he sank to the ground and held his arm cradled to his chest.

"By the taking of your blood, I owe you one answer. Choose your question." The sexless whisper was no less frightening now than it had been the first time it spoke to him.

"Who is the Shadowed?" Phoran asked.

"He that gives his soul and spirit for power and eternal life. The Hungry One."

"I know that, that's not what I meant, and you know it," Phoran snapped. It would be useless to protest. He should have found a better way to frame his question. There was always tomorrow. He closed his eyes against the dull, consuming ache in his arm. "Give me a name."

"I give you all the answer I have," it said, and faded into the night.

CHAPTER 14

Ielian walked beside Lehr, his bow on his shoulder. It was still barely light, and the air was chill.

When they were out of sight and sound of the camp, Ielian asked, "Why me? Why not Jes or Rufort?" Either of them knew twice what he did about hunting.

"You don't do so badly," said Lehr, and Ielian took his words for the compliment they were. "Jes is still fretting because Mother and Hennea intend to go to the library on their own today. If I took him, like as not I'd turn around, and he'd be gone. He's done it before. If there's danger about, you can always count on my brother—but if it is just work, he gets distracted pretty easily. Toarsen and Kissel won't leave Phoran—and Papa needs too much help in camp for me to take all three of them."

"And Rufort?"

"Rufort is a fine hunter, but he takes no enjoyment from it." Lehr grinned suddenly. "Besides, Papa can use a strong back more than we can."

"What are we hunting today?"

"I thought we'd find a nice fat deer," Lehr said. "Since we'll be here a while, we can take time to preserve the meat."

Farther from Colossae the trees began to grow closer together, forming a sparse forest.

"I have a question," Ielian said.

"What is that?"

"Your mother talks about six Orders—and I was taught there are only five."

Lehr laughed. "I'd forgotten that. There are Falcon, Raven, Owl, Cormorant, Lark, and Eagle. The one you wouldn't have heard of is Eagle. Mother says that Travelers don't talk about them much, not even among themselves. Never to outsiders." His face grew somber. "The Eagle—the Guardian—is different, more difficult to bear."

"Your mother calls Jes, Guardian, sometimes."

Lehr nodded. "Jes is Eagle."

"He's . . ." Ielian tried to come up with a polite way to say it and failed.

"Slow?" Lehr offered. "He can seem that way sometimes. Mother says that he's not always paying attention, that he's always carrying on a running conversation with the Guardian half of himself. The Colossae wizards created the Orders, and I guess they didn't do the Eagle Order correctly. The Eagle is supposed to protect his clan—Jes can be pretty awesome in a fight."

"I saw him the night the Path fell," said Ielian.

"Then you know—ah, here's what I've been looking for. There's been a deer past here recently. Time to start the hunt."

"Let's explore the rest of the building before we start on this room," Seraph told Hennea, surveying the main room of the library. At least she hoped it was the main room. It would take them a long time to look through, and she didn't want to find any bigger rooms. "Wizards are a secretive lot. If they were working on something new, it might be in some obscure corner of the library, either high up or down in the basement."

Hennea pursed her lips. "If we're looking for something about the Orders, it won't be in bound books anyway. Otherwise, we'd have found *something* in the *mermori* libraries. It will be in parchments or handsewn notebooks of some sort. Maybe in a laboratory or work area."

"I'm glad I'm not a *solsenti* wizard," Seraph said. "I don't have the temperament to draw endless runes and mix potions in a laboratory. So, do we stay together or split up?"

"It'll take half the time to look if we split up," Hennea said, then she smiled. "Of course, if you are worried about being alone . . ."

Seraph snorted.

Hours later, Seraph was feeling as frustrated as any *solsenti* wizard.

She'd been right about the kinds of places wizards liked, and the section of the library that she'd found abounded in such places, small alcoves that were obviously private studies, laboratories with shelves full of jars and baskets of spell components, and slightly larger rooms where two or three wizards might have worked together. She'd walked leagues of maze-like halls that twisted and turned, with unexpected stairways and half stairways.

Everything as perfectly preserved as it must have been the day that they had left. She could not conceive of the power that had taken.

"You were here weren't you, Isolde?" Seraph murmured to herself as she walked through yet another narrow twisting hallway. "I wonder what you saw and where you were going? Did you know what they were doing, those great wizards who created the Stalker? Were you one of them, or did you protest futilely?"

She trailed a hand on the wall until she came to another door. The room was mostly empty, though it still smelled of some sort of incense or tobacco.

"I wonder where the Stalker is," she mused. "And why neither my Falcon nor my Eagle feels it anywhere." It hadn't struck her as odd until just that minute. Her sons could feel shadowing and, less reliably, the Shadowed, but they hadn't said anything about the Stalker at all.

There was a small desk and a chair on one end of the room. Someone had carved two letters in the wood of the desk. Remembering the scolding she'd given Jes and Lehr for carving their initials into the floorboards at home when they were about Rinnie's age, she smiled.

Some young person had sat here, she thought, brushing her hands over the chair, but keeping a lock on her talent for reading objects because she didn't know how the wizard's preservation spells would affect it. That didn't stop her from speculating. A student had been sent here to work, perhaps, and had taken his eating knife and carved his initials here instead, finding a kind of immortality in the act. *Look,* he said, *I was here, I left my mark.*

She stepped out of the room and shut the door gently.

"Excuse me, can I help you?" said a male voice in softly accented Common.

Seraph spun on her heel and stared at the young man who stood in the hallway behind her.

Except for his clothes, he looked every inch a Traveler. Silvery blond hair, not two shades off her own, hung to his shoulders, where it wasn't caught up in beaded braids. His eyes were a pale, pale grey, and he looked only a little older than Rinnie. He was naked except for a wraparound kilt of bright colors secured with a plain brown belt. Even his feet were bare.

"Who are you?" she asked, centering herself in case she needed her magic.

His small polite smile widened a bit, and he ducked his head without dropping her gaze. "You may call me Scholar. May I help you find what you need?"

Only then, when the first shock of fright had passed did she realize what her senses had been trying to tell her: this was not a human.

"Illusion," she said, reaching out to touch him lightly. His skin was soft, warm, and gave beneath her touch as if he had been a real boy and not a magical construct. The magic felt very familiar—just like the *mermori*. "Hinnum made you."

"Indeed," he answered her politely. She found it impossible to look at the illusion and not designate him as male, though she knew it was foolish. "May I help you find something? You seem to be searching."

"I need to find out about the Orders," she told him. "My husband's has been damaged, and I need to repair it."

"You have many Orders," the Scholar said neutrally.

"I am Raven," Seraph said confused.

"You carry many Orders."

Her hand went to the bag where the gems the Path had created lay. How had an illusionary construct sensed them? She narrowed her eyes at him. "I do. There have been many Travelers killed, and their Orders bound to gemstones so that *solsenti* wizards could use them. I have them here. I hope that if I find out enough to help my husband, then I can see these Orders are properly released as well."

The boy said nothing, just waited in silence. His small smile was unchanged, and she suspected that she'd been mistaken when she'd thought it had widened earlier.

"Why were you left here?" she asked him.

"I am here to help others find information from the library."

"You know what information is stored here?" Seraph felt a stirring of excited hope that the first sight of the library full of books had extinguished. If she and Hennea had to sort through the books for ones they could decipher, then read them, Tier would die of old age before they finished.

"I know what is in the library," he answered.

"Good," she said. "Do you know where Hennea is? My friend who came in here with me?"

This time the answer didn't come immediately. "I know where the Raven is," he said at last.

"Take me there," she said. This was better than a notebook full of the scribblings of wizards.

Hennea had chosen to explore the basement. They found her seated at a table, a magelight hanging over a loose-bound sheaf of papers. Her hair was mussed, as if she'd spent time crawling under tables.

"Raven," said the Scholar, before Seraph could announce them. "You are welcome here."

Hennea marked her place with a finger and looked up with an expression of mild inquiry. She didn't look at all surprised to find a stranger addressing her. Seraph had never admired her aplomb more.

"This is the Scholar," Seraph said, wondering if Hennea would see what she had seen.

Hennea frowned and set the papers aside, shifting her weight in her chair as she stared at him. "You look familiar," she said at last.

"No," Seraph corrected her gently. "He feels familiar."

Hennea straightened. "Hinnum," she said.

"The Scholar is here to help people find information." Seraph smiled. "Phoran said that wizards tend to be very well organized."

* * *

The Scholar led them back to the main room, the first room they'd been in. "This is a good place to start," he told them. "What would you know?"

"Tell us about the Stalker," asked Hennea.

He bowed shallowly. "Pray have a seat, Raven."

He was talking to Hennea as if he no longer noticed Seraph was in the room, his eyes locked on Hennea's face. As she sat on the cushioned bench beside Hennea, Seraph wondered if it was some aspect of his creation that he paid attention only to the one who questioned him.

"There were once two brothers, twins born of the Eastern Star and fathered by the Moon. They were mirror images of each other, the light twin and the dark. We called them the Weaver and the Stalker, though those were not their names."

"Why not call them by name?" asked Hennea.

"Do you know this story?"

"No." But Hennea frowned and rubbed her forehead as if she were trying to recall something.

"I've never heard of the Weaver," said Seraph. "Only the Stalker."

"Names have power." The Scholar's voice was as polite and even as his small smile. Seraph was finding that the Scholar's expression, which had first been almost welcoming, was starting to make her uncomfortable.

He continued in that same quiet voice. "To speak the names of the twins is to call their attention to you, and it should not be done lightly."

When neither Seraph nor Hennea commented, he continued. "The Weaver held the power of creation. Whenever he spoke a word or had a thought, he created. The Stalker held the keys of destruction. Whatsoever the Weaver created, the Stalker numbered its days so the Weaver's creations did not grow to such an extent that the All of Being was made to Nothingness."

"I remember that," said Hennea. Her hands were on her temples as if they ached. "I remember that. If creation was given no limit, ultimately everything would cease to exist."

The Scholar's focus on Hennea was starting to bother Seraph. Though his expression never changed, his body leaned toward her, just a little. Seraph could see no magic passing from him to Hennea, but she watched him closely.

"One day the Stalker was walking when he came upon a woman washing her clothes. She was more beautiful to him than any other thing his brother had ever made, and so he took her to wife.

"While he had her the Stalker was the happiest of men, but, since she was his brother's creation, her days were numbered from her birth. When she was an old, old woman, the Stalker went to his brother and pleaded that the Weaver would break the power of destruction, the Stalker's own magic, that she might not die.

"But this was something the Weaver could not do. If he broke this power, then he would destroy them both. Because for the All that Is to exist, the power of creation can never overwhelm destruction.

"Since the Weaver had not saved her, his most perfect creation, the Stalker vowed that all of the Weaver's creations would be destroyed. But he stayed his hand while his wife yet lived, because he could not stand to lose her one moment before he had to.

"As she lay dying, his wife gave her husband a drink the Weaver had prepared, and the Stalker fell asleep as the last breath left her mouth."

It was a romantic story, but the Scholar told it the same dry fashion Jes had used to recite his lessons—perhaps with even a shade less enthusiasm.

"The Weaver knew that without his brother, his powers would also destroy the All of Being, so he drank the same potion the Stalker had drunk. They slept, the Weaver and the Stalker. And while they slept, the Weaver dreamed a weaving to cover them both and protect his creations from them when they next awoke."

The Scholar quit speaking.

"That doesn't sound like the end of the story," Seraph said.

"The story of the Weaver and the Stalker will not end until the All of Being ends," said the Scholar. "And at that time there will be no one to tell its end."

Hennea sighed and started to say something but was stopped by noise from the stairway.

Gura was the first to reach them, whining and wagging his tail and trying to wriggle his way onto Seraph's lap. Since he outweighed her by a couple of stones she was hard put to save herself until Tier hauled him off by his collar.

"Gura, down," he said, and the dog dropped to the floor and looked repentant for a moment. Seraph sat up and rubbed his side with the toe of her boot, and he wagged his tail cheerfully.

Jes had come with Tier, and the Guardian was staring at the Scholar, who had not changed his expression—or his focus on Hennea.

"Where are the others?" she asked.

"I left them cooking steaks at camp. Since we'll be here a while, Lehr brought down a buck. Jes and I came to get you for dinner." Tier glanced at the illusion, then he looked again, frowning. "Your friend is welcome to come with us."

"Thank you," said the Scholar, turning toward Tier as if he'd just noticed him. "But I do not need to eat, and I may not leave the library." He paused. "It is good that you stay outside of the city. The dead walk the streets at night."

"It's an illusion," Hennea told Tier. "One of Hinnum's."

"It told us a story," said Seraph. "I think you ought to hear it. Scholar, would you tell the story of the Weaver and the Stalker?"

"Of course."

When the Scholar finished, Tier rubbed his jaw, and said, "So the Stalker wasn't something created by the wizards here?"

"No," said the Scholar.

"The stories are wrong," Seraph said.

"So why did the wizards leave?" Tier asked Seraph. "Why freeze the city this way? Why is the library the only thing that isn't frozen in time?"

"There was nothing here for them. It was part of the price for what they had done. They could not bear to lose the library forever."

Hennea frowned. "If they didn't create the Stalker, what had they done?"

For the first time, the smile fell from the illusion's face and left something very old peering out of the young eyes. "They killed the gods," he whispered; and then he was gone as if he'd never been.

The Guardian growled.

Back at camp, Tier told the story of the Stalker to the others, as they cooked venison over the fire. As far as Seraph could tell, he used the same words the Scholar had twice used.

"I thought the Stalker was supposed to be evil," said the Emperor, feeding the last of his fire-roasted meat to Gura, who accepted it with more politeness than enthusiasm. The dog had discovered during their trip that Phoran and his guards were not as hardened to pleading eyes as his usual family and had been making use of this new power throughout supper.

"That's what the stories I've always heard say," agreed Seraph.

"So it isn't the Stalker that caused the fall of the Elder Wizards?" Lehr leaned back on his elbows and stared thoughtfully at the fire.

"Ellevanal told me the Travelers killed their gods and ate them." Seraph braced her elbows on her knees and leaned her chin on her hands. "My father just told me there were no gods, but Hennea—and the Scholar—say the gods are dead."

"I don't know where I heard it," said Hennea, and Jes rubbed her shoulder gently.

Hennea had been quiet since they left the library, but then, being a Raven, that wasn't unusual for her. Seraph would have dismissed her suspicions that Hennea was upset about something, except Jes had been fussing over her.

"The Shadowed is evil," said Lehr with conviction. "He killed a whole town, a town larger than Redern. He killed Benroln, Brewydd, and all of Rongier's clan. He taught the wizards of the Path how to steal Orders."

"The Shadowed is evil," agreed Seraph.

Phoran cleared his throat, and Seraph turned to look at him. He glanced once at the setting sun, then said, "I ought to mention that the Memory came last night. I asked him if he knew who the Shadowed was, but he didn't. I wonder if you have a question you would like me to ask him tonight?"

"I do," said Seraph, before anyone else could say anything. "I'd like to know the details of the second part of the spell that steals the Orders to tie them to the gems."

That night, when the Memory beckoned Phoran, Seraph went with him. She made everyone else stay back in camp.

"If it was willing to come out with everyone here, it wouldn't force Phoran to come to it," she said, staring first at Jes, then at Toarsen and Kissel. "I will see to it that Phoran comes to no harm—and he will do the same for me."

"Now mind you," she told Phoran as they tromped up to the little rise he'd gone to the night before "Jes is going to follow us anyway. There's nothing I can do about that—but he'll stay out of my sight, and hopefully not interfere with the Memory."

Phoran smiled down at her. "If *I'd* tried to leave Toarsen and Kissel behind, we'd still be arguing."

"Yes," she agreed. "But you are only an emperor, after all, and I am Raven."

He couldn't tell if she was teasing or not. He rather suspected not.

The Memory came again. It said nothing to him, nor did it appear to notice Seraph. It fed from his wrist this time. Phoran had thought it would be less awful with Seraph there, but somehow it was worse. As if, he thought, someone was witnessing his rape, it increased the humiliation and feeling of violation. The pain was as bad as it ever had been.

When it was finished, the Memory said, "By the taking of your blood, I owe you one answer. Choose your question."

Phoran staggered to his feet and felt Seraph's arm come round his waist to help support him.

Phoran tried to remember what Seraph had told him she needed to know. "There are three parts to the spell that the Masters use to steal the Orders from Travelers and bind them to gemstones. What happens in the second of the three parts."

"The Masters take the gem, already bound to the Order, and they place it in a man's mouth. He is the sacrifice to power the spell. They cut his throat, and when he is dead they remove the gem." The Memory swayed and its voice changed, rough with remembered agony. "They took it, still warm from the dead man's last breath, and touched me with it. I could feel it pull, I knew that something bad was happening."

"This happens immediately," asked Seraph urgently. "You knew right away?"

"Yes," said the Memory, but it didn't sound like the Memory anymore. It sounded like a man in pain.

"Tier would have known if it started before that night in the Tavern."

Phoran didn't think that Seraph was speaking to the Memory anymore, but it said, "Yes." And it was gone.

"Come," said Seraph, stepping away from him until she held him by the arm rather than around the waist. "I need to talk with Lehr and Tier."

Phoran felt so tired, so weary, and the camp seemed a long way away.

"Come," Seraph said more gently. "Your Memory has give us a different clue than I expected."

"What do you mean?" Phoran started the long trek back to camp.

"I thought I'd learn something of the magic they used," she said. "And I did—though nothing that I can use. But it might have given us a clue about the Shadowed."

They hadn't gone far before Jes joined them. Without asking, he pulled Phoran's arm around his shoulder.

"Lean on me," he said.

Toarsen and Kissel came next.

"They didn't listen to *you* either," Phoran whispered to Seraph.

She laughed. "At least they didn't bother arguing."

They set Phoran down upon his bedroll, and Seraph tucked him in with all the expertise that his nurse had had when he was a child younger than Rinnie.

"There now," she told him. "Go to sleep."

But he didn't, he just closed his eyes and listened.

Seraph moved away from Phoran and lowered her voice. "Lehr, Olbeck was Shadowed when you found him attacking Rinnie and Phoran."

"That's right," he agreed. "That's what Jes says. I told you Akavith said Olbeck killed poor Lukeeth."

"Lukeeth died the day Tier was stricken," she said. "As best I can piece it together."

"What did you find out?" asked Tier, putting a hand on her shoulder.

She held his hand with her own. "Wait," she said. "Lehr?"

"I don't remember exactly, but either that day or the day before," he agreed.

"Tier, do you remember anyone touching you the day we noticed there was something wrong with your Order?"

"I was at the shop all morning, Seraph," he said. "Of course people touched me."

"Tell me who," she said turning around to face him so he could see her urgency. "Tell me. Not everyone you talked to, just the ones who touched you, Tier." He was a Bard. He could remember them all.

"Alinath and Bandor, of course," he said slowly. "The Brewmaster came with breadmother to replace the one we lost. The miller brought flour. Ciro and his son. Those were the only ones who touched me—that I remember, anyway."

"What about at the tavern?"

"Regil touched me when he gave me his lute. I shook Willon's hand."

"One of them was the Shadowed," Seraph said.

Phoran sat up. "The Shadowed is a Rederni? Redern is a very small place, Seraph. Surely someone would notice that one of them wasn't aging as he should."

"Willon." Rinnie's voice was very soft. "Willon's store is right below the Temple of the Five. Those tunnels weren't just below the temple, they were behind his shop. Maybe he found them when they dug his shop deeper into the mountain."

"Willon was in Taela when I found Tier imprisoned," said Phoran. "I saw him at his son's shop."

"The Shadowed wouldn't have a son," said Hennea. "Birth is not one of the Stalker's powers."

"Master Emtarig isn't really Willon's son," said Phoran slowly. "I don't remember who told me, but Willon's wife died without giving him children, and he adopted one of his apprentices, an orphan."

"Willon told me about the plague at Colbern," Tier said, sounding stunned. "They rode past Colbern on the way back from Taela, he said. But surely Lehr or Jes would have noticed if Willon were the Shadowed."

"They didn't know what he was until the Memory had stripped him of some of his magics." Hennea tapped her fingers impatiently. "But if it were Willon, where are the bodies? The Shadowed has to feed upon death."

"Colbern," said Lehr.

"He used to leave a couple of times a year," said Seraph. "He could have been off hunting, then."

"The temples," said the Guardian. "I sat outside his temple in Redern and felt the feeding, but I didn't understand what it was. I didn't remember enough. The Stalker was not the Lord of Death, but the Lord of Destruction. The Unnamed King did not just feed upon death, but upon the pain and suffering that came before the death. Emotions feed the Shadowed—hatred, envy, the kinds of things that consumed Bandor before Hennea freed him from the taint."

"Willon came to Redern just after I returned from the wars with Seraph," Tier said. "He could have followed us after I killed the man who the Path sent for Seraph when her brother died. But I thought the Shadowed wasn't supposed to age? Willon is older now than he was then."

Seraph shook her head. "Illusion. He wouldn't need much, not enough I'd notice anyway. There's a little bit of magic around Redern all the time."

"Mehalla," said Jes, his voice a low throbbing growl that raised the hair on the back of Seraph's neck.

Seraph felt as if someone had clubbed her. He was right. Oh, sweet Lark, he was right.

"She was so sick," Tier whispered. "She got sick in the spring and just never got better. She lingered for months and months."

"She had convulsions," Lehr said. "I remember watching Mother hold her down so she wouldn't hurt herself."

"Who is Mehalla?" Phoran asked.

"My daughter," whispered Seraph. "My daughter the Lark. She was just a toddler. He must have thought she was easy prey."

Tier's arm slid across the front of her shoulders and pulled her back against his chest. "He killed my daughter."

Tier was behind her, but she saw Phoran meet his gaze.

"My Emperor," said Tier in a silky-sweet voice. "We will see you freed of your Memory as soon as we return to Redern."

CHAPTER 15

"The Scholar felt a lot of guilt and despair for something
not alive," said Jes, who had appointed himself escort to Seraph
and Hennea, as the three of them walked to the library. Everyone
else, including the dog, had gone out exploring together.

"Hinnum created him," Hennea answered Jes before Seraph could. "He was the greatest of the Colossae wizards. I
suppose if he could create the *mermori,* he could also create
an illusion that empaths could feel."

"Why would he do that to something that exists to help people find information?" Jes asked rather reasonably—for Jes.

"Is that why you insisted on coming today?" asked Seraph.
She wasn't ready to put limits on an illusion created by Hinnum either, but she also found herself agreeing with Jes.

"The Guardian doesn't trust him because he has no scent,"
Jes said with a shrug. "I explained the Scholar is an illusion,
but neither the Guardian nor I think that an illusion should be
so interested in Hennea."

The main room of the library was empty when they arrived,
but there was a book lying open on one of the tables.

Seraph picked it up. It seemed to be a general treatise of
some sort on magic, open to a chapter on the "Aspects of

Man"—whatever that meant. However, it had obviously been
left out for them, so she started reading.

Hennea hovered briefly over her shoulder, then walked to
one of the bookshelves and began perusing titles. Jes paced
restlessly back and forth for a while.

Finally, he came to stand in front of Seraph.

"If you want to go out and explore, go do so," she told him
without looking up. "Just be careful. We'll be fine. It doesn't
look as though the Scholar is going to come out today."

He sniffed the air. "All right," he said. "But I'll be back in a
little while."

She heard his rapid footsteps down the stairs and the click
of the outside door as it shut behind him.

"I didn't finish the story of the Stalker yesterday," said the
Scholar's voice as soon as Jes was gone.

Seraph looked up from her book to see the illusion standing in front of Hennea.

"Nor did I tell you why the wizards were forced to sacrifice
this city," he said.

"No," agreed Hennea, reshelving a book she'd taken out. "I
wondered why you didn't."

The Scholar stared at her with that half smile that seemed
more of a mask than an expression. "Make yourself comfortable, and I will tell you."

Seraph set her book aside and sat down on the other end of
the bench where Hennea was sitting down.

"The Weaver created a binding that would keep both him
and his twin from interacting directly with his creations. But
he could not completely isolate them, because eventually their
power would build and destroy his bindings. Instead he created six gods who would control the power of the Weaver and
of the Stalker."

The Scholar paused.

"The Orders," said Hennea hoarsely, though Seraph
couldn't see anything in what the Scholar had said that ought
to have bothered her. "The Raven, the Owl, the Falcon, the
Eagle, the Lark, and the Cormorant. Magic, music, the hunt,
the guardian, healing, and storms."

"Magic, music, hunt, war, healing, and wind," corrected
the Scholar.

"The Guardian is not an Order of soldiers," Hennea argued.

"No," agreed the Scholar, but he did not elaborate upon his answer.

"Something broke the bindings on the Stalker," said Seraph. "The Elder Wizards sacrificed the city to bind the Stalker. Not because they created the Stalker, but because something they did loosed the god of destruction." Or so she'd been taught.

"The gods ruled this world for a very long time," the Scholar said, and Seraph couldn't tell if he'd even noticed what she'd said. "Long enough for a small village to become a town, then a great city. Long enough for the wizards to become arrogant and fall away from the worship of gods. 'What good praying to the Cormorant who might or might not answer?' they asked themselves. 'If you bring your gold to Korsack or Terilia or one of the other wind witches, they will do your will as long as you are the first or most generous with your gold.'"

The Scholar reached out as if he might touch Hennea, but then pulled both hands behind his back.

"It didn't help that the gods no longer granted the gifts they had once freely given. The great city had no desperate need for a legendary warrior or a gifted healer. They did not depend upon their crops to survive, and so they needed no god-gifted weather mage. So the gods gave less, were worshiped less, but they were not unhappy with Colossae— perhaps just indifferent."

The Scholar closed his eyes. "Except for the Raven, for Colossae was Her city. The city of wizards."

No matter what her magic told her, Seraph was having increasing difficulty in believing that this was an illusion—or at least *just* an illusion.

"Children were taken to the Raven's temple on their name days," he said quietly. "The Raven's priests would tell them if they were mageborn or not. If they were, then the oracle would tell them what areas of magic would be their specialty. Sometimes, the Raven herself came and blessed them with a gift of her own magic, which the child could use without need of study or ritual."

"Like the Raven's Order," said Seraph.

"Yes."

There was a long silence.

"What happened?" whispered Hennea intently, and she leaned forward. "Something terrible happened."

"Yes." The Scholar took a half step away from Hennea. "Something terrible happened. There was a boy. He had the power to be a successful wizard, having been blessed by the goddess herself, but he had no dedication. He would not study—he had no need to earn a living because his father was a great wizard and so had accumulated great wealth."

He turned his back to them and stared at the great rows of books. "This boy fell in love with a maiden who loved him in return—so long as his father's gold was more than that of any of her other suitors. The day came when she found another, richer, man. When the boy reproached her, she told him that she preferred a man adept in the fighting arts rather than a half-trained wizard."

The Scholar sighed. "The boy could not bear the rejection. If she wanted a fighting man, he would become one. Remember though, that he was a lazy young man, used to buying his way through life. So instead of hiring an instructor and learning, he went to the war god's temple."

"The Eagle," said Seraph.

"Aythril, the god of war," agreed the Scholar, his back still toward them. "The war god's priestess laughed at the boy's plea for the gift of martial arts. The war god would never have given his gifts to a man so obviously unworthy. She told the boy that if he trained for a year and a day, she would petition the war god on his behalf. The boy was angry and offended, for he was proud."

The Scholar bowed his head. "He went to his father, an old wizard and powerful. People walked softly in his presence because he was quick to take offense—and the priestess's words offended him greatly."

"Hinnum?" asked Seraph.

The Scholar turned back and met Seraph's eyes. "No, not Hinnum, though there are sins enough to lie on his shoulders. Ontil the Peacock was the wizard's name. He saw the priestess's words as an attack on his standing, and so he vowed to take the gifts that the priestess would not willingly give. He hid himself here"—the Scholar waved a hand around the library— "and for a year he studied and buried himself in obscure texts."

He looked at Hennea again, though she wasn't looking at him at all. She was staring at her hands.

"The old wizard had help in his endeavor. He was not well liked, but, as I said, he was powerful, and there were many who feared him or sought his favor. One night, with four dozen lesser mages, he called the war god's power to his son. But the power of the war god is not held lightly—fifty mages died that night. Fifty mages and a god."

"Do you remember, Raven?" The Scholar leaned forward and touched Hennea lightly on the shoulder.

Seraph frowned, but there was nothing magical in the Scholar's touch, she would have felt it. Why did he think Hennea would remember any of this?

Hennea flinched away from his hand and came to her feet. "Thank you," she said in a distracted tone. "I'm going to take a walk."

The Scholar watched Hennea disappear down the stairs and continued to watch until the sound of the outer door shutting rang through the room.

"You are not just an illusion," said Seraph.

The Scholar looked at her, no smile upon his face at all. "A child was born that night. A little girl. Rage such as no child should have gave power to her voice, the rage of a murdered god, and the very walls shook with His power in a baby's cries. She was taken to the Lark's temple, where the Lark Herself sent her to sleep until something could be done."

Seraph sat back down, abandoning her half-formed intention to follow Hennea. "Guardian," she said.

The Scholar shook his head. "Almost, you understand. A god is immortal, we thought. They cannot die. But Ontil proved us wrong. Only the Stalker and the Weaver are immortal. And that part of them that made the Eagle a god survived his death, though it survived broken and torn, tainted by the wrath of a murdered god."

"In the child."

"Years passed." The Scholar gave Seraph the same intensity of attention he had given to Hennea. "Years in which it became obvious to the wizards that the god of destruction was awaking. Not just in Colossae, but all over the world we heard of mountains falling to the earth and oceans heaving themselves beyond their boundaries."

"Hinnum, the city's greatest wizard, went to the Raven for help—as he had all of his long life."

"He was four centuries old," Seraph said.

The illusion's eyes brightened with temper. "Four and a half. I—*He* knelt before Her statue in Her temple and pleaded for aid." Seraph realized it had not been temper alone that had brightened his eyes because a tear slid down his face. "She used to walk with him in the gardens here, because Hinnum was Her favorite. They would argue and bicker like children and when his third, most beloved, wife died, She held him through the night while he cried."

"She loved him," Seraph whispered.

"Like a son," he said. "Her love and Her Consort was the Eagle."

Seraph sucked in her breath, caught up in his story. "And wizards used the gifts She had given them to kill Him."

The Scholar nodded. "She blamed Herself, and She blamed us." He closed his eyes briefly. "She was so angry. While Hinnum prayed, he heard others enter, but until the Owl spoke he didn't realize who had come into the Raven's temple. It was the first time he'd seen any of the other gods."

He sat down beside Seraph, taking her hands in his own. "The Owl was . . . was like your husband. Even frightened as I was I could not help returning Her smile. She lifted me to my feet, and I saw the Others." He paused, and Seraph decided not to point out that he'd claimed to be Hinnum again. She would wait until he was finished with what he had to tell her. Hinnum, she thought, Hinnum would know how to save her husband and how to kill the Shadowed—and somehow this illusion was Hinnum.

"The Hunter was not a big man"—the Scholar was saying—"nor did He speak much, but when he was in the room, I was always aware of him, even in the presence of the other gods. The Cormorant looked just like the statue in His temple—they all did really—but the Cormorant looked as though a smile belonged on His face. He wasn't smiling, but I could see that was the expression he was most comfortable with. I didn't like the Lark. I don't know why. Maybe it was the way that She held the child who slept in Her arms, the child who bore the rage and power of the god of war—as if she were a stone or rock, not a child who suffered for other people's sins."

The Scholar pulled his hands away from Seraph's and covered his face. "The Owl called my Lady, and forced the Raven to come to Her Call. Ah, Raven who was, that I could have died before that day."

He sighed and let his hands fall limply to his sides. When he spoke again, he continued his story with more dispassion.

"When the Raven came, the Lark showed Her the sleeping child, and said, 'I am no more powerful than your consort was, Raven. In another month I shall not be able to hold His anger asleep in this child. And then his power will ravage this world, and nothing will be able to hold it in check.'

" 'This isn't about the child, or about the Eagle.' said the Cormorant. 'It is about the Weaver and the Stalker. The Eagle's death has weakened the binding that holds them. We must restore the balance.' "

The Scholar looked down at his lap. "Then the Weaver spoke. I don't know what he said because his voice overwhelmed me, and I fainted. When I came to myself, only Raven was there, sitting beside me and stroking my hair."

Tears fell again down the Scholar's face, but he seemed not to notice them. "The Raven told me, 'We give mortals small pieces of our godhood all of the time: you call them gifts: the toddler who can sing a song note perfect; the warrior whose reflexes are faster than most; the midwife whose patients never die of birthing fever.' " The Scholar stopped speaking because his voice grew too thick to continue.

"She killed the other gods," said Seraph, stunned as she realized what must have happened. "Ellevanal said that the Travelers killed their gods and ate them—and he was right."

"We killed them, the Raven and I," agreed the Scholar. "They chose to die because it was the only way to save the All of Being. They sacrificed themselves and their souls flew free, leaving only their power behind. The Raven showed me how to divide the power and bind the Orders so when the mortal who bore them died, they would find another Order Bearer."

"But the Eagle's power was corrupted," Seraph whispered. "He was not a willing sacrifice and would not leave His power." *Oh my poor Jes,* she thought. "Empaths. You gave empaths the power and rage of the war god's ghost."

When Hennea rushed out of the library, she didn't know what had upset her, just that she could not bear to hear one more of the Scholar's words. The flood of anger, of pain, was so strong—she had no idea where it had come from.

She walked rapidly with no goal other than to wear out her body and give herself a chance to think. To become calm. A Raven had no business allowing herself to become so upset. Disastrous things happened when a Raven was out of control.

She followed a narrow footpath behind a hedge of roses, found a small fountain, and sat upon the small stone bench in front of it. The roses in the hedge were opened wide to the sun and had no smell at all.

It took a long time, but gradually peace seeped through her bones, leaving her feeling more like herself. She put a hand into the water of the fountain, then drew it out dry. There was a barrier of time between her hand and the cool water where small fish had once lived. She couldn't touch the water because it didn't exist in this time, not really.

The memory of how the spell worked was hers. She could break it if she wanted to. She didn't remember where she'd learned it: she hadn't known it yesterday.

She didn't hear him come. There was nothing to warn her, until his hand closed around her wrist, and he pulled her to her feet.

"Jes?" she whispered though she knew better. The hand that gripped her so carefully was burning with cold.

"No." The Guardian examined her face as pounding fear washed over her, through her, without touching her because she could never fear him. "Jes is where he cannot be hurt."

She was wrong, she was not immune to fear. The Guardian's words terrified her.

"You can't do that," she said. "You can't lock him away. He's an empath—he needs to be with you."

The Guardian's lip curled in an expression she'd never

seen on Jes's face, though it was familiar. Achingly familiar. Where had she seen it?

"I do not need advice from *you* on how to protect Jes," the Guardian said, and she finally realized he was angry with *her*—a rage so deep that he'd locked Jes away from it.

"What's wrong?" she asked. "Is there something new wrong with Tier?"

He snarled at her, the growl of an enraged mountain cat out of a human mouth, then turned on his heel and began striding away, pulling her behind him.

"Papa is dying—or didn't you know that?" His voice was soft with menace. "Isn't it important to you?"

"You know me better than that," Hennea said, trying to answer his anger with control.

As if the calmness of her voice were more than he could bear, the Guardian jerked her to face him and shook her once. The small act of violence only seemed to increase his frustration—he growled, a low, angry sound.

He bent his head and kissed her. It was a hard kiss, born of rage. She felt her bottom lip split under the pressure. When he tasted her blood, he hesitated, then shoved her away from him—though he didn't release his hold on her wrist.

He was still for a moment, then began striding forward again. "Papa leaves his lute in its pack, and my mother cries herself to sleep every night. They pretend and pretend all day long so they won't hurt us." His voice was so low that she felt it as much as heard it.

"That is no different now than it was this morning," said Hennea. "But your mother and I are getting closer to the answers we need. We know who the Shadowed is. Guardian—"

She let her voice trail off because she recognized the streets the Guardian had taken, she knew where it led—and she didn't know how she knew.

She looked at Jes's face and saw that he would not listen to her now, not until he'd given vent to his rage—and maybe not even then. It was not a good thing that he'd locked Jes away. Strong emotions were such a danger to the Eagle: love, hatred . . . betrayal. She took hope from the long-fingered hand that was wrapped around her wrist: not once had it tightened enough to bruise.

She watched that hand, and let Jes direct her to the end of the street, where a temple much like the one they'd found their first day in Colossae presided. Jes led the way through the temple's open doors into the antechamber which was covered in thick carpets. There was a second set of steps, four of them, and another doorway. He didn't pause as the carpets gave way to white marble, but walked to the far end of the room. He grabbed her shoulder with his free hand and held her before him so she stood directly in front of the black marble statue on the dais of the Temple of the Raven.

Like her sister goddess the Owl, the Raven was clad only in a skirt caught with a belt bearing the device of her totem, but there was no paint on this statue. One hand rested at her side, and the other, held up toward the room, bore a raven with ruby eyes. In contrast to the merry expression the Owl had worn, this goddess's face was serene, Raven-like.

Her features were Hennea's own.

"Alhennea it says on her belt," said the Guardian. Jes would not have been able to read the belt. "Did you shorten it when you came to my family? Why did you come to us? Were you bored? Decided to play with the lives of mortals for a while?"

Shock held her still, then she dropped to the floor under the sudden weight of the memories Hinnum had long ago stolen from her. She hit the floor hard enough that she knew, dimly, she would have bruises tomorrow.

Stronger even than the memories were the accompanying emotions.

"I do not know you at all," he snarled, and even in the richness of her banquet of despair she heard him, heard the anguish that underlay the anger in his voice. "You could have healed my father. You could have killed the Shadowed in Taela and saved Phoran from his Memory." He waved his arms, and she saw Jes filter through the Guardian's eyes. "You could have destroyed the Path before it was born. You could have saved my mother's clan."

"Jes," she said hoarsely. "I am not She."

"You are," he insisted, and it was Jes she talked to. "Do you think because I do not *have* to read your feelings when I touch you that I cannot do so if I want to? I felt you recognize this place. You knew. You *are* She."

Her eyes were drawn again to the statue. "I—I think I was once."

She looked back at Jes and tried to pull out words to lessen the agony in his eyes. He was listening, listening, when the Guardian would have protected him from her. Seraph had been right, her son was strong. There were not many Eagle Bearers who could wrest control from the Guardian.

"I will swear in front of your father, who is Bard still, that I did not know who I was until just now." She would have said something more, but a memory overwhelmed her. She cried out, a shuddering, inarticulate cry and bowed her spine until her forehead hit the marble floor. Part of her felt the pain of the impact, but a clear image of a red stain spreading in the Owl's colorful skirts held most of her attention. She could almost feel the cool haft of the knife even yet.

Then, somehow, she was back in the present, and Jes was curled around her, pulling her into his lap.

"I have never betrayed you, Jes. I don't play games with people I—with people I love," she managed to say. "I don't have that kind of power anymore, I gave it away." The words spilled out of her faster and faster. "We took my power and divided it so it balanced with the others. There was no more war god, and so the other gods had to die, too. I had to direct the spell to sacrifice the city, though; no one else knew how to do the spell. But I was supposed to die. Hinnum swore he would kill me, but I think he could not bear to do it. He took my memories instead."

Jes kissed her forehead, and it was too much, because she knew her uncontrolled emotions were hurting him. She didn't want to hurt Jes, couldn't bear hurting him.

She pulled herself free of his lap and stumbled away from him. Her nose was running and her face was wet, she pulled up her shirt and wiped all the moisture away and kept moving away from Jes until she could lean her face against a wall.

"I was supposed to be dead," she said calmly, pressing her cheek against the cold marble. Then she hit the wall as hard as she could with the flat of her hand, savoring the pain that was so much easier to bear than her memories. "I was supposed to be dead!" She screamed it, felt it roar through her lungs and release the pressure just a little. She would have hit the wall again, this time with her fist; but a gentle hand caught her wrist, opened her fingers, and laid her palm flat on the wall before he let go of her again.

She stared at her hand.

"I am so *old*. I have failed so many times, I—" She broke off. She had no right to burden him with her pain, he had enough of his own. She would mend what she could. "I am no longer a goddess, just very old." She was babbling. She took a deep breath and felt the lines of her face relax as her control returned. "I am so poor a thing I could not even kill the *solsenti* mage-priest Volis, because I could not break free of his magic. I thought at least I might help your mother understand what had happened to Tier. I didn't think she could rescue him; I thought she could spread the word to the other clans."

She waved her hand helplessly. "I expected to cause a little trouble for the Path, for the Shadowed, a slap, you understand, because I could do nothing more. I am not used to asking for help, nor having it offered to me. Travelers are not a generous people. They do as they have to, as their history demands, but they take little pleasure in it. I did not expect your mother to help me."

She had to take another controlling breath. She was glad he stood behind her so she didn't have to look at him. "I did not expect what happened—but I did *not* sit back and watch while your family risked everything, Jes. I helped with every power I had."

She stopped speaking because there was nothing more to say, and because if she allowed herself to say another sentence, she would scream her throat raw. She hoped what she'd told him was enough to allow Jes to keep the fragile balance he'd ridden for so much longer than most of his kind. She should have stayed away from him, should have left after the first time they kissed.

"I've never seen you cry before," said Jes's soft voice, then his hand was touching her cheek. When it touched her skin, he hissed softly, as a man who burned himself on a cinder might.

She tried to pull her emotions under control, tried to step away so she wouldn't hurt him. She didn't want to hurt him any more.

"Shh," he said, putting his hands on her shoulders and turning her.

She resisted because she didn't want him to look at her, her face blotched, her eyes swollen. She didn't want to look at him and see the distance that the knowledge of what she once had been would put between them. But he was stronger than she, and persistent. In the end, she chose to keep what little dignity she had left rather than fight him.

His face was too close for her to see his expression, she only caught a glimpse of velvet-dark eyes before he bent his head to lick gently at the cut on her lip.

"I don't want to hurt you either," he said. "Neither of us does. I'm sorry. I believe you, I believe you. I was almost certain you wouldn't betray us—but the Guardian had to believe, too. He wouldn't listen to me. Hush now."

He kissed her, a kiss as different from his last kiss as a palace from a midden: closed mouth and soft lips, tender and loving.

"My mother says Ravens are good at keeping secrets; I think she is right," he murmured. "My *father* says it's not safe to keep secrets from yourself. I think he is right, too."

His hands drifted from her shoulders when she stopped pulling away. Lightly, his right hand slid over her breast and stopped just over her navel, as if he sensed the hot ball of grief, pain, and anger she'd buried there.

"I'm hurting you," she said, but she couldn't force herself to back away from his touch. "I don't want to hurt you. Give me some time, and I'll—"

"Bury it again?" he said, his voice a soft rumble against her ear. "I don't think that is wise." He kissed her ear and down her neck, nibbling gently as he loosened the tie that kept the neckline of her dress shut.

She would have sworn passion had nothing new to teach her, but she found under Jes's inexperienced but intuitive touch, she was wrong. He had barely begun, and she trembled, caught in the fear that he might stop: stop touching her, stop talking to her in that velvet voice . . . stop loving her.

"Please," she said, her voice no louder than his. *Please don't let me hurt you. Please touch me. Please love me.* She would allow herself to say none of it.

He met her gaze and smiled, Jes and Guardian both.
"Don't worry so," he said, before continuing the journey he'd
just begun.

His mouth followed her skin down her throat to her collar-
bone while his hands trailed heat down the curve of her spine,
then across to her hips. He stopped with his mouth over her
navel, his head against that ache of grief and memory his hand
had found earlier.

"Here," he said. "So much hurt. Let me loosen it for you."
He pressed his forehead against her, just below her ribs. And
the warmth of him softened the old pain gently, then the
Guardian's coolness eased the ache.

"Don't keep your hate and pain so tightly," the Guardian
said, his voice as gentle as Jes's had been. "I share my rage
with Jes, and it lessens. Some hurts need the light of day, Hennea, so that they may be counted and let fly."

She sighed and felt the ugliness she had carried for so long
in secret, hidden even from herself, writhe under the light he
would bring to it.

"So many dead," Jes said, his voice subtly softer than the
Guardian's. "Too many to keep here." His calloused hand
brushed tenderly over her heart. "They were beloved by you,
and loved you. It would hurt them to know they caused you
such anguish. Let them go."

"You can't read my mind," she said, shaken by the accuracy of his words.

"No," he said. "But I feel what you feel, and I remember
the ones I have lost along the way, and the pain is the same.
The cause the same." He smiled against her cheek; she could
feel his dimple. "Selfishness."

"Selfishness?" It stung as if he were trivializing her suffering. She tried to pull away.

He laughed, low in his throat, and pulled her more tightly
against him. The vibration of the Guardian's quiet laughter
touched something deep inside, and she yielded to him again.

"Selfish," he said again. "I do not know where the dead go."
Jes laughed this time, the sound less graceful, less beautiful, but
more joyous. "But they do go and leave their bodies behind,
I've seen it. I've *felt* it. They go in joy, Hennea, the pain and fear
is left with the ones who stay behind and mourn. You and I. And

the pain we feel is for ourselves. I will never again see my little sister, Mehalla, who died the year Rinnie was born, and it makes me sad. For me. And I mourn even now, though she is eleven years dead. It is not bad that I mourn, but it is selfish." He slid down to kiss her belly, then rubbed his cheek against her, his afternoon beard stubble catching on her shirt.

"Let their deaths go," he said. "Let them leave off their haunting of your heart."

He waited, as if he were listening for something she couldn't hear. His patience, and the warmth of his arms around her—as if he were protecting her from all harm—was too much to bear.

"Ah, that's it," he said, coming back to his feet so she could bury her face against his chest as she sobbed. "We cry, too, the Guardian and I." He rocked her softly and sang a lullaby, like a mother soothing an overly tired child. He wasn't Bard, but his voice was lovely all the same.

When she pulled back, he wiped her cheeks with his hands. "You need to forgive them," he told her. "They are long dead, and your anger harms only you. Forgive them for dying and leaving you behind. Forgive Hinnum, if it was he, who loved you too much to allow you death to salve your pain."

Hennea felt raw. "You are a child," she whispered. "How can you know such things?"

The step she took away from him was more of a stumble than the firm distance-setting stride she'd intended, but it served its purpose. His touch was too unsettling, too necessary.

He smiled. "Some truths are truths, no matter who says them. My father knows a lot of them. 'Forgiveness benefits you more than those you forgive' is one of his favorites."

The smile faded, and his eyes darkened. "You lost so much," he said, and she couldn't tell who spoke, Jes or the Guardian. "Is there nothing you found afterward? Were no gifts given to you?"

She stared at him, trying to maintain her dignity; but he waited patiently, a smile lurking just below the surface of his eyes.

"You," she said.

He smiled again and closed the distance between them. As he pulled her into a hug that was more exuberant than sensual, he whispered, "Next time you want to look dignified, you might tie your blouse closed first."

He laughed when she pushed against him with an indignant huff. "Come," he said. "I know of a place that'll be more comfortable for what I have in mind than this marble floor. I did a bit of exploring before we noticed the face on the statue was yours—the black color threw us off."

"You just weren't looking at the face," she said, and he threw back his head and gave one of his joy-ridden crows of amusement.

"Jealous of a statue?" he asked, and picked her up. "A man likes something softer and warmer than marble—no matter how beautiful."

She let him carry her up the stairs of the dais and through the half-hidden door beyond. He took her through the halls and into a room built around a serene pool. The afternoon light reflected off the water from hidden skylights, giving the walls a dappled appearance.

"I remember that this was always my favorite room," she said, as he laid her on one of the thick mats that covered the ground.

The Guardian buried his face under her hair, between her neck and shoulder, and inhaled. "I love your scent," he growled.

"Wait," she said, pulling away from him.

He let her go, though his hands clenched, and he grimaced.

"I have to tell you," she said. "I have to tell Jes."

"Jes is listening," rumbled the Guardian, rolling until he was on his belly, his face hidden in his arms. "That is the best we can do right now."

Hennea sat up and rubbed his back, then pulled her hand back because it was distracting to touch him and feel him shaking with passion under her fingers—and she needed him to understand just what she was before he made such a commitment to her.

"There were six of us in the days of Colossae. Raven, Eagle, Owl, Cormorant, Lark, and Falcon. We kept the world safe by the balance of our powers."

She folded her legs and made herself small as she organized her newfound memories and composed a story that would make sense to Jes without losing itself in useless details.

"Colossae was my city, and I loved her. I loved the wizards who lived in her. They asked me for power, and I gave it to them."

The Guardian turned onto his side so he could watch her. His body was relaxing slowly from the tension of passion.

"The only thing I loved more than my city was my Consort. We were created for each other. There was balance between us: Eagle for Raven, Owl for Cormorant, and Lark for Hunter. Then my wizards, using the power I gave them, killed my Eagle."

"How?" The Guardian's breathing had picked up, but not from passion.

"Like the Path took the Order from its bearer, the greedy wizards stole the Eagle's power. They died in the doing, but it killed my beloved, too."

He turned his gaze to the pool of water, his face neutral, she could not read what he thought.

"The power we held was immortal, Jes, but we learned that we were not immune to the Stalker's gift. We lived, the six of us, to keep the greater gods in check. Our world is old and brittle; if the power of the Weaver and the Stalker were loosed upon it now, it would shatter like an old, dry pot. We maintained the balance that kept the gods bound."

"One of you died." It was Jes who spoke now, though she could feel the Guardian's presence in the chill that raised goose bumps on her arms.

She nodded. "When the war god was murdered, the Elder gods stirred. People died all over the world. The old god's power is involuntary, like the dread that always hangs about the Guardian whether he wills it or not: the Weaver creates, and the Stalker destroys, they have no choice. It's what they are. They came to us, those of us who still lived, and asked us to help them restore the balance."

"To sacrifice Colossae."

"The bindings that kept the Elder gods in check were failing, day by day, because there was no balanced outlet for their power. We had two problems to fix. We needed to create a new binding and a new balance. Colossae's sacrifice was necessary to create the binding—as long as she stands frozen, so will the gods be bound."

"But one of the gods was dead, so there could be no balance."

"That's right." It sounded like a story, Hennea thought, except she could remember it as if it had happened yesterday. "The Lark suggested the Weaver create a new Eagle."

Even so many years later the rage she'd felt at that—as if her beloved were no more than a broken bowl that could be replaced with a potter's wheel and kiln—was hot in her breast.

"Why didn't he?"

"He couldn't," she said. "The immortal power of the Eagle was still here, hosted in the mind of a child born the day my beloved died and held to sleep by the Lark. My beloved would not release his power, and not even the Weaver or the Stalker could force him to do so."

"I was so angry with them all." She remembered holding her grief and guilt and hiding them behind her anger. "It was my fault," she whispered. "And it was for me to correct though we would all pay the price for my folly."

"What did you do?"

"The Orders were created before the wizards left Colossae, Jes. I made them. I took the powers of my fellow gods and tore them from their bodies as my beloved's power had been torn from him. Because I was the goddess of magic, I could take them cleanly, pure power with nothing of the soul clinging to them. But I could not take them without killing the gods."

She closed her eyes and remembered how it was, working magic with a pale and shuddering Hinnum, who aided her in doing what must be done. "They sacrificed themselves because five gods could not hold the bindings and keep the Elder gods confined, but if I took our power and divided it and bound it to mortals, then the balance would be served."

"So Colossae died to confine the powers of the Elder gods, and the Orders were created to keep them confined."

"Yes," whispered Hennea.

Silence grew until Jes looked at her instead of the pool. "You didn't stop us for this."

She shook her head, but she couldn't bear telling him yet, so she shared the lesser of the evils she was responsible for. "I was supposed to die, too, Jes. Hinnum helped me divide my power and create the Ravens, leaving only what I needed to direct the spells that sacrificed Colossae. I think that my survival is why the Shadowed is able to draw power from the Stalker. My survival left a hole in the bindings."

Jes sat up abruptly and gathered her into his arms, but she had the feeling his attention was on his own internal dialogue. "No," the Guardian said after a moment. "It wasn't your life. You were the Raven, and had the Raven survived, it would have destroyed the balance. A Raven survived, Hennea, but not the Raven."

She considered his words carefully, but could find no flaw in his argument. "All right," she whispered. "All right. But something went wrong."

"Hennea?" he asked, his lips against her ear. "Why is the Eagle Order different?"

"My fault," she said, glad he'd found the worst of her crimes before she'd had to confess. "It is my fault, and I beg your forgiveness."

Jes held still behind her, but he didn't push her away when she leaned against him. "When my sisters and brothers died, their spirits and body fell away, leaving only their power behind. When the wizards murdered the Eagle, they ripped his power and spirit from his body together. I could have divided his power into such small sparks it would have been no more than a glint in the eye that gave a person just an extra mote of courage or strength. And they would never have felt the remnant that was Him, and not just his power. I could have given him into the care of the warrior born, let loose his gifts on the field of battle. But this was *my* beloved."

"So what did you do?"

Surely he knew, she thought, but she owed it to him to confess her guilt in full.

"I divided his power until his rage at his murder was small enough it did not instantly overwhelm the mortal who would hold it, then I gave him to the only people who could know what it was they held. The only people who might comfort him."

"Empaths like Jes," said the Guardian.

She nodded, awaiting his judgment. He pulled her into his lap and rocked a little as he thought.

"If," whispered the Guardian "*if* you had given me a warrior to bind to, blood would have flowed like rivers until there were none more to kill. I remember generations of being only rage, incapable of coherent thought. Without Jes to love me, that is all I would ever be."

"I know, beloved," she said, holding his arms against her. "But so many have paid the cost of my decision. So many Eagles have lived short lives. Jes—Jes has paid such a price for a debt that was not his."

"Hmm," Jes said. "Papa says everyone pays a price for living." He nuzzled behind her ear. "I like who I am, Hennea. I cannot imagine life without the Guardian. I think it would be terrible and lonely if I did not have him. Right now, in this room with you in my arms, I would trade my life with no other man alive. Do not ask for my forgiveness, because you have not sinned against me. Do not ask for our anger because there is none. We love you."

CHAPTER 16

Much to Tier's relief, the clouds seemed to be keeping their water to themselves, and there was even a growing area of blue sky to let the sun out to warm his bones.

He hadn't been away from home this much since he'd been a soldier, but, moments of terror and worry aside, he didn't really mind it. Perhaps when his wife decided she could not go back to being a farmer's wife, he'd become a Traveler's husband and roam the world with her.

He missed his farm—missed the smell of the earth turning and the plants growing.

He deliberately turned his attention to the city.

The University District had evidently been where the wealthy lived. From his perch on top of a garden wall, he had a good view of most of gardens belonging to a three-story stone manor house. The lack of birds and insects bothered him, but did not diminish the elaborate beauty of the carefully laid out flowers and trees.

The real benefit of his chosen position was not the local flora, but the ability it gave him to keep an eye on all of his charges, who had a tendency to scatter as something interesting caught their attention.

Rinnie left Lehr, half-hidden by a hedge at the far end of the block near the boundary Tier had declared was as far as they could go until everyone was ready to move on, and had started toward him with Gura at her side.

A moment later Phoran trailed laconically after Rinnie and Gura with the look of bored cynicism—a mask left over from earlier times—that he wore whenever he remembered that he was the Emperor, and not merely another of Tier's boys. The work and riding Phoran had been doing had thinned down his face, showing wide cheekbones and a narrow, elegant nose. He wasn't handsome, but his tanned face had an angular cast that would be more interesting than mere handsomeness—especially when he smiled.

Though he still dressed in his flamboyant colors, they had grown worn over the weeks of work and riding. He'd given up on the elaborate hairstyles of court and taken to tying his hair back. The overall effect was more that of a rogue than an emperor.

Behind him, as usual, were Kissel and Toarsen. Ielian would be somewhere near, but not too near, always aware of where the Emperor was. Tier saw him leaning casually on a garden wall on the other side of the street. Rufort had taken the other side of the block and, like Tier, had found a position that allowed him to keep an eye on everyone. Tier smiled, proud of his Passerines. They would do to guard the Emperor's back.

Rinnie was getting closer, and Tier's smile widened to a grin as Ielian fell in to trail casually behind Toarsen and Kissel. *He* knew they were guarding Phoran, but to an outsider it would look as though Rinnie were very important.

She stood on the street just under Tier and shaded her eyes. "Papa," she said, "Lehr says he's solved the mysteries of the places where the buildings have fallen, but he won't tell me until you come."

"All right." He knew the chances of anyone else being in Colossae were slim, but the silence made him wary, and he took one more good look around before dropping off the wall.

He followed his daughter, her emperor, and his guards down the cobbled street to the end of the block, where Lehr awaited them. Rufort, he noticed out of the corner of his eye, was strolling along behind them.

"Look, Papa," Lehr said, his voice tight with excitement as soon as Tier could see around the bushes to the small plot of land with another of the rubble-covered places where a house had once stood.

Lehr pointed to the surrounding fence that was modest in comparison to its neighbors, being only waist high and made of wood. The fence was elaborately painted with green vines and small white flowers that wove in and out of the evenly cut slats.

Tier frowned; he'd seen a fence like that before, but for a moment he couldn't think just where. Lehr waited expectantly while Tier put a hand on the wood and bent to look more closely at one of the painted flowers. No, he thought, it hadn't been a fence. If his memory had been its usual self he would have had an easier time of it.

"Benroln's *mermora,*" he said at last. He'd seen it virtually every night on the trip from Taela until Benroln had led his people to Colbern. "Rongier the Librarian's house has this pattern on the windowsills."

"And the lines of the building match the house, Papa. I think the buildings that have fallen are all the wizards' houses. If we get Mother, I bet we could figure out where all her *mermori* belong."

"What's a *mermora*?" asked Phoran.

Rinnie and Lehr both started to explain. Rinnie would have stopped and let Lehr continue, but Lehr reproved her for being rude and talking over the top of him.

Tier let them work it out while he took a few steps out into the middle of the road and tried to see, in his mind's eye, what it would have looked like with Rongier's house in place of the scattered stones that were all that was left of his house.

He wondered if Rongier's house had been here first, and all the estates had grown up around it—or if the estates had been here and one of the owners of the properties on either side had given this land for Rongier's use. Certainly the relatively modest house must have looked out of place while Rongier had lived there.

He half closed his eyes and visualized it. His hands warmed and tingled as the picture formed—no, not just picture. Suddenly the sounds he'd been missing were here, the

wind in the trees and the birds twittering. He smelled the
sweet scent of herbs and flowers and a faint tang of manure.
The street wasn't busy, only the people who lived on it and the
people who did business with them came here.

A horse was tied outside Rongier's house, smaller than the
horses Tier was used to, and lighter built. Its mane was plaited
with ribbons, and the horse's tack was whitened leather. It
flicked its tail and stomped a back hoof, trying to dissuade
some irksome insect.

"So the wizards found a way to take their *libraries* with
them when they fled?" Phoran's voice broke Tier's concentration. "All I managed was two changes of clothes, my sword, a
fat purse, and four guards to spend it on."

"They were killing their families," said Rufort slowly. "Libraries seem . . ." He floundered for the right word.

"Petty," supplied Ielian.

"They couldn't bear to lose everything." Tier said. The
scene of the past had gone as soon as Phoran caught his attention. "If I were forced to kill my family and survive them,
which is almost the most terrible fate I can imagine, then I
would want some keepsake—something to show that once
they had lived."

"Isn't that what they sacrificed?" asked Lehr holding on to
the fence. "Mother says magic is about patterns, and along
with the lives of the people who lived here, it was the patterns
of everyday life, all the things that made Colossae their home,
that they sacrificed."

"The library wasn't sacrificed," said Rinnie. "It's not part
of the spell. Maybe the *mermori* are like the library."

Phoran smiled, and said wryly, "Maybe, but my uncle said
if a wizard had a choice between rescuing a book or his only
child from a flaming building, the wizard would save the—"

Phoran's voice broke off, and Tier was suddenly looking
up at the branches of a tree.

"Papa?" Rinnie's voice was small and scared.

"I'm all right," Tier said, instinctively answering the fear
in his daughter's voice before he'd had a chance to assess the
situation.

He hadn't realized he was being held down until his arms
and legs were released. He was lying on his back in the street,

with the boys crouched around him and Rinnie's tearful face looking over Lehr's shoulder.

"Another fit, eh?" he said. He sat up too suddenly, and if Phoran's hand hadn't shifted unobtrusively behind his back, he would have fallen again. There was blood in his mouth, and he could feel a cut on the inside of his cheek.

"This one was bad, Papa," said Lehr. His voice didn't tremble, and there were no tears, but Tier could see he'd scared Lehr as much as he'd scared Rinnie.

"Kissel caught you before you fell," said Toarsen. "But it looked to me as if you hit your head pretty hard before I could steady you."

"Thank you," Tier said, putting a hand on Phoran's shoulder and using it to pull himself to his knees. When he didn't feel any dizziness, he got to his feet.

"I'm all right," he told the worried faces gathered around him, and Bard that he was, he knew that he lied.

"The Raven could have set the magic upon Colossae herself," said the Scholar, answering Seraph's question as he paced the short distance between Seraph's bench and the stairway. "But that would not have been a sacrifice capable of binding the Elder gods. Only the wizards could make the proper sacrifice of the wizards' city. The Raven directed the spell, and Hinnum served as the focus—but the power of the spell came from the wizards of Colossae."

"They killed their loved ones," said Seraph, trying to imagine how it was. "They destroyed all they held dear. How did you persuade them all?"

"We gathered them in the Raven's temple and explained what had happened. They knew the Weaver and the Stalker were unbound—no one could deny it by then, all of nature was in tumult."

"They didn't all agree," said Seraph, trying to imagine a roomful of Ravens agreeing on anything.

He stopped at the head of the stairs. "No," he said heavily, and she heard death in that one word and saw it in his bowed shoulders. He took a deep breath, though she didn't think he really needed to breathe. "We left Colossae by the University Gate. And then we sacrificed her."

"But not the library, not even the wizard's personal libraries," she said slowly putting together the pieces as a Raven did, taking facts and using them to intuit beyond what she knew for certain. She remembered the way the Scholar focused on Hennea, and his voice as he spoke of his goddess. As if he were here, she could hear Tier say that he thought Hennea was *old*.

"And not the Raven. She planned on dying, didn't she?" Seraph whispered, awe rushing through her. *Hennea* was *the* Raven. "After she'd seen the whole of the business finished, she wanted to die like the other gods."

"I couldn't bear it," said the Scholar. "I couldn't bear that she die, too. I loved her."

"So what did you do?"

"I took her memory instead. As you have seen, she still doesn't remember. I changed her face—just for a while, until all of those who would have known her for what she was were gone. So many of the wizards died that night, and those who lived were all damaged one way or another. She wasn't the only one to have lost her memory. There were wizards who never again worked magic, a handful who went blind. One who never said another word."

"Isolde the Silent," said Seraph.

He turned then and stared at her. "How do you know of Isolde? Are you of her house?"

Seraph nodded.

He smiled, remembering something with pleasure, she thought. "No. It wasn't Isolde who was struck dumb. Isolde could have studied under the Owl's wing—she had a singing voice like crystal strung to sound in the wind. In the days after Colossae fell, her songs comforted us all. We called her the Silent because she never said a word that didn't need to be said." He paused. "You don't look like her, but you have something of her manner."

Seraph pursed her lips. "I don't know how you are doing it, but you *are* Hinnum, himself."

"Yes."

Seraph leaned back, assessing the situation. She had in front of her the greatest wizard of Colossae, and she was going to make good use of him.

* * *

"Man is made of spirit, mind, and body," said Seraph, "To see spirit, the wizard must push past the barriers that block his sight." She set the book down with an ill-tempered thump. "Nonsense," she told it—and her new instructor—irritably. "Moreover, it is useless nonsense. No real details, nothing except a collection of high-sounding poetical nonsense. I have done everything it says to do, and I cannot see anything other than my Order—which is *not* spirit."

"It isn't nonsense," said the illusion Hinnum wore mildly. "And if you are to keep your husband alive until I am capable of working magic, you need to know how to see spirit. All it takes is a little study and self-discipline."

She turned to look at him, and he smiled at her—just like Tier. No one else laughed at her temper.

For Tier she would learn how to do this or die trying. And Hinnum, she reminded herself firmly, was the only wizard who could teach her—unless Hennea suddenly recalled herself. Seraph thought it would have happened already if it were going to.

It would probably be a kindness, Seraph thought, *if Hennea never remembered.* From what Hinnum had told her, Hennea had no more power now than any other Raven: her memory of what she had been would gain her nothing but pain.

Hennea wasn't the only one who had lost when Colossae was sacrificed. He hadn't gone into detail, but the damage he'd sustained from the spell had been bad enough he'd chosen to stay here alone rather than go out into the world.

The illusion he'd built to house his intellect—his spirit, he'd said, tapping the miserable book she was slogging through—was not capable of much magic. Which was why he'd begun the process of awakening his proper body as soon as he'd seen Tier and the Order-bound gems. Hinnum knew something of how to fix both problems, he'd told her, but he didn't know how long it would be before his body would recover. For the gems there was no rush, but Tier did not have much time left.

Thus she found herself sitting at a table like a fledgling *solsenti* wizard under the tyranny of his master.

"It's not that difficult," he said now, and handed her the piece of chalk she'd thrown across the room. "An apprentice of thirteen would be able to master this easily. But not if she was too busy throwing tantrums to listen."

Seraph simmered with ill temper as she drew the arcane glyphs across the gleaming surface of the table again. She hadn't had a teacher since her own had died, and Hinnum seemed to take particular delight in being obscure.

This was worse than learning the runes for warding—at least then she could feel the power gathering under the runes so that the runes themselves told her if she'd drawn them correctly or not. This was just scribbling nonsense.

"That figure turns the other direction," said Hinnum, tapping the drawing in the book. "See there? And the little bit right here needs to be a hair longer."

"If you told me what we were trying to do," she said, not for the first time, "this might not be necessary."

"It's in the book," he told her. "But you told me the book doesn't make sense to you—thus the figures." He leaned over the marks as she made them. "That's better. Only three more figures, then I'll teach you the words."

"Could Hennea do this?" she asked.

"I don't know," he told her. "You can, of course, wait for someone else to fix all of your problems if you aren't willing to put in a little time and effort."

If he hadn't been an illusionary construct, if he weren't the only hope she had of saving Tier, she would have done something unpleasant to him.

She started trying to reconstruct the next random assortment of squiggles and angles.

Hinnum gripped Seraph's cheeks and pushed, forcing her mouth into an unnatural position. "Like this. If you don't get the sounds just right, they won't work."

She jerked her face out of his grip and tried again. *Rhythm, tone, pitch, pronunciation, no wonder* solsenti *wizards were a nasty bunch.*

Staring at the meaningless shapes she'd drawn on the table, she once more focused all of her attention on getting the words just right. It sounded to her exactly as it had the first twenty times, but *this* time something happened. Magic rushed through the chalk marks and into her in a stream of power that pushed the stool she was sitting on back a few inches.

It was different from the runes. The runes were *hers,* and they did as she bid.

The shapes and words of this kind of spell weaving distracted her, then stole her magic and twisted it into a new shape. She didn't like it—a Raven controlled her own magic. She didn't like it, but she saw and understood the pattern the symbols and sounds were trying to make of her power. There were flaws here and there, and she fixed them as she tugged her magic until it was once more *hers.*

"I've got it," she said, turning to Hinnum.

But instead of the half-grown Traveler boy, she saw instead a net of magic, a complex pattern of strings and knots that gave form to the Scholar. The violet fabric she'd always seen as the Raven Order was there as well, beneath the netting—or so she thought at first. She got up from her chair and walked toward him. She could see now it wasn't the same as the Order, not quite.

"It's not the Raven Order, but it is akin to it," she said.

"I was goddess-touched," he said, seeming to follow her meaning. "The gift of the Raven is very like the Raven's Order. What did you do? This magic doesn't feel like the spell you were working on should!"

"I fixed it," she said, bending closer, fascinated. "Pardon me," she said absently, as the reality of what she saw began to give meaning to the passages Hinnum had made her read.

"What did you do?" Hinnum sounded fascinated, examing her magic as closely as she was examining him.

"Not right now," she said. "Let me look." It took concentration, as if she had to pay attention in order to focus her eyes on anything. It was draining, too. She wouldn't be able to do this for long periods of the time. It was akin to the way Ravens *looked* to see Orders, but it went deeper.

"I see the spell binding you to your illusion," she said after a moment of thought. That must be what the net that encompassed the rest of him was. "Beneath that the—Raven's touch, I suppose you'd call it—and under . . ." The violet sheathing became transparent, fading from her view as she chose to look at different things. "I see a bluish light and a dark core beneath."

"Describe it to me." Hinnum's voice had lost the note of caution and become eager.

Seraph lifted up her hand and pushed it through the net to stroke the light with a fingertip. "Give me your hand," she told him. If his goddess touch worked like the Order, she should be able to show him what she had done so he could do it himself. It would be easier than trying to explain it to him.

It was her turn to be the teacher, and she hadn't forgiven him for grabbing her cheeks.

He took her hand, and for a while she wondered if his not-quite-an-Order, his not-quite-human, and his not-able-to-work-magic were going to hinder her.

She found out quickly that he was right about the magic, but if she split up what she wanted to do, everything worked. She showed him the form of the magic she used for this new, extended vision, and though he couldn't work the magic himself, she knew from his "Ah" of pleasure, that he understood. Then she showed him what she saw, the same way she could have shown it to anyone, even someone who didn't happen to be mageborn.

She took him slowly through the net of his magic and past the Raven's touch and brought him to the pale blue fire surrounding a darker form.

"The light blue is spirit," he said. "That's what you needed to be able to see. I have no idea what the other is . . . soul? Perhaps. Or perhaps it is something that has happened because I've kept my self in this form . . ." His voice trailed off.

She closed her eyes and separated her magic gently from Hinnum, then dissipated the spell she'd used. She blinked twice before her eyes returned to working properly—and took two steps back so she was no longer nose to nose with the Scholar.

While Hinnum still had a dazedly pleased expression on his face, Seraph asked, "If the Stalker is not evil—then why is the Shadowed?" He'd avoided answering any question she'd tried about the Shadowed; she hoped taking him by surprise would yield better results.

His expression returned to alertness with disappointing speed. When Tier had that look on his face, it took him much longer to return to his usual quick-witted self.

"How would I know?" he asked. "I've been here since the end of Colossae."

"Not quite, I think," Seraph said. "There was a Shadowed with the wizards who survived, and the stories tell us you are the one who killed her. So why are the Shadowed evil?"

She should probably have left the questioning to Tier, but the expression on Hinnum's face had led her to try. She had nothing more to lose now by trying to bludgeon information from him. He *knew* about the Shadowed in general—and he knew about Willon in particular. She hadn't forgotten that Willon had come to Colossae. Willon had had the same maps that she had, and he was a wizard. Of course he had come to the library.

Hinnum had had a hand in the creation of her Shadowed, Willon, who had crept into her home on the pretext of his friendship with Tier and killed her daughter. Hinnum would tell her all he knew if she had to pry it from him one word at a time.

Something of that determination must have been on her face, because Hinnum sighed. "There's a flaw in the veil we drew between the Elder gods and our world when we sacrificed the city. I felt it—and so did the few great wizards who survived. One of them used the hole to draw upon the power of the Stalker."

"What caused it?"

"We did. I did." Guilt was one of the expressions she'd seen on his face quite often, given she'd only known him for part of two days. "It took me a long time to figure out what happened." He sat on a bench, his head bowed. "I had been experimenting with an illusionary form that not only reproduced an object perfectly to all the senses, but could be set into a silver object to be called and recalled without degrading the illusion."

"The *mermori*," said Seraph.

Hinnum nodded. "I'd found that by destroying the object I intended to reproduce, the spell required very little more power."

"Forming the *mermori* destroyed the wizards' houses." Seraph rubbed her forehead, which ached from the spelling she'd been doing. "Since it took little power, it was not such a big thing to work it into the Raven's spell, and you formed the *mermori* at the same time the city fell. The sacrifice wasn't perfect because the wizards' houses weren't part of the eternally preserved city."

"And then there was the library," Hinnum said.

Seraph rubbed her forehead harder. "Stupid."

"Yes." Hinnum sighed.

"You were going to tell me why the Shadowed is evil."

"A wizard—not just any wizard—but a powerful, smart, well-schooled wizard, can under certain circumstances slip through the hole in the veil and touch the power of the Stalker, can touch destruction. Being destruction, it kills any mortal being who holds it for long."

"But the Shadowed doesn't die," Seraph said.

"Most wizards who touch it release it immediately and never seek it again. But if the wizard gives the death that is the price of the power of destruction to another person, then he can use the power for a while."

"He chooses to kill others to keep the power," Seraph interpreted. "And anyone who would do that—"

"Is evil." Hinnum glance up at the skylights. "It's getting late," he said. "You'd better find your family."

" 'The dead walk the streets at night,' " she quoted him softly.

He nodded. "The dead have a lot to be angry with in this city."

Lehr walked just behind his father, Rinnie's hand clutching his. She was still breathing in jerks from the tears she'd tried so hard not to let Papa see. The moment that the fit had struck his father was close to the worst moment in his life.

It wasn't the first fit his father had had, but it was the worst—and the first time it had happened without Mother there to give them direction. And after the fit was over, Papa had just lain on the pale cobbles. He hadn't been breathing until Kissel hit him in the chest.

Phoran walked just on the other side of Tier, and on some pretext or other had managed to get a firm grip on Tier's arm to steady him a little.

"Are we going back to camp?" Ielian asked Lehr in a subdued voice.

They hadn't discussed it. Phoran had helped Papa to his feet, then said, "Let's go." But he hadn't said where.

Papa had been a little dazed, and he'd slurred his words—but he wouldn't let any of them help him further. He'd gotten better as they walked; well enough to carry on an animated conversation with Phoran.

"We're going to find my mother," said Lehr.

Phoran caught Lehr's eye and nodded slightly.

"Papa, what's wrong?"

Lehr looked up to see Jes and Hennea hurrying over.

Papa smiled. "Do I look that bad?"

"Yes. You smell of sweat, and you are pale," Jes answered with his usual bluntness.

Hennea wore her usual inscrutable face, but Lehr noticed that her eyes were puffy. She was almost as pale as Papa except for her nose, which was reddened. She'd been crying, which was something he could hardly imagine. On a different day Lehr would have wondered about it, but he was too worried about Papa.

"I had another fit," Papa admitted to Jes. "Judging by the way they are all hovering around me, it must have been pretty bad."

Phoran started walking again and pulled Papa forward with a gentle tug. Jes picked up Rinnie and put her on his shoulder, then he and Hennea fell in with Papa.

Lehr waited and took up the tail end of the procession beside Rufort. He'd come to like the quiet man; besides, he didn't want to walk too near Jes.

Sometimes Lehr reveled in the powers that had grown in him since he'd found out that he was Hunter. Sometimes, though, he wished that his senses didn't tell him quite so much.

He hadn't wanted to know what Jes and Hennea had just come back from doing. It was bad enough he knew too much about his parents; he didn't want to know about his brother, too.

Brewydd would have laughed at him, he thought. He could almost hear her voice ringing in his ears. "So where do you think the babes come from, my lad—under a mushroom?"

He could feel his ears heat up even more—his cheeks were probably bright red. Not for the first time he wished for his father's darker skin.

"I hope that your mother can help him," Rufort said, either too worried about Tier to notice Lehr's flushed face or too polite to press him.

"Me, too," Lehr said.

"I thought he was going to break something," Rufort said, then gave Lehr small smile. "Possibly me."

Lehr smiled back and felt a little better. The worst was over for now. "Ielian was the one who was outmatched," he said just loud enough Ielian could hear him.

The smaller man made a rude sign with his hand, then waited for them to catch up.

"I never thought being a guardsman was going to be more interesting than working for the Path," said Ielian.

"Better," said Rufort.

"Mmm." Ielian glanced around as they entered an intersection of streets, looking for danger. Colossae still unnerved Lehr, too. "But being a Passerine was better than being a clerk for my uncle's steward. Paid better, too."

Rufort stiffened, his mouth tight, but before Lehr could ask him what bothered him, he relaxed again. "This will be a story to tell my grandchildren," he said. "And they will pretend to believe me because their mother has told them to humor the old fool so she can get dinner on."

His mother was standing at the top of the stairway into the main room of the library as if she'd been about ready to go to camp herself. The young man who called himself the Scholar was with her.

Her gaze swept them all, and she stepped back. Without a word she commanded them all up the stairs and into the library, where they scattered among the benches, stools, and tables.

Lehr didn't think that Hennea intended him to hear her whisper to Mother, "You know, don't you? You know about me."

Lehr had found a seat, and so he saw his mother take in Hennea's reddened eyes and Jes's easy posture. He didn't think that she could tell what they had been doing, as Lehr had, but he didn't put it past her.

Mother smiled coolly, but Lehr could tell she was pleased about something—which, after all the lectures Papa had given both boys about how to treat women, he felt was a little unfair.

Then Mother said something very odd. "Hennea, you of all people should know that Ravens like secrets."

Papa sat on one of the tables, his legs crossed at the ankles. Phoran sat on the floor, and Rinnie curled up beside him and put her head down on his knee. Gura lay down on Phoran's other side with a sigh and took the other knee.

Lehr thought that the Scholar intended to stand with Mother, but she sent him off to a bench, too.

"I have had a productive day," Mother told them, her eyes dwelling on Papa's ravaged face. "But why don't you tell me what you have found? Jes?"

Jes smiled widely, and Lehr was momentarily horrified by what his brother would say. With Papa for a father they all had learned not to lie, but Jes was sometimes too honest.

"Found the Raven's temple," he said. "Not far from here." He glanced down at Hennea. "Different from the Owl's temple, all black-and-white stone, but the same idea."

Lehr saw relief cross Hennea's face and knew she'd had the same worry that he'd had. Unexpectedly, she met his gaze across the room, blushed, then gave him a rueful smile.

"Tier?" asked his mother.

"Lehr discovered what those damaged buildings are," Papa said.

Mother looked at Lehr, so he explained about the fence and the shape of the house that once had stood there.

"We'll take Rongier's *mermora* there tomorrow," was all she said when he finished.

"I thought you were of Isolde's house?" asked the Scholar suspiciously. "Why do you have Rongier's *mermora*?"

Mother gave him one of her looks. "I told you the Shadowed has been systematically killing Travelers. He killed the last of Rongier's clan a few weeks ago. The *mermora* came to me."

"Rongier's line is gone?"

"I hold two hundred and twenty-nine *mermori*," Mother said. "They are all *gone*."

The Scholar dropped his eyes. "I'll be able to work magic for you tomorrow afternoon," he said.

"Good." Mother looked at Papa and raised an eyebrow. "You look better," she told him. "I wasn't certain if you were going to survive the trip up the stairs."

He grinned. "All right, Empress," he said. "I had another fit. If Kissel hadn't been quick and caught me before I hid the cobbles, I guess I'd have a worse headache than the one I do. That's nothing new, love. Tell us what you've learned, we've been waiting long enough."

CHAPTER 17

"It happened like this." Seraph gave Tier a quick smile as she used the words that he began most stories with.

He was looking better—he could hardly look worse without being dead. Watching Phoran half-carry him up the stairs, she'd realized they were running out of time even faster than she'd thought.

She condensed the story of Colossae and left out as much of the drama as she could—it looked to her as if most of them had had all the excitement they needed for the day. She also left out the part about Hennea and the Raven being one and the same. It sounded as if Hennea, at least, had figured it out. She would check later to make certain Jes knew, too, and she would tell Tier because she didn't keep secrets from him. Hennea could decide if she wanted to tell anyone else.

As she spoke, Seraph's eyes kept trying to linger on Tier. She didn't use the new *seeing* spell she'd learned, because it would have taken too much of her concentration, but she *looked* and tried not to panic at how frail Tier's Order had grown.

He knew it was bad, too—she could tell by the lines around his eyes and the too-casual pose. Panicking the others more wouldn't help anyone, so Seraph didn't wring her hands or rage, though she wanted to do both. Tomorrow, Hinnum would help them if she had to hold his beloved library hostage. Tier could hold on one more day.

She finished the story, then gave them Hinnum's insights into the Shadowed, the Stalker, and the mess the wizards had made with the *mermori* and the library.

"So," said Phoran heavily in the silence that followed. "My uncle was right. They killed their children and saved the books."

"To be fair," said Tier, who was watching Hinnum carefully. A Bard, thought Seraph, had a way of seeing through illusions. "I imagine they were told their families had to die—and no one said anything about the books." Then he smiled at her. "But that's not all you learned today, you're too smug, Empress."

Seraph looked at Hinnum. She'd given Hennea the choice to keep her past to herself. Somehow it didn't seem right not to do the same for the old wizard.

"Introduce me to your family," he said.

"Sir, may I make you known to my husband, Tieragan, Bard of Redern." She caught Ielian's frown and realized she should have introduced Phoran first. It was too late to correct that mistake, but she named him next.

"Emperor?" asked the Scholar.

Seraph supposed it said something about you when you could shock a wizard as old as Hinnum, even though he'd spent the better part of ten centuries buried in a library. "I forgot to tell you about him," Seraph said, quickly explaining why the Emperor was a part of their quest. When she finished, she looked around trying to remember who was next in rank for introductions. She gave it up for hopeless and decided settled for age instead.

When she had named everyone including Gura—at Rinnie's insistence—she turned to Hinnum, and said, "These are my family. My family, may I make known to you Hinnum, the Illusionist of Colossae."

"I thought you said he was an illusion?" said Tier frowning. He stared at Hinnum. "He *is* not real, Seraph—I can tell that much."

"This is an illusion," Seraph said, waving vaguely at Hinnum's body. "But the puppet master is Hinnum himself."

"You mean he's alive," whispered Hennea.

Seraph saw a rush of feelings that were quickly tucked away behind Hennea's impenetrable calm. Jes—or the Guardian—pulled Hennea closer to him and watched Hinnum with brooding intensity.

"Yes," Seraph told them all. "Hinnum has agreed to help us. He told me that he could definitely help with Tier's problems and the Order-bound gems." Though if Hennea had remembered everything, whatever everything was for a Raven who used to be a goddess, they might be dependent upon Hinnum's help.

She looked at the old wizard in the young boy's form. "But it is with the Shadowed he can help the most. You know him, don't you? He came here a few centuries ago, a young, powerful mage who was searching for someone who could teach him."

Hinnum met her eyes, his face impassive.

"You enjoy teaching," she said. "I don't know what his name was then, but we know him as Willon. He's smart and charming."

"He was an illusionist," Hinnum whispered. "Wizards see illusion as lesser magic—something to fool the eye rather than change the world. To be a great mage, to have so much power and to have the other wizards who could barely scry in water if they were given the Bowl of Ages to do it in snigger with contempt of your abilities is a hard thing. Even in Colossae we were looked down upon—until I showed them all what an illusionist could do."

"You taught him," Tier said, taking over. She left him to it gratefully. He'd know how to pull every last detail out.

"I did."

Tier tilted his head. "I'll wager you didn't teach him how to become the Shadowed."

"No."

"There aren't any other people here," said Tier. "Seraph told us that the Shadowed cannot hold the Stalker's power without death. Whom did he kill?"

"My other apprentice," Hinnum said. "I didn't know at first. I thought they both had left. You aren't the first to find Colossae. They come, sometimes, when I get too alone. I call them here, teach them, and bind them to silence."

"Will you help us bring him to justice? To stop his killing of the Traveler clans? To stop him from stealing the Orders?"

Seraph saw guilt cross Hinnum's face. *Of course Hinnum was the one who taught Willon how the Orders worked,* thought Seraph. *Who else would know how to do it?*

"He wanted to know about the wizards," said Hinnum. "About the gods who died. About the Orders. I didn't teach him how to take them, he didn't have that kind of power, then. He asked me about the Travelers."

"You didn't tell him about the Eagle," said Jes suddenly. "Volis didn't know about Eagles, and none of the gemstones Hennea and Mother have belong to Eagles."

"Of course not," Hinnum said indignantly. "The Eagles are to be shielded, protected. The burden you bear is difficult and not of your choosing."

"He was here, wasn't he?" asked Lehr. "Didn't he explore the city? If the Owl and the Raven have temples, didn't the Eagle?"

"The Eagle's temple was razed," said Hennea. "After they killed the god, they destroyed His temple. Why should they worship a dead god?"

"Hinnum told us that much," lied Seraph cheerfully. She wouldn't let Hennea reveal herself just because she was upset. Hinnum would know that she lied, Hinnum and Tier. Neither of them would tell.

"Papa," Jes said. "What would the Shadowed want with the Orders?"

Tier smiled, and Seraph knew they'd both caught something that she'd missed. "Right, son." He held Hinnum with his eyes. "I'm not a Raven. Nor yet a Traveler, for all I bear the Owl's Order. But I am a storyteller."

"In the story of the Shadowed it seems there were three people of interest." Tier held up one finger. "The first is you, who taught an illusionist how to use his power. You did it because you were once as he was, because you were lonely, and because he flattered you."

He raised a second finger. "Then we have Willon, who became the Shadowed for power—but I know Willon. He made a fortune as a merchant because he always planned things carefully. He always has a goal in mind. He has kept himself hidden—as opposed to the rather direct approach favored by the Unnamed King, for instance—but we know some things Willon *has* done. For instance, he had a secret society that purposefully increased the unrest in the Empire and stole the Orders from Order Bearers."

"Raven save us, he's trying to destroy the veil," said Hinnum with sudden intensity. Then he paled and glanced at Hennea. He cleared his throat. "The purpose of the Orders was twofold. The first was to provide the balance that kept the veil in place. The second was rendered moot by our folly when I saved the library and built the *mermori*."

"What was it?" asked Hennea. "I don't remember."

"The veil keeps the Elder gods from working in our world, but their power must be used. Without an outlet of some sort, eventually the veil would be overcome. So the six gods were made to drain the power of the Stalker and the Weaver. The Orders were to serve the same function, but, because of the imperfection in the veil, the Elder gods' power seeps out on its own."

"The Weaver's as well?" asked Phoran. *It was a good question,* thought Seraph. *If destruction escaped, why not creation?*

Hinnum crossed his legs and sat on his feet on the cushioned bench. "Let me tell you what I see. A Raven married to a *solsenti* Bard—and the Orders were tied to the bloodlines of the Colossae wizards. They have three Ordered children, each a different Order. The Orders were to scatter among the Travelers. They travel with the Emperor—who is afflicted with a Raven's Memory, which, through a strange twist, must kill the Shadowed." He looked at Hennea, then away. "You are not the first people to find Colossae—but you are the only ones whom I have not called here."

"You think that this is the Weaver's work?" asked Hennea intensely.

Hinnum nodded. "I do." He looked at Tier. "You think the Shadowed is going to try to destroy the veil by confining as many Orders as he can to these rings?"

Tier nodded. "I think that depends upon the third player. The Stalk—" His face went blank.

Lehr was out of his seat before Seraph really understood what had happened. Jes pulled Tier down off the table and onto the floor. For a moment he lay still, staring blindly up at a skylight.

Hinnum caught her by an arm before she could go to Tier and jerked her back.

"There's no time," he said urgently. "Seraph, look at his Order—He's too close to losing it all. It will kill him if he does. You need to work the spell I taught you. Find out how the Shadowed is stealing the Order and stop him."

She jerked her arm free and ran to Tier. The boys were holding him down to try to keep him from hurting himself. She saw Hinnum was right; Tier's Order was almost gone. There was no time to wait until the old wizard could help with this. If Seraph couldn't find some way to stop the spell, it would be irreversible, and Tier would die of it.

She stuffed her terror deep, where it would be a source of strength rather than a distraction. Then she called the magic Hinnum had taught her and tried to ascertain what the Shadowed and his minions had done to her husband.

She'd believed the Shadowed's spell was simply destroying the connection between Tier and his Order. Now that she could view both spirit and his Order she understood she'd been wrong.

Each strand of the Shadowed's spell was cloaked in spirit; a pale gleaming sheath around a darkly-malignant core. Just as she had wrapped her magic in her Order so she could affect Tier's, so did the Shadowed wrap his spell in spirit. The spirit had hidden the spell from her earlier attempts to discover it. Tendrils of the spell insinuated themselves into the warp and weft of Tier's order, worked into its fabric as tightly Tier's own spirit.

Wrapped in spirit, the spell was able to bind to the Order as Tier's own spirit did. It had worked deeply into Tier's order, but where his spirit was passive, the spell was not. The spell wasn't attacking the connection between Tier and his Order, instead it was ripping it away from Tier by force. The threads of Tier's spirit were being slowly broken, strand by strand as Shadowed's spell inexorably rent Tier's Order from him, leaving severed bits of spirit behind.

Her old teacher would have considered the spell crude, relying on power rather than finesse. But, however crude the spell, it was working.

The Shadowed's spirit-magic twined around the threads it had stolen, forming a rope of magic, spirit and Bardic Order that stretched between Tier and, presumably, whatever gemstone the Path's Masters had attached his Order to. A small gossamer ribbon Tier's spirit broke and fell away from the Order, darkening as it did so. It curled down limply against Tier's body.

"Seraph? Let me help?"

It was Hennea. Seraph nodded twice and felt the Raven's hands close on her shoulders, feeding her power.

She could have tried to darn Tier's Order to him again, she could do a better job now because she understood what was needed—but, as before, it would only help him temporarily. Eventually both her magic and Tier's spirit would fail, and Tier, his spirit damaged beyond healing, would die.

Instead, with Hennea's strength to aid her, Seraph threw herself, magic, spirit, and soul down the twisting rope that connected Tier and the Path's gem. She lost all sense of time and place as she followed the rope, until her journey began to seem endless. Only her fierce determination to find the end of the rope kept her going.

Then, without warning, she found what she sought, a gem the color of cinnamon. Grey-green strands of Bardic Order formed a tight ball in the center of the stone, with a few stray fragments of Tier's spirit still woven in it. She had no idea how to retrieve what it had stolen.

To her magical self, the gem was enormous, but she knew physically it would be small enough to be set in a ring or necklet.

She could take it, she thought. She held it in her magic now—if she could make herself just a little more physical, she could just steal it from wherever it was and pull it back with her.

There was danger in what she intended. She might find herself wherever the gem was—and she was in no shape to face the Shadowed alone. Or she could fail to make herself real enough to take the gem and too real to go back to her own body.

As she hesitated, the cord pulsed and turned, and the ball of Tier's Order in the gem became just a little bigger.

She'd never done anything like this before, but all a Raven had to be able to do was conceive of possibilities and let magic fill the patterns she conceptualized. For a moment the stone eluded her, as if it feared her touch, but finally her fingers closed upon it, a power-warm, sharp-edged, and slick-sided garnet.

It was hers. For a moment she just held it, stunned it had worked. Then she released her hold on her magic, both the *seeing* spell and the power that had allowed her to follow the Shadowed's trail. She came back to herself with Tier's cry in her ears.

It took her precious moments to realize why the gem warmed until it was hot in her hands, moments while it pulled more of Tier's Order to it. The gem's proximity strengthened the effectiveness of the thieving magic.

"Hold him so he doesn't hurt himself." The Scholar's voice had altered a little, deeper tones added to give weight to his commands.

Hennea's hands slid from Seraph's shoulders and wrapped around her hands instead.

"Let me ward it, Seraph," said Hennea.

Seraph opened her cupped hands and allowed Hennea to touch the gem. A simple warding would have just severed the connection between Tier and the stone, and she was too tired to be clever. Let Hennea work the subtler magic necessary.

"There is too much of him, spirit and Order already in the gemstone," Hennea said worriedly, showing she understood as much as Seraph herself did.

"You can see it?" asked Seraph, then thought, *Of course you could.* Seraph was still trying to absorb the implications of who and what Hennea had been; possibly Seraph's slowness had hurt Tier. If she had just let Hennea try—Hennea, who used to be the goddess of magic. Perhaps she could have really unworked the Shadowed's spell.

"I followed your magic and remembered." Hennea released her hold and stepped back. "I couldn't have done it myself, not until I saw what you had done. What I've done to the stone should keep it from hurting Tier more for a while. But it is not a permanent situation. I don't know how to reverse the Shadowed's spell."

"Neither do I," admitted Seraph readily as she reached out to touch Tier's face. "Yet."

He opened his eyes at her touch. He smiled at her, then looked at Phoran, who sat on Tier's legs, and at Jes and Kissel, who were holding his arms.

"It's all right, you can let me go," Tier said. "I'm all right now . . . I think."

They looked at Seraph and waited until she nodded before letting Tier go.

"Last time we thought he was done, too" said Phoran apologetically. "He was quiet for a little while, then went into convulsions again."

"I thought you were going to break apart, this time." Lehr's voice was taut as he helped his father to stand.

Tier moved his left shoulder a little gingerly. "Nothing so dramatic—though I might have pulled a muscle or two." He looked up at Seraph with a smile of ironic amusement. "You *did* learn something today. I usually feel worse after one of those instead of better. What did you do?"

Seraph opened her hand, so he could see the gemstone in it. He took the unset, rust-colored garnet from her hand gingerly.

"They might have chosen a prettier stone," he quipped, then, seeing Seraph's face, he gathered her against him, letting her use his shoulder to hide her tears.

"I almost lost you," she said. "Almost."

"I'm here," he told her. "I'm right here."

She let him comfort her, but she could see the remnants of his fragile Order sway to the tugging of the gem in her hands.

Phoran eased his way out of the chaos of the general meeting that followed Tier's almost demise. Rinnie didn't need him anymore, she was clinging to her father. And Phoran, being neither Traveler nor mage, had nothing he could add to the discussion—which was currently about how to destroy the Shadowed.

He knew they wouldn't leave him alone for long, though Toarsen and Kissel had appeared to be thoroughly fascinated at the thought of meeting a wizard who was old before the Empire had even been a twinkle in the eye of the cunning old farmer who had been the first Phoran.

Phoran welcomed the silence of the old city, outside of the library's door. A sunset, pale and subdued compared to the ones in Taela, lit the eastern sky.

He thought he'd grown accustomed to amazing things on the trip—a lonely mountain haunted with the remnants of ghosts, a legendary city frozen in time, a wizard older then the Empire—but Seraph had just proved him wrong.

It wasn't the magic. Though he was sure that she had done something to help Tier, he hadn't seen anything. He'd noticed the magic Seraph worked was usually less showy than the magic of the court mages—probably because Seraph had no patron to impress.

No, what Seraph had done was even more remarkable than her magic, at least from Phoran's view.

"Introduce me to your family," the old wizard had said—obviously expecting Seraph just to announce who he was. Phoran had a lot of experience with court wizards and their sense of consequence. It would never have occurred to Hinnum that Seraph would take his invitation literally.

"This is my family," she'd said.

She hadn't meant it. She couldn't have meant it. Tier would have, but then Phoran had listened to Rinnie's stories and realized Tier's behavior with the Passerines was nothing new. He adopted any stray creature that wandered past him, be they giant black dogs or fumbling, dissolute emperors.

Phoran *knew* she hadn't meant it, but it was precious to him just the same. Ever since his uncle died, Phoran had known that he was alone. Oh, there was Avar, but Avar didn't make Phoran feel safe and . . . and *loved*. "My family," she'd said, as if Phoran were one of her own children.

He heard someone come out of the library and sighed to himself, though he'd known Toarsen and Kissel wouldn't leave him alone for long. A furry black head dropped onto Phoran's boot, then Gura sighed, too.

"Phoran," said Lehr, quietly from behind him.

He turned to look at the dark young man—if not the last person he expected to see, he was close to it.

"Get tired of the noise?" Phoran asked.

Lehr smiled, but didn't admit it aloud. "Hinnum thinks if Mother can round up a Lark, a circle of all six Orders might be able to call upon the Elder gods. They were supposed to work that way, to keep the power of the Elder gods from growing too great. But once the surviving wizards realized there was a hole in the veil, it didn't seem necessary, so they never developed a ceremony that worked. Hinnum thinks the Weaver's power and the six Orders might be able to destroy the Shadowed."

Phoran looked back out at the sunset. "I heard some of that. Sounds like she, Hennea, and Hinnum are going to take a good try at fixing both Tier and those stolen Orders tomorrow. They need the real names of the Elder gods, or some way to get the rest of us out of their hair, so they're planning on sending us out to find the Owl's Temple because the names are in the temple somewhere."

"Etched into the dais in reverse," said Lehr. "She says we can get a rubbing with some char and someone's shirt." Then he said diffidently. "I can do it myself. There's no need for anyone else to . . ."

His voice trailed off, and Phoran realized some of his irritation at having his private moment interrupted had made itself felt. Lehr thought it was because he resented Seraph's assigning him tasks without consulting—which was something, thought Phoran, he really ought to be a little upset about since he was the Emperor and she was a farmer's wife. But she had called him family: as far as he was concerned, Seraph could command him all she wanted to.

"Have you ever watched three wizards work together?" asked Phoran.

Lehr hesitated, and said cautiously, "No."

"That's because they can't. I don't want to be around when that old wizard, your mother, and Hennea start arguing." It was Jes who didn't like being touched, Phoran remembered, so he slapped Lehr on the back reassuringly.

Lehr gave him a slow smile.

"Seriously, Lehr, I don't think any of us should be running around alone in this city. It's not like the woods, where you and your brother know the kinds of things you'll face. I know we haven't run into anything threatening yet, but there's something about this city that gives me the creeps."

"All right," Lehr agreed. "Actually, I came out here because

I thought you might answer a question for me. I thought I'd ask Toarsen, but since I have you alone . . ."

"Ask."

"On the way to the library today, Rufort and Ielian were talking about being a Passerine. Ielian said something that bothered Rufort, but I don't know exactly what it was or why it bothered him."

"Tell me," Phoran invited again.

"Rufort said that he liked being one of your guardsmen, that it was much better than being a Passerine had been. Then Ielian said he liked it, too. But being a Passerine had been better than being a clerk for his uncle. It bothered Rufort, but he didn't let Ielian see his reaction."

Phoran knew who Ielian's uncle was, but then so should Rufort. Like Phoran, he didn't see anything wrong with what Lehr had said. "Did he say why he liked being a Passerine better?"

"He said it paid better."

"I thought we'd found all of those," said Phoran, dismayed.

"All of what?"

"The only Passerines who were given coins by the Path were paid for killing people—or frightening them. Most of them were the older Passerines: Kissel and Toarsen knew who they were. Ielian is younger, from this year's crop. We didn't think that any of the youngest group were doing that sort of work."

Kissel and Toarsen had both gone out to frighten people. "Bruised a few knuckles" was what Kissel had called it. But killing—particularly the kind of killing that the Path had been behind—was a different category.

He couldn't trust Ielian anymore.

"It's all right, Lehr," he said. "Thank you for telling me. I'll let Toarsen and Kissel know."

"I like him," said Lehr. "Not many people stand up to Mother."

"I like him, too," said Phoran. "I'll talk to him about it before I decide what to do. Thank you."

Night had fallen while they talked. Phoran turned to go back into the library, and the Memory was there.

"Ah," he told it. "I hadn't realized how late it was getting."

Lehr watched the Memory, but he hadn't jumped or shrieked or anything else. Phoran remembered the first half dozen times the Memory had come to him and wished he'd been half so calm. Gura whined, but stood his ground.

Phoran rolled up the sleeve on his left arm; his right had been aching all day today, and that was his sword arm. He didn't remember the ache lingering as long when the Memory had fed before, but he might just have forgotten it.

But it felt worse again as the cold mouth closed over the wound it had made in his arm. The icy chill was more pervasive, the pain more intense than last night. Surely he would have remembered if it had been so bad last night.

Phoran found himself seated on the ground, half-leaning on Lehr.

"By the taking of your blood," said the Memory, its voice as dry as old leaves. "I owe you one answer. Choose your question."

"Phoran?" It was Lehr's voice, intensely quiet, like it got sometimes when they were nearing their prey on a hunt. "Look between those two houses across the square. Do you see them?"

Feeling dizzy and slow, Phoran stared at the houses Lehr was pointing at. Vaguely conscious of the dog, growling at Lehr's side.

"Yesterday, Hinnum warned us not to be here at night," Lehr was saying. "I'd forgotten—I'd wager Mother and Papa have as well. Hinnum said the streets belonged to the dead."

It looked almost human, thought Phoran. It was the right height and shape, but some primal instinct told him that whatever it was that watched Lehr and him from twenty yards across the cobbled avenue had not been human for a very long time.

"How do we survive this?" asked Phoran, looking at the dead man who had haunted him for better than half a year and never, ever, scared him as much as the thing—no, his eyes finally told him, Lehr was right there was more than one of them—things, then.

"Go inside," it whispered. "They are coming, and I have no power over the dead. They will come demanding a gift or your lives."

"What kind of gift?" Phoran asked. But the Memory had evidently given him his answer, such as it was, because it said nothing.

Still holding his arm, and staggering a little, Phoran stood up. "I hope your mother knows something about the dead," he said.

"I know about predators," said Lehr. "Don't turn around until we reach the door. Keep your eyes on them—and don't hurry."

Abysmally slowly they backed the few feet to the library door. Lehr opened the door, and Phoran took a last look at the gathering things slowly blending into the shadows of the buildings as twilight faded and darkness held sway on the streets of Colossae. Then he was inside, the wooden bulk of the door between them and whatever hunted them.

For the first time, the library struck Phoran as welcoming, the gentle glow of magicked lights tucked unobtrusively behind bits of carving in the ceiling and walls providing a sense of protection from the dark.

Seraph didn't hear the door open or shut over the babble of voices, but she saw Jes stiffen and look toward the stairs.

"Lehr, Phoran, and Gura," he said. "They smell of fear and blood."

His voice was loud enough that Hinnum and Hennea stopped the calm-voiced argument—an argument so heavy with unspoken guilt and anger that Jes had been forced to leave Hennea's side and stand alone away from the rest of them.

Phoran topped the stairs holding his left arm as though it hurt. Lehr stood just behind him with Gura. The dog's hackles were raised, and it kept looking behind them.

"It's night," Phoran said. "There are dead walking the streets. And I am hoping that's not as bad as I think it might be."

"Magic has no hold on the dead," said Hennea, speaking quickly, though there was no panic in her voice. "Hinnum, can they get in here?"

"They haven't bothered me before," said Hinnum. "But you, they will follow. The door might hold them for a while, but not after they've smelled blood. Magic can work on them a bit, no matter what the stories say, Hennea. Seraph, you will know what I mean when I tell you they are creatures of spirit."

She did. Difficult to work, but if the Shadowed managed to cloak his magic in spirit, then something could be done. As long as there weren't many of them.

"Of course," said Hennea, sounding rattled. "I'm sorry. I had forgotten. Like at the Mountain of Names. It's hard to remember everything. Jes, come back away from the stairway."

"I have safeguards that can keep them out of the library," Hinnum said. "But I haven't used them since your Willon left, and I cannot raise them as I am. I have no need of the safeguards myself; the dead are after flesh and blood, and, in my present form, I have none to tempt them."

"What happens if they find us?" asked Ielian. He'd gotten to his feet and loosened his sword. Steel worked against some creatures of a magical nature, but it wouldn't help against the dead.

"It's not a good thing for the dead to touch the living," Seraph said, giving them the extent of her knowledge. Her old teacher had been more worried about mistwights, water demons, and the like.

"There are a few ghosts in Colossae," said Hinnum. "But they are largely harmless and stay near their homes. I don't have a name for these—necromancy was never an art I was drawn to."

"I don't remember much about the dead," said Hennea.

"They killed all the wizards who chose to stay here with me after the city died," said Hinnum. "Running doesn't work; neither does most magic. It took me long time to learn how I might shield my apprentices, and it will take me too long to try to teach it to you. We have minutes before the doors give way, not days."

"The Memory said they will demand a payment for our lives," offered Phoran. "For whatever good that does us."

"Seraph," said Tier, his deliberately calm voice cutting through the rising tension in the library. "I left my lute in my packs at camp. Is there any way you or Hennea could fetch it for me?"

Seraph stared at him. Under the circumstances, it seemed like an odd request. Maybe she had misheard him. "What?"

He put his arm around her shoulders and smiled down at her, the tiredness in his eyes lifting a little. "There are a lot of songs about the dead, Seraph, and more stories. Phoran says the Memory told him that they are coming for a gift. The only gift I've ever heard any of the dead accepting is music."

"I've heard that," said Toarsen quietly. "My nurse used to tell us a story of a bard who tried to survive a night in a haunted castle by singing to the spirits until daybreak." He hesitated, then said, "He stopped a moment too soon because he was distracted by the song of a nightingale."

"I know that tale, but, fortunate souls that you are, there are no birds in Colossae to distract me," said Tier. "So fetch me my lute, love."

"They come," said a strange, toneless voice.

Standing in the middle of the library was a creature of blackness. Too tall and thin for a human, it was shrouded in mists of night-colored darkness that moved as if some unfelt wind blew them here and there. It looked out of place, as if it belonged along the edges of the room where shadows gathered rather than out standing in plain view.

Phoran stepped forward, between it and the rest of the room, and she realized it was Phoran's Memory. It looked more substantial than it had last night, as if it were closer to being a living creature than a dead one.

Just then there was a hollow boom, which echoed in the room and made Jes growl.

"Seraph," said Tier. "I think I'd better have that lute as soon as you can."

Seraph opened her mouth and shut it. Tier knew the state his Order was in. He knew that the convulsion fits happened more often when he sang. He didn't need her to tell him again.

She bent her head and closed her eyes.

She'd never done this before she stole the gem, and she wasn't certain how to find Tier's lute without a cord of magic, however fell, to show her the way. But it had been a day of new things, and she took her magic and told it what she wanted.

Tier's lute was almost as much a part of him as his brown eyes and his dimples. It was easier than she expected to find it and call it because it wanted to be with him. She suspected

Tier might have been able to call it himself. She opened her eyes and saw it had placed itself on the polished floor at Tier's feet.

Tier bent down to pick it up. He grimaced, then rose more slowly than he'd bent down. Another thud came from the outside door.

"I'm getting too old for this much adventure," Tier said. "Thank you for the lute, my love." He looked around. "Let's get everyone gathered together here."

He took a seat on the table, and made himself comfortable.

"Sit down," he told them. "I want them looking at me, not at you. And that means you as well," he told the Memory.

To Seraph's surprise, it collapsed to the floor. When Tier said something in that tone of voice, apparently even things like the Memory listened. Seraph sat on a bench next to Tier's table as he tuned the lute.

Phoran sat down on the floor, and his guardsmen spread around him. Jes and Hennea sat on the far side of the group, and Lehr took up the other, even though it left him nearest the Memory until Hinnum settled in between them.

"Rinnie, why don't you come here next to me," offered Phoran. "I think your mother might have her hands full before this night is over." So the most vulnerable of Seraph's children was seated in the middle, and Phoran took a good hold on Gura's collar without Seraph having to ask him.

Tier was still tuning the lute when the door failed, with the shriek of nails tearing free and a crack Seraph assumed was the wood of the door frame breaking. They all looked at the stairs, but there was nothing to see, no sound except for Tier's fingers on strings.

A wave of terror washed over her, worse by far than anything Jes had ever caused.

Tier played a quick scale and began tuning again. "I left it sit too long," he muttered. "The strings don't want to stay in tune."

"Papa," said Lehr, staring at the stairs. "Play."

A mottled grey hand appeared over the top of the stair, and it pulled its body behind it.

"Run!" Ielian came to his feet, but Rufort and Kissel each caught him by an arm and pulled him back down again.

The thing emerging from the stairway looked more human than the Memory, thought Seraph, and oddly the more horrible for its increased resemblance. It had a pair of eyes and what must once have been a nose. A few strands of grey hair stuck out from the top of its head. It looked at them and snap-snapped its jaws.

"Sit," hissed Toarsen at Ielian, who fought to get up again. "Running won't help."

"No," agreed the Memory, his voice like dry leaves in the wind. "Death walks the streets of Colossae by night."

"Thanks," snapped Phoran to the Memory, as Ielian made another abortive attempt to run. "That helped. Why don't you be quiet, eh? Ielian, sit still. Gura, *down*."

Gura and Ielian dropped to the floor with equal unwillingness. Rinnie curled up and buried her face against Gura's side, and Phoran reached over awkwardly to pat her on the back with the hand that wasn't holding on to the dog's collar.

"Mother, the Guardian wants to come out," said Jes. "But I think everyone is frightened enough."

"Let him come," said Seraph, the dryness of her mouth making her voice crack. "He can hardly make this worse."

Someone, it might have been Ielian, squeaked, as Jes flowed into the shape of a black wolf just a hair smaller than Gura. The Guardian glanced once at Ielian and bared his fangs before looking at the thing on the stairs. His low growl was a continuous rumble that echoed oddly off the high ceiling.

Rufort jerked and slid backward a handspan before he stopped himself.

"Something touched me," he said softly.

"Tier, isn't that damned thing in tune yet?" asked Phoran just as the creature pulled its flaccid legs over the stairway and began dragging itself forward.

The pressure of the presence of the dead crowded upon Seraph, bowing her shoulders under the weight. There were more of them than the creature they could see and the one that touched Rufort. She could feel them all around her.

"Tier," said Phoran, as the thing closed the too-little distance between the stairway and their huddled group.

Jes stalked around until he stood between it and them. As he growled louder, the stench of rotting meat filled the library.

Tier grinned fiercely, and his fingers moved on the lute strings.

The thing mewled at the first note, fading from sight just as the foul odor lessened. But Seraph could feel them waiting.

Tier played a mournful song first, a song about a girl wed to a sailor who left on a ship and never came back alive. It was melodic and slow, and Tier's fingers never faltered. Nor did his voice.

Toarsen sucked in his breath once, but when Seraph glanced quickly at him, she couldn't see anything wrong. He hunched over and bowed his head, but he didn't look like he was ready to run.

The immediate crisis seemed to have been put on hold by Tier's music. Seraph worked the spell that allowed her to see spirit again—and the library lit like a field of bonfires in winter. The dead were there, a ring of shapes made of spirit and something else she could see but not define, a haze of red alternating with gold. She managed to pull her eyes away from them long enough to make certain Tier's Order was behaving itself, then returned to her watch, making certain that the dead stayed away from them.

When Tier was finished with that song, he glanced around at his audience—the one he could see. Then he began a soldier's marching song Seraph had never heard before. It had a catchy chorus, and as he started into it for the second time, Tier said, "Join in if you'd like."

Lehr and Jes both did, and Rinnie sang a soprano harmony. Seraph found herself humming along. At the top of the fourth verse, Tier said her name, instead of the word that should have been there, and she realized that he was fighting.

"Seraph," said Tier again.

She pulled her gaze away from the dead and saw his Order had pulled almost entirely away from him, held only by a few lonely strands of his spirit and the last threads of her magic. She grasped the cord that ran between Tier and the gem and pulled hard toward Tier.

"Better," said Tier, before throwing his voice into the chorus again.

She held on. She might be able to help Tier better if she knew how spirit and Order interacted on a healthy Order Bearer.

She'd been too busy watching the dead before Tier called her to pay much attention to anyone else.

She looked up, intending to study Lehr—but her gaze stuck on the Memory first. She could see the Memory's form, but with her *seeing* spell its form was deep purple rather than black. Crouched beneath the shelter of Order was a sharp-featured Traveler who gleamed a soft spirit-blue. He met her eyes, looked startled, then whispered in her head, "Have him tell *The Fall of the Shadowed* as he told it for me."

"Tier," she whispered so she didn't interfere with his song. "The Memory told me to have you tell *The Fall of the Shadowed* the way you told it for him."

Tier looked a little surprised, but he nodded. As he sang, she noticed Tier's spirit had steadied and grown more solid where it attached to the tattered grey-green bits of his Order. Seraph wondered if, once the Shadowed's spell was restrained, Tier's music helped fight the drag of the spell.

Tier finished the song, then, striking a minor chord, began an ascending scale that built to a haunting arpeggio, the music forlorn and plaintive. His clever fingers flew over the gut frets of the lute, and the notes fell into a less disturbing tone as he began the story of Shadow's Fall.

"It happened like this."

Seraph had heard the story dozens of times before, so she paid little heed to the words. She surveyed the dead, but they seemed to be content with the lute-accompanied story, because they stayed where they were. The upper courses of Tier's lute wove bits of heroic ballads and festival songs into a single melody over a subtle throbbing bass that gradually began to take on the rhythm of a heartbeat.

"This young man was a good king, which is to say that he promoted order and prosperity among his nobles and usually kept the rest from starvation." Tier's voice blended into his music.

When she was certain the dead were satisfied with Tier's storytelling, she resumed her interrupted task of looking at Lehr to see how the Order was supposed to look in relation to spirit.

The smell didn't startle her at first, though if she'd been paying attention, she'd have realized there was no reason for the library to start smelling like horses.

"I smell flowers," whispered Lehr.

Once he said it, Seraph did, too. She looked up, but none of the dead had come closer.

Ah, she thought, returning to her examination of Lehr, *no wonder the Path's Masters had such a difficult time retrieving just the Order, no wonder it took months to separate spirit from Order—spirit is woven between the threads of Order like warp and weft.*

She heard the sound of sword meeting sword, but when she looked up, she could see nothing that would account for the sound—or for the sudden smell of the sweat of combat.

"None of his guardsmen or nobles could stand against him with sword or staff," said Tier.

Seraph looked at him incredulously, and she realized that even as she had restricted the magic she used for most of the two decades she and Tier had been married—so had he.

"He established libraries at every village," said Tier, and the scent of dust and mildew overwhelmed that actual scent of the library they were in, which smelled only of leather, parchment, and preservation spells. "And in his capital he collected more books than had ever been assembled together then or since. Perhaps that was the reason for what happened to him."

She was so in awe of what he was doing, it took her a moment to realize the cord of the Shadowed's magic she'd been holding steady, the one binding Tier's Order to the gem, was trying to pull away from her—and before she pulled it back, she realized it was pulling the wrong way. It was pulling back toward Tier. She released it.

"Time passed, and the king grew old and wizened as his sons became strong and wise. People waited without worry for the old king to die and his oldest son to take the crown." Tier stilled his fingers for a moment, so that his silence waited like the people had waited for the old king to die.

Two beats of silence . . . three, then he began a run of minor chords, echoing the melody he'd used to begin the story. "One evening the king's oldest son went to bed, complaining of a headache. By the next day he was blind and covered with boils; by that evening he was dead. Plague had struck the palace, and, before it left, the queen and every male of royal blood were dead." The familiar melody twisted with a weight of sorrow. An occasional plucked harmonic rang like a widow's wail.

Then, Lehr's startled gasp made her look away from Tier, where she'd been caught by the magic of his words and music.

She saw Hinnum and the Memory, so different from the others who huddled at Tier's feet. She saw the dead. She saw her children, Phoran, and his guardsmen. She saw Gura. She saw them all in glittering lights of spirit, Order, and the dark core that she had decided might be soul.

And before them all, untouched by Seraph's magicked sense of sight, stood the Unnamed King's daughter, Loriel. Seraph didn't know how she knew who it was, just that the woman who discovered what her father had turned into stood before them all. Brought before them, real as life, by Tier's power. Seraph watched in awe as Loriel fled the monsters who now filled her father's castle.

The music became momentarily militant, sharp percussive taps of the lute's face evoking drums and marching troops as Tier told of the army Loriel formed, one whose core would go on to fight to the end. Abrupt, discordant, wild strains starting and stopping suddenly followed by a cacophony of strident squeaks and slides, as Tier told of Loriel's death. Always, throbbing steadily beneath the other sounds, was the rhythm of the Unnamed King's heart.

It was hard to keep her attention on the reality of the Shadowed's spell when Tier's rich baritone called for her attention. Still, she watched him as the power of his music slowly forced the Shadowed's spell to yield its prey. Seraph pulled the gem out of the belt pouch where she'd put it, and it was warm in her hand.

A man's scream pulled her attention back to the battlefield the library had become. She couldn't tell if the noise had been made by one of their boys, the dead, or by some quirk of Tier's storytelling magic.

Seraph recognized the wide field they'd ridden across a few days ago, but this time there were bodies lying everywhere, and the stench of death made Seraph's gorge rise.

The bass courses of the lute continued to measure the steady pulse of the Shadowed, but the melody faltered, quieted. She saw Red Ernave fighting the Shadowed King, who was even more frightening than she'd ever thought he could be. Tier's fingers played a melody that stuttered and strained, falling a bit behind the beat, as if too exhausted to continue, the proud strains of military airs made aching and painful by their very slowness.

Under his red beard, Ernave looked like Tier a little, and Seraph thought that might have been why she cried when he died at the end of the battle. Or maybe it was because the garnet in her hand had shattered into minute shards, and Tier was covered head to toe in the grey-green fabric of his Order.

CHAPTER 18

"*Well,*" *Tier said, his fingers picking out bits of melody* that seemed to be keeping the dead away from them all while he caught his breath. "That went better than last time."

He looked at Seraph. "Something's different. What did you do?"

"I should be asking you that question," Seraph said. "You told me you learned a few things while you were alone in the Path's dungeons, but that was extraordinary. I know Bards are supposed to be able to make their stories feel real. I suppose I never realized what that meant."

"I've seen a Bard or two who could build pictures, sights, or sounds with their power," said Hennea. "But I've never seen any of them build truth from their stories."

Tier grinned. "I don't know about truth. But it's pretty disconcerting, isn't it. When I saw I'd gotten the details right on where Red Ernave died that first time I told the story this way—it fair made my heart stand still. I could have warned you, I suppose," he said. "But I haven't tried anything like that since the first time it happened. I wasn't certain it would work as well." He looked at the Memory. "What did you think?"

"Your control is better," it said. "You didn't leak power all over for anyone to feed upon."

"And I didn't get caught up and need rescuing." Tier's fingers found another song, something instrumental that was light and airy that seemed to clear the depressed atmosphere left by the death of Red Ernave. "Maybe it was adding music to the mix."

"Kissel, where are you going?" asked Toarsen.

Sure enough, Kissel was up and walking slowly toward the rows of shelving. "She needs us," he said. "Don't you hear her crying?"

Jes darted forward and stood in Kissel's way, growling at something in front of them.

Then Seraph heard it, too. A woman's brokenhearted weeping.

Seraph climbed over Tier's table since it was the shortest route, waving back the others, who all started to get up to help.

"Play, Bard," suggested Hennea. "Sing something. Something cheerful."

Tier started a common drinking song.

With Jes blocking his path, Kissel had stopped moving forward, but tears were flowing down his cheeks. "She's so sad," He told Jes. "Why can't we help her?"

The thick ruff of hair down the black wolf's back was standing straight up. Seraph moved slowly to Kissel's side, not wanting to startle him into doing something. He was fighting the enchantment, or else he wouldn't have stopped, Jes or no Jes.

With her spirit sight she could see one of the dead stood a few feet from Kissel, she thought Jes saw it, too, because his attention was focused on just the right place. Either Tier's music was keeping it back, or something about the way it fed required its victim to come to it. Either was possible from the little Seraph knew about such things.

Seraph slipped her hand into the crook of Kissel's arm. "It's like a painting," she said quietly. "It makes you sad or moves you, but you can do nothing to change it. The woman who weeps died a long time ago. There is nothing you can do for her."

"She will weep forever unless someone helps," he told Seraph, but he sounded more alert, more like his usual self.

"No one can help her, Kissel," Seraph said, tugging a little on his arm. "Come sit down."

He turned and shuffled back to his place, with Seraph guiding him and Jes guarding their backs.

"She was so beautiful," whispered Kissel as he sat down. "So sad."

"I know," said Jes.

Toarsen put an arm around Kissel and gave him a quick hug before releasing. He nodded once at Seraph—either telling her thanks, reassuring her that he would watch out for Kissel from here on out, or both, she wasn't certain.

Seraph released the sight magic with a sigh of relief; it was giving her a throbbing headache. She glanced down at Jes. "Did you see her?"

He nodded, curled up next to Hennea, and rested his snout on her knee. "She was beautiful."

Seraph bent down and rubbed him behind the ears, taking the moment to look over the others. They looked a little shaken, but Tier's drinking song—a silly, slightly risqué piece—was doing its job. Lehr and Phoran were singing along, and after a few verses Toarsen joined in as well.

Seraph worked her way back through the crowd to Tier's table. She patted Ielian then Phoran on the shoulder as she passed because they looked as though they needed it. She sat down on her bench and leaned her cheek against Tier's knee and let the melody his fingers coaxed out of the battered old lute sink through her like the knowledge of everyone's safety. Tier was safe.

She had a good idea now of how the Orders caught in the Path's gems might be cleaned so she and Hennea could release them. They knew who the Shadowed was—and that he awaited them in Redern. Hinnum and Hennea, for all their arguing, were pretty sure they'd come up with a way to destroy the Shadowed, so Phoran could be free of his Memory. All they had to do was find a Lark, and Hennea knew of a young man who would be willing to come though it might take her a few months to find him.

"Seraph," Tier said, as his clever fingers finished the song he'd been playing and began his between-song chord playing.

"I feel better. Tell me you managed to do something more with the Shadow's hold on me."

She smiled at him. "Ravens are arrogant," she told him. "When there is a problem, we tend to believe we are the only ones who can solve it." She opened her palm, where she still held the remnants of the garnet. "You broke the spell yourself while you told the story of the Fall of the Unnamed King."

"Huh." He raised his eyebrows in surprise. "Just the same, I think I'll stick to more mundane music for the rest of the night." His prosaic words didn't cover the relief she saw in his eyes.

He picked a sweet ballad written by a young man to his love, who was supposed to wed another. It suited his range, and the song was soothing, the perfect foil for the press of fear the dead still raised.

She slid off the bench and made her way to Rinnie. On the way she glanced at the Memory, but without the spell that let her see spirit and other things, it looked just as it had when it had come into the library.

Rinnie was curled up asleep on Gura, who was still watching the dead Seraph could no longer see. But the dog didn't look upset, just watchful. His alert pose mirrored the wolf settled comfortably next to Hennea. Seraph yawned and curled up on the floor next to Rinnie, found something soft and warm to lay her head upon, and let her eyes close while Tier's music kept her safe from harm.

Phoran must have fallen asleep sometime not too much after Seraph had. He woke up to the smell of something wild and sweet, and opened his eyes to see Seraph's hair and realized the light drumming he heard was her heartbeat. Hastily he straightened and took a quick glance around to see if anyone had noticed.

Not that waking up with somebody else's wife was a unique experience for him, and this was much more innocent than those instances. But still, her husband and children were in the room.

Jes, a human Jes, stretched out on his side next to Hennea, gave him a friendly smile, and lifted his finger to his lips. He was the only other one awake.

"Did you stay up the whole night?" asked Phoran, in a near-voiceless whisper.

Jes nodded, though he looked none the worse for wear. Phoran lifted and shifted and wiggled and finally managed to untangle himself from Seraph. He got up and stretched out most of the kinks in his back.

Tier slept on the table, the lute resting on his middle. Phoran smiled, then realized that the pile of sleepers was short a few people. He remembered the Memory leaving after Tier's incredible song. Ielian and Lehr must have awakened already. Hinnum, he decided, was none of his concern.

He waved at Jes and walked outside. By the angle of the sun, he could tell it was no later than midmorning. *Who would have thought it, we survived the night.*

"Morning," said Lehr, who was leaning against the wall of the library next to the broken door. "I heard Ielian get up, but by the time I could make myself move he was gone."

Phoran nodded. "Probably headed back to camp. He'll be hot that he was the only one who tried to run."

"Except the dog," said Lehr.

Phoran grinned. "That fool dog wasn't running; he was trying to attack."

The others began stirring not long after. When everyone else was awake, Jes woke up his parents, and they all trudged back to camp.

Phoran hadn't noticed it so much last night, but in the clear light of day, both of the Ravens looked drained, and Tier wasn't much better. Seraph caught his concerned look and smiled at him.

"It's all right, just too much magic yesterday and not enough sleep."

"Two days here, and we've found almost everything we came here for," he said. "Truthfully, I didn't think we'd find anything after Shadow's Fall. Not Colossae, not Hinnum, not the identity of the Shadowed."

She smiled, and her whole face lit up—he'd never seen her smile like that. For a moment she was beautiful.

"To tell you the truth, Phoran," she said, "there were times I didn't think we would either."

*   *   *

"Thank you for talking to Mother, Phoran," Rinnie said, one hand on Gura's back and the other in his.

"Anytime," he told her.

They'd left camp a little earlier than Seraph had planned, but Hennea had come up to him after breakfast to see if he would mind going earlier.

"Tier, Seraph, and Jes all need more sleep," she'd told him. "They won't get it with everyone up and about."

So he'd gathered everyone else, including Rinnie and Gura, and set off for the Owl goddess's temple. Ielian, who'd been in camp when they arrived from the library, had managed to work out whatever embarrassment or anger he felt over his behavior the night before. He suggested they pack a lunch and do a little exploring since they had some time to do it.

Lehr had the city map memorized already, and Phoran decided that if they all survived—and, at the moment, it looked as though they might—he wanted to get Lehr to map out the palace in Taela. Maybe Lehr could find his way to the southwest tower that no one had been in for at least thirty years because no one knew how to get to it.

Since they had all spent yesterday exploring in the University District, they just walked straight through and found their way down the ramp into the lower city.

"This is interesting," said Rinnie.

Phoran had to agree. They'd wandered through the Merchant's District for an hour or so and encountered mostly houses, closed up and impossible to enter. But the street they'd been following as it wandered along the bottom of the cliffs that divided the city had taken a sudden turn and dumped them into the middle of a market square, just as Lehr had promised.

"I'd sure like to get Lehr to Taela and watch him run a maze," said Ielian slapping Lehr on the back. "I'd make a few golds on you, I'll bet."

The market was paved with tiles rather than cobbles. Bright colors designed to raise a person's spirits, Phoran thought, judging from his own reaction. Once, he supposed, the whole empty expanse had been covered in stalls and tents where food and goods were sold. They would have been put away for the night, he thought, or perhaps the day Colossae had died had not been a marketing day.

"I've won a few bets in mazes," Toarsen was saying. "Though this isn't quite as interesting as the last thing I found in the middle of a maze."

"What was that?" asked Rinnie innocently.

Toarsen's smile dropped from his face. He cleared his throat. "A fountain. Uhm. With birds."

The most famous maze in Taela—at least among the young noblemen—was the one at the White Bird, a whorehouse that catered to the rich and bored. They held orgies in the largest of the parks inside the maze, but you could make assignations in the more secluded places, too. Phoran had done both a time or two.

"I've never seen a maze," said Rinnie, wistfully.

"Come to Taela, Rinnie, and I'll take you to some mazes." Not the White Bird. "If Lehr wants to come to Taela, I'll hire him to explore the palace for me—now *that* is a maze."

"I've been through enough mazes," said Kissel. "Last one I had to cut through trees to get out."

"That was you?" asked Phoran, impressed. "I'd heard that the White Bird had to hire a wizard to undo the damage."

Kissel smiled, not a nice smile. "I don't like being confined. They thought it was funny I couldn't find my way out. So I did."

Phoran saw Rinnie examining Kissel as if he were more interesting than he'd been a few moments ago. "That sounds like something my brothers would do."

Kissel grinned, a startling sudden grin. "I thank you for the compliment, Rinnie Tieragansdaughter."

Rinnie shook her head. "No, the boys are called after their fathers and the girls after their mothers."

"Ah," said Kissel. "I didn't know that."

"Mother says it's silly because that is not how the Travelers do it," Rinnie said. "I think it is fun to be named after my mother. People are *afraid* of my mother. They don't know that it's Papa they ought to be most careful of."

"Look," said Ielian, peering under the curtain blocked the nearest doorway. "Toys."

* * *

After the boys and Rinnie left, the camp was quiet. Tier was asleep, or dozing, at least, with his head in Seraph's lap. Jes had disappeared; he was probably sleeping somewhere just outside of camp. Hennea was sitting cross-legged by the coals of their campfire meditating.

Seraph hadn't meditated in a long time, and it had never been easy for her—mindless peace was not her natural state. Nevertheless, she thought it might be a good idea since she was too wound up to sleep. So she straightened her spine and relaxed her shoulders.

She didn't really meditate, but she closed her eyes and blocked the rest of her senses so she could organize her thoughts. They had learned so much in such a short time, and she needed to let it all settle into place. Tier was safe. Hennea was the goddess of magic. Hinnum was alive and well. Tier was safe. Hinnum would come to help release the Orders from the rings. *Hennea* was the *goddess* of magic. Tier was safe.

"You're thinking awfully hard," murmured Tier, from the vicinity of her lap.

"Tier," she said, without opening her eyes. "What do you think the Stalker wants?"

"Why ask me?" he asked, his tone lazy and warm, like a cat in the sun. "Until yesterday afternoon, I didn't even know what the Stalker really was."

"Yesterday when you were talking to Hinnum and you said there were three players in the story. Hinnum, Willon, and the Stalker. You had that last fit before you could tell us what you thought the Stalker's motivations were."

She heard him take a deep breath and let it out in a tired sigh. "Hinnum taught Willon about the Orders, Seraph. But Hinnum didn't think he taught Willon enough to allow him to steal them."

"I didn't teach him how to see spirit," said Hinnum. "I would have thought that was necessary to steal an Order."

Seraph opened her eyes and saw the old wizard standing in front of them. He'd had come upon them without her hearing. Or Jes hearing—which meant he'd used magic of some sort. Tier didn't bother opening his eyes.

Hinnum continued. "I spent all this morning and half the night—once I knew Tier's music would appease the dead—trying to see how he could put what I taught him together and steal Orders from Travelers."

Seraph noticed Hennea had opened her eyes, but she stayed where she was.

"I don't see how he managed it," Hinnum said. "I only knew because of what those fools had done to the Eagle. And because I helped the Raven to create the Orders in the first place. Willon is not a Raven, who can take the story of the Orders and know how it was done. At least he didn't have access to a Raven's power until *after* he'd already discovered how to steal the Orders. He'd have needed specifics. Rituals, words, and runes—*something*. I did not give them to him."

"Hinnum," said Hennea.

He turned to her and, to Seraph's eyes, seemed to shrink a little. Then he caught himself, stood up straight, and looked her in the eyes. "I could not kill you, Raven. In all the centuries I paid my allegiance to you, there was only one thing you asked that I did not do. I could not do."

Tier opened his eyes during Hinnum's speech, looked up at Seraph, and raised an eyebrow. *Centuries?* He asked without words. *Raven? Is Hennea the Raven? Is that what Hinnum is saying?* Twenty years of marriage allowed her to read all of that in his face.

She nodded.

"What a story," he mouthed. "I knew she was old."

She smiled and touched her finger to her lips. "I'll tell it to you later," she mouthed back.

He smiled and closed his eyes again. She couldn't tell if he was going to sleep.

"I don't remember most of it very well even now," Hennea told Hinnum, her face wearing its Raven mask. "Some things," she said slowly, "are as clear as yesterday. I can see the Eagle's face and hear his voice, but I don't remember the Falcon or the Cormorant. When Seraph looked at Tier's spirit, when she brought back the gem, I thought, 'I remember how to do that.' But there is much I ought to know that is simply a blank, fogged by time's passage. I doubt I shall ever remember some of it."

Hennea stood up and left the fire so she could face Hinnum. "But I do remember *you*. I remember you beside me during the black days before Colossae's end. I remember finding peace in the knowledge that I would die when Colossae did—because you promised to kill me. And you always fulfilled your promises."

Hinnum made a soft sound and turned away.

"For four and a half centuries, Hinnum, you were a man of your word." She touched his shoulder, and he cringed under her hand. "And this beautiful morning, I cannot find it in me to be anything but grateful for the one time you were not."

Tier sat up, yawned, rubbed his eyes, and looked at Hinnum. He rubbed his eyes again and looked some more.

"I see why you chose to stay here," he said after an awkward moment.

Seraph looked, too, but Hinnum appeared no different to her than he originally had. Which, she realized, was odd, because he'd told her that something had happened to his body that kept him from leaving Colossae with the other wizards. He must still be using an illusion, even if it was his own body he wore that morning.

Hinnum lowered his eyebrows and looked down at Tier. "I love music," he said heavily. "Last night you told the story of Shadow's Fall with such power that I cried for the death of a man I never knew. Even so. Even so, *Bards* are the *bane* of my *life*. I am an *illusionist,* and Bards see truth."

Tier shook his head. Whatever he saw must have been bad, because his reply was without the touch of humor he usually threw in. "My apologies, Hinnum. I won't reveal what you want hidden."

If Tier said he wouldn't tell them what he had seen, he would not. If she was not to know what had happened to Hinnum, Seraph would rather talk about other, more important matters.

"If you did not teach him how to steal the Orders, how did he find out?" she asked.

"It was the Stalker," said Tier.

"The Stalker?" said Hennea.

"Who else could it have been? I've been thinking about it a lot."

"The Stalker is not evil," Hinnum said.

"I didn't say that he was. You told us the Elder gods' powers are constant, almost involuntary. If there are holes in the veil that keeps the Elder gods from destroying the world, then

I believe it is possible for a wizard to feed off the Stalker's power without the Stalker's consent. You also told Seraph that the Stalker is caught behind the veil against his will."

Hennea took a seat beside Tier. "The Weaver told me the world was too old, too brittle for the stresses He and His brother would bring to it. Their powers would destroy it."

"The Weaver told me His brother did not care if the world died," Hennea continued. "Death is a part of the Stalker's power and is a natural process. But the Weaver loves His creation—so He found a way to bind them both and restrict Their powers so that His world could survive."

She patted the ground beside her, and Hinnum sat down as she began speaking again.

"The substance of the veil is the power of both of the Elder gods: what else could restrain Them? If the Stalker had agreed, He and the Weaver could have re-created the veil Themselves after my consort died. Instead, the death of Colossae served as proxy for the power of the Stalker—taken from Him by force. The Weaver wove the other half of the veil Himself."

"The Stalker wants free," said Seraph.

"That's what the Weaver told me on the night we decided that Colossae and her gods would die."

"So why would . . ." Seraph's voice faded off as she saw what Tier had seen yesterday. "The Stalker couldn't stop the Shadowed from feeding off his power, so he might as well make use of him. Willon was an illusionist, angry at the limits of his magic. So the Stalker offered to show him how to steal the power, of the Travelers. Why didn't he tell him of the Guardian Order?"

"A lot of the Ordered gems don't work," said Hennea slowly. "If the Elder god chose to show Willon how to steal the Orders, he would certainly do a better job of it."

"No," said Tier. "Because the Stalker doesn't care if the Orders are useful or not. He just wants them bound to inert objects rather than Order Bearers. Because the Orders do serve a purpose."

"They keep the balance," Hinnum said. "Without the balance to anchor it, the veil will fail, and the Elder gods emerge."

"Ah," said Hennea thoughtfully, "If Willon wore one of each of the Orders, he could draw on the power of both of the

Elder gods instead of just the Stalker. The Stalker ensures he never attains that goal by making certain the Shadowed cannot have all six. Many of the Ordered stones do not work—the Lark not at all so far as we know—and the Shadowed doesn't know about the Guardian Order."

"Clever people, those Colossaen," said Toarsen, as they left the Owl's temple.

It was later than it ought to have been, because they'd spent a couple of hours in the Merchant District, where the entrances to the shops had been curtains rather than doors. Most of the curtains left a space above the floor that they could slide under.

Some of the shops had been just like their counterparts in Taela, some had not. Phoran had been particularly struck by the mercantile that had fabrics the like of which he'd never seen before. There were brocades and velvets, but also some sort of shiny fabric with a luster like a silk, but it changed colors from gold to green, depending on what angle he viewed it from.

Toarsen teased Phoran because of his fascination with some of the more exotic fabrics—but he'd always had a flair for fashion and saw no need to change his mode of dress simply because he'd become respectable. His only regret was due to the nature of the spell holding Colossae, all of the fabrics were stiff as wood, and it was impossible to tell how they would feel against skin.

"They had knowledge that was too dangerous," continued Toarsen, and Phoran pulled himself away from his daydream. Some men dream of fair women, he thought with self-directed humor; he dreamed of fabrics.

"Speaking the true names of the gods is a bad thing—" Toarsen continued as self-appointed lecturer. "—but not being able to call upon them if you needed to was equally bad. So they engraved the names on the Owl's dais backward and colored it so most of the indentations aren't easily seen. Then we come along with a white shirt—"

"*My* white shirt," said Rufort in a not-quite-whining tone. "I hope that char comes out because I only brought one other shirt."

"I can clean it," said Rinnie, sounding resigned. "Mother

can, too—but she'll give the chore to me. She doesn't like laundry or sewing."

"At least she doesn't make *you* butcher the pig," said Lehr.

"—With *Rufort's* white shirt," continued Toarsen cheerfully over the top of all the others, "and a charred piece of firewood, and now we have the names of the gods." He held the shirt up so they could see them more clearly.

"Ielian," called Lehr, "you're going the wrong way."

Phoran looked away from the shirt and saw Ielian ahead of them. He must have kept walking while Toarsen paused to admire the rubbings on Rufort's shirt. Ielian must not have heard Lehr's call because he disappeared down the street he'd chosen without pausing.

"Remind me not to bet on Ielian if he decides to run in a maze race," said Kissel in disgust. "I suppose we'd better go get him." He looked down. "Come, Rinnie Tieragansdaughter, let's go rescue Ielian."

"It's Seraphsdaughter," she told him in a patient voice.

He nodded. "But Tier is the one people really need to worry about—and I suspect that there will be a lot of young men worried about you one of these years, lady."

Rinnie looked pleased.

They came to the street Ielian had taken and found him engrossed in the elaborate carving on the door of a house that stood next to a narrow ally.

"Ielian," called Phoran. "Lehr says this is the wrong way."

"You have to come here," he replied. "I've never seen anything like this."

They were within a few yards of Ielian, who was still absorbed in whatever had caught his attention, when Phoran saw Lehr stiffen, sniffing the air.

"What's wrong, Lehr?" Phoran asked.

"Run!" said Lehr, his voice urgent.

"Stop," said another, almost-familiar voice.

Phoran, who would have rather followed Lehr's advice, found himself helpless to do anything except follow the second command. His body refused to move.

"We should try an easy one first."

Seraph had the Ordered gems spread out on a blanket from

her bedroll. She began sorting them quickly into piles according to Order. Hennea, sitting on the other side of the blanket, began helping.

"I meant to ask," Seraph inquired as she put a ruby necklace in the Falcon's pile. "Why are there so many fewer Larks than, say, Ravens?"

"For magic to work," Hennea answered, "the Order could be a very small part of the Raven's power. It is the ability to work magic—not magic itself. So there are more Ravens, each with the smallest part of a god of any Order—and it is Raven who is most easily bound to the gems. Healing is different. There were always only a few Larks, because a lesser gift would not have functioned."

"So the Lark gems failed," Seraph said. "As they were meant to fail."

She used her seeing spell so she could see spirit again. The small pile of Lark gems lit up with spirit, brighter by far than any of the others.

"Their Order holds more tightly to the spirit," she told Hennea. "And so the rings behave as if they are haunted." She picked up the tigereye that used to warm to her touch. "I wonder if this is my daughter's Order?" she asked.

Tier's hands closed over her shoulders, as Hinnum said, "I don't think there's a way to tell."

"We should begin with the Ravens," said Hennea. She picked up a brooch set with a pale green peridot that had only the faintest wisp of spirit.

Some of the gems were still in their settings, but others had been in armbands or heavy jewelry that were bulky and made them difficult to conceal. They, Hennea, Brewydd, and she, had pried the stones out of the largest settlings.

Seraph watched Hennea coax the bit of blue out of the violet Order.

"There's a little bit more," Hinnum said, peering closely at the brooch. "Yes, right there."

"Now," said Hennea. "Do you think that breaking the stone is enough, or do we have to unwork the spell binding the Order to the gem?"

"Unworking the spell is safer," said Seraph, setting down the tigereye ring in a pile all its own. Hinnum was right, there was probably no way to know for certain if the tigereye held Mehalla's Order and part of her spirit.

She could see how it had happened. Willon had a Lark born right under his nose, a child. He'd have been frustrated because when the Path had managed to find a Lark, they could not use the Order they stole from her. Maybe a child would be easier.

She'd started to get sick in the spring. No matter what herbs Karadoc had given her, no matter what Seraph could do, Mehalla just kept fading away. She'd had fits in the end.

Seraph had almost forgotten that. Mehalla was weak by then. She would just stiffen a little, her eyes rolling up into her head. It hadn't been dramatic, like Tier's fits, but then Mehalla had been a toddler, not a full-grown man.

"With magic strong enough to imprison an Order, it is better to be safe," agreed Hinnum. "I—" He jerked his head up. "Did you feel that?" he asked.

Phoran heard footsteps approach them, and he decided whoever it was had been hidden around the corner. He couldn't see anyone because he couldn't move at all.

"Breathe," said the voice.

Phoran realized that he hadn't been breathing only after he took in a deep gulp of air. He was almost certain the voice belonged to Willon, but it sounded wrong. He heard Lehr, who had been standing next to him, take a harsh breath, too.

Gura whined unhappily, and he felt the big dog brush against his leg. The dog, it seemed, had been impervious to the spell holding Phoran and the others.

The footsteps stopped just in front of Phoran. "You can move your eyes," the man said. "And blink. I am not a cruel man, not when I think about it. I may have to kill you, but I don't gain anything by torture."

Phoran blinked—and moved his eyes. The only people he could see were Rufort, who had been just in front of him, and the wizard. For a moment he thought he'd been wrong, and the wizard who held them was a total stranger. The man's dark hair and lithe, muscular body didn't belong to the Willon he knew. Then the wizard turned, just a little, and Phoran saw his face. It was Willon, but a much younger Willon.

Willon had been an illusionist when he came to Colossae, thought Phoran. Of course he would protect himself by appearing to age.

"What's this?" asked Willon.

"A rubbing from the Owl's temple. The names of the Elder gods." Ielian's voice came from somewhere behind Phoran.

"Ah. I don't think those should be left loose where anyone can read them, do you?"

The smell of burning cotton came to Phoran's nose.

"Ielian, you have done well," said Willon, reappearing in Phoran's view. "All of them at once without Tier to see through my illusions or the Ravens who could break them. Now, you are certain Hinnum has taught Seraph how to make the Ordered gems useful?"

"Yes," said Ielian, who had moved just behind Phoran. "I don't understand how it worked, Master. But I know Seraph was certain she could clean them, she said as much."

"Good work, my lad," said Willon. "If she can do that, it will be worth the trouble they caused me when they brought down the Path. I gave them all the gems except for Tier's own in the hopes that a pair of Ravens and a Lark might do what I could not."

"But they didn't," said Ielian. "Of course they couldn't."

Willon smiled. "Of course not. So only Hinnum knew how, but he'd never teach me, and he has no one I could threaten. No one he cares about."

"So you gave them the maps and sent them here."

"No," said Willon. "I merely left them where they were— where Volis put them after he stole them from me. When nothing Seraph did would heal Tier, I knew she'd come here, looking for answers—and find Hinnum. I'm just surprised that they won Hinnum over in so short a time—secretive bastard that he is. They haven't been here two days, and Hinnum stole Tier's gem from me."

"Seraph did that, Master, not Hinnum. Then Tier broke the spell entirely while he was singing *The Fall of the Shadowed*."

Willon frowned. "Tier freed himself? You must be mistaken. A Bard can break illusions, but that spell is not an illusion."

Ielian said, "I'm no wizard, Master. I can only tell you what they told me."

"Perhaps Hinnum did it and allowed them to believe it was Tier," mused Willon. "Makes no difference."

He looked up into Phoran's eyes. "You needn't worry, Phoran. I owe you greatly for bringing my Passerine where he could spy for me. How else would I ever have found the Guardian Order? There is nothing written about them, no story told about them. None of the Path's prisoners spoke of them. When Volis began muttering about an Eagle, I thought he was deluded. Imagine my surprise when I found that Jes is slow, not because he is defective, but because he is a Guardian. How unexpected to find an Order Bearer so ill equipped. If Hinnum were still speaking to me, I'd chide him for it."

He looked over at Lehr. "None of you will die if you do as I ask. Tell your mother, boy, if Seraph cleans all the rings she has." He paused. "And if she shows me how it is done. None of her children will die. You tell her that. Tell her you and your family have nothing to fear from me, if she does as I bid her."

"If not . . ." He walked just behind Phoran and whispered something Phoran couldn't quite hear.

"My father will kill you after my mother boils you in oil," said Rinnie, and Phoran's heart twisted in fear.

He knew that she struggled because she bumped against him.

"I don't think so," Willon purred. "I think she will do exactly what I ask because otherwise you will pay the price."

She was a child, and Phoran could do *nothing*. A bead of sweat slipped into one of Phoran's eyes, burning it, but no matter how hard he struggled, he could only move his eyes.

"Bring her," Willon said. "Meet me at the top of that tower. I'll go to the Owl's temple and see to it that no more enterprising explorers happen onto the names of the gods." He walked back in front of Phoran, but without Rinnie. He must have given her to Ielian. He stood down so he could see Lehr's eyes. "Lehr Tieraganson, tell your mother we'll be up there in that tower, waiting for her answer. Her daughter and I."

"There're ghosts and whatnot here in the city," said Ielian. "It might be better to find a place outside."

"I assure you that I know how to keep them away," said Willon, straightening. "I lived here for five years, once. I learned how to deal with the ghosts. Bring her up to the tower."

One moment Willon was standing in front of Phoran, and the next there was a golden hawk where he had stood. The hawk crouched and, in a graceful swoop of wings, took flight.

Everyone knew wizards couldn't change shape, thought Phoran. Apparently the Shadowed didn't need to worry about what everyone knew.

"Traitor, *oath breaker*," said Rinnie, her anger almost hiding the fear that made her voice shake.

Ielian laughed. "No, they're the oath breakers: Toarsen, Kissel, and Rufort. I took my oath to the Masters of the Path, and I've never broken it."

"He's the *Shadowed*," Rinnie said. "How can you serve the Shadowed?"

"Because," said Ielian, his voice slick and hungry, "he gives me people to kill."

Gura whined again, clearly agitated at Rinnie's fear, but Ielian was supposed to be a friend.

"Rinnie, Rinnie," Ielian chided. "Did you think I wouldn't notice the gathering clouds? You're a Cormorant, a weather witch. But I noticed something while I was riding with your family. Do you want to know what it is? Unless you're a farmer, Cormorants are all but *useless*." His voice became mockingly sympathetic. "It takes such a long time to build a storm. And all it takes to stop you is—" There was the dull sound of flesh hitting flesh—and Phoran couldn't *move*.

Gura could.

Phoran heard the threatening growl and the sound of a scuffle. A grunt—dog or human he couldn't tell. Phoran's frustration rose to new heights. A body fell to the ground.

"Gods that felt good," said Ielian. He appeared in Phoran's view, splattered with the dog's blood, a hunting knife in his hands.

He rolled his head, first one way than the other, like a fighter loosening up his neck muscles before a battle.

"I've forgotten how good it feels." His face was flushed with agitation, his hands vibrating with some extreme emotion. He spoke rapidly, almost unintelligibly. "I can't kill Lehr. The Master is right. Seraph would never cooperate if we hurt her son. And the Emperor might be useful. Can't kill the Emperor."

With a strike as swift as a snake, Ielian slit Rufort's throat. Blood spurted, and Ielian jumped back with an excited laugh. Rufort stayed standing as he had been while he bled out with the beating of his heart. At last he fell face forward into the puddle of his blood that covered the cobbles.

Ielian crouched beside the body. "What did that feel like, Rufort? Did you feel helpless? Did you feel death coming to take you? Or were you lost in disbelief?" He looked up, meeting Phoran's eyes. "I could have killed you a thousand times, Emperor. That makes me a very powerful man indeed. More powerful than you could ever be. Do you know what it is to hold a man's life in your hands?" He reached out and ran his fingers through Rufort's hair. "No one will ever love him more than I did at the moment of his death. How could I not love someone who gave me such pleasure? Did you see how he stood, soldier-straight until death took him?" He shuddered with pleasure at the memory, like a man might when recalling a particularly good whore.

He stood up and shed that strange aura of intensity and looked calm and competent. "I'd better get going. The Master is expecting me." He walked past Phoran. "Here," he said. "Why don't you hold this for me? I'll leave it in to slow the bleeding. Maybe the Master's spell will fade before you bleed to death."

Kissel or Toarsen, thought Phoran. Ielian had stabbed one of the two. Phoran struggled as hard as he'd ever struggled in his entire life, but he couldn't move so much as a fingertip.

Ielian appeared again, blood staining his shirt. He had a limp Rinnie over one shoulder and an expression as peaceful as any Hennea had ever worn. As he left them there, he softly whistled one of the songs Tier had sung last night.

CHAPTER 19

"No," said Hennea. "I don't feel anything. What's wrong?"

"The Shadowed is here," Hinnum said. "I know the magic of my apprentice."

Tier's hands tightened on Seraph's shoulders. "Here? In Colossae?"

Hinnum nodded and looked at Hennea. "I am no match for the Destroyer's power, not in a man who has had it for two hundred years. I can buy you time to run, my lady, but you must run far and fast. Find your six Ordered and destroy this monster I helped to make."

"We can't go without Rinnie and the boys," said Seraph.

Hinnum looked at her and nodded toward the city where a group of low-lying clouds were forming. "He has them already," he said gently. "There is nothing you can do. A Falcon and a Cormorant have no chance against him. No more do two Ravens, a Bard, and an Eagle. Even if one of you used to be a goddess, even if I give you all the help I can. I tell you that I have seen the power of the Shadowed before. If the Unnamed King had not been mad, Red Ernave and Kerine would never have been able to kill him. Our Shadowed is no Unnamed King. I'll do my best to delay him, but you have to run."

Seraph's hand closed on the tigereye ring. "We need a Lark," she said. "I have one here. My daughter or whoever this Order once belonged to would have given her life to destroy the Shadowed. If you can help my children, we can destroy him now."

Phoran stood in helpless, hopeless anger. He had *promised* Seraph no harm would come to her daughter. An emperor should keep his promises—but Willon's spell held him firmly.

Willon was an illusionist. What had he said? Tier could see through his illusions. Did he mean that this spell would not have held Tier? Could this spell be some form of illusion?

Phoran had grown up in a court littered with mages of one sort or another. The illusions he'd seen had been minor magic, when it wasn't outright legerdemain and not magic at all. It was common knowledge that disbelief would break an illusion—one of the reasons that illusionists were considered second-rate mages.

Phoran tried to convince himself the spell was just an illusion, something he could break. *Of course I can move—I've done so all my life. How can a magician stop me with one word?*

The problem with disbelief was that Willon quite obviously had managed to stop him with one word—it was hard to disbelieve something true. This would be a story to tell his children—whose future existence was in serious doubt: The story of how the lowborn wizard overcame the Emperor with one word—because the Emperor was so weak-willed as to allow it.

Anger began to stir, and Phoran welcomed it. He was Emperor, no wizard had the *right* to force his will upon him. Phoran pushed aside his recent realizations of how little difference there was between a farmer and the Emperor. He wasn't a Bard. This wasn't about *truth,* it was about a peasant-born trader-illusionist who thought he had the right to command an emperor.

No one commanded *him.* Hadn't he killed thirteen Septs who believed they had more power than the Emperor?

Phoran closed his eyes and took the deepest belief of the drunken sot he'd once been and held it to his heart. An emperor was superior to any wizard born. He was Emperor Phoran the Twenty-Seventh of that name. No one, *no one* commanded him!

He stepped forward, knowing with utter certainty, that his right foot would lift, and his weight would shift. He stumbled forward and opened his eyes. He'd done it.

He rolled Rufort over, but his body was limp, his eyes open and covered in the blood he was lying in. Phoran closed Rufort's eyes.

"Sleep sweet, my friend," he said, and went to tend Ielian's other victims.

Kissel had the handle of a knife sticking out of his chest, which was covered in blood.

Phoran hurriedly drew his own knife. "Don't worry," he said as Kissel's eyes widened. "I'm not putting you out of your misery. I'm just getting bandage material before I pull that knife out."

He stripped off his own shirt and sliced it into strips. The fashion for sleeves was full that year and he thanked the tailors for it as he folded the sleeves up into a pad. A quick glance at Kissel's back showed him there was no blood. The knife hadn't gone through then, so he only had one wound to worry about. He tried not to think of internal damage as he tied pieces of his silk shirt together until he had a long strip of bandaging. He cut Kissel's shirt so he could get a good look at the wound.

Stop the bleeding, he told himself. The others would have to see to the rest.

"I'm going to take the knife out," he told Kissel. "Brace yourself."

He did it from behind, so if he overbalanced Kissel, the captain would just fall against Phoran. He pulled it as fast as he could, and cringed at the sound of steel against bone. When it was out, he dropped Ielian's knife to the ground and held the pad made of his sleeves as hard as he could against the wound as he wrapped Kissel's chest with the strip of cloth.

When he had the bandaging tied as tightly as he could, he rocked Kissel back against him. Kissel was not a light man, but though he easily outweighed Phoran, Phoran managed to lay him on the ground without banging him up much.

As soon as he'd taken care of Kissel, he went to Gura. The big black dog was still breathing, but his eyes were closed, and there was too much blood on the cobbles.

"I have to get Rinnie," he told the dog, hesitated, then took his knife to Toarsen. "I need your shirt."

It took him too long to bandage the dog, but at last he was satisfied that he'd done what he could.

"Don't come after me," he told them. "I require your obedience as your emperor. If and when this spell wears off, go get Tier and Seraph and tell them what has happened. I'll get Rinnie if I can. If not, I doubt that Willon will kill her, not if he wants Seraph to do anything for him."

He started to go after Rinnie, then stopped and turned back. He couldn't leave without telling them what he'd learned.

"The spell is an illusion," he told them rapidly. "As soon as you believe, really believe you can move, then you can break the spell."

He walked backward as he spoke. When he finished he turned and ran.

Phoran was not Lehr, but he didn't need to be. He could see the tower Willon had pointed out; it rose from the top of the cliffs above them. Ielian had walked in Rufort's or Gura's blood, and though the blood trail didn't last for more than three or four steps, it gave Phoran all the direction he needed. He headed for the alleyway that looked to be where Ielian had been heading.

The alley was narrow—only wide enough for two men walking abreast, and it ended against the cliff edge, where a steep, zigzagging stairway had been carved into the cliff face. He shielded his eyes and saw a small figure climbing near the top.

Phoran drew his sword and started up the cliff. There were no railings on the side of the stairway, which was narrower than that alley had been. By the time he'd passed the third flight, he was high enough to make misstep fatal. He kept his eyes on the steps before him and tried not to look over the edge.

The past few months had melted much of the self-indulgent fat from his body, but even in his best shape, Phoran would never be a great runner. His build was more like Kissel's, good for power but not stamina; but with Rinnie's life at stake, he made the best speed he could. Lack of air made him dizzy and forced him to slow his pace. Legs aching, a stitch in his side, focused on climbing, he might not have noticed the Memory if it had not grabbed his arm and pulled him to a stop.

Its hand touched his mouth when he would have said something. The cold touch caused Phoran to jerk his head back with a reflexive shudder. But when he heard the scuffle of feet above him, he knew what the Memory had been trying to tell him. Someone was coming down the stairway.

Phoran waited, trying to catch his breath. As soon as he stopped, the Memory faded from sight.

Ielian's clothing was bloody, his pant leg ripped over his thigh where Gura must have bitten him, but his smile was genuine. "My emperor," he said, "you needn't have bothered coming. The Master sent me to release the rest of you." He held out an amulet with the hand that wasn't holding his sword. "This will break the spell. I'll give it to you, shall I? Then you can go release the others yourself."

Phoran didn't say anything. Their relative positions on the stairway gave Ielian the advantage. Phoran knew from the morning training sessions with the Emperor's Own that Ielian was the better swordsman. Even as he acknowledged the advantages Ielian held, Phoran set those worries aside.

He had no intention of taking the amulet and meekly going back to the others. Even if Ielian was telling the truth, the others were adults and likely not to come to any immediate harm. He had given his word to protect Rinnie.

The Memory resolved itself a couple of steps behind Ielian.

"No," said Phoran as he lunged. "This one is mine."

He didn't use his sword, as Ielian had been waiting for him to do. He just ducked under Ielian's blade and thrust his shoulder into the side of Ielian's knee, toppling the lighter man off the open side of the stairs. He screamed as he fell.

By the time Ielian died, Phoran was climbing again.

"The Shadowed is here," said the Memory, climbing just behind him. "But I cannot kill him, he is too powerful."

Phoran took a second to look back at it. "What good *are* you then?"

"The last time someone killed a Shadowed he did it with an army at his back, a Raven at his side, and a dead wizard's power guarding him," answered the Memory. "It will take more than a ghost and an emperor to kill the Shadowed. More than all of us combined."

"Encouraging, aren't you," Phoran said dryly. "I agree with you, as it happens." He'd hoped to catch up to Ielian before he'd delivered Rinnie, but it had taken Phoran too long to break Willon's spell. "Maybe, just maybe, though, we can distract him long enough to allow Rinnie to escape."

They came to the top of the cliffs at last. The watchtower was farther back from the edge than it had appeared from below. Stairs wound around the outside of the tower, but they were wider than the ones he'd just climbed. Even better, handrails edged either side of the stairs. The top of the tower was half-enclosed, with the open half looking out over the edge of the cliff, giving whoever was watching a clear view of the lower level of Colossae and most of the valley.

"He's up there," Phoran said.

"Yes," agreed the Memory. "He is there."

"I don't suppose you could take a message to Tier," asked Phoran, but he wasn't surprised at its answer.

"No, that is not within the compass of my purpose. I *am* that I may destroy those who killed me."

"You saved me from assassins," said Phoran. He was beginning to get his breath back.

"You are my tie to life and without you I will cease to exist, my vengeance unsatisfied."

"Bringing Tier and the Ravens here might save my life," he suggested.

"Not directly," answered the Memory. "If I could feel sorrow or regret, it would be for this. However, I will come with you and save you if it is possible for me to do so."

"Better than nothing," said Phoran. He put a hand on the rail that edged the stairway winding around the tower. "Let's go."

The tower was fifty or sixty feet tall, and when he was halfway up he slowed to a walk. He wanted to be rested when he reached the top. The Memory had not followed him up, but he trusted it would keep its word to help and give him another weapon against the Shadowed.

Near the top of the stairs, he slowed further, his sword in hand. Not that he expected his sword would do him much good against a wizard who could freeze him with a word, but the familiar grip felt reassuring.

He stopped before the guardroom came into view and crouched, listening. From where he stood, Phoran could see out over the city to the river they'd crossed to enter Colossae's valley.

"Have some tea, child, you'll feel better."

"No, thank you," said Rinnie in a polite but extremely firm voice.

Willon laughed. Phoran closed his eyes against that laughter because it reminded him of the affection he'd always had for the old man who came to Taela two or three times a year to visit Master Emtarig, for the man who always took time to share a story or two, who always had some exotic sweet for a lonely boy emperor. It had been Willon who had made his uncle's funeral bearable for Phoran. He'd taken Phoran's hand and said quietly, "Your uncle loved you, boy, for all that he wasn't the sort of man to say so. He told me he thought you would be a great emperor."

All the while it was Willon's machinations that had caused Phoran's uncle's death—and Phoran's father's death, a man Phoran vaguely remembered as the smell of horse and fresh air, and as the feel of strong arms hoisting him onto a shoulder. There was a portrait of Phoran's father hanging in the art gallery in the palace, but the painting was of a stranger with Phoran's nose and fine, midbrown hair.

"My father will see you dead," Rinnie said. It wasn't the most wise thing she could have said, Phoran thought.

"You've said that before, and it becomes tedious. The fact of the matter is that Tier is a Bard. He is a fine Bard. Over the years I've heard many Bards sing, and none was as good as your father." Willon's voice lowered and became cruel. "But a Bard is no match for me. He can't sing me to death, Rinnie. He can't touch me. And as long as I have you, neither can your mother or the Raven."

"People worry about my mother," said Rinnie, sounding far more adult than a child of ten should be able to. "And they should worry. My mother says people underestimate my father. They see the entertainer, the singer, the cheerful, easy-tempered man; and they don't realize that all of that hides something different. When my mother was a girl her whole clan died except for her and her brother. Then her brother died, too. She told me that after all of that, the only safety that she could find was in my father's arms. Remember, remember that the Raven ran to my father for safety."

The wind had picked up, Phoran noticed, as it blew chill and strong on the back of his neck.

"I remember," said Willon, dismissively. "I was there, and I remember a woman little more than a child who looked to an adult man to take care of her. A Bard is a record keeper, child. His duty in the clan is to keep their secrets and to remind them of what they once were. Tier is a Bard."

"My father is a Bard," agreed Rinnie softly. "But he is not only a Bard."

There was the sound of flesh on flesh that brought Phoran to his feet and moving.

"Do not play games with me child," said Willon. "Sit and be quiet."

Phoran moved as quietly as he could, and he was rewarded by the sight of Willon's back not four feet from him. Rinnie was on the ground, her face already bruising from her treatment at Ielian's hands. Blood dripped from what looked, to Phoran's barroom-brawl-educated eye as a fresh split in her lip.

But Willon turned before Phoran could attack, and he smiled. "I thought it was about time for you to arrive. Tell me, where is my Ielian?"

If a lie would have won them anything, Phoran would have lied. "Dead," he said.

Willon's face hardened. "Pity. He was useful to me."

"How did you hide him from Jes and Lehr?" Phoran asked. "They can feel the taint of shadow." *Keep him talking*, Phoran thought, *let Rinnie gather her storm*. He didn't look at Rinnie again after that first, anxious glance. He wanted to keep Willon's attention on him.

"He wasn't tainted," said Willon. "I did not have to do anything to make him mine. He was one of those who is drawn to the power of the Stalker, the power of destruction. I have others, but he was a promising boy, deserving of the rewards I cannot give him now."

Phoran snorted and walked toward the open half to look over the thigh-high stone wall that was all that stood between him and the bottom of the cliffs. "He was no proper servant for a man like me or even like you. He didn't obey orders—he killed the dog and Rufort. If he hadn't done that, likely I wouldn't have been able to break your illusion."

"Death always serves the Stalker," said Willon, following Phoran's movements. "He was a bit overzealous, perhaps, but he was loyal."

Phoran allowed his lip to curl. "He liked to kill. That is all. He served you because you gave him people to kill. But if he had been given the opportunity, he'd have just as soon killed you."

He had managed to turn Willon, so that the Shadowed was no longer between Rinnie and the stairs.

"But it is so much more interesting to work with tigers than with sheep, Phoran, don't you think?"

"You are a peasant," replied Phoran coolly, walking farther from the stairway as if he were not afraid of Willon at all. "We have not given you leave to address Us, familiarly. You are a peasant and a cheap illusionist—your spell couldn't even hold Us—who have no magic at all. The Unnamed King ruled the world, Willon. It took the whole of humanity and the death of a great mage and a great warrior to defeat him. He was a king. You have had twice the amount of time that he had, and what do you rule? A crazy boy who lies dead at the bottom of these cliffs. A secret society of fools who serve themselves and fell to a *Bard* who was their *prisoner.*" And when Phoran saw the light of rage cover the Shadowed's face he said, in the same tone of voice he'd been using. "Run, Rinnie." Then he continued, "Where are the terrible beasts that answered the Unnamed King? You are a failure, a small mind with a little power."

"You are emperor of *nothing,* Phoran. You are nothing but a drunken sot who thinks he should be ruler. You have no power, otherwise you would not be here." He waved his hands eloquently.

Phoran didn't hear Rinnie's footsteps and he couldn't afford to take his attention off Willon to see if she had taken advantage of the little distraction he could grant her.

"I think I tire of you, Emperor," continued the Shadowed. "Die."

When he said the last word, Phoran found that he couldn't breathe.

"No!" shouted Rinnie. "Stop it!"

A gust of wind came from nowhere and hit the Shadowed, knocking him to the ground—and Phoran could breathe again.

He sprinted, grabbed Rinnie and pushed her toward the stairs. "Run!" he said, and headed back toward the distracted wizard.

Maybe if he hadn't tried to push Rinnie toward safety he'd have made it, but he was only halfway across the distance he had to travel when the wizard stood up and made a gesture at him and said something that sounded dark and ugly.

Something hit Phoran in the chest with the force of a kicking war stallion. He stumbled back, and the half wall hit the backs of his legs. If the power the wizard had thrown at him had lost any of its force he might have still been all right, but it just kept pushing him until he tipped off the edge.

"We can't run," Tier told Hinnum, and was surprised at how calm he sounded. Seraph was stiff and shaking under his hands. He whistled, a clear, two-note sound he used for calling the children in for meals or work. Even if he were asleep, Jes would answer it.

"You can't win," Hinnum said. "That ring does not a Lark make, whether it was your daughter's Order once or not."

"Nevertheless," said Tier collecting his sword and lute—a Bard needed a lute upon occasion. "My children need me."

"You are the world's only hope," said Hinnum. "You cannot sacrifice the world for your children." He paused. "I had grandchildren who died with Colossae."

Seraph slipped the tigereye ring over her finger. "Sometimes sacrifice is necessary," she said. "Sometimes. But everyone is not always asked to make the same sacrifice, Hinnum. Colossae's death was the only way to save the world. Without your children's death, everyone would have died. My children's death would serve only to buy us time." She turned to look where the storm clouds were dissipating. "You and Hennea think the only way to defeat the Shadowed is with the names of the Elder gods—and we don't have those."

The strain of yesterday showed on her face. Her cheeks were hollow, as if she had not been eating well for months, dark circles ringed her eyes, and her hair was mussed in its braids. Tier thought she was beautiful.

"The temptation in fighting," Tier told Hinnum, "is to adopt the enemy's successful tactics." He opened the corral gate and took Skew out and began saddling him. "Willon could have faced us the night we destroyed the Path in Taela, but he chose to run and pick a time and place that better suited him. It seems to me he has been very careful to hide all these years—perhaps that is why he left. I don't know. If we follow his tactics, we should abandon our soldiers in the field, pick up, and run until we are more ready for him."

"Yes," said Hinnum.

Seraph and Hennea let him talk while they saddled their own horses.

Tier shook his head at the wizard as he tightened Skew's cinch. "We cannot win that way, Hinnum. There is no victory in playing to your enemy's strengths. Willon doesn't age: he can afford to wait. You tell me that he is here now. If we leave to ready ourselves, to prepare for certain victory—we'll never find him. He's hidden his presence for years, another fifty will make no difference to him." He took in a breath. "It may not be for us to destroy him. Perhaps that chance died when Willon killed Mehalla all those years ago. Perhaps it was destroyed this morning when we let Lehr, Rinnie, and the others go off to find the names. But if we abandon our own, it will not be for victory over the Shadowed. You sacrificed your children for the world. I might be willing to do the same—but not for the mere chance of saving the world."

Jes came. "Papa?" He stiffened, looked at Seraph, and the Guardian asked, "What's wrong?"

"Willon is here," said Tier. "It looks as though he might have taken Lehr and the rest."

The Guardian drew a deep breath. "I want to go after them."

"No," said Hinnum. "You have no chance if you meet him alone."

"Go," said Tier, knowing full well that he might be sending his son to his death. "We'll follow as fast as we can. We'll head straight to the Owl's temple."

The Guardian flowed into wolf form, shook himself once, as if to get a feeling for the shape of the wolf, then ran.

Hinnum threw up his hands. "You would feed your children to the Shadowed one by one."

"No," said Seraph. The rage she felt was so strong her voice shook with it. "Jes is almost immune to magic. He'll buy us the time we need to get there."

"I'm ready," said Hennea swinging onto her horse.

"Wait," said Hinnum. He stared at his feet for a moment, then knelt before Hennea. "I failed you once, lady. I'll not do it again. Like the Guardian, I'll go to hold off the Shadowed until you get there, or die in the attempt. I think it foolish. I don't believe it will work. But I will go."

"You've never failed me," said Hennea, her voice tender. "Never once."

Hinnum stood and then, like Jes, he changed form. A magpie, ebony-winged and black-eyed, replaced the boyish form, and then took flight.

"Wizards can't change form," said Tier. "Not even Ravens."

"Hinnum can," Hennea said. "Hinnum can do a lot of things other wizards never dreamed of."

Rinnie watched in shock as Phoran fell off the wall. She'd been so glad to see him, though she'd known, really, that he couldn't rescue her from the Shadowed.

Something cold grabbed her by the shoulder and jerked her to her feet. "Fly, Cormorant," hissed the Memory in her ear. "Fly!"

And he threw her off the tower as the Shadowed screamed his rage after her.

The winds that had been comforting her ever since Ielian had dumped her on the floor of the guard tower caught at her hands and feet.

Trust us, they said, and then, like Phoran's Memory they said, *fly, Cormorant, fly!*

And she did.

"Help Phoran," she demanded of her winds and they let her speed down the tower, down the cliff, all but falling so that she didn't lose sight of him. She landed, overbalanced, and then tripped and stumbled, trying to keep her feet. She landed on her knees not ten feet from Phoran's body. She didn't bother to stand up, just crawled to where he lay.

There's no blood, she thought, surely there would be blood if the winds hadn't obeyed her fast enough. If he was dead there should be blood. But if he wasn't dead, he should be breathing, shouldn't he?

"Phoran?" she said.

His eyes popped open in an almost comic expression of surprise. He still didn't seem to be breathing, but he rolled to a seated position. His eyes watering, he sucked in air shallowly— and Rinnie sagged with relief. She recognized the signs, having fallen out of the rafters of the barn a time or two.

"You've just had the breath knocked out of you," she said. "You'll be all right."

"The Shadowed is coming," said the Memory from somewhere just behind her.

Phoran, still not breathing quite right, got to his feet. Rinnie grabbed his hand hard when she saw what lay just beyond him.

Ielian wasn't going to be stabbing anyone again.

She turned away, but was caught by Phoran's hand briefly. "Wait. He had an amulet—no, don't look."

He left her for a moment and returned, shaking his head. "No use," he said taking her hand again and setting off at a jog.

"What were you looking for?" Rinnie asked him.

"An amulet that was supposed to release the Shadowed's spell."

"How did *you* break free?"

He smiled at her, though his eyes were tired. "No one commands an emperor," he said. "It is unbelievable, inconceivable."

Rinnie tried to put his answer with her question, but she couldn't see how they connected.

"His spell was an illusion," said Phoran helpfully. "When I didn't believe it anymore, I could move."

"He hurt some people before he took me," Rinnie said. "I remember blood and Gura barking."

Phoran's hands tightened on hers. "Rufort's dead. Kissel, I think, will be all right. I bandaged Gura, but he'd lost a lot of blood."

"Look, there's Lehr," said Phoran.

Rinnie looked ahead and saw her brother running toward them. Phoran straightened a little more and sped up until they were running. Lehr caught up to them and turned to run with them.

"The Shadowed is coming after us," Phoran told her brother. "We need to get out of here."

Being able to breathe again made Phoran more aware of his surroundings, so he saw Toarsen and Kissel before they saw him. Toarsen had managed a more professional bandage than Phoran had taken time for, and Kissel was on his feet.

Kissel didn't look like a man about to die, which was terrific. On the other hand, he didn't look as though he was going to be running back to camp either.

"Gura," Rinnie ran to the shaggy, black beast, but it was ominously still.

The scream of a hawk echoed through the empty streets. Phoran looked up in the sky toward the tower, but couldn't see the bird anywhere.

"On top of that building across the street," said Lehr, sounding grim. "It's him, isn't it."

"Yes. We're going to go back anyway. Toarsen, watch Kissel," said Phoran, not taking his eyes off the watching bird. "Is Gura still alive?"

"Yes," said Lehr reluctantly because he knew, as Phoran did, that the right thing to do was slit the dog's throat.

"Can you carry him?" asked Phoran.

Willon was playing with them. They were none of them a match for the Shadowed. Only Rinnie and Lehr had any magic at all. Lehr's bow was back at camp—and a hunting knife, which was the only thing their Falcon was armed with, was no match for Willon.

"Yes, I can carry him," said Lehr softly.

If we are going to die, thought Phoran, *we'll do it together.*

"The dog was hurt trying to defend Rinnie," Phoran said aloud. "We'll get him out if we can."

"That's the Shadowed, isn't it?" asked Toarsen. "Why is he just watching us?"

"Maybe he's waiting for us to kill the dog," said Phoran.

CHAPTER 20

Lehr grunted as he picked up the dog. It must have weighed 140 or 150 pounds, thought Phoran. He couldn't carry the dog all the way back to camp. No more was Kissel in any shape to walk far.

Phoran glanced at the hawk watching them. Probably carrying the dog was going to be the least of their problems.

"Phoran. Where are you going?" asked the hawk. "Run, Phoran, run. It will do you no—" Something that Phoran couldn't see hit the bird and knocked it from its perch.

A magpie flew from somewhere behind Phoran and landed on the ground before becoming Hinnum.

"Run, boys," he said without taking his eyes off the great bird that floundered on the ground in front of them. "I can't hold him for long."

"Go," said Phoran, voice cracking with relief.

"This way," said Lehr, and led off with Gura in his arms.

The journey was nightmarish. They walked because that was the best Kissel and an overburdened Lehr could do. Phoran took the rearguard position, walking backward so he could watch behind them.

The skies, so bright and blue that morning, had turned dark and threatening. Since Rinnie was muttering softly to herself and had a tendency to stumble over nothing, Phoran was sure she had something to do with the growing storm. He remembered Lehr's tale of the lightning that had struck the troll threatening them, and decided that Ielian had been proved wrong: Cormorants had more to offer than good weather for a farmer. Give Rinnie a little time to work, and she was a formidable opponent.

There were sounds and flashes of light from the vicinity of where they'd left Hinnum facing the Shadowed. A few of the noises were accompanied by vibrations that shook the ground beneath their feet.

When they reached the base of the ramp, Phoran said, "Lehr, give me the dog, then take my sword. Keep an eye on Kissel. You might have to help brace him from the other side."

He took the dog and began the long climb. What had seemed an engineering marvel to Phoran the first day they'd come into the dead city was now torturous.

Kissel tried his best, but he'd lost a lot of blood, and their progress was abysmally slow. Lehr slid his shoulder under the one Toarsen wasn't supporting before they were more than a dozen yards from the bottom.

"Give me the sword," said Jes, startling everyone badly.

Phoran hadn't seen him, and neither, he thought from the look on Lehr's face, had anyone else.

"Don't *do* that," said Lehr irritably as he held out the sword to his brother who had, in broad daylight, suddenly appeared from nowhere.

"Keep going," said Phoran.

"Mother, Papa, and Hennea are on their way," said Jes. "Hinnum felt the Shadowed's magic and went ahead to help if he could."

"We saw him," said Phoran, breathing in huffs as the steep climb made the dog feel heavier and heavier. "He attacked Willon so we could escape. They've been making a lot of noise."

"I heard it," agreed Jes shortly. Phoran was always surprised at how different this Jes was from the slow, soft-spoken boy he usually was.

"I haven't heard anything since we started up the ramp," said Lehr. "I hope it's not bad news."

As he spoke a bedraggled magpie flew up and landed on Rinnie's shoulder. "Go," it croaked, swaying unsteadily. "Go."

Kissel staggered, and brought Lehr and Toarsen to their knees.

"Jes, take the dog," said Phoran, pushing the limp animal into Jes's arms before the other man had a chance to protest. Then he bent down and put his shoulder into Kissel's belly and hoisted him up.

"Toarsen, draw your sword. Lehr, take mine back from Jes before he drops it or the dog. Rinnie, steady that bird before he falls off altogether."

Kissel outweighed Phoran, but not as much as he out-weighed Toarsen and Lehr. His calves already hurt from climbing up the cliff and the guard tower, and his ribs were sore from his fall, but Jes had said Tier was coming.

"Let me take him, Phoran," said Toarsen, as the ramp ended at last. "You're about done in."

Phoran shook his head. Toarsen was all wiry muscle, but he wasn't big enough to carry Kissel for long.

"How's his bleeding?" Phoran's breath was coming in heaving gasps that made it hard to talk.

"Not good," Toarsen said. "He's unconscious. I—"

"Hush," said Jes, setting the dog on the ground and looking back down the ramp. "He's coming."

Then he shifted into the shape of a black mountain cat as large as any Phoran had ever seen.

"No," said the magpie. "No. They will need all six Orders, Guardian. I'll stop him."

He launched off Rinnie's shoulder with an uncertain flap of wings that steadied on the second stroke.

"Toarsen, take Gura," said Phoran. "Let's go."

He wasn't sure how far they'd come. Phoran's world was rapidly reducing itself to putting one foot in front of the other. When he heard the sound of galloping hooves, Phoran knelt and very carefully set Kissel on the cobbles.

"You'll be all right now," he told him. "Tier's here."

Skew slithered on the slippery cobbles, and Tier was off the horse and bending over Kissel before Skew had quite stopped.

A pulse, too rapid and too faint, beat against his fingers and Tier looked up, taking in the rest of the party.

"Rufort and Ielian?" he asked.

Toarsen set Gura down gently beside Kissel. "Rufort's dead," he said. "Kissel and I both picked Ielian out of the Passerines as a loyal man. We failed in our responsibility. He killed Rufort."

Phoran, pale and drenched in sweat, held up a hand. "I knew that there was something wrong. He told Rufort that the Path was paying him—I found out last night and didn't confront him. I bear equal responsibility."

"Ielian was the Shadowed's man, Papa," said Rinnie.

When he opened his arms, she ran to him. Her little face was bruised, a black and swollen knot on her chin. Her bottom lip was split and puffy. Tier looked from her to Phoran.

"Ielian again," he said. "Willon is responsible for the split lip, though."

"Tell us," said Seraph. She began a gentle examination of Gura, though Tier saw that her eyes blazed with rage. "Sit down, Phoran. If you keep swaying half-up, half-down, you'll fall. What happened, Lehr?"

"Ielian lured us out of our way—I suppose he and Willon had arranged something of the sort. Before any of us knew something was wrong, Willon froze us where we stood."

He took a deep breath. "Papa, Willon told us why he ran from Jes and me that night in Taela. He wanted us to succeed. He sacrificed his people so Mother would get all the Ordered gems. He couldn't figure out what was wrong with them, but he thought Mother, Hennea, and Brewydd might. He knew that Volis had the maps. When Mother and Hennea couldn't fix the gems, he wanted them to come here. He attacked you to force us to come here. Hinnum knew how to make the gems work right, but he wouldn't talk to Willon. Willon sent Mother to talk to Hinnum."

"What good did that do?" asked Hennea. "We won't talk to him either."

"Mother has people she cares about," replied Lehr. "Willon promised not to harm any of us if Mother fixed the gems so that they worked for him. He took Rinnie hostage and left us to break free of his spell and tell you what had happened."

"He took Rinnie?" asked Hennea, crouching beside Kissel. "Then why is she here? Did Hinnum rescue her?"

"No," Rinnie said. "That was Phoran. He broke free of the Shadowed's spell and came up to rescue me."

"*Phoran* rescued you from the Shadowed?" Hennea sounded incredulous.

"Not exactly," said Phoran wryly.

Tier tightened his hand on Rinnie's shoulder; he'd come so close to losing her. "What happened?"

"He broke free of the Shadowed's spell and told us how to do it, too," said Toarsen, with a respectful nod in Phoran's direction.

"It was an illusion," Phoran explained, giving Tier a sheepish grin. "Some parts of me aren't very nice, sir. The idea that a peasant, trumped-up parlor illusionist with delusions of godhood would try and command me, the Emperor, just seemed wrong. I couldn't believe it would work—so it didn't. The others had broken free by the time Rinnie and I got back. I don't know how."

Toarsen laughed, though there were tears in his eyes. He'd sat on the road next to Kissel, and now he touched him lightly. "Kissel, broke free before any of the rest of us. He said anything you could break free of couldn't hold him. He talked the rest of us free."

Phoran nodded soberly. "I chased after Rinnie. There's a stair carved into the cliff, just below that guard tower over there." He pointed to the second tower to the south. "I met Ielian, who was coming down the cliff as I came up. I tossed him off the cliff—"

"Too bad," murmured Seraph.

"He's dead," Phoran told her.

"Thank you," she said. "But I could have made it more painful."

Phoran half bowed. "The next one I will save for you. I couldn't be bothered with him because I knew Willon had Rinnie." He shrugged. "Not that I was much help. We exchanged a half dozen words, then he tossed me off the tower."

Tier turned to look at the tower in question again. "Down the cliff, too? You look good for a man who just fell several hundred feet."

"Thank you," said Phoran. "I feel good, too—relatively speaking." The Emperor tilted his head and looked at Rinnie with a smile. "I think it was Rinnie who saved me: we've been too busy trying to run to stop and exchange stories to make certain. But instead of being splatted unpleasantly on the ground, I was lying at the base of the cliffs trying to catch my breath, and Rinnie was there."

"The Memory threw me off the guard tower after you," Rinnie said.

"*What?*" Phoran's eyes flashed, and his hand went to his sword hilt. "It did what?"

Tier was feeling pretty murderous himself.

Rinnie grinned, first at Tier and then at the Emperor, looking more herself. "It grabbed me where I was cowering on the stairway and threw me off and said, 'Cormorant, fly.' I think if it hadn't said that, I'd have fallen and squished right on top of you. As it was, I wasn't sure I had been soon enough for you. You weren't breathing and I was sure you were dead. Then you sat up, and your eyes were bulging and watering—I thought you could have been the walking dead, like the ones last night. But no, you started breathing and grabbed me without so much as a thank-you."

All in one breath, thought Tier. Amusement won over the horror of hearing that something had thrown his daughter from a tower. It helped that Rinnie had survived.

Phoran bowed. "Thank you, my lady. I was remiss when I forgot to thank you earlier—though I believe the fear for your life took precedence at the time."

Rinnie looked pleased, and said smugly, "I can't wait until I get home and I can tell people that I saved the Emperor's life."

Lehr smiled at her. "No one will believe you, pest."

"Where is Hinnum?" asked Hennea.

"The Shadowed was coming," said Jes, who had exchanged his wolf form for the mountain cat. "Hinnum was already hurt, but he wouldn't let me go."

"Speaking of which," said Phoran. "Should we continue going?"

"No," said Hennea. "What we do, we can do here as well as anywhere. Seraph, this is as good a time as any to see if that ring will work for you. Phoran, where are the names from the Owl's temple?"

"Willon burned them," said Toarsen. "He said he was sealing the temple so no one else could get them again."

"I remember one of them," said Phoran.

Hennea frowned at him. "You know how to read the language of Colossae?"

He smiled. "I'm not just a drunken sot, my lady. *I* am an *educated* drunken sot. I couldn't read the maps or the gates, but the alphabet is the same as Old Oslandic, which I do know. If Toarsen has that piece of char still, I can write it on the stones."

Toarsen fumbled in his belt pouch and handed Phoran the charred stick. Phoran wrote some odd lines on the ground that might have been letters.

"Do you know to which one the name belongs?" asked Tier.

Hennea shook her head. "I don't remember."

"Ah, well," said Tier. "Either would work I suppose. So what exactly do we do?"

"The six of us, you, Jes, Seraph, Lehr, Rinnie, and I hold hands. Then you speak the name of the god—I'll tell you how to pronounce it." Hennea sighed unhappily. "The rest of it we'll have to improvise, I don't know what will happen. The Orders are not the gods of Colossae."

"We should wait until Willon comes near?" asked Tier.

Hennea nodded.

"Is there something I can do?" asked Toarsen. "He's not going to make it." He'd lifted Kissel's head onto his lap and he touched his forehead lightly. "Lost too much blood. I need to have a hand in the destruction of the man who killed him."

Tier hunkered down beside the big lad and put a hand on his too-cold cheek. He looked at Seraph, who nodded.

"Don't give up on him, yet," Tier told Toarsen. "Kissel's survived worse than this—and we'll have a Lark to help him, eh, Seraph?"

"I don't intend for the Shadowed to kill any more of ours," said Seraph.

"So there," said Phoran. "Seraph has said so—Kissel won't dare to fail her."

A faint smile appeared on Kissel's face.

"See," said Tier. "All men must bow to my wife's whims. You'll do, lad." He looked up at Toarsen. "I think this battle will be beyond steel, but I've no objection if you keep your sword handy and use it if you see a moment to do so."

Toarsen nodded solemnly.

"Seraph," Tier said. "If you're ready, Kissel has been doing his best to hold on, but he could really use some help."

Seraph fingered the tigereye ring and closed her eyes, trying to feel what was different, but she felt the same as she ever had. Just the same as she had when she'd tried to work some healing upon Gura a few minutes ago.

She looked down for a moment upon the young man who'd fought by her side against the Path that night in Taela. When she settled next to Kissel, Toarsen looked up at her with all the welcome of a bitch guarding her pups from a stranger.

"I'm not going to hurt him," she told him, though she wasn't at all sure of that.

"There's not much that will hurt me at this point," murmured Kissel unexpectedly, with the subtle humor that he liked to employ. He always seemed best pleased when his audience wasn't quite certain he was trying to be funny.

"I'm glad to hear it," she told him, though she wasn't at all sure he was still conscious.

She tried to remember what Brewydd had done when she had been repairing Tier's injuries—but she'd been distracted and hadn't paid much attention to the Healer.

"Lehr?"

He sat on his heels beside her. "What do you need, Mother?"

"Did you ever watch Brewydd heal?"

"She's a Lark, Mother," said Lehr. "Can Ravens heal, too?"

Seraph held up her hand so he could see the ring she wore. "I'm a Lark today, too. But I need your help."

"The Lark rings don't work," said Jes. "You and Hennea need to clean it first."

Seraph turned to look at him. "Willon killed Mehalla to steal her Order, Jes. All those years ago. Something in this ring

knows me, and I believe it means that this was once Mehalla's."
She paused. "We need me to be a Lark today, but even if the
gem contained nothing but the Order, I could not use it to become a Lark—any more than Volis was a Raven when he wore
a Raven's gem. I need to see if the person, Mehalla or not, who
haunts this ring will help me be a Lark, just for today."

"Try putting your hand on his wound," Lehr suggested.
"We're going to have to take off the bandage."

"Wait, let me do it," said Tier. "I've a little experience at
field dressings."

He sat beside Seraph and cut through the cloth that held the
pad over the wound. Then he tugged gently on the padding.

"The pad is stuck down, but not badly—because he's still
losing blood. That would be bad if we didn't have a Healer."
He smiled at Seraph. "As it is, it makes it easier to get the pad
off—but you need to get your hands over that wound. Lark or
no Lark, the boy's got to have some blood in him if he's to
live. Are you ready?"

"Yes."

He took the pad off and, as he'd indicated, the wound began to ooze blood. She put her hand over the wound and
sealed it with the palm of her hand.

Everyone waited, even Seraph, but nothing happened.

"Try visualizing the healing," Hennea suggested. "Think
of Kissel well and whole."

She tried and felt her magic stir, but magic could not heal.
She could have used it to bandage the wound though, and
would if she could not heal him—but he was so pale, and there
had been so much blood. If it came down to making do with
magic rather than healing, she suspected that he would die.

"Hennea has part of it right," Lehr said. "But this isn't
magic. I think, from watching you and Hennea, that being a
Raven must involve a lot of thought. But Hunting is almost instinctive for me. I look, then I see the trail. I don't have to
think much about it. Jes gets upset, and the temperature anywhere near him drops to freezing. Papa starts singing, and
people stop whatever they are doing to listen. Just let your
body do the work."

Seraph closed her eyes and tried to relax, but the more she
tried not to think, the more she thought.

Tier got up, but she didn't look to see what he was doing. He was back in a moment and began playing his lute. He picked one of her favorite songs, an evening song that had lulled their children to sleep when they were teething or sick. The husky, soft tones slid over her and soothed the tension from her neck and shoulders. She let his voice coax her away from the blood and danger and back into their home and evenings when, with the work of the day done, she and Tier would sit on the back porch. Gura's wire coat tickled Seraph's bare feet as the setting sun colored the mountains red.

As she relaxed something stirred at the tips of her fingers, a whisper at first. She coaxed it with a breath of interest just like she'd have puffed at a reluctant spark when she was trying to light a fire the *solsenti* way.

"He's stopped breathing."

Toarsen's voice, thick with grief.

But when she would have paid attention to him, Tier's song brought her back to her little spark of . . . healing. See, she coaxed, directing it to the flesh under her fingers. *I have something for you to do.*

Fire shot up her shoulders so unexpectedly that she jerked and gasped, but someone's hands locked on her wrists and held her hands against Kissel. She opened her eyes and knew the damage Ielian's knife had done, though it was buried under her hands and beneath Kissel's skin.

The power of the Lark eased through Seraph's hands and into Kissel's body, repairing the gross damage to the tissues first, then moving on to smaller things. His heart had stopped, but her power hit it and it could not resist her and began beating.

There isn't enough blood, Mother. He won't live without more blood.

"Who said that?" asked Jes.

"Said what?" Lehr whispered. "Keep your voice down, Jes, you'll distract her."

Mehalla? Seraph asked, uncertain whether that soft voice had been real or imaginary. There was no answer.

Whoever it had been, she had been right. Kissel needed blood the Lark could not supply him with.

But Seraph wasn't a Lark, or at least, not only a Lark. Leaving her right hand, the hand with the Lark's ring to cover the closed hole in Kissel's chest, she brought her left hand, covered with Kissel's blood, to her lips and touched it with her tongue.

She called her magic to hand. *Find this,* she told it, showing it Kissel's blood. Her magic took the dried blood from the bandages, from her hands, from Kissel's bloody clothes. She touched her tongue again. *Make it like this.* The dried, dead blood became clean and alive again. *Put it here.* The part of her that was Lark found the collapsing blood vessels and showed the magic where it needed to be.

Seraph took a shuddering breath. "Let go," she told Lehr, who held her wrists in a bruising grip. "He doesn't need me anymore."

Lehr released her, and she pulled her hands away. Kissel's chest looked as though the wound was weeks old. She was a little disappointed that there was a mark at all, but remembering Brewydd's insistence that Tier's knees heal the last bit on their own, she thought that perhaps it was just as well.

Kissel opened his eyes. "I don't think I'll be up and fighting today," Kissel told Seraph. "But maybe tomorrow." He tried to sit up, but didn't quite make it. Toarsen caught his head before it hit the ground. "Then again," Kissel said weakly, "maybe next week or the week after that."

"You'll do," said Tier, breaking off his singing.

"Thank you," whispered Toarsen, and there were tears in his eyes.

"I told you I wouldn't lose anyone else to that bastard," she said coolly.

"Where'd all the blood go?" asked Rinnie.

Seraph patted Kissel's bare shoulder. "Back where it belongs," she said. "Let's try Gura."

Gura was at once both easier to heal and more difficult: easier because she knew how to call upon the ring now, more difficult because she was tiring, and there was more damage. Ielian had broken Gura's ribs and completely severed a muscle in his shoulder.

She was deep into the final connections that the Lark knew would allow the dog to control his leg as well as he had before it was injured when someone spoke to her.

"Seraph?"

It took her a moment to pull far enough out of the healing to know that it was Tier.

"Seraph, Hinnum has come back." Tier's voice was soft but urgent. "Can you help him?"

Seraph looked up and saw Hennea on her knees, tears streaming down her cheeks, holding a limp black and white bird in her hands. "Seraph?" she said.

Seraph stumbled to her feet and Tier put his arm around her until she steadied. She knelt beside Hennea and put her hands on the magpie.

She felt the Lark's power wash over the bird, but like oil repels water, the healing washed over him without touching him. She tried again.

This time she noticed the differences between him and Kissel. Age and magic entwined his body and kept her from healing him. She saw that it would be difficult to heal a *solsenti* mage because of the alteration that magic, without the filter of the Raven's Order, worked on a mage's body. She understood how it was that a strong *solsenti* mage would live for many years beyond a normal life span as magic reinforced aging flesh, ligaments, and bone.

"He is too old, and magic too deep in him to allow for healing," Seraph said, stricken. "I can do nothing."

Hennea smoothed his feathers and crooned to him. Bright eyes dulled, and Seraph could feel the exact moment his heart ceased beating.

Darkness approached, and Seraph looked up in alarm, but it was only her son. The Guardian crouched behind Hennea and wrapped his arms around her as she wept.

"Jes couldn't be here," he told her. "But I can."

The magpie's shape fell away and in Hennea's lap was a child who looked to be no more than four years old.

"Ah my poor Hinnum," Hennea whispered. "How cruel was this? Such a price you paid for magic, my friend." She looked at Seraph. "When he was three centuries old he stopped aging and began to get younger. It was good, until he began getting too young. When I last saw him he looked as though he was Rinnie's age—he found it humiliating." She looked at the toddler in her arms. "He would have hated this."

"He was a great wizard and the world is lessened by his death," said Seraph.

"He was the greatest mage who ever lived," Hennea's voice was thick with grief. "I was the Raven, and I never dreamed what power an illusionist could wield. He could work other magics, but illusion was the heart of him. He took the point for the spell to sacrifice Colossae because I no longer had the power to do so. Fifty Ravens would not equal his power."

"When this is over," said Tier, "you'll tell me his story, and I'll sing it so that his fame will never die. He died protecting my children, he died trying to defeat the Shadowed. Such a man deserves to be remembered."

"I remember him," Hennea murmured. "I remember him."

"He'll be coming soon," said Lehr.

"If he did this to Hinnum," said Hennea, "then we have no chance."

"He could kill us without our ever seeing him," said Phoran. "He stopped the breath in my body. If Rinnie hadn't startled him, I'd be dead."

"He hasn't gotten what he wants yet," said Tier.

"The gems?" Seraph shook her head. "Without Hinnum to guard the library, all he needs is to read through the books. He'll discover what he needs."

"You're Ravens." Tier got to his feet. "You don't need the kind of study that a wizard does who is learning new magic. The Willon I know is meticulous. He'd never just jump in and try something new. He's a merchant, a successful one. He'll think of negotiating for what he wants before he'll try it himself. He still has the advantage. It would have simplified things to have Rinnie with him. But he doesn't need to do it that way."

He walked over to the horses and unsaddled Skew. Taking the blanket, he unfolded it, shook it out carefully, and brought it to Hennea.

"This is covered in the sweat and hair of a humble and faithful servant. It is not the silk Hinnum deserves, but I think it is not entirely unsuitable."

Who but Tier could make an old horse blanket seem a fitting shroud for Hinnum of Colossae? Seraph blinked back her own tears. She hadn't known Hinnum long—but she'd known of him all of her life. Wetness struck her face, and she looked up to see the skies dark with heavy rain clouds, as if they, too, were mourning the death of the old mage.

Tier laid the blanket on the cobbles and took Hinnum's body from Hennea's unwilling arms. He set the small form in the middle of the brightly colored blanket and wrapped him in it. Picking him up, he carried the small bundle to the side of the road. There was a house with a small yard with a bush. Tier hid the body behind it.

"We'll keep him out of sight," he said. "Let Willon wonder if he will be coming back to help again. Hennea, I think Lehr is right. Willon will rest up a little, but it won't be long before he comes. You need to teach me how to pronounce the name of the Elder god."

"We have to hurry." Seraph stood up. "Hennea, Hinnum gave his life to give us this chance."

She waited until Hennea was coaching Tier, one syllable at a time so as not to attract the god's attention prematurely, before going to Phoran. He sat, with Toarsen and Kissel, leaning against one of the buildings that fronted the small winding street. Rinnie was sitting next to him, as she usually was. They all looked half-asleep.

Lehr crouched next to Phoran on the balls of his feet, talking quietly with Phoran. He broke off as soon as he heard her approach.

"You can be used against us, too," she told Phoran. "And you are defenseless against a Shadowed. I want you to stay where you are. Don't draw attention to yourselves if you can help it. I don't know if we can protect you—and I'd rather never have to find out."

Phoran shook his head. "Willon doesn't know you."

She'd expected arguments—in her experience men didn't like to be told they were helpless. Phoran's remark didn't seem to have much bearing on what she'd said.

"Of course he does," she answered. "For twenty years we have lived in the same town."

Phoran smiled, the sweet smile that doubtless had seen him through more trouble than any ten children. "Yes, but he doesn't know you. He knows a quiet, cold woman, commanding and strong, who cares for nothing except for Tier and her family."

"And?"

"The woman he thinks he knows would never put her family in danger. Not for an emperor, and certainly not for his guards." The smile widened, and his tired eyes lit up. "And he'd be right—except that you don't see us as an emperor and his guards. I saw your face when we told you Rufort was dead—but Willon didn't. He won't know you care about us at all because he cares for no one. He won't try and use us as hostages."

Then he did something utterly unexpected. He stood up, brushed off his pant legs, and took two steps forward, bowed low, until his mouth was level with her face, and kissed both of her cheeks. "He thinks Tier is soft, and you are hard—and he's wrong on both counts."

She could feel the flush that rose under her skin.

"We know you," he said. "But he doesn't."

"Well," she said, flustered, and was almost grateful for Jes's low, rumbling warning.

"He's coming," said Lehr, standing up. "I feel it, too, Jes. He's not trying to hide from us."

"Just keep low," she told them. She held out her hand for Rinnie. "We need you with us," she told her. "Come, Lehr."

At Hennea's direction, they stood in a rough semicircle with Tier in the center. As Willon strolled into view, Seraph tightened her hands on Rinnie and Lehr. She saw Jes take Hennea's hand, and, finally, Hennea and Tier held hands. As soon as they did so, Seraph felt it happen. Just as Hennea had told her it would, a connection snapped between her and the other five Ordered who stood in front of the Shadowed. In so much, the Lark ring allowed her to stand in for their missing Order.

"I mean you no harm," said Willon, stopping a dozen feet from them. He was young, Seraph saw, with dark hair tied at the nape of his neck. There was a bruise on his forehead, and he moved stiffly: Seraph took pleasure in knowing he had not come out of the battle with Hinnum unwounded.

"Tier," he said. "You are a Bard, you know I speak the truth. I've never wanted to hurt you. I only need your wife to fix the Ordered gems so that they will work for me—or, better still, give them to me and show me how it is done. I'll leave you in peace until the end of your children's children's days—my word on it."

"We are Travelers," said Lehr, in a growl that sounded as if it could have come from his brother's mouth. "We cannot let the Shadowed go free."

Willon threw up his hands. "The Shadowed, the Shadowed. The Shadowed died five centuries ago, a fool who was trying only to stay alive, and so he drained the life from everything else. Killing all those he cared about to preserve what was worthless without them. I am not like that. Tier, you know me. I wouldn't do something like that. I enjoy a challenge, Tier, I enjoy a song in the evening. I'm not like the Shadowed King."

"Perhaps not yet," said Hennea. "But he wasn't always the Unnamed King either. He was a good man who worried for his people. He saw a way to ensure that his kingdom would prosper."

"He killed them," said Willon. "He destroyed his kingdom. I would never hurt anyone."

"Tell that to Rufort," said Rinnie.

Seraph squeezed her hand hard. She did not want the first attack to settle on her daughter.

"Your guardsman and the dog were killed by Ielian. I did not command their death."

"Colbern," said Jes, in a voice so soft and low it beat upon Seraph's ears like far-off thunder. "A whole town died to feed you."

"They were nothing," he said. "No one I knew. No one you knew."

Seraph felt Lehr take a breath, and this time *he* received her warning squeeze.

"What of Mehalla?" asked Seraph. "My daughter, whom you killed."

The affability fell off Willon's face as if wiped by a cloth. For a moment his expression was entirely blank. He started to say something—a lie, because he stopped when he glanced at Tier. "Mehalla was a mistake," he said.

"I don't think so." Seraph kept her voice soft and pleasant. "I think you killed my daughter, watched her die for almost a year, then came to my home and told us how sorry you were for her death."

"You will be sorry for her death," said Tier. "For her death and for all the dead you have caused since you became the Shadowed. When you take the Stalker's power, Willon, you become evil."

"No," he said. "You become powerful. You don't understand the good I can do, Tier. If I have the gems, if I can work all the Orders in the gems, I can heal, I can build, I can raise cities or even empires."

"You could," said Seraph. "But would you? Death follows you like maggots follow rot."

"So, Tier," said Willon, "do you let your *woman* do your talking now? Women should be taught to be silent while a man conducts business."

"I would never say that, never even dare think that," said Tier. "It might make Seraph angry. If *I* said it. But you'll not make her mad because she doesn't care what you think. Without the Stalker you are nothing."

Seraph felt the power Tier poured into his words and saw Willon take a step back. She also felt herself regain control of her instinctively hot reaction to Willon's words.

"You killed my daughter," Tier said, his voice as hard and cold as Seraph had ever heard it. "I will not bargain with you."

"I didn't mean to," Willon said. "She wasn't meant to die."

"No," agreed Hennea. "She was meant to stand here with us, so that we could destroy what you will become."

"She stands here anyway," said Seraph softly. "To watch you *die. Sila-evra-kilin-faurath!*" She said the word that had killed the troll, heard it echo in the streets of Colossae.

Willon staggered back, but he was no troll who was used to his natural magic immunity to stand still under the word of power, and Seraph had no vast store of magic to draw upon, as she had drawn upon the wards of her home. She hurt him, but he did not die.

Willon licked the blood off his lip. "Stupid Traveler bitch," he said, spittle flying from his mouth. "Shut up. Just shut up. If you would be quiet, it would all be arranged. Your family would be safe. Why won't you just shut up?"

"Because you aren't worth listening to?" said Phoran laconically, and much too closely. She couldn't take her eyes off Willon to look, but he'd left his safe place near the buildings—and if he'd left, surely Toarsen and Kissel were not too far behind. She should have gotten his promise rather than let Phoran distract her.

"You couldn't even keep Rinnie and me when you had us. What kind of wizard can't hold on to a child and a has-been drunkard like me?" Phoran asked.

If Seraph hadn't had her shielding ready, Phoran might not have lived to regret those words. The magic Willon threw at the Emperor was strong, and Seraph felt her hastily redirected shields begin to give beneath it. Then Hennea's magic aided hers and turned Willon's attack aside.

"Now, Tier," Seraph heard Hennea say.

"Lynwythe," Tier said.

"Lynwythe," he said, and hoped something would happen.

It wasn't at all what he expected. As soon as the words left his lips, Rinnie's and Hennea's hands disappeared, as did Willon. The familiar weight of his lute was gone as well. Tier was alone.

He stood in a long, wide room with walls, ceiling, and floor all of dove grey and strangely featureless, as if someone merely thought about a room, rather than a real room.

Instinct made him want to return to his family—but Hennea and Hinnum had both thought his speaking of that name was the only possible way to defeat the Shadowed. He disciplined himself, looked around, and began walking.

His sturdy boots left marks on the featureless floor: not quite footprints, just a marring of the surface where the hard edge of his heels touched down. For a moment he felt ashamed, embarrassed that he, a farmer, should dare tread such hallowed halls at all, let alone mar the floors.

He stopped and took a deep breath. "I do not belong here," he said in a more pleasant tone than he felt like using. "I know it, as do you. However I doubt a few marks on the floor are going to bother you much. I am a Bard, sir. I know how to influence people—and I know when someone tries to influence me. I'll thank you to stop."

No one replied, but the feeling that he ought to be cringing and scuttling forward on hands and knees because of his great inadequacies left. Conscious of the danger his family was in, he walked quickly forward. Though there was nothing in the room that he could see, he felt this was the direction he must walk in.

"Why did you call My name, Bard?" The voice was deep and rich.

Tier stopped walking and turned to face the god who'd appeared next to him without a sound or any warning, just his words in a rich bass that part of Tier could not help but want to hear in song, just once.

There was not much else impressive about him. He appeared to be a man a little shorter than average and slight of build. His hair and eyes were as dark as Tier's own.

"Why do you hesitate, Bard?" He said with a small smile that sent chills down Tier's spine. This was not the Weaver. "Do you seek to form lies that might please Me?"

"No," answered Tier truthfully. "It just occurred to me that I'm not certain what the real truth is. The simple answer is that we only had the one name."

"So you called upon Me because you could not call upon My brother? Is there another answer?"

Tier decided to trust his instincts. "I think the barrier the Weaver created limits His ability to work in this world. I think He has interfered all that He can already. If we'd had both names, we would have called upon the Weaver." He took a deep breath. "And we would have failed. The Weaver can do no more to help us."

The Stalker raised his hands. "And you think that I will? Now when My servant, My slave has loosened the bonds that hold Me? He will not have to take many more Orders before I am able to do whatever pleases Me."

"He is not Your servant, nor Your slave," said Tier. "He is a thief who snuck into Your prison and stole Your power without so much as a by-your-leave."

"Even as you have called My Name, Bard, so I must answer like a dog answers the call of his master." The words were bitter and angry, but neither emotion was reflected in the Stalker's face or voice.

"While we speak my family faces the Shadowed on their own," said Tier, then sucked in a breath. *You can do better than this,* he thought. "I can only apologize for my discourtesy. Offending You is the last thing I wish to do. We need Your help to defeat the Shadowed."

"Indeed," said the god. "What will you give me for this help? Who will you sacrifice? Your wife? One of your children? The Emperor, perhaps?"

"I will not," Tier said, his blood turning to ice in his veins. "But I will give you myself."

"Will you?" said the god, his voice hushed. He reached up to cup Tier's chin in his hands.

Pain snaked down Tier's spine, and he heard himself cry out. Nothing, not even Telleridge's hammer slamming down on his knees, hurt so badly. He fell to the ground, and the god knelt with him, keeping that gentle touch that rent and tore without a physical wound.

"Pull away, Bard," said the Stalker. "Pull away, and the pain will stop."

Tier closed his eyes against the voice, pull away and lose any chance for victory. He could not, would not do it.

In the end the god released His hold and stood. "If I could do something about the thieves who take My power without asking, I would have long ago. There is nothing I can do."

"I am a Bard," whispered Tier, curled in a sweating ball on the clean, cold floor. "I can tell when You lie."

For the first time, Tier saw honest emotion on the face of the Stalker: anger. "You overstep yourself, Bard. I am the Lord of Death and you are in My realm."

"Binding the Orders to the gems hasn't worked to loosen the veil that keeps you imprisoned," said Tier a little desperately. It sounded like truth to him, and he found the reasons why. "I think that if they had loosened, You would already have destroyed Willon yourself. Hinnum told me that You are not evil. Surely what the Shadowed does with Your power offends You."

From somewhere he found the strength to sit up, though his muscles were still twitching, waiting for more pain.

"If your wife destroys the gems without freeing the Orders, it will loosen the barrier," said the Stalker.

"Willon wants my wife to clean the spirit from the gems so that he can use them all," Tier told him. "He knows about the Guardian Order. If my wife does not show him, he will learn how to do it eventually. He has all the time in the world, because death has no hold on him. Eventually he will take all the gems and eat their power—the power that belongs to You and to the Weaver. Then he will destroy You both."

He'd read Willon's intention when he first realized what it meant that Willon was not looking for six spirit-cleaned gems, but all of the gems clean.

The Stalker turned away, jerking his eyes from Tier's as if Tier had some sort of hold on him.

"You told him how to bind the Orders to the gems," Tier said. He wasn't certain he could stand, so he didn't. "If You had not done that, the Travelers could have dealt with him eventually. That is the task they bear for their imperfect sacrifice. Their greed for knowledge, for the libraries and Hinnum's *mermori* left the possibility open for a Shadowed to exist. It is a task they have carried out since the fall of Colossae. But there are few Travelers left now, thanks to Willon. If You had not told him how to bind the Orders, he would be no threat to You now."

"You said it yourself, Bard," the Stalker said bitterly, "death has no hold over him. I can do nothing to him so long as he holds My power."

"So what can I do to him?" asked Tier. "How do we stop him for You?"

The god sighed. "I can help." He said. "I will sing with you and we will withhold my power from Willon for a time. You have proved to me that you can withstand the pain of My song inside you. While we hold the power back, Willon must be killed."

"Lehr?" asked Tier.

"Only the war god can kill an immortal," said the Stalker regretfully. "There will be sacrifices before the Shadowed is dead, Tier."

"The Guardian believes that if he kills someone, it will destroy Jes," said Tier.

"The Guardian is right," agreed the Stalker. "Hennea is as much My child as she is My brother's or Jes is yours. I would not cause her more pain if I could help it."

* * *

"Lynwythe," Tier heard himself finish the word and realized that the entire episode had taken no time at all.

Everyone paused, waiting for something to happen. Tier released Rinnie's hand, then Hennea's. He pulled the lute, which was once more on his back, over his shoulder and began to pick a melody.

The Stalker had told him the song didn't matter, but Tier picked a soldier's song, one of those pieces with eight lines of chorus for every two lines of verse, and the number of verses was limited only by his memory for risqué puns. He could sing it from now until sundown.

He bent his head to tune a string, and said, very softly. "Jes, when I start the second chorus, the Guardian will be able to kill Willon."

"It didn't work," said Willon. "The Stalker didn't answer you."

"Did you think He would?" asked Tier. Of course Willon would know the god's real name. He would have to have both names if he were to steal their power. "Why would He answer me?"

"I can do it," said Lehr, who had also heard Tier's words.

Tier shook his head and began singing.

"What are you doing?" asked Willon, but Tier could tell that Seraph wanted to ask the same thing.

He could answer neither one of them because the god's power burned through his throat like fire. He understood why the Stalker had tested him with pain because this song hurt, the Stalker's power no lighter for him to bear than it was for the Shadowed—and Tier would take no other person's life to make it easier.

"What are you doing?" asked Willon again, and this time he was angry, certain Tier was making fun of him with his choice of song—a silly thing about a soldier who goes out into a strange village looking for a woman to lie with.

"He is a Bard," said Seraph suddenly. "Music is his gift, Willon."

Out of the corner of his eye, Tier saw Jes release his hold on Hennea, then vanish from sight.

Willon had been watching, too.

"Two hundred and twelve years," said Willon, "and I never knew that there was a sixth Order. I thought Volis was talking about the Stalker when he called him the Eagle. If it hadn't been for Ielian, I never would have known that I was missing one. Where did he go?"

"He's still here," said Seraph. "Can't you feel the ice of his breath on the back of your neck?"

Bless her, thought Tier, as he forced his pain-laden finger to exert the proper pressure on the neck of his lute. She didn't know what he was doing, but she knew he was doing something. The longer she kept Willon distracted the better.

"I told you to shut up, *woman,*" said Willon in a vicious tone that broke through his merchant-smooth manner and rang true as a bell to a Bard's senses. He gestured at Seraph.

Nothing happened. Tier was no mage, but he had a Rederni's keen sense where magic was concerned, and he felt nothing at all.

"Bitch!" snarled Willon, obviously placing the blame for his failure upon Seraph. He sucked in a breath and pulled the merchant's mask back over his face. "But I am more than just the Stalker's avatar. I am a wizard who bears the Raven's Order."

He ripped open his tunic neck and Tier saw that he wore a necklet covered with gems. Hennea made a small sound, so Tier could only suppose that they were all Ordered.

"I can't," the Guardian said into Papa's ear. "I can't risk Jes." Jes sensed the Guardian's cold terror before it was buried beneath the avalanche of the Guardian's protective rage. A Guardian defended those he considered his—and Jes belonged to him.

"Only you can do it," said Papa in a quick whisper between verses. "The Stalker said only the Guardian can kill him."

Jes understood than. Somehow the god his father had called upon had given Papa's music the power to hinder the Shadowed. But the power came at a terrible cost, the shimmering waves of agony that rolled over Jes were only a taste of what his father felt.

The Guardian couldn't perceive Tier's suffering as Jes did, but he could see the sweat that dampened their father's tunic and the lines of pain around his mouth. And all of Papa's hurt was to make a way for them to kill the Shadowed.

We can't let him suffer for nothing, Jes told the Guardian. *We have to kill the Shadowed while we can. It doesn't matter if I die as long as we take the Shadowed with us.*

<No.> Jes could feel the Guardian's absolute refusal, and beneath it the echoes of memories of the other Order Bearers, driven mad by the Guardian's actions. He couldn't bear to lose Jes that way.

Jes was helpless, held prisoner by the Guardian's unwillingness to put Jes at risk.

Look, Jes told him in mounting frustration, *look at Papa's pain.*

"*We* are Ravens," his mother was telling Willon, her voice laden with disdain as she nodded toward the Ordered gems the Shadowed wore. "*You* are *nothing.*"

She was trying to keep the Shadowed's attention on her, to let Jes do what Papa had asked. She did it with the weapon best suited to the task—her tongue.

"You are a *solsenti,*" she told the Shadowed in the voice Papa always said could freeze a man to death quicker than any blizzard. "A mere *illusionist* who can only ape his betters by stealing magic that doesn't belong to him."

Jes felt the impact of her words, the fury loosed in the Shadowed in response to his mother's mockery. He tried to urge the Guardian to action, but the Shadowed's response was swifter.

The *solsenti* wizard gestured and Seraph flew backward, slamming into the road. She bounced once, then lay still.

With a soundless snarl the Guardian raced to her side, still camouflaged from view. The relief of seeing her ribcage rise shook the Guardian's resolve. Mother was his to protect as well.

"You are not but a dirty little thief," said Hennea, who had stepped between the others and the Shadowed.

Willon, still enraged, screamed out a smattering of unintelligible syllables that both Jes and the Guardian knew must be some sort of *solsenti* spell. The Guardian, knowing himself helpless, watched Hennea hold up her hand.

Nothing happened to her.

"A dirty little thief," Hennea said again, dusting her hands.

Rain began to fall from the clouds Rinnie had been gathering. As the cold drops hit his mother's face, she opened her eyes. After a moment she sat up slowly. The Guardian started to touch her, but his attention was drawn back to the Shadowed as Willon suddenly staggered and fell.

For a moment Jes thought it was something Hennea had done, but then he saw a knife on the ground and realized Lehr had thrown it with such force it had knocked the Shadowed off his feet. The blade hadn't penetrated, though, just cut the cloth of Willon's tunic so the links of chainmail showed beneath.

Phoran sprinted forward, Toarsen a half step behind; but it was too late—Willon had recovered from his surprise.

Hennea shouted, a wordless sound, and Jes could feel her desire to protect the others, but Willon's magic still sent all three men stumbling backwards. Hennea swayed and he knew the sharp pain that sliced through her at the backlash of the Shadowed's imperfectly deflected spell.

Mother struggled to get up, and the Guardian helped her to her feet.

"Papa wants me to kill the Shadowed," the Guardian told her urgently, as he steadied her. "But it will kill Jes or drive him mad. An empath can't take another's life—not a strong empath like Jes."

She shivered as if she were cold, the mist of her breath a testimony to the Guardian's distress. Unable to break through the Guardian's protective concealment. "You underestimate Jes," she said. "He is stronger than you believe."

Yes, said Jes.

Papa, still singing, walked between Willon and the Emperor, setting himself in front of Willon. He walked with a limp, and Jes knew his left knee ached from the old injury. But the knee was as nothing to the torment of the Stalker's music. He tucked the lute against his body to shield it from the rain as best he could.

Willon raised his hands again, and Rinnie ran between them, shouting, "No!"

It was too much for the Guardian. For Rinnie, for Papa, for his family, both he and Jes were willing to die.

Lightning struck Willon with a deafening crack. He staggered and sobbed, his flesh smoking in the chill of Rinnie's storm. Lightning struck again, but Willon didn't fall down. He ran at Rinnie.

But the Guardian was there first. There was no finesse in his attack, but none was needed. Willon didn't see him until the Guardian hit him the first time. As his fists hit flesh, the fever of battle rose, and the wizard, half-stunned by Rinnie's lightning, was not much of a challenge—not as long as Papa kept playing so Willon had no access to the Stalker's power.

"Wait," said Phoran's Memory wrapping a hand around the Guardian's wrist, stopping his strike.

As soon as he was still, the Memory released him. "Hold him for me," it said.

At the sound of the Memory's voice, the Shadowed took a step back. The Guardian stepped in and took him in a wrestling hold, pinning the struggling mage to the ground.

The Memory settled beside them and took Willon's head in its hands. The wizard showed the whites of his eyes and a rising tide of fear poured off him. The Memory bent over him.

Willon screamed and Jes pulled the Guardian around him, letting the Guardian protect him from the worst of Willon's experience. The firmly muscled body beneath the Guardian began to shrink, the softness of flesh replaced by something dry and hard. When at last the thing the Guardian held quit struggling, and the Memory pulled away, the Shadowed bore no resemblance to Willon, merchant of Redern.

Thick dark hair had been reduced to a few strands of white on his scalp. He looked as though something had sucked all the moisture from his body. His skin was color of oiled wood and had the texture of parfleche. His lips had shrunk with the rest of him, leaving his teeth exposed. He looked like a corpse left to dry in the sun, but Jes knew he was very much alive.

The Guardian released his grip before the Shadowed's terror had a chance to damage Jes.

"I cannot kill him," said the Memory. "That task is yours, Guardian."

"I'll do it," said Lehr.

The Guardian smiled at his brother, then met Hennea's gaze briefly.

"No," he said. "Death is my gift." And he snapped the brittle neck.

Jes screamed, ripped from the safe cocoon the Guardian had tried to envelope him in. The pain was far beyond anything he had ever undergone, but that wasn't the worst of it.

Something reached up from Willon at the moment of his death and grasped onto Jes, wrapping itself around him. When it touched him, it felt as if someone had torn away his skin and pressed him into the man Willon had been. No man should ever know another as Jes knew Willon at that moment. He couldn't hide, couldn't distinguish himself from the Shadowed.

Cold hands touched his face and he felt Willon draw away, as if Willon's ghost had no wish to come in contact with those hands.

"His death belongs to me," said the Memory. "Give it to me."

"Yes," agreed the Guardian and gave way to Jes.

Cold lips touched Jes's and he opened his mouth even as he struggled against the Memory's hold—not because he wanted to, but because he couldn't help himself. He had no words for the sensations he felt then as Willon was drawn from him like a sword from its sheath.

Only when he was empty, did the Memory release him. Jes stared at it, unable to look away. The Memory had become a darkness so solid, Jes could hardly bear to look upon it. Rain glistened on it like wet ink.

"I am avenged," it said, and it was gone.

Papa quit singing midword. He walked over and put a hand on Jes's shoulder. Raw as he was, even such a light contact hurt, but Jes needed the reassurance more than he needed freedom from pain, so he leaned against his father for a moment.

When he pulled away, Hennea was there, slipping a hand through the crock of his arm and resting her cheek against his shoulder. The cool grace of her presence washed over him, soothing the raw places Willon's death had left. He sighed with relief.

Mother came and gave him a sharp once over. "You'll do," she said.

He smiled tiredly at her, or maybe it was the Guardian who smiled.

"And so," Papa said, his voice hoarse and his face unreadable. "And just so died the Shadowed who was once Willon, merchant of Redern."

Mother took Papa's hand and brought it to her lips. "Well done, my love."

CHAPTER 21

They brought their dead out of the city.

While Hennea and Seraph set about making a meal, Tier got a camp shovel and began digging. Lehr joined him a few minutes later with another shovel.

"Who are we burying?"

"Willon," Tier answered.

"We won't have to bury him too deeply," Lehr said. "There's nothing left that would attract carrion feeders."

"There's all sorts of carrion feeders," said Phoran, coming over in time to hear Lehr's last remark. "I think six feet might be deep enough. I'll spell you when you get tired."

When Jes wandered over, his eyes soft and happy, they had dug down about halfway and had to leave the digging to one man at a time because there was no room in the grave for two. Jes crouched so his head was level with Tier's.

"Are we going to bury Rufort and Hinnum?" he asked.

Tier sighed at the thought of digging another grave through the hard soil. "Let's wait and ask what their customs were. Hennea will know what to do with Hinnum. Phoran, do you know what Rufort's people do?"

"No." Phoran shook his head. "But Kissel will. He's sleeping now, but I'll ask him when he awakes."

"Kissel's up," Jes said. "I can hear him complaining about his shoulder. It itches, and he can't reach it under the bandages. Toarsen—"

"—is coming over to help," said Toarsen. "Hop out of there, old man, and let me take a turn. I didn't get to kill him, but I'll have my part in the burial. I don't want him crawling back out of his grave."

Tier knew better. He did. But when the rest of them turned to make sure that Willon's body had not moved, he did, too.

Swearing, Tier jumped out of the hole and handed his shovel to Toarsen. "Dig," he said. "And take it as punishment for that thought."

They buried Willon deep in the earth. Hennea muttered something over the grave as they filled it. She didn't use the usual words of an eulogy; it was more of a good-riddance-and-stay-in-your-grave-forever which she enforced with magic that Tier could feel envelop the grave.

No one wanted to sleep before their dead were tended, and there wasn't much time before dark to collect a lot of firewood. So Hinnum and Rufort burned on a pyre owing more to the power of the Ravens than to the sparse pile of wood while Phoran, Toarsen, and Kissel told what they knew of Rufort's life. When they were through, Hennea got up and spoke of Hinnum, the last wizard of Colossae.

Seraph and Hennea spent most of the next day freeing the Orders from the gems, but they stopped before dinner.

"It's going to take a long time," Seraph told Tier, as she ate Jes and Lehr's rabbit stew. "We worked all day, and I think we freed four of them." The first one, the Lark's tigereye, Tier had watched.

"That's all right, Mother," said Jes, looking up from feeding Gura. They'd all taken turns babying the limping dog, but Kissel wouldn't let anyone but Rinnie baby him. Tier had derived considerable amusement watching Kissel's bewildered looks as Rinnie made him lie down while she tucked his blankets against him.

"There's no hurry," Jes continued. "Hennea is staying with us."

We could spend this fall building Jes and Hennea a cabin,

Tier thought. *Jes would like something farther in the woods, if the forest king wouldn't mind.* But he looked at his wife and didn't say anything. She was all Traveler now, her hair in braids and her skirts traded for Traveler garb.

She had given up her people's ways for twenty years, and he supposed that he could give up his farm for the next twenty or thirty.

"You have to come visit me," said Phoran, eating as though the rough stew was a gourmet dish from the palace's kitchen. "Give me five or six years to tame the Septs a little, then I want Lehr to map the palace for me. I don't want any more secret societies lurking in passages that no one remembers."

"We'll do that," said Seraph. "But you come to us, too." She nodded at Toarsen. "That one has ties in Redern. When Avar comes to visit his lands, come with him." It wasn't a suggestion, Tier noticed, watching Phoran's lips curl up. Rinnie wasn't the only one who'd grown comfortable commanding the Emperor.

"I'll have you help me weed," said Rinnie.

Phoran laughed. "I'll do that. Toarsen, Kissel, and I will ride back to Redern with you and see you safely home. Then I think we'll ride to Gerant and return to the palace with the Emperor's Own at my back."

"There will be more Ielians," Tier warned him.

"I know." Phoran's smile dimmed. "But as long as there are more like Kissel, Toarsen, and Rufort, who have been a priceless aid to me, I can take the bad with the good." He nodded at Tier. "You could come help me sift them out," he said. "I'd see to it that you would be well paid."

"No," Tier said. "I'm not a soldier anymore, I'm a farmer." He hesitated and glanced at Seraph. "Or I'll be out on the roads with my Traveler wife." He meant to sound casual, but his wife knew him too well.

She stiffened and put down her stew. "Is that what has been bothering you?" she said hotly. "You'll do no such thing. I tell you, I'm through paying for the sins of people long dead"—she glanced at Hennea—"or mostly long dead. I have no intention of being homeless ever again. If you want to wander around, you go right ahead. I'll keep a candle in the window so you can find your way back when you've had enough of nonsense."

Tier heard the *truth* in her words, lifting the weight of the world off his shoulders and smiled. "I guess, Phoran," he said, "we'll see you in Redern."

That night, in Hennea's temple, a Bard sang of heroic deeds, of lost loves, and mourning for the dead. Sometimes he sang alone, sometimes with his children, who were not Bards, but were children of Redern with voices that were true and pure. When the sun rose the dead departed.

They lingered a while, exploring the city, but before the first hint of autumn was in the air, they left the old city and closed its gates, trusting that it would guard its secrets for another age or so.

Tieragan of Redern took his family home.